FALLEN ONES

ORDER OF THADDEUS
BOOK 11

J. A. BOUMA

EmmausWay
P R E S S

PROLOGUE
BÜREN, GERMANY. APRIL 1945.

Hans Kammler pulled in a satisfying drag off the cigarette sandwiched between his lips, the smoke laced with cinnamon and cloves dancing across his tongue and soothing his rising anxiety, telling him all would be well. Telling him today would be the day when the miracle weapon would show itself true, and the Power behind it would rise to revelation.

The chamber shook with the force of Thor's hammer and the power of his sons, the gods of old. Telling him otherwise.

For years, he had pursued these arcane Powers, the ancient knowledge of an unseen realm bursting with possibilities buried in the collective unconscious of the German *volk* stretching back millennia and humming within the Universe. Encouraged by Reichsführer Himmler himself, he had sought weapons inspired by their shared Germanic mythology to bring the völkisch struggle to a conclusion, leveraging these Powers.

Now all was being threatened.

And all because of mismanagement and ego, the one fueling the other.

He pulled another satisfying drag, an Indonesian brand of tobacco by way of their Japanese allies who had occupied the chain of islands in the South Pacific. Milk and bread were hard to come by these days. More so fuel for the Luftwaffe air forces and panzer tank brigades, even metals for bullets and weapons.

Thank the Universe for an open supply line of cigarettes for such moments.

Another rumble vibrated through the ancient cut stone, sending rivulets of crimson wax winding down tall, stout candles anchored to the walls. Perhaps it was only thunder, the rapid expansion of air surrounding the path of a lightning bolt slicing through the heavens.

He blew a hazy cloud and stayed his shaking hand—listening, discerning, intuiting the cause of such perturbations.

There was rain, the soft pitter-patter of the drops smacking against the glass windows high above the vaulted ceiling. Yet he sensed the rumbles were not from storm clouds.

No, Kammler knew intuitively why those rumbles continued roiling through the stone chamber. For he knew who was causing them.

They were closing in, the Allies arrayed against their just and worthy Cause to raise up a single race of men who would rule on behalf of the gods!

And Kammler was so close. Finally...

There it was again, the world's foundations rumbling in the distance. Flames flickered in the dim darkness, the pale light barely making purchase in the stone chamber, windows above shrouded by storm clouds and too narrow anyway to make any difference—what little light there was reflecting off from a white sheet draped across the object of this afternoon's gathering.

Normally a round table with twelve chairs was anchored at the center. Herr Himmler's pathetic attempt to recapitulate the Arthurian legend of the King and his Knights of the Round Table. The Reichsführer was crazy about medieval fantasy. Kammler never understood why. Perhaps Himmler saw himself less a Knight and more the King. Less the Reichsführer and more the Führer himself.

Only time would tell...

Kammler blew another hazy cloud, lifting his head toward the ceiling and smiling reverently at the symbol adorning its center, the symbol of power that was also an ancient religious one.

The swastika.

Taking the form of an equilateral cross with its four legs bent at ninety degrees. A sacred symbol of such spiritualities as Hinduism, Buddhism, and Jainism, it had been used as a decorative element in various cultures stretching back to at least the Neolithic period. For Kammler, the symbol held all the divine promises of these pre-modern cultures for such a time as this.

Directly beneath the dome, in the middle of the room, was the chamber's crown jewel: the ceremonial basin. Normally, it served as a baptismal pool for the rite opening the storehouses of divine knowledge and power. Not this day.

Instead, the fruits of Kammler's arcane labor would be unveiled, witnessed by the assembled Brotherhood from amongst the highest ranks within the Third Reich. Perhaps then they would take him seriously.

Oberth, Hess, Dornberger, even Wernher von Braun, the fabled rocket scientist who had blessed the Führer with its first ballistic missile. The others had been steeped in the precious, but misunderstood, sciences that existed at the borders of modern knowledge. They tapped into the ancient revelations of the völkisch people of old, of Thor and his sons. Of the principalities and powers of this present dark world that had guided humanity for ages.

A passage from an ancient book sprang to mind. One that was wholly ironic in its own right, given the current struggles, but revealed the magical weapon that would bring the Cause to completion.

Regardless of where the arcane knowledge had arisen, Kammler had memorized it, feeding off the revelation-insights that would reveal the magical weapon sought by the Führer. He recited it to himself:

And it came to pass when the sons of men had multi-plied that in those days were born unto them beautiful and comely daughters. And the angels, the children of the heaven, saw and lusted after them, and said to one another: "Come, let us choose us wives from among the children of men and beget us children."

Yes...the children of heaven, the sons of God, the Fallen Ones who had dared raise up a special race of men upon Earth. The true *Übermensch* laying hold of human destiny!

These ancient gods did not leave men without recourse. Instead, they equipped them with the technology they needed to rise to a higher consciousness, one that would rule the entire world. From Azazel to Hermani, Semjaza to Kokabel, Shamsiel to Sariel...These were the gods of old who had taught men to make weapons of war, enchantments and magic, knowledge of the earth and sky!

The ones Kammler had summoned to forge the *wunder-waffe* anchored at the center of the room.

The miracle weapon that would win the war and finalize the Cause!

One of the men stood. The only man that mattered in that moment. Heinrich Himmler.

Not a commanding man, by any means, with those narrow eyes and weak chin, falling several inches below the height of most men of fighting age. Gold medals lined his left breast pocket, their glinting hue set starkly against his black suit coat. A circular signet was pinned below, a black swastika set against white, ringed by crimson and set inside gold. The same insignia was plastered to the man's left arm.

The room quieted, not because he commanded their respect, but because he elicited their fear.

Clearing his throat, he announced, "Heil Hitler!"

The man stiffened and violently threw an arm into the air, palm flat. The salute.

The rest did the same, rising as one from chairs arrayed around the chamber with the same announcement: *"Heil Hitler!"*

Returning to their seats, Himmler announced, "We have a collective secret of which the whole German people are already aware. Details are certainly not known, and it is too early to speak with certainty about the debut of these new weapons. However, today we are reporting on the next stage in our search for a miracle weapon to end the war. The Führer demands it."

An unsettled murmur rippled through the chamber.

"If it pleases you, Reichsführer Himmler, I would like to be heard."

All eyes snapped to a tall man with a generous gut. He wore a modest charcoal suit, not the military garb of the others, with a white shirt and black tie. Which made sense since he wasn't a military man, but rather a political minister. The Minister of Armament, Albert Speer.

Himmler crossed his arms, eyeing the man suspiciously. "Go on," he simply said.

This should be good...

"You know that I think in real terms," said Speer, his voice polished and enticing. The voice of a politician, not that of the people. "You know that I would not like us to fall into the psychosis that ascribes too much meaning to the new miracle weapons. I am also not of the opinion that they should now play such a prominent role in the propaganda."

Himmler nodded toward the man. "Go on," he said again.

Speer clasped his hands behind himself now, the man towering above the others.

"The faith in the soon-to-come deployment of new militarily decisive weapons is spread generally across the troops, as well as high-ranking officers. They expect this deployment in the next few days. However, it is questionable whether it is the right thing to do, in such a difficult moment, to create disappointment that cannot but have an unfavorable effect on our military morale by encouraging hopes that cannot be fulfilled in such a short time."

A rumble of discontent outmatched the rumble of those sorties bombing towns in the near distance.

"Same for our beloved *volk*," Speer went on, "who similarly await daily for the miracle of new weapons. I question whether this propaganda makes sense, whether we should continue with the charade. Not only amongst the German people, but also with the Führer himself."

More discontent rippled through the chamber, the flickering flames snapping in sync with the growing irritation at the man's wet blanket.

"I have said my piece. I shall say nothing more." Speer slumped down in his chair, making good on his promise.

The room continued with quiet whispers. Himmler for his part remained as impassioned as ever, casting a cool, steely, assessing eye across the chamber.

Until it landed upon Kammler.

"What say you, Herr Kammler? Any news?"

His moment had arrived. And he would stop at nothing to unveil the fruits of his research and preparation before the gathered. Even if it meant defying Speer.

And humiliating him.

"Today, I am most pleased to report to you the long-promised secret weapon, the magic weapon the Führer himself and our esteemed Himmler have been anticipating. A weapon truly steeped in the magic of the unseen realm that will snatch victory from the jaws of defeat!"

There was a rumble of surprised approval.

Kammler chuckled to himself, grinning outwardly but inwardly shaking his head. For they knew not the full nature of this magic weapon.

The beloved German composer Richard Wagner, a favorite of the Führer himself, bestowed upon his final opera a certain name that rings true amongst the völkisch.

Götterdämmerung.

Twilight of the Gods.

The piece was emblematic of the folklore revival amongst the common folks, as well as the intelligentsia of the Third Reich, that Wagner inspired. The title was derived from the Old Norse Ragnarok, which connoted the fate of the Gods. The fate of which culminated in a final, cataclysmic battle foretelling the birth of a new era. One where the gods and humanity would live in peace, and wickedness would cease while food would flow in abundance.

Still more: Humanity would join the gods in power.

Thunder rumbled overhead, shaking the stone floor beneath. At least that's what it seemed.

Kammler knew better.

The enemy was coming.

Making his work on the magic weapon all the more urgent.

And its presentation.

Tossing his cigarette to the floor, Kammler stepped to the center of the chamber and approached the fruits of his arcane labor.

He thundered, "Herr Himmler, and other assembled grup-penführers, I present to you...*der Glocke.*"

Without waiting for approval, Kammler let slip a white sheet draped across the *wunderwaffe*, the miracle weapon that would end the war and birth a true *Übermensch*, a race of men who would rule the world.

God-Men, born not of natural descent but of the hidden, arcane Power.

A murmur of confusion rippled through the chamber, the gathered clearly not grasping the significance of what they were casting their eyes upon.

Until they did.

Kammler closed his eyes and chanted lowly, a Power suddenly coursing through the room and rising from behind, all around—within his very soul, even.

And the miracle weapon lifted from the ground, rising high into the vaulted chamber toward the symbol of the Third Reich and emitting a charge that would lay waste to the enemy!

Gasps filled the void of the gruppenführers' confused murmurs. Then an immediate rushing to stand, followed by the snapping of feet to attention.

Throwing their flattened palms out in front, they chanted as one:

"Sieg Heil! Sieg Heil! Sieg Heil!"

A satisfied grin stretched across Kammler's face. Hail victory, indeed...

There it was again. A bassy rumble in the bowels of the earth itself, brought on by the relentless machinations of war.

This unveiled *wunderwaffe* would surely hand the Third Reich its worthy victory.

And yet...

If he failed, he would flee. Because what he discovered, the arcane knowledge of the gods, must be preserved for the future.

The fate of humanity depended upon it.

For in the fullness of time, the true *Übermensch* would rise.

Aided by the stars.

CHAPTER 1

WASHINGTON, DC. PRESENT DAY.

S ilas Grey was running late. Again.

He was supposed to meet his partner in crime for dinner at a fancy French bistro in Dupont Circle. Had been meaning to try the joint for months. Yelp reviews were good and the missus-to-be had been craving French food for ages. He was more of a meat and potatoes kind of guy himself. Would even settle for an MRE when in a bind. But there was a dish of boeuf bourguignon with his name on it waiting for him. Made reservations weeks ago at 1700 hours to make sure they had a table with their name on it!

He'd blown past that appointed time long ago.

This time it wasn't his fault. Really, it wasn't!

An oversight committee hearing of muckety-mucks with the Order of Thaddeus board of directors proving to be the bane of his existence had raked his backside across the coals from here to kingdom come. It was the climax of several months of inquiries thanks to an activist board member, Ekhard Weiss, and some of his cronies who weren't too keen with how he had been handling his role as Order Master since assuming it after Rowen Radcliffe's death.

If money makes the world go round, the grease in the skids

of everything from school boards and homeowner's associations to non-governmental organizations in the foreign field and government ones back home on the range—well, then committees are the gravel in the gears that mucks up everything that is holy and just in the world!

He'd seen it firsthand as a professor at Princeton University, where everything from how many plies the toilet paper rolls should have to the necessity of this or that annual professional guild meeting was argued to death. Then before that, as a sergeant with the Army Rangers, Silas had seen how ruling by committee had real consequences when life and death were on the line and split-seconds were standing between the former and the latter.

Thankfully, he'd been spared much of that grief at the Order of Thaddeus, where his motley crew of SEPIO agents guarding the Christian faith flew under the radar of both governmental and ecclesial organizations—by design, given the connections with the Vatican and their powers of persuasion. But this latest gamut with Weiss and his cronies shattered that illusion. Especially after his latest backside-raking.

No wonder it hurt hustling down Massachusetts Avenue after all he'd been through!

A chilly wind raced through the corridor of steel and concrete high-rise buildings housing lobbying firms and consultancies, stirring up piles of leaves milling about the urban monstrosities. The urban beasts took care of them entirely, taxis and Metro buses scampering along the road crushing the dead foliage beneath their rubber paws. Blaring horns screaming with selfish intent and a bout of black exhaust from one of those buses sent Silas recoiling with a wince and cough. What he wouldn't give for a log cabin in the woods and a six-pack right about now...

After his last operation saving small-town America from no uncertain doom, he'd had something of a change of heart about big-city living, thinking it would be mighty nice to settle down with a few acres of land on the outskirts of civilization. Maybe raise grass-fed chickens alongside a quiver full of kiddos. Something about the slower pace of life and noiseless streets, the local watering hole where everyone knows your name and they're glad you came—

Silas chuckled to himself. Now he was reduced to channeling the *Cheers* theme song. Things must really be bad!

Earth and those dried leaves mixed with the scents of roasting meat and garlic joined by baking bread and coffee snapped him back to the moment—his stomach throwing up a growl and a reminder that dinner awaited with the most amazing woman on the planet, the reason for his hustling down Massachusetts Ave.

Celeste Bourne. Who was a Bourne far before Bourne was a Bourne, as she had introduced herself the first time—a reference to that amnesic special forces novel character. She was also his right-hand woman with the Order, serving as his director of operations, a post she'd held with a firm and steady hand after Radcliffe recruited her from MI6 years ago. The evening's committee meeting came rushing to memory, that comment Weiss had made at the end of their remarks on their findings—the one about Celeste.

'*Regrettably, Ms. Bourne was not Rowen's named successor. Although Order of Thaddeus tradition has always allowed the Master to name the one who would carry Jude Thaddeus's torch preserving and defending the Christian faith, and although it might have been unorthodox for a woman to assume such a role, we cannot help but conclude that it would have been a more prudent choice to tap Ms. Bourne to succeed Radcliffe as Order Master...*'

Silas's stomach sank with the truth of the matter. He was right. She would have been a better choice than him.

Speaking of which...

Twisting his arm around, he shoved back the sleeve to his

black suit that was freshly pressed for the hearing and glanced at his watch—a cheap, faded fake gold-plated Seiko clinging to his wrist. It had been a high school graduation gift from Dad now pockmarked with age from over a decade and three tours of duty with the Rangers across the Middle East, and then even more operations defending Christ's Church. Didn't want to know the full measure of his lateness, but he figured he should rip the bandage off.

Dang it!

Yep. Definitely late.

Celeste was going to kill him...

Sure, she'd understand. She'd been standing alongside him as his partner in crime as much as his soon-to-be wife—defending him before the board, counseling him with how to navigate all the politics of it all, serving him gin and tonics like only a Brit could. Hated it though, putting her second when his career was on the line. Especially since they were supposed to be wrapping up the final details to their wedding at that French bistro!

Darting across an intersection at a blinking orange cross-walk, Silas reviewed all that had gone down the past few months with his credibility and career on the line. For a second time in as many years.

It all started earlier in the year when Victor Zarruq, a former Libyan bishop that was his liaison with the board of directors—babysitter, more like it, though he was a wise, encouraging ally—when he had reported a development that brought flashbacks of his time at Princeton University.

An imminent no-contest vote.

Victor had reassured Silas he was "doing a smashing job" executing Saint Jude Thaddeus' original vision to contend for the once-for-all faith. Assured him plenty more board members shared his sentiment, believing Silas to be the right person for the job—yada, yada, yada.

Of course, there was a *but* right at the end of all that; there always was.

But...some of the board members—one or two according to Victor's original tally that turned out to be five—would rather that Silas and the Order focus on more 21st-century issues than previous-century ones. Hadn't a clue what Victor or Weiss and his cronies meant, but it was clear that issues of justice and equity and inclusion were high on his list. The more social elements of the gospel.

"As if contending for Christ's once-for-all faith doesn't also cover those issues..." Silas grumbled hustling down Mass Ave toward Dupont Circle with the same original irritation he had with Victor, heat rising back up his neck at the memory.

The bishop agreed with him, but the man revealed it was more than that. There were more players involved at the top who were asking questions about him and his leadership.

As in Vatican players.

Questions were being raised from certain sectors of the Holy See about the amount of money being spent, which apparently still controlled the purse of the ecumenical Christian order—who knew? Silas certainly hadn't. He was too busy saving the Church from no uncertain doom than to worry about whether the Order's profit-loss statements balanced—which apparently was running into the red. And a number of cardinals back in Rome were throwing up a stink about it, giving plenty of fodder for Weiss's own inquisition agenda.

Again, Victor had reassured Silas all would be well, that the drama was less about the Order than the internecine struggles between factions within the Vatican, not to mention the broader Church. Regardless, all the administrative, bureaucratic bull had been one big headache that had eaten up most of his year.

What's the saying? A committee is a group of men who can't

do nothing on their own but as a group decide that nothing can be done at all. Yep. That!

In the case of the Order, there was a real possibility their mission would be reduced to blog posts on WeShare and WeTube videos defending the faith, and academic conferences catering to the ivory-tower class of tweed jackets and sweater vests—God forbid! All while Weiss's committee was paralyzed with indecision simply because of some bad press optics and pissing contests between old men.

If the past few years revealed anything about the true nature of the Church's struggle—the principalities and powers of this dark world that fed and fueled the flesh-and-blood actors staging an all-out assault against Christianity and its beliefs—it was that sometimes car chases and gunfights and battles with wicked actors were all that truly stood between the Church flourishing or folding.

Which took money and sometimes led to bad press. But such was life contending for the once-for-all faith. What did the board expect?

Silas kept up his pace, clenching a fist and wiping his brow beading with sweat. From a rising anger at all the bureaucratic nonsense and second-guessing as much as from his hustling pace.

He'd given his all when he joined the Order—gave *up* it all, putting it all on the line for the Church. To what end?

Instead of thanking him for all he'd done—from shoot-outs and car chases to recovering lost relics and saving the Church —the board had handed him his backside on a silver platter, landing him in the hot seat of another committee that nearly sacked his backside.

Nearly.

Because somehow, purely by the grace and influence of the Holy Trinity, he was still Order Master.

Barely.

The vote was split. Five for and Five against his continued tenure, with one abstaining.

That one hurt the most. It was Victor Zarruq. Man said he was trying to keep the peace without taking sides. Silas didn't buy it.

Because in not voting to take his side, he had taken theirs by default!

Coming to a crosswalk with a halting orange hand, he pulled out a cigarette and lit it. Celeste hated the nasty habit he'd picked up in Iraq with the Rangers. Wasn't much else to do whiling away the hours on nation-building duty; wasn't much else to ease the pain when said nation building went to pot. He'd kicked the habit after his honorable discharge but picked it up again—ironically, after joining the Order.

Silas shoved the stick between his lips and struck his lighter, holding it at the end and fueling the burn with an intake of oxygen.

"FUBAR is what it is..." he muttered to himself.

Flubbed up beyond all repair, is right.

Waiting for the light to change, he took another drag, the end glowing orange in the night and nicotine already working its magic to ease his frustration and anxiety. The sharp scent of burning tobacco and spice was almost as much of a balm, the smoke triggering a memory of Dad's pipe. Man, what he wouldn't give to be able to call him up and ask for advice. What would he do in Silas's shoes? What *should* he do?

Had not a clue.

Something rubbed against his leg, snapping him back to the moment.

He looked down to find a large cat pressed against his dark pants, white fur left behind from the animal's affection.

The pedestrian walk light turned white, but Silas was too taken by the beautiful Persian still seeking his attention. He took another drag on his cigarette and bent low, rubbing its back. The feline threw up a pleasurable purr, clearly relishing the affection.

"Aren't you a beaut. Yes, you are. You remind me of my old kitty. Barnabas is his name."

Silas had rescued the cat while serving in Iraq after it ambled into his barracks. Was beat up real bad until he nursed it back to health, bringing it back to the States upon discharge. Gave it up to his old assistant Miles when he joined the Order, figuring with all of his globetrotting he would be a bad caretaker. But man...what a pal that cat was.

He took another pull off his cigarette and flicked it into the street. "What's a kitty like you doing out late at night on your own, huh? Looks like you've lost your way. I bet your owner is worrying—"

A truck with a growly muffler ambled by with interruption, the beast grunting something fierce as it turned their way and rumbled on by. Startling the stray, its back going rigid and legs bending as if it were about to pounce away.

Just as the crosswalk turned orange again and traffic shuffled back into action.

Silas saw it before she did—and anticipated what she was about to do. And what would happen!

"No, wait!"

Bent down to snatch it before it got a chance, but it was no use.

The Persian leaped from his grasp and darted into the intersection.

And he didn't think twice before reacting.

Darting after his new feline friend, Silas reached the cat before a black Mercedes did, grabbing her by the mane with a grip that threw up a pained scream and angry hiss.

The car laid on the horn something fierce as it screeched to a halt and swerved to avoid him.

"What the hell is your problem!" Silas yelled at the driver, throwing up his empty hand in a fist.

A middle-aged man smoking a pipe flipped him off without a word and sped off.

"Yeah, right back atcha!"

A few cars waited patiently for him to clear the intersection, so he carried his new friend to safety on the other side.

"You gave me a scare, little lady." He set her on the sidewalk and gave her head a pat. Then off she went, scampering away without a sound or parting glance.

"Suppose I did my one good deed for today."

His pants pocket buzzed with attention. His phone, which he pulled out—and frowned.

Celeste!

Thankfully, the bistro was just up the block, so he silenced the device and took off running, reaching it as she emerged onto the evening street.

And looking drop-dead gorgeous.

A slimming indigo dress hugging her fit frame fell to her knees, her long legs accentuated by lipstick-red stilettos. A hot choice that didn't surprise Silas; he had learned she was much more into fashion than he expected, far more than him. A string of white pearls ringed her neck, and her wavy chestnut hair was spun up into a pile of thick locks, with two gold pins holding it all in place.

How could he be so luck...

Her eyes caught his, and he snapped back to the moment.

Silas ran up to her out of breath. "Hon, I'm so sorry!"

"You alright, love?" she asked in her perfectly posh British accent, face scrunched up more with worry than irritation.

"Committee meeting went way longer than I thought it would."

"I'm just grateful you weren't marooned on the side of Massachusetts. You gave me quite the fright!"

"Sorry, I should have texted. But you know me and communication."

She smirked. "Don't I know it."

"And here you've been waiting for, what, half an hour?"

"Try an hour."

"Dang it. Late again."

"Seems to be a theme with you."

"I know! But not when we're married. First thing to go, I promise."

"Well, you're smartly dressed," she said, drawing close and grabbing his overcoat collar, "and looking more dashing than normal, I might add. So I suppose I'll give you a pass."

Silas laughed, putting his hands on her hips. "Thanks for accommodating my tardiness." He drew her closer, feeling better already. "I must say, you're looking mighty fine yourself, Ms. Bourne."

Celeste smiled and whispered, "I love it when you say my name."

"I'll love it even more when I can say Mrs. Grey."

She grinned widely now. "Me too..."

Heat raced up Silas's neck and spread through his body. And not because of hustling across twenty DC blocks and saving a cat from no uncertain doom. Marriage was going to be magical!

Wrapping his arms around her, the couple embraced, the familiar scent of jasmine and vanilla at her neck relieving Silas's cares now—

Until Celeste promptly pulled away and frowned, huffing with disapproval.

"Have you been puffing on a fag?"

He chuckled at the characterization, still not getting over her British slang for his bad habit. But he fessed up, nodding and hanging his head in shame.

She put a finger under his chin and lifted his head. "That bad, was it?"

"You have no idea, darling. But, hey, I saved a cat from getting crushed by a Mack truck. That should count for something."

"A cat? Sounds like you've had quite the go of it this evening."

"You have no idea..."

Celeste stuck out her bent arm and offered him its crook. "Come along, love. Let's get a round of gin and tonics."

Silas grinned and slid his arm inside. "Yes, please..."

CHAPTER 2

Silas opened the bistro's heavy walnut door, a tinkling bell above announcing their arrival and a hot breath of succulent food washing over him with invitation. Grilled beef and roasted lamb, joined by a mixture of saffron and sage, garlic and onion, topped with stewing tomatoes and squash—all of it sent his head dizzying with hunger and stomach rumbling for relief.

"After you, my lady," he said, motioning inside.

"Such a gentleman," Celeste replied. "Although, I'm quite sure your chivalrous gesture is more about observing my backside than proper manners."

"You know it!"

He wrapped an arm around her waist and gave her firm hips a squeeze; she threw up a giggle and scampered to their table.

A mainstay of the fashionable DC neighborhood of high-end retail shops and cuisine, the bistro was bustling with patrons and servers alike, the dark wood soaking up the dim light and bouncing the hushed conversations in various languages around the long, narrow dining room. Some would call it cozy; Silas thought it cramped, the walls seeming to close in compounded by the suffocating heat.

Hated being cramped, which was probably a holdover from his days with the Rangers and the nightmare accommodations in the desert. It also stemmed from a rule he had about always knowing the way out—again, thanks to his military background sussing out high-level targets and needing a quick extraction when things got hot and heavy, but also thanks to his three years with the Order. Again, needing a quick extraction when things got hot and heavy—probably more so with the ecclesial organization that landed his backside in more hot messes and near-death endings battling the Church's goons than he'd care to count.

Following after Celeste, Silas took off his wool charcoal overcoat, fixed his tie, then settled in for a night with his bride-to-be planning their future.

Drawn white lace curtains hung from the large picture windows flanking the street, and white lace tablecloths draped small tables arranged in neat rows along the window and wall flanking an open kitchen. Again, cozy but cramped. Stoves flaring with culinary activity, and cooks speaking in rushed French slung orders along with dishes. Every table was taken by couples but one lone man sitting off in the corner with a *New York Times*, apparently content to dine with Old Lady Grey than any significant other. Sounded like a good way to end the day after the drumming he'd just had.

But alone time could wait. Tonight was about his future with his partner in crime, his soulmate, his future wife. And there was no place he'd rather be.

A server took their drink orders and promptly left— Tanqueray with Q Tonic and extra lime for them both. Leaving the engaged couple to plan for that future.

Celeste asked, "So, what's the word from old miser Weiss?"

Silas took a sip of water, readying to dive into the details.

Didn't much want to, but he was trying to open up to her more, share his feelings and frustrations. Never had been too keen on such rigamarole. Didn't come easy or natural. Mostly didn't see the point after having traveled from base to base following his father's military career, not making many friends and no long-lasting connections, other than his brother. And even that relationship had been obliterated, the two pitted against one another in a Cain-and-Abel rematch.

Probably all stemmed from deep-seated abandonment issues stemming from his mother's passing after giving birth to him and his brother, and then his father dying in the Pentagon attack on 9/11. But he was trying to open up more, trying to share what he was thinking and feeling, what irritated the snot out of him and made him stay awake at night—which Celeste seemed to appreciate.

"Ringing Doctor Grey..." she said with a wry grin, head tilted in wait.

"Sorry," Silas said with a chuckle. "A bit distracted from it all."

"I can tell. So what happened that has you so distracted?"

Leaning back in his chair, he covered the highlights—from concerns over spending to the optics of their operations that had led to open gunfights and car chases, drones exploding into buildings and half their headquarters sinking under the power of an IED, even putting civilians in harm's way to accomplish their last operation. He left out the part about Victor, and the prospect he could still be fired. Too painful to voice yet, and his mind was still stewing in silent contemplation.

The server returned with their drinks. Silas promptly threw back a mouthful, the piney taste of juniper and tart lime a balm for his frustrations.

"Sounds wretched," Celeste said, taking a sip of her G&T.

Silas threw back a swig himself and nodded. "It was. It is.

Who knows what will happen. But that wasn't even the worst of it."

She raised a brow. "There's more?"

"Thanks to the questions Weiss and his cronies are raising, some are even starting to target SEPIO."

"What? Are they bloomin' mad?"

Silas had to smile. Once Celeste started in on her bloomins, the world better watch out. Especially since Project SEPIO had been something of her baby the past several years, the late Master Rowen Radcliffe having established it half a century ago and hiring her away from MI6 to take it to the next level in operational know-how.

Radcliffe's vision had been to position it as a more muscular, deliberate outworking of the Order's mission from the founding apostle himself, Jude Thaddeus. *'Contend for the faith that was once for all entrusted to the saints,'* he had written in his letter to the churches of Asia Minor, a clarion call that had become the core mission of the religious order he established. SEPIO was meant as a more muscular effort at that contending mission. Celeste was the reason it had succeeded so well. A little too well, by Weiss's estimation.

He explained, "According to Weiss and his cronies, all that contending the past few years has had a cost."

Celeste scoffed. "Defending the faith usually does! Are they bloody serious going after SEPIO—after all we've accomplished protecting and promoting the essential elements of historic Christian orthodoxy?"

He suppressed another grin. Bloomin' had leveled-up to bloody. Weiss better watch out!

"Except the Vatican and Weiss are balking at the costs—financial, yes, but also *optical*, the fallout from various operations over the years not playing all that well in the press."

She huffed and threw back the rest of her G&T, then raised her glass at their server for another. Couldn't blame her in the slightest. Silas joined her, draining his drink and handing it off for a second.

"Zarruq counseled all would be well," he went on, "that it was more about conflicting camps within the Church vying for power—political and theological struggles taking up their cause with the Order."

Now she threw up her hands. "Well, tell them to rain on somebody else's court and leave SEPIO well enough alone! Who do they think they are?"

"I know. That's what I told Victor, but he insists the inquiries are less about us and more about the bigger ecclesial picture."

"And what do you think?" she asked, leaning in.

He shrugged. "I'm not so sure."

"Go on."

"You know what it's like, given your years with MI6. If it was anything like mine, my experience with the Army and the academy tells me these sorts of struggles have a way of spinning out of control—"

"And blowing things to kingdom come, I reckon!"

"Especially when committees are involved!"

The server returned, setting down two more gin and tonics.

Celeste raised hers. "Cheers."

Silas clinked her glass with his and promptly threw back a mouthful, the piney juniper taste stronger than the tart lime this go around. Which meant more gin to soothe the soul. Fine by him.

A silence settled between them, the pair contemplating the turn for SEPIO and the Order in their own way.

But for Silas, it was more than that. More than just the internecine political games within the broader reaches of the Church. It was personal, the pain from the accusatory panel stretching beyond just the Order of Thaddeus.

Things had gone south with his brother, Sebastian, who was now headlining the Church's greatest nemesis, Nous. The pair had a falling out years ago when he was a bit overeager in his proselytizing efforts to bring Sebastian back to the faith. Silas had a sort of conversion experience serving overseas—or more like a rededication experience of his faith while at an on-base chapel service. Both had been regular attenders at the Falls Church Catholic parish in Northern Virginia as teenagers; their father had made damn sure they were raised proper in the Church. But after his brother left the faith, for good reasons that had made headlines in recent years, Sebastian never looked back. And now they were bitter enemies—literally, the pair on opposite sides of an eternal struggle between good and evil.

Things had also gone south with his former employer, Princeton University. Had been skating on thin ice for some time with his dean, but the Order was what broke the ice. His exploits saving the Church and the world from no uncertain doom had forced him to sideline his university work, leading to his firing. Didn't matter in the slightest he proved Jesus rose from the dead or found the lost Ark of the Covenant. Dean McIntyre had finally gotten his way.

Now he'd come full circle. On the verge of being sacked again.

Throwing back another mouthful of G&T, Silas looked up and around at the others gathered over drinks and meals, wondering what they all did for a living that didn't put their backsides on the line fighting global conspiracies. Accountants, professors, politicians, most likely. Maybe some doctors and NGO professionals stationed in far-flung countries that carried risk. Mostly just suites and skirts, working nine-to-fives that sounded mighty nice after his whooping. Even the single dude in the corner probably lived a quiet life, just him and his newspaper enjoying a drink.

Newspaper and a drink. Boy, did that sound nice right about then.

"Cheer up, Charlie," Celeste said, snapping his focus back to his bride-to-be. "All will be well, I'm sure of it. And I'm saying that to myself as much as you, love."

Silas nodded. "I suppose."

"Victor's got our back. As does the Holy Spirit."

Strike the newspaper and drink. He had all he needed sitting across from him.

He grabbed her hand and smiled. "Enough about me and my problems. We're here about us. About you, and all you have planned for our special day. So, let's hear it."

"You sure you're still up for having a chat about it all? Not sure I would be after Weiss and his minions had a go at me and my leadership competency."

Nodding, he gave her hand a squeeze. "Absolutely, hon."

Celeste grinned and gave a girlish squeal. "Right, let's get on with it."

Her countenance instantly transformed into a young girl who had waited her whole life for her special moment— bridesmaids and bouquets, vows and violins strumming Pachelbel's *Canon in D*, dancing and drinks, and all other manners of nuptial flare. Reaching below her chair, she hoisted a whole armful of books and folders, pamphlets and guides to the table. Everything from dresses to tuxedos, venues to menus, even flower arrangements and proper colors for winter. She grinned and held them aloft, waiting for an answer.

"You sure you are ready?" she asked.

Silas promptly drained his G&T and raised his glass for another.

"Let's do this."

And she did, jumping headlong into an extended conversation about the finer details of weddings, their wedding. From the color scheme (winter white and boysenberry) to the venues (the Anglican church they had been attending and a "posh" country club that would accommodate three hundred guests, which sounded expensive and relationally overwhelming); from the dinner menu (three courses, with a choice of salad and quail or bison, neither of which sounded appetizing, but it was her deal) to even their choice of getaway vehicle (a Mercedes A-class sedan, black). The only thing that focused his attention was the after party: the honeymoon week they had planned in Cabo, Mexico.

Felt bad how distracted he was, his mind wandering to the accusations and possibilities with the Order, eyes roaming the tight bistro and noticing the gentleman in the corner again—the man seeming to eye him back, them even.

Which was odd. Especially the way he had snapped that newspaper up above his face after Silas caught his eyes glancing above the parapet of the newsprint. And the man's drink hadn't been touched, either. A cloudy liquid with two limes bobbing in an iceless pond. Gin and tonic, by the looks of it, with its ice having melted and the outer glass sweating with perspiration. Yep, definitely hadn't touched it since they had arrived.

He stared in the mystery man's direction, waiting for another glimpse of the man.

There it was! Newspaper lowering a hair, the man's wavy salt-and-pepper, slicked-back hairdo coming up for air until the whites of his eyes met his own.

Instead of snapping the newspaper back to clandestine attention, he did something curious.

He eased it down further, then took a drink.

Locking eyes on Silas's own before snapping his head every-so-slightly toward his right shoulder. As if asking him to join.

Which was super creepy.

There he was, having drinks with his fiancé, planning their wedding—and some dude was giving him a come hither?

Suppose he could be eyeing Celeste, which made him even more mad.

"Silas..." Celeste said, taking his hand.

He startled. "Huh, what?"

She smiled and gave him a squeeze. "You're distracted."

"N–n–no, I'm not."

"Yes, you are. I see it all over your bloomin' face! And your eyes are casting about, everywhere but these books and pamphlets. What do you think—"

He shifted in his seat as Celeste kept talking, but he wasn't paying any attention. Instead casting his gaze at his drink before glancing back over her shoulder for another look-see.

Dude was still there, eyes still engaged with his own.

And that damn come hither again! This time joined by eyes widening with an exclamatory flit, as if saying get to it.

A shiver ratcheted up his spine. What's with this guy?

"—pregnant. With your child."

That got his attention!

"Huh, what?" Silas exclaimed, nearly sending his drink overboard. "Pregnant, really?"

A couple next door glanced their way.

Celeste scoffed. "No, you bloody moron! We haven't shagged once since dating, leaving it at snogging until we tie the knot, you know that!"

Now the whole row was looking their way, sending heat racing up his neck and blooming in his cheeks.

Silas quickly scooted to the edge of his seat. "OK, I'm here. Fully present."

She raised a brow, knowing him too well.

"I mean, I am having drinks with the hottest gal on the planet," he said, trying to recover. "So, yeah, I suppose I'm distracted."

Celeste giggled, pushing a stray lock of hair behind an ear. "That's not it, silly. I know you better than that. No worries, love. This whole thing with the Order board of directors will blow over, just you wait. I'm sure of it."

"That's not it," he muttered, looking back at the guy who had returned to his newspaper.

"Then what is?"

Silas took a drink and gestured with his glass. "The dude behind the newspaper giving us looks from across the room."

"Dude? What dude?" She sat up and glanced around.

"Have to say, that British accent of yours makes even dude sound like a million bucks."

She threw him a grin. "Where's this *dude* of yours, this bloke that's got you so distracted?"

He nodded across her shoulder. "Guy is in the corner, holding up a *New York Times*. Can't get a good look at him with the shadows, but he keeps glancing our way. Creeping me out the way he's eyeing you."

"How do you know he's not eyeing you, hot stuff?" She tossed him a wink before easing around for a look, the man setting the paper down now and the light catching him just right.

Mystery Man was tall and tan with trim salt-and-pepper hair, putting him mid-forties to early fifties. A Burberry patterned scarf tossed around his neck indicated class and money, as did the Montblanc pen nestled in the pocket of his blue gingham patterned shirt and Tag Heuer watch. An interesting choice that probably put him overseas. European, maybe British.

He said, "The John's trying to look all nonchalant, but he looks sketchy as all get—"

Celeste cut him off with a startled breath and stood, the chair throwing up a scuffing squeak at her sharp movement. She took a step toward the mystery man, then another—as if she recognized him.

Now the man raised a hand, a sort of hello gesture that shouted familiarity.

But why?

Without looking back at Silas, she closed the gap.

"Nicky McGrath?" he heard her say with confused recognition.

The night just went from frustrating to intriguing in no time flat.

CHAPTER 3
BORDER OF TURKEY AND IRAQ.

Matt Gapinski was not a happy camper. Because Matt Gapinski hated camping.

The bugs, the heat, the cramped quarters. The sweaty shirts and shorts, not to mention the sweaty underoos sticking to his backside like a bad high school girlfriend. The stiff necks and aching back, the barking dogs and joints, the bugs and plain-Jane food that was never enough to keep him full. Then there was the whole rigmarole of filtering their water with a pump, making fire like an embarrassing *Survivor* challenge, and crapping in the woods that brought back bad memories of basic training at Parris Island, South Carolina.

Did he mention the bugs?

Yet there he was, flopping over onto his side in a cot made for a twelve-year-old girl, trying to catch what little shuteye he could snatch in the middle of a terrible night's sleep thanks to said cot and a skeeter hissing sweet nothings in his right ear since dusk.

"Why I ever agreed to shlep my fat backside to the Turkish wilderness for a camping trip on steroids is beyond me."

Except he did know why.

Silas Grey.

His boss, who had asked him as a personal favor to join Naomi Torres on a "chance of a lifetime opportunity" to dig up old bones, as he framed it. Didn't understand half of what he was going on about—christological anthropology this, antediluvian bone fragments that, "chance of a lifetime opportunity to work on cutting-edge research that would help the Church contend for the once-for-all vintage Christian faith." Silas's go-to line spiel that guilt-tripped you into seeing things his way. How could he not say yes after the prospect of making sure baby Jesus was safe and sound from the seven-headed dragon from the Book of Revelation?

Besides, the way Gapinski figured it, he could help his bro out while also sitting pretty in some Four Seasons on the outskirts of Istanbul. Why not offer up some security muscle during the workday, then trot off to eat chocolate-covered strawberries with a bottle of scotch at night watching reruns of *The X-Files* in a terry cloth bathrobe? The Order of Thaddeus would foot the bill, he'd come back with a tan, maybe toss a few pounds overboard from all the running around—and save Christianity in the process.

He flopped over onto his other side and snorted a laugh. Yeah, right. Not even close.

Not only were they stationed in a sweltering big-top tent digging trenches through soil that made his teeth rattle and joints scream something fierce, hundreds of miles away from any sign of civilization. They were definitely nowhere near chocolate covered strawberries and scotch and terry cloth bathrobes! Accommodations were that girly cot, inside a tent that rattled with every breeze, eating freeze-dried yogurt balls and beef jerky.

And that damn mosquito!

Naw, what the trip really was about was Silas staying

behind to plan his wedding with his chickadee—his other boss. Dude was in punch-drunk love, is what he was, and they had dresses to pick and color schemes to plot and reception menus to prepare. So, stay Silas did, and off Gapinski went to a dig site on the border of Iraq.

Which was fine. He was all about the bro code of honor. Soon his duty would be done anyway, and he'd get back to the States and then spring for a vacation. Definitely some place on the cooler end of Earth's spectrum. Maybe an Alaskan cruise. Definitely an ocean view suite chock full of chocolate-covered strawberries, bottles of scotch, and terry cloth bathrobes. And lots of *X-Files* reruns.

And no skeeters!

Flipped to his back now, cranky and stewing as the full moon painted one side of his tent a faint silver. Wouldn't be long before the crew outside would start banging and clanging away on their equipment and he'd be joining them, pickaxe in one hand and a handful of freeze-dried yogurt balls in the other.

Except...

Gapinski bolted upright, tilting his head and sniffing a warm breeze of something that had gusted into his tent.

What was that smell?

He sucked in a startled breath, wondering whether his nose was deceiving him. Then stuck his sniffer higher in the air for confirmation.

Nope. Dead on the money! Both ends of his mouth curled upward with greedy hunger, with instant recognition.

Bacon and eggs, baby!

But in the dead of night? Did not compute in the slightest. No matter. He'd get the 411 on the midnight snack right after he put his pants back on.

Bolting to his feet, he slipped into a pair of well-worn Army surplus fatigues and hustled through the billowing tent flap—searching the dig site with bated breath but knowing full well he could very well be hallucinating given his hunger pangs. Been there, done that, got the beer koozie from basic when he could've sworn the Golden Arches were throwing up Big Macs and french fries just over an Appalachian ridge line after a sleepless night scavenging berries and leaves and boiling bark.

Nope. Instead, he'd stumbled across a dead moose with half its guts spilled on the forest floor, a rotting and maggot-filled corpse that smelled nothing like Mickey Ds.

He sniffed again, neck going this way and that scanning the barren tan Turkish wilderness that was their camp bathed in moonlight—eyes moving from tent to beat-up, second-hand military jeeps to the center of camp.

Where he caught sight of the faint glow of fire.

Taking a step, he squinted. Was that Torres? And working a griddle?

His face widened into a ravenous smile. It was!

Working a griddle piled high with frying pork with one hand, she poked at a cast iron pan with her other filled to the brim with billowing mounds of scrambled eggs topped with cheese. There was even one of those white-speckled blue coffee pots you see on old Westerns, a gust of hot nighttime air confirming it was filled to the brim with black Joe.

"Come to papa..."

Wasn't a long walk, thankfully. Didn't have a clue why Torres was playacting June Cleaver all of a sudden, especially at four in the morning. But he wanted to kiss her feet just the same! And boy, was he glad she was on their side of things. Because after all the operations they'd been on together, she knew how to work a Sig Sauer that's for sure! And apparently a skillet. Who knew?

"Didn't know you were the cooking type," Gapinski said,

reaching his partner as she tonged the last few strips of bacon onto a platter.

"*Buenos días, muchacho,*" Torres said standing. "I can work a skillet of bacon. That's about it."

She was wearing a pink bandana around her head. Hair hadn't grown back yet after several months of wicked chemo treatment for breast cancer. Missed those dark Latin locks of hers, but she'd kicked cancer's ass like the champ she was and got back into the ring to save the world. A real She-Ra Turner, that one was. Glad he was at her side again fighting for the faith.

"What's with the early morning rise?"

She wiped a line of sweat from her forehead. "Last day on the job means an early rise. It's the way I've always worked my digs. A few of us have been working the past few hours, so I thought I should make breakfast."

"Past few hours?" Gapinski shuddered, a wide-mouth yawn reaching up at the thought. "God's not even up this early, and certainly no Gapinski ever was."

She went to respond when his gut intervened, throwing up an embarrassing rumble that sounded like it was coming out places no chick should know about.

Heat raced up his neck, and he blushed with a chuckle. "Stomach. Does that after a week subsisting on freeze-dried yogurt balls."

She threw him a raised brow and thin smile, but let it go.

He went to grab the platter when she snatched it from his mitts.

"*No lo creo, muchacho!* This isn't for us, it's for the crew up bright and early."

"What? I am the crew up butt-crack-of-dawn early!"

She frowned. "You're management, Hoss. It's a special thanks for busting tail the past week."

Gapinski scoffed, offended now. "What do you think I've

been doing the past week, playing tiddlywinks and crocheting my granny a Christmas scarf?"

Torres huffed and muttered something in her family tongue. "*Bueno*. Two pieces. That's it."

He opened his mouth to protest but knew he wouldn't get anywhere. So, he snapped it closed and swiped two strips of fried pork, then promptly scooped a pile of eggs on a plate before she could say otherwise.

She spun around and made for the massive tent glistening silver in the moonlight at the other end of camp.

"*Vamos,* Hoss. We've got work to do!"

Barely got his first piece of bacon down, but he knew how to pick his battles. Especially with Torres. "Coming!"

But not before a cup of Joe...

Nearly burned his mitts pouring the dang thing, and then singed off all his tastebuds after throwing back a mouthful to wash down his eggs, but the earthy mud wasn't half bad. He was gonna need it after the fitful night of sleep and final day of work.

Shoveling the rest of his food along the way, Gapinski reached the main dig site, a big-top bonanza-style tent that reminded him of those Ringling Bros before they went belly up after animal rights activists ate their lunch. Couldn't much blame them for their protests. Even as a kid when Grandpappy brought him to see the circus when it rolled into town, he thought making elephants and seals and tigers perform on cue was a bit cruel.

Below the massive tan canvas structure, the ground opened up like a heart surgeon putting in a pacemaker. A generator grumbled and mumbled with as much protest as Gapinski being up that early, juicing up a handful of tripods throwing up yellow LED light casting wicked shadow puppets across the canvas walls. A pit had been carefully excavated at the center, along with adjoining square plots roped off and marked with colored flags that meant something. Half a dozen Order archaeologists and anthropologists were working away.

Didn't have the slightest clue what it all meant. Didn't even know what the gig was all about. Just a worker bee like the rest who was on security detail. But seeing the fruits of all their back-breaking work, the piles of dirt and plots of vacant earth —Gapinski threw up a whistle, craning his noggin around for a look-see at all they had accomplished.

Torres had descended a rickety wooden ladder into one of the open graves and was on hands and knees scraping away dirt again. Another guy in a dirty T-shirt with thick braids slung over his shoulders, Jamar if he remembered right, was hunched over in another pit.

Wasn't sure what they were doing. Looked boring, whatever it was. Never wanted to touch another sand pile again after all he'd scraped and hauled away the last week. As far as he was concerned, sand was meant for building castles and digging your toes inside on the ocean shore, cigar in one hand and mojito in another.

Just what the doc ordered, actually, after all they'd—

"Don't just stand there!" Torres shouted up to him, snapping him back to the task at hand. "*Vamos, muchacho!* Lend a hand, would ya?"

Throwing back the rest of his brew tasting of old socks now, Gapinski climbed down the ladder he prayed to the good Lord above would hold his girth, then joined his partner to offer a helping hand.

"What do you need, sister?"

"Move all the sand and dirt I'm taking away from this final specimen."

"Roger, roger."

He stood and stretched the scream from his spine, shirt already pasted to his back and forehead dripping with sweat. "A hot one already, geesh. Dry heat at least. None of that swampy, humid crap from back home."

Head down and focused on her digging, Torres replied, "Beats salvaging lost ships, that's for sure."

"Oh, yeah. Forgot about that. Knew you were some anthropologist or archaeologist—"

"Both," she said as she kept removing a layer of hardened dirt.

"Well, there you go. Bet you and your uncle made bank."

Torres wiped a line of sweat beading at her brow. "You could say that. The work also put me on the radar of all the major exploration, salvage, and archaeological groups. Including the Order of Thaddeus."

"Ahh, so that's how you got to be an Order agent. Sounds like a story with that one."

"Radcliffe, God rest his soul—" she crossed herself before continuing, "he had been acquainted with my grandfather from his time serving as a Jesuit archbishop in the Vatican's Congregation for the Doctrine of the Faith. Apparently, Abuelo had put in a good word for me, telling him about my deep faith and commitment to the Church. And having read about my archaeological exploits in the news and hearing from *mi abuelo* about my experience with the Israeli Defense Force as the daughter of my ethnically Jewish mother, Radcliffe came calling and the rest is history."

Gapinski snorted a laugh. "He could be persuasive."

She nodded. "I was pretty resistant to the invitation. Reluctant, really, having devoted years of academic work and vocational energy to preserving the culture of my father's people in Mexico."

"That's right. Your pops was from south of the border. Before he died—I mean..." He cringed, knowing how Torres's parents' death had hit her as a teenager—literally the family getting hit by a drunk driver. "Sorry about bringing up old memories…"

She flashed him a weak smile before returning to her work. "No worries, Hoss. And yes, *mi papa* was Mexican. Anyway, after sitting down with Radcliffe and Celeste, I was intrigued by the idea of offering my talents for historical inquiry and anthropological preservation in service of the Church."

"And here you are," Gapinski said, spreading open his arms. "On a dig site in Turkey digging up some bones of some saint I don't know a lick about. Sure he's some important dude who—"

He stopped short, squinting at what Torres had uncovered.

"Is that a full-length skeleton?"

She stood and brushed the dust off her hands. "*Sí.* But not of any Christian saint."

"Who then?"

"Someone who lived almost five millennia ago."

"Five hundred years?"

Torres smacked his arm. "Try five thousand years. A millennium is a thousand not hundred."

"My bad. But that's wicked cool."

"Got a tip a few months ago and here we are."

Gapinski crouched for a look-see. "Where the heck did you get a tip like that?"

She shrugged. "Old contact who swims in foreign intelligent circles."

He counted off the years with his fingers. "I suck at math, but if I figure it right—" Another few fingers, then another. "Doesn't that put him, like, way old? As in Moses old."

She smirked. "Try again, Hoss. You're looking at a specimen that died during the flood."

"The flood? As in…the flood flood? Noah and his ark, all the animals dancing the conga line two by two?"

"Something like that. Initial radiocarbon dating we

performed up top puts the bones between 4500 and 4800 years ago. And these tools, see these here?"

"Yeah. Looks like a pot and some knives."

"A cauldron, actually, made of solid bronze. You can see that greenish patina there."

"Looks like mold."

"A chemical reaction with the copper that changes the surface. Think of the Statue of Liberty."

"Gotcha. So, what, our mystery dudette was cooking when God rained down the funk on Earth?"

"A man, actually." She pointed to the middle set of bones. "That pelvis ain't made for childbearing, Hoss."

Gapinski shuddered at the thought. Had a kidney stone once the size of a peppercorn that hurt like a mother. Couldn't imagine pushing anything bigger out down there!

"My bad. Figured if you got ancient cookware, then Wilma Flintstone must be around somewhere."

Torres crossed her arms and threw him a glare. "That's not sexist at all."

"Just saying! Suppose Wilma could have brought home the saber-tooth bacon and Fred cooked it."

Now she cracked a smile. "Something like that."

"Is that unusual, a Bronze Age fella manning the stove?"

"Yes, but now you're editorializing. Have no idea what he was doing when the waters rose. Could have been forging the cooking utensils for all we know."

"A regular blacksmith, ehh?"

"A sort of smith, yes. Not black. They only worked with iron. This dude's not old enough."

"How about that..."

"At any rate, we're about done here. Just have to pack up the bones and other archaeological findings, then we're good to go. A good week's work, I'd say."

"Except you forgot something, sister."

"Yeah, what's that?"

"His brother chillin' next door."

She furrowed her brow and looked around the cleared floor. "What do you mean? What brother?"

Gapinski pointed. "Isn't that a finger bone poking through the sediment?"

Torres went to her knees and grabbed her trowel and brush, then started at it. He looked on as she worked her magic. She was like a female Michelangelo working a slab of marble, chipping and brushing away the dirt for the goods below.

Took some doing, with a whole lot of silence that grated on Gapinski's nerves. But he held on and held his tongue, letting her work. Dirt seemed softer here, so the bones emerged more easily. One finger after another until—

"Holybamoly, Batman! Is that what I think it is?"

She finally sat back and took a breath, wiping her forehead wet with sweat again. "You see it also?"

"Sure do! No way I could miss that sixth digit sticking out on that dude's paws. Or dudettes, as the case may be. Hey, you think that dude had a six-finger wife?" He snorted a laugh and shook his head. "Sounds like a country song..."

"No sé, Hoss. No sé..."

She fell silent, staring at the weird hand thingy. Then got back to it, scraping and brushing and clearing away the dirt until an arm was revealed, leading to a shoulder on toward a yapper that was hanging open like it was nobody's business. Tiny thing, too. Looked like no mouth he'd ever seen.

Finally, she rested on her laurels, leaning back and shaking her head while muttering something under her breath.

"What was that?" Gapinski said, annoyed at her keeping her cards close to the chest. "Don't leave me in the dark, sister!"

Torres turned to him, muttering again, *"Hombre desconocido, Hoss. Hombre desconocido..."*

"No comprendo, chica. My español is a little rusty. Whatcha saying?"

"What I'm saying—" She faced him now, eyes wide and face white. "I think this very well could be a new kind of human group."

"Like some German dude come to soak up the rays at an Airbnb? Or some African or Indian come to—"

"No, no, no," Torres said, waving her hands. "Not a different *Homo sapiens*, some other race or ethnicity."

"Then what?"

She took a beat, then a breath before answering: "*Homo ignotus*."

Gapinski twisted up his face. "Como say what?"

Another beat, another glance at the specimen.

"Unknown man."

Silence settled between the pair, the truth bomb doing some major damage in the bowels of their dig site. The chatter above from the crew and flatware on plates was the only soundtrack for their noodling on the meaning of their find.

Until—

Gapinski gasped. "Wait a hot second..."

"You see something, Hoss?"

He reached for the trowel and brush. "May I?"

She hesitated but gave up the goods. He took them and started scraping at the sediment. Probably too hard and fast for Torres's liking, but he didn't care. He could see it in his mind's eye fully unearthed even before it emerged, but he wanted to be sure. That hand, then that mouth had sparked something that made him attack another part of the remains.

The head.

More specifically, the skull.

Took some doing, Torres patiently waiting for Gapinski to work his own magic. But soon it emerged.

Exactly what he feared.

"*Que es eso?*" Torres said lowly, as if she'd come face to face with ET.

Which was about right on the money.

Gapinski plopped down hard on the sandy ground, head spinning with what it meant. Spinning with the memory of what he was *sure* it meant. And yet—

No way was this happening.

Again...

CHAPTER 4
WASHINGTON, DC.

Who the heck is Nicky McGrath?

Looked like Silas was about to find out.

The tall, lanky man nestled in the back corner fumbled with his paper, putting it back together even as his eyes darted around the dining room. He straightened back his broad shoulders on their approach, and his rolled-up sleeves revealed a tattoo with Arabic characters. Candlelight glinted off from green eyes set above angular cheekbones that cast dark shadows across his clean-shaven face. A handsome fella who looked like one of those guys who thought he owned the world, head raised and cocksure with that glare of his he had thrown Silas's way.

Nicky McGrath, he assumed.

But who the heck was this guy? More importantly, how the heck did Celeste know him? And why did it look like the guy was interested in them—in him, even her?

Silas wasn't sure he wanted to find out.

Celeste sure was interested in finding out, though, reaching his table and planting her hands on her hips.

"Nicholas McGrath, what the bloomin' blazes are you doing here?" She said it with an air of disbelief as much as irritation.

Like they had history. Maybe at Oxford or MI6—romantic, even?

The man shushed her, putting out a staying hand before motioning for her to have a seat.

"Crikey, keep your voice down, would you?" he said with a British lilt, much like Celeste's.

Not Cockney, the accent of working-class Londoners. Queen's English. The kind hammered and honed in preppy boarding schools like Eton and Winchester College, then refined at Cambridge or Oxford for lock-jawed, black-suit service in some commercial trade or media conglomerate—government, even.

Silas had encountered enough of those blokes in Iraq during Operation Iraqi Freedom—or UK code-name Operation Telic, their boys making up the Coalition Forces that had cooperated with Kurdish forces in the north to atone for 9/11 and nation-build the country into the 21st century. One of his best friends during his tour was a British soldier, Eli Denton. A man he had met during the on-base chapel service that changed his life—who then went on to betray him in his second operation with the Order.

So, to see this man with that accent in that French bistro, 3600 miles from home, someone Celeste clearly knew from whatever part of her past—the encounter threw up all sorts of signals and red flairs from the back of his lizard brain. The one not only trained by Uncle Sam during his tenure with the Rangers, but by his ancestors chasing down mastodons and saber-tooth tigers.

In other words, Silas was ready for anything.

"Don't dawdle, standing there gawping at me like you're mental," Nicky complained. "Sit, sit!"

Celeste threw up a sighing huff and slid into a chair opposite him. Silas grabbed his chair from their table and joined her. So much for wedding planning.

"What are you doing here?" she said, voice tinged with the sort of no-nonsense edge he'd come to expect from her—both on and off the job.

"How about we start at the top," Silas said, getting down to his own business. "Like who you are and why you were eyeing me from across the way."

"Suppose introductions are in order." She gestured to the man, explaining, "Silas, this is Nicholas McGrath. Former partner with MI6—"

"And lover..." the man interrupted with a wink, one end of his mouth curling upward.

Crimson instantly rushed to Celeste's cheeks. He could see the embarrassment even in the dim light. She pushed a stray lock of hair behind her ear, a nervous tick he'd come to learn, and love.

"Yes, well, that was a long time ago," she said. "And my question still stands. What are you doing here, Nicky?"

"Come to fetch you, that's what."

She crossed her arms, clenched her jaw, and furrowed her brow. Saying nothing but at the same time saying all she needed to say.

Explain.

Nicky's mouth flattened into a thin line of understanding. He took a sip of his warmed drink, then another. If he was MI6, this could get interesting...

"I've come for a favor," he said above a whisper. Leaning in, he added, "Not personal, mind you, but professional. For Her Majesty's government."

She scoffed. "I'm retired, you know that."

"You know how this works, Celeste. No one ever really leaves the Circus. Once a spook, always a spook, in the parlance of you Yanks."

"The Circus?" asked Silas.

"Nickname for the Secret Intelligence Service," Celeste

explained. "And I settled my debts, Nicky. Fair and square. So, if the Chief has an issue, he can come fetch me himself."

Nicky took another sip of his warmed-over drink and put up a hand. "This is an off-the-books operation, not from the Chief."

She relaxed for the first time and leaned in, resting her arms on the table. "Off the books? For what sort of nonsense?"

The agent shifted, looking over her shoulder and then over Silas's, glancing across the space as if he were looking for listening ears. This was too weird for words.

Now at a whisper, he asked, "Does the name Project Condign mean anything to you?"

She held her stare, the seconds ticking by before she finally blinked. "You're speaking of the secret UFO study undertaken by the British Government's Defence Intelligence Staff, aren't you?"

"That's right."

Now Silas shifted in his seat and crossed his arms. "Secret UFO study?"

Nicky shushed him and glanced over their shoulders again. "How about you invite CNN to broadcast our conversation whilst you're letting the cat out of the bag!"

"What cat are you referring to?"

He took a breath, then glanced at Celeste. "The one where I need your help, Celeste. And the Order of Thaddeus's."

"And what kind of assistance are you meaning?" she asked.

"The kind that cracks open and stays the hand of a conspiracy that threatens to undo the very fabric of Western civilization—all of civilization, really."

Celeste sputtered her lips and crossed her arms again. "Enough of the theatrics, Nicky. Get on with why you're really—"

"A government entity," Nicky went on, raising his voice for the first time, clearly frustrated. He sighed a curse and continued, "A government is interested in what I have to share as it poses the utmost national security threat. That's not even touching on the political implications, the social ones—as well as religious."

That got Silas's attention.

Celeste leaned in again, saying above a whisper, "What's happened, Nicky?"

The man cast Silas a sideways glance. "Can he be trusted?"

Celeste nodded. "Trust me and you can trust Silas."

The MI6 agent leaned back now, crossing his arms and looking at him with those piercing green eyes of his. "Professor Grey, isn't that right?"

Silas looked at Celeste, then nodded. "That's right."

"Master of the Order of Thaddeus, ancient propagandists of Christianity. Before that, professor of Christian history at Princeton University, earning his PhD from Harvard under the direction of Henry Alfred Gregory. A man who was tragically killed at the hands of religious terrorists. Before that, tours in Iraq and Afghanistan with the Army Rangers, where you discharged out at the level of sergeant. Does that sound about the long and short of your biography, Master Grey?"

Silas smirked, leaning back himself with the same cross-armed pose. "Looks like you've done your homework, *Nick*."

"Truth be told, I did the same homework on you as well, Celeste."

"Nicky, what are you playing at?" she asked.

"You recall having a visit with me at The Hague this past summer?"

"Right..." She threw Silas a sideways glance. "We interrogated the bloke who stole the relic bones of Polycarp. What of it?"

"And you were quite surprised to find me manning an operation hunting down religious artifacts."

"I was. As were you, if I recall, not expecting me to show up on your turf."

Nicky shrugged. "Not really. I knew you were working for the Order all along. In fact, I recruited you specifically for the assignment with INTERPOL."

"What?" she exclaimed, nearly flying out of her chair. "You little bugger!"

"Now, now. Don't be so dramatic. I needed to see if you still had it, and your religious outfit was a match for my needs."

"For MI6?"

He nodded, saying nothing more.

"So, you played me for a fool."

"Not intentionally."

"I'm sorry, but hold on," Silas interjected, head swirling with the night's direction. "You mentioned *needs*. What are those, exactly?"

The man shook his head. "Not here. Now that I've made contact, it's best if we return to the British Embassy."

Silas went to protest when slamming car doors just outside caught his attention.

Heavy doors, and four of them. One right after the other. The kind that come from something big and bulky, from men with solid arms and on a mission.

He glanced toward the sound and was alarmed that a couple a few tables down had parted the lace curtains and were pointing outside.

"Hold that thought."

Standing, Silas edged around Celeste's chair to one of the picture windows flanking the street. He peeled back a white lace curtain for a look outside.

Not at all liking what he saw.

Men in black were assembling outside a large vehicle. Four of them next to a black Chevrolet Suburban. Couldn't get a read on the plates, but Silas knew government-issued schmucks when he saw them. Dressed in black suits you'd find at any Nordstrom, with dress shoes made for running and hair trimmed close to the scalp. Along with dark shades that were out of place at that hour of night.

And one more thing. Something he glimpsed glinting in the streetlight.

One of the newcomers had brushed back his jacket and shoved a Glock 17M at his waist.

Not good...

Silas let the curtain slink back into place and withdrew his own weapon. A Beretta holdover from his days with the Rangers. Not Army-issued, but he appreciated the Italian-made weapon that had saved his backside on more than one occasion in the Middle East. Much more preferred it to the German ones other SEPIO agents used. And he never left home without it, thanks to the advice Gapinski offered one operation after he was caught flat-footed.

"We've got company," he revealed.

"What?" Celeste said, twisting around with wide eyes. "Who?"

"Men in black."

"Bloody hell," Nicky said, bolting to his feet and withdrawing a weapon of his own. Silas snorted a laugh. Looked like a Sig Sauer. Figured.

He shuffled to the window now as Celeste stood, the man yanking back the lace curtains for his own look.

Celeste went to their table and retrieved her purse. Opening it, she withdrew a Sig Sauer of her own. Supposed if his own fiancé fancied the weapon, he shouldn't look down his nose at their new British friend.

"Who do you figure it is?" she asked lowly while Nicky scoped out the street. "Nous? Those upstart religious whackos, the Church of the Theotites?"

Silas shook his head, noticing the patrons around them staring and shifting and talking in whispered rushes.

"Not sure, but they looked more official than upstart."

"Official? As in..."

"As in government official. American by the make and model, though I couldn't tell which agency."

"Bloody hell..."

Nicky jumped back from the window. "They're coming."

The man hustled past diners looking worried now toward the entrance, reading his weapon.

No way they were getting out the front door. Not with at least four hostiles, or government agents, or whoever they were gathering on the street. And if they were the feds, last thing Silas wanted was a shoot-out. Just the sort of scenario Weiss would slobber all over, sealing his fate for sure.

He scanned the dim room for an alternative exit, catching sight of the only other door available when a server came through it bearing a tray of food.

Kitchen.

Which would surely have an exit out onto some back alley, fire code and all.

He put a hand at Celeste's back and started off. "This way!"

She followed, withdrawing her cellphone. "I'll call for backup."

"Good idea."

The night just kept getting better and better...

The pair hustled past their original server as others stood now with assessing concern, one woman giving a startled scream as Silas padded past. Assumed she had glimpsed the pistol clenched at his side.

"Come along, Nicky," Celeste said. "Unless you'd rather enjoy your sunset years in a US black site."

"No, thank you..."

He joined Celeste hustling through the kitchen door, a

suffocating breath of humid, cuisine-laden air smacking them in the face upon entrance. Silas stopped for a parting glance, weapon raised now.

Just as the four agents he had glimpsed outside came bursting through the front. The men quickly fanned toward the back corner where they had been located. Almost as if they had gotten a tip on Nicky's location.

One agent spun around and locked eyes on Silas.

Not good...

"Federal agents, stop!" he yelled, pointing his weapon.

Silas snorted a laugh. Yeah, right. Then he took off after Celeste—

Smacking into a server with plates of coq au vin—baked chicken, mushrooms and carrots, Burgundy wine and all tumbling to the floor and smearing down his front, staining his white shirt brown.

The server cursed him in French, hands going this way and that with annoyed irritation, but he paid him no mind. An exit stood at the end of a long, wide kitchen filled with a maze of faded steel stoves and ovens, sinks and refrigerators. Celeste and Nicky were running toward it, bobbing and weaving through a gauntlet of cooks dressed in white chef coats stained brown.

He made a mad dash to join them—

When a hand clenched his arm.

"Not so fast, pal."

Silas spun around and smacked the hand away with his raised forearm.

Finding a pistol aimed at his face. That Glock 17M he had glimpsed earlier. Government-issued, with a pasty white face sagging from years at a desk to match.

He quickly shoved his Beretta at his back, then showed the man his empty hands.

"What seems to be the problem, officer?"

"What's your name?"

"Puddin' Tate. Ask me again and I'll tell you the same."

The fed didn't like that, the man tightening his grip and working his clenched jaw with irritation. Knew it was all for show. No way would he shoot in the confined space, with the cooks and servers standing in stunned silence behind. Too much possibility of collateral damage, as they say.

Or so Silas hoped.

"Where is he?" the agent growled.

"Where's who?" he said, backing up and glancing around for leverage.

"Don't move, Marty McFly," the agent commanded, giving his outstretched Glock a shake for good measure.

Silas smirked, taking another step back and glimpsing something that might work. "You're not going to shoot me. I'm a civilian who poses no threat, someone who was enjoying a nice dinner with my fiancé until you came barging in."

Another step back, another glance.

"Not another move!" the agent shouted.

"It's a little thing called rules of engagement, pal. And shooting me ain't going to hold muster."

Now the agent smirked. "I decide the rules of engagement, McFly."

Silas clenched his jaw with resolution.

Me too...

In one motion, he grabbed for a skillet bubbling hot on the burner to his right, yanking it from its perch and whipping it at the fed. The burning hot liquid made instant contact. Splashed clear across his face, the man throwing up a painful scream he'd not soon forget.

"Hey!" another agent shouted.

Another goon in black with government-issued hair from behind the poor soul whose face was melting off. Literally, skin peeling away from the boiling liquid.

Couldn't worry about that now or have empathy for the man. Had to keep his head in the game and eye on the ball. Which was getting the heck out of Dodge before ending up in a CIA black site, or FBI holding cell, or whatever alphabet soup government agency was bearing down on them!

The one fella kept screaming, both palms covering his face as the other goon's government-issued Glock rose to engage.

Without waiting for what came next, Silas barreled into the one man he already hammered with the boiling pan, head low and connecting with his sternum.

Sending the dude stumbling into his partner.

Who pinched off a *one-two* shot!

Didn't expect that. Not from the feds. Though in his experience, most never saw combat up close and personal like he had overseas, and were too trigger-happy when they did.

Bullets never drew close to Silas, but one shot straight into an exposed pipe that started hissing something fierce.

He twisted around for a look, hoping to find water spilling down to the floor.

Nope.

Just air, probably gas.

Just his luck.

Which made this thing a whole other thing. Not what you want in the back kitchen of a French bistro filled with cooks and servers and patrons. And open flames!

But first things first.

Twisting back and finding Goon Two struggling under the weight of Goon One, Silas slugged both in the temple. A smack to the skull that instantly flipped the lights to dim. Both men were out cold without issue.

Jumping to his feet, he pointed at a large man in a white coat stained brown and red and yellow. "You, get these bodies out of here and clear the dining room!"

"Who do you think you are?" he replied in an accent that

sounded more Brooklyn than anything resembling French. "I've gotta restaurant to run, Mac!"

"You're not gonna have a restaurant left, Mac. See that pipe?" He pointed at the black tube racing from one end to the other with a chipped tooth still hissing. "That's natural gas. Which means this thing is going to blow!"

That seemed to kick everyone into high gear. Pots overturned and plates crashed to the floor in the everyman-for-themselves shuffle.

Silas went to retreat himself when the Brooklyn chef grabbed his arm.

"What are you, the feds or something?" he asked.

He looked at the bodies on the floor then shook his head. "Or something. Now get the heck out of here! And get them out of here, too."

Yanking his arm back, Silas gestured to the prone bodies and fled for the exit.

Where Celeste and Nicky were waiting in the shadows behind a large rusting dumpster smelling of that boeuf bourguignon he had been craving.

She ran over and threw her arms around Silas's neck. "You're safe..."

"For now."

She gave him a peck on the lips; he returned the favor with more than a peck.

Nicky snorted a laugh. "Don't expect the same love from me, mate!"

Celeste let go and Silas made for the MI6 agent, jaw locked and fists clenched with more than enough punch left to knock those crooked British teeth clear through his skull.

"Thanks to you, that bistro is going to blow to kingdom come after the feds nicked a gas pipe!"

"Bloody hell," the agent cursed, running a hand through his hair.

"What the heck have you gotten us into?"

"*I* got us into nothing. It's your bloody government who has made a royal mess of things!"

"Which we—" Silas gestured with angry hands between him and Celeste. "—have nothing to do with!"

"You have more to do with this than you can possibly imagine."

"What the heck—"

"Boys!" Celeste shouted, her voice echoing through the alleyway. "Let's put away the swords, shall we? We can sort this out later when we find safer ground."

"And when will that be?" Nicky complained.

"Called HQ ten minutes ago. Shouldn't be long."

"Why don't you get your MI6 pals to extract our backsides?" Silas growled. "After all, you're the one who got us into this train wreck!"

A Mercedes G-Class SUV raced toward them and screeched to a halt with intervention. Black and big and looking like it meant business. But definitely not the feds, who preferred domestic-bred vehicles to the European counterparts. Looked much more familiar, much friendlier.

It was Greer, a big, bulky black man with an eight-ball head who could break Silas in half in no time flat. He had also saved his backside the first time he'd met the Order, the man driving him out of harm's way in a similar ride.

He rolled down his window and grinned. "Looks like you three could use a lift."

"Boy, am I glad to see you," Silas said.

"Your chariot awaits." The doors unlocked and he jerked a thumb inside. "Hop in!"

"Don't have to tell me twice..." said Nicky, yanking the door open and climbing in first.

Silas scoffed. Real gentleman, that Brit was.

Celeste followed, then Silas.

"Thanks for answering the call of—"

"Federal agents!" a commanding voice interrupted. "Don't move!"

"You got the feds on y'alls backsides?" Greer said, shaking his head.

Silas jerked a thumb at Nicky. "He did. Now get us the heck out of here."

Greer hesitated, clearly uncertain about defying an order from law enforcement.

"You think that's a good idea, boss?"

He twisted around for a look. Two of the four he'd seen from the start were padding toward them with outstretched weapons. The others must still be out. Which made it two-to-one odds. Not bad. But the last thing he wanted was a shootout with the feds after what he was facing back at the farm.

"Professor, I implore you," Nicky said. "Get on with it! What I have to share is a matter of life and death."

Silas closed his eyes and heaved a breath. Moment of truth...

"Hit it, Greer. Get us back to HQ."

Greer sighed but threw the SUV into *Drive*. "I knew I shoulda listened to my mama..." he muttered before flooring it, tires squealing with protest as the beast jerked forward with resolve.

Right before bullets splintered the glass like angry hornets, white blobs dotting the rear like spit wads. But the bullet-proof glass didn't break.

Yet.

A jerk of the wheel and Greer spun the Mercedes out of the back alley and onto a service road that led to Massachusetts Ave. Shouts of protest joined his tire squeals as he peeled out onto the main artery. Then honking cars and screeching brakes, even the smacking of front ends against rear ends.

Which the man somehow avoided himself. At least they were out from under the fed's guns.

For now...

Celeste slugged Nicky in the shoulder, the man yelping in protest. "What the bloody hell have you gotten us into, Nicky?"

"Oy, mate! I gave you fair warning, didn't I?"

"You said a government entity was interested in what you had to say, and that it posed the utmost national security threat."

"Exactly!"

"Except you failed to mention said government entity was the United States of America!"

"Did I? Oops..."

She slugged him again; he yelped on cue.

Silas twisted around for a look, squinting through the white bullet marks left behind by—whatever government entity had shot at him in the closed kitchen quarters that went against all the rules of engagement he knew.

Which meant this was a major law enforcement operation. Maybe FBI, even CIA depending how hot this intel was and knowing a foreign agent with a rival foreign intelligence service was working on US soil.

An explosion split through the night.

Silas's stomach sank through the floor at the sound; his face fell with it.

A fireball bloomed high in the sky, trailed by a mushroom cloud of acrid black smoke visible even from there. Splintered wood and bricks seemed to float on a pillow of explosive force as they returned to their place of last repose.

He just hoped those poor patrons hadn't joined them in that final destiny.

Celeste moaned. "Weiss sure isn't going to fancy the optics of this turn of things, I reckon."

He frowned. No, he wasn't...

CHAPTER 5

I f it's not one thing, it's another.

Silas ran a hand through his overgrown hair. He had meant to cut it for their date that evening, his locks growing far too long for his taste—and Celeste's—but Weiss had called that special committee nonsense last minute. Wanted to unveil their findings, with the unexpected no-contest vote at the end, which threw his male grooming plans out the window.

Now they were racing back to Order HQ under the cover of night-time darkness after defying the direct orders of some mystery government agency, their French bistro date venue blew to high heaven after a melee with said mystery govern-ment agency, while harboring a mystery foreign agent with a rival mystery government agency spouting off about some UFO nonsense.

He sighed and rubbed his face with both hands. If it's not one thing, it's another is right.

But par for the SEPIO course.

Which meant nothing good was in store.

In the fast-approaching distance, Order HQ shone bright like a beacon of hope. A full harvest moon cast a brilliant silver hue against the Kentucky limestone of the Cathedral Church of Saint Peter and Saint Paul. Better known as the Washington National Cathedral, America's default ecclesial icon that housed the Order of Thaddeus's headquarters and operational nerve center of SEPIO, its more muscular arm. Nearly lost it to a terrorist attack a few years ago, too.

Again, par for the course with the Order of Thaddeus!

Blowing through a stop sign, Greer took a sharp left into a drive entrance near the base of the north transept to the cathedral, the sacred structure looming large in the dead of night. Suddenly, the van disappeared through the black maw of a parking entrance and took a dip, moving swiftly underneath the national Christian architectural icon.

The narrow passage was edged by LED lighting, leading the way beneath the massive building. Old stonework shone in the faint light before curving into a spiral that revealed newer masonry. Turning ever downward, soon they reached a large parking garage of gray cement. Several cars, all black, were docked in spots beneath white lights, SUVS matching their own military-grade one.

"Right, we're here," Celeste said, the SUV sliding to a halt.

"And where, pray tell, is that?" Nicky asked as they exited.

"The Church's Navy SEALs for Jesus," Silas said, leading the way to a set of frosted glass doors.

"Oh, goody…"

Before they reached them, they *whooshed* open. Victor Zarruq rushed through the doors to meet the arriving crew.

The man was rather tall and widely girthed, skin bronzed a lighter shade of ebony from his Libyan homeland and face covered with a salt-and-pepper bushy beard—heavy on the salt. A wide smile stretched underneath, polished white teeth gleaming through a widening smile along with deep-set eyes that shone with delight. He was shrouded in billowing light brown vestments, an interweaving pattern of green and black and blue running down the center. Resting on his bald head was a matching hat embroidered with the same pattern, his outfit marking him as a bishop.

A jolt of anger ratcheted through Silas seeing the man who could have put the whole no-confidence vote nonsense to rest. He knew good and well it was all bull. Yet he didn't lift a finger to help.

He clenched a fist and took a breath, knowing that didn't matter right now. His personal drama had to take a back burner to—whatever the heck the Holy Spirit had dragged to their doorstep.

"I was worried when Zoe Corbino got the call to mobilize Greer and his expeditionary force," Victor said in a North African lilt. "Thank God, you made it safe and sound!"

"Safe, yes," Silas said before glancing at Nicky and adding, "Sound? That's to be determined."

"For heaven's sake, what was all the ruckus about, anyway?"

Celeste answered, "We've had a bit of a go of things, I'm afraid."

The bishop furrowed his brow and shook his head, waiting for more.

Nicky stepped forward and cleared his throat. "I'm afraid I'm to blame for the brouhaha at the bistro."

Celeste chuckled. "Sounds like a '90s British boy band."

"It does, doesn't it?"

"Perhaps cook up some bangers and mash between shows."

"Why not serve cream tea between sets?"

The pair shared a laugh, their high and heady British chuckles echoing around the cement car park.

And grating on Silas's nerves.

Wasn't at all liking how cozy Mr. Bean was getting with Celeste.

"Sorry to pour water on your nationalist camaraderie," he complained, "but we almost got our backsides handed to us by the feds. CIA, FBI, DIA—who knows. So how about we keep it professional until we hear the full scope of the train wreck we're in."

He spun to the doors and took off. "Debrief at my study in five."

The glass doors gently swooshed open on his approach, the scent of sanitized air smelling of a summer thunderstorm a balm for his nerves.

The slate gray hallway was washed in the same dim, white light as the garage, and midnight quiet. Silas hurried forward, guiding the party down a hallway lined with windowless, nondescript doors, each armed with a keycard entry pad. It was as secure as any of the military installations he'd worked at during his military career before joining Princeton and then the Order.

Silas arrived at a set of double doors at the end of yet another hallway and placed his hand on a palm-reading security device. It pulsed a light blue hue before turning a solid green. Then the doors opened, revealing a very different room.

Instead of the sanitized slate gray, the space was entirely clad in dark cherry wood and lined with floor-to-ceiling bookcases. At one end was a large, dormant stone fireplace, though Silas wished a fire was crackling away. At the other end, an ornately designed desk was piled high with books and paperwork. Behind it, three monitors lay sleeping for the night. Commanding the center of the room was a sizable Persian-style rug with two burgundy leather couches, complemented by well-worn, overstuffed burgundy leather chairs. Flanking the arrangement was a minibar nestled inside the bookcases.

He went for that straight away.

The others filed in as he fixed himself a Scotch whiskey, neat. A 30-year Balvenie that probably threw up all kinds of red flags on Weiss's TPS reports, but he didn't care. He poured two fingers worth, then added a third. Figured he'd earned it, and it would give him an excuse to buy another bottle soon enough.

Take that Weiss...

Silas carried his drink over to the huddled couches and chairs, along with Nicky's by request. It was go time.

Settling into a well-worn, overstuffed leather chair that Radcliffe once commanded, he threw back a swig. Intense oak and spice washed across his tastebuds and hit his stomach hard, realizing he never did get that boeuf bourguignon.

No matter. The whiskey was already working its magic. Now it was go time.

"Let's have it, Nicky," he said. "What mess have you dragged us into?"

Celeste crossed a leg and crossed her arms, eyes drilling him with the same question. That's my darling!

Nicky threw back a swig. "First things first. Who, pray tell, are you lot—precisely?"

Silas smirked. "A little late for an intel download, don't you think?"

"I didn't plan on being dragged against my will down beneath some stone edifice to a dead god!"

"Well, we didn't plan on our wedding planning being disrupted by some British spook with too much time on his hands!"

"Boys..." Celeste said. "I understand nerves are frayed from the day, but Silas is right, Nicky. Get on with it. Why did you seek our help?"

Nicky finished another swig of scotch. "I didn't seek your help." He gestured around the study with his glass before landing on Celeste. "I sought yours. Followed you to that French bistro. And I must say, it was quite the delight with you in that posh frock of yours."

He smiled and winked; she blushed and pushed a stray lock of hair behind an ear. Silas wanted to puke.

But he kept his cool. "What did you want with Celeste?"

"As I said in the bistro. Her Majesty's government is in need of her services."

"Which are?"

"Counterintelligence."

"Of the religious sort? You made reference to the Order, so we must have something to do with it."

"Supernatural, not religious."

Silas threw a furrowed-brow glance at Celeste. She shrugged her shoulders.

"Which begs an answer," Nicky continued, "to the question I asked at the start."

Silas sat back and threw back another swig. "Which is?"

"Who are you people? I just thought you were a bunch of tweed-wearing, four-eyed, ivory-tower uni types. Not the sort to organize an extraction in the throes of battle."

"You're welcome for that, by the way."

Nicky chuckled and raised his glass. "Yes, well, cheers to saving my life from a CIA black site." He threw back a swig and asked, "Perhaps a better question than who is *what* are you?"

"Ordo Thaddeum," Celeste said.

"Order of Thaddeus. Yes, I know that is what you mentioned at our little meet-and-greet in The Hague. But I never heard of you until you popped up on my radar."

"And you wouldn't. We've been working in the shadows as much as our archnemesis has—Nous, they're called. Protecting and preserving the memory of the Church from nearly the very beginning of her existence."

"Who is this Thaddeus fellow? I presume that's who it was originally built around. Like the Franciscan and Benedictine monks."

Celeste nodded with a grin. "Impressive, Nicky."

"Once in a while I sail the ball across the pitch into the goal."

"Thaddeus was a disciple of Jesus, better known as Jude. He wrote the letter to the churches in Asia Minor that bears his name."

"And he was the founder of this religious sect of yours?"

"Order," Silas corrected. "But, yes, as the patron saint of lost causes, Thaddeus was acutely aware of the forces already pressing in against the Church and the teachings of the faith. In his letter, he exhorted Christians to '*Contend for the faith that was once and for all entrusted to God's holy people.*'"

A rise in emotion caught Silas by surprise. He had memorized the verse early in his Christian journey, drawn to its passion, to its conviction that there was an essence to the Christian faith that needed to be contended for. It's what launched him into his academic career in the first place. The one that originally brought him to tirelessly work to authenticate the Shroud of Turin, his original ambition that brought him to the Order in the first place. It was a good reminder why he did what he did—regardless of the bureaucratic nonsense Weiss was pulling.

"Contend for the faith," Nicky said. "Sounds a right bit dodgy, if you ask me. Much like those Knights templar whackos, or Islamic jihadis that roam the earth looking for marketplaces to blow themselves up in."

"That's not what we're about," Silas corrected. "The Order's objective is to preserve not only the faith itself, but the shared, collective memory of the faith. Thaddeus had already seen evidence for the need to preserve and protect this memory. More recently, the Order launched a more—shall we say, muscular arm to help promote and defend the memory of the Christian faith."

"Like the bloke who galloped in on his white horse to save our backsides?"

"That's right. Greer is a SEPIO agent, we all are."

"SEPIO?" Nicky asked with furrowed brow.

Celeste answered, "Project SEPIO. *Sepio, Erudio, Pugno, Inviglio, Observo.*"

"I don't—"

"It's Latin," explained Silas. "For protect, instruct, fight for, watch over, heed."

"So, what is it? Some covert Vatican special-ops team?"

"You could say that," said Celeste. "Around a decade ago, the Order realized it needed to take greater steps to preserve and protect the memory of the faith through faithfully passing it along and combating heresy. It's what Radcliffe, the former Order Master, recruited me out of MI6 to lead."

"Much to the chagrin of the Chief."

She blushed, playing with that lock of hair she had pushed behind her ear.

"So you really are some sort of Navy SEALs for Jesus, then?"

Silas took over, explaining, "*Sepio* is Latin for 'surround with a hedge.' That's SEPIO's mission. To surround the memory of the faith with a hedge. To preserve and protect objects and relics of the faith, as well as the memory itself."

"We're mostly research-based," Celeste continued. "We also dabble in a bit of propaganda, you could say, seeking to broadcast the memory of the faith using new media, preservation mechanisms, and other exploits. But we also take seriously the 'P' in SEPIO."

"Which is?" asked Nicky.

"Fight for," Silas said.

"I assume that's where the special-ops part comes into play."

He nodded toward Celeste. "Celeste has been heading up the SEPIO operational arm to fight for the memory. Technically, this more...kinetic aspect of the project falls under the Papal Gendarmerie Corps. The policing unit of the Vatican."

"So SEPIO is a Vatican-run initiative?" Nicky asked.

"We're an ecumenical mission," Celeste corrected, "with

members from every Christian denomination. Protestant, Catholic, Orthodox. We even have some Southern Baptists on the force."

He snorted a laugh. "Figures. But it all sounds just right up my alley. And it makes me think our encounter was meant to be."

"For what, exactly." Silas said, drilling the man with searching eyes as he finished his drink.

Celeste nodded. "Right, Nicky. How about we get on with it? Tell us why you've come calling after all these years."

"Something about a different project than ours. Project Condign, if I remember right."

Nicky threw back a swig and nodded. "Right. Project Condign. Are you familiar?"

"Never heard of it."

"I only recall bits and bobs," said Celeste. "Something about UFOs, as you yourself mentioned."

"Project Condign," explained Nicky, "was a commissioned report running nearly five-hundred pages. Beginning in 1996 and running until the end of 2000, the report was an attempt to properly catalogue and scientifically study all the evidence the Ministry of Defense had accumulated concerning UFOs since the Ministry originally set up its office. It was then tasked with coming to a definitive conclusion about the unidentified phenomena that has captured the world's attention."

Silas put up a hand. "Wait a second. You said, 'originally set up.' You mean to say the British government took all of this UFO business seriously?"

"Oh, yes. Along with every other Western nation, the British Ministry of Defense set up an office for investigating UFO phenomena in the 1950s, around the same time that the United States established Project Blue Book."

"Project Blue Book?"

"I'll get to that soon enough. However, whilst you Yanks

shut down your program the next decade later, the British government kept their investigation going far longer. Or so we all thought."

"What does that mean?"

"Again, in a minute."

Silas sat back in a huff, irritated at the cloak and dagger nonsense from this guy.

Nicky took a swig of whisky and continued, "In 2006, Project Condign was released to the public in an unclassified manner. The Executive Summary from that report states, *'That UAP exist is indisputable.'* UAP being another name for UFO. Unidentified Ariel Phenomenon. The report goes on to suggest no evidence had been discovered to suggest the objects were *'hostile or under any type of control.'* However, it also admitted *'The study cannot offer the certainty of explanation of all UAP phenomena,'* leaving the door wide open to further explanations on whatever the bloody hell they are."

"And what are they?" asked Celeste.

"In a minute—"

"You keep saying that," Silas said with irritation.

Nicky answered, "Yes, well, it's all quite complicated, really. And the most important part pertains to your government."

"The reason for your inquiry?" asked Celeste. "The reason you want my help."

"Her Majesty's government," Nicky replied with a wry grin. "But, yes, I have it on good sources that the American government has kept secret tabs on UFO sightings and has continued to investigate such phenomenon well after it said it did. I also have it on good authority that entities are about to blow the lid on the whole operation."

"Government entities?" asked Silas.

"Not sure. I need to know what the US government knows about UFOs and extraterrestrial biological entities, what they have been covering up and why, what said US government enti-

ties have gleaned from UFO technology, and—more importantly—stop any disclosure of said UFOs and the existence of
alien entities before it destabilizes Western civilization. After
hearing about the nature of your own agency's mission, I am
more certain our partnership is vital."

"Why is that?" asked Celeste.

"Because, my dear, if we fail, and the American nincom-
poops posing as responsible, respectable leaders disclose their
discoveries—well, let's just say disclosure will be a shock reli-
giously as much as politically."

Silas's head was spinning. UFOs and extraterrestrial biological entities, and their cover up? The American government
gleaning information from UFO tech—and the disclosure of
UFOs and aliens? Not to mention civilization destabilized at
their disclosure—it was all crazy talk!

The landline phone chirped on a glass end table for his
attention, interrupting a reply.

"Excuse me a second." Silas punched the phone to speaker
mode and barked a hello.

It was Zoe Corbino, their resident operational support wiz,
along with her partner in crime, Abraham Patel. Between the
petite Italian with oversized baby-blue glasses and her Indian
partner who was a bit scatterbrained but more than adept at
hacking his way into anything that bled ones and zeroes—
between the pair, their tech know-how and operational expertise had gotten SEPIO through more operations than he could
count.

"I'm sort of in the middle of it here, Zoe. Can it wait?"

"No can do, chief. Urgent matter from the field."

"Which field is that?" Celeste asked.

"Turkey," Zoe replied.

Silas threw a worried glance at Celeste. "You mean
Gapinski and Torres?"

"That I do."

"What's happened? Please don't tell me they've been kidnapped by my brother or some other religious conspiracy thriller entity that would give Rollins a fever dream."

"Uh, I don't know what a rollins is—"

"He's referring to James Rollins, dear," explained Celeste. "One of his newest author obsessions. His yarns give SEPIO a run for its money, that's for sure!"

"Genre fiction..." Nicky *tsked* and shook his head. "Wouldn't have expected such low-brow slop from someone as distinguished as yourself, professor."

Silas frowned, heat racing up his neck. He drained his drink and turned to the phone. "What's going on, Zoe?"

"They've found something," she answered. "Well, *somethings*. And one of them..."

Zoe trailed off, going silent but for some fidgety background noise, as if she were uncertain how to proceed. Wasn't like her in the slightest. Always a straight shooter, especially with urgent matters from the field.

"Zoe, we've had a go of it already this evening," said Celeste, "and are in the thick of it here. So we really aren't in a position to be faffing about. Get on with it, would you?"

Clearing her throat, Zoe revealed, "They've uncovered two skeletons."

"Skeletons?" Nicky exclaimed. "What sort of work are you involved with?"

"An anthropological project," explained Silas, "on a need-to-know basis."

Nicky sank into his chair with a frown, getting the message. Which gave Silas a small amount of satisfaction.

"What of it?" he asked. "Are they what we hoped they were?"

"Yes and no," Zoe said.

"What does that mean?"

"The first does indeed look to be from about five thousand years ago. Antediluvian, but I'll let Torres explain."

"Sounds great. What's the problem then?"

Another bout of silence, more background fidgeting.

"Zoe..." Celeste said. "Word on the second skeleton, if you please."

Another clearing of the throat before: "The second one—well...that one isn't of this world."

The characterization snapped everyone to attention. Silas, Celeste, and Nicky straightening and sliding to the edge of their seats. All three leaned toward the phone as one.

Nicky threw Silas wide eyes. "Not of this world?"

Silas frowned and returned to the phone. "Come on, what does that mean?"

"It means what Gapinski says it means."

"Which is..."

"That the second remains are—well, *alien*."

If it's not one thing, it's another is right.

CHAPTER 6

S ilas pounded through the light gray corridors wondering what other measure of crazy the Lord had dragged his way. He took a stabilizing breath as he hustled, the dueling scents of plaster and paint from a rebuild effort from earlier in the year still competing for attention.

Couldn't help but think about what had gone down earlier in the evening—especially with Zarruq's abstention. The thought sent a cold spread of anger through his veins, settling hard in his stomach with churning waves of disbelief.

Couldn't believe Weiss and the other board members were going after him like that, after all he had done for the Order—after all he had done for the Church. Not only preserving and contending for the once-for-all faith, taking more enemy fire and gut punches than he had as a Ranger. But also as a leader who neither wanted the title and responsibility nor sought it out for himself, offering a steady hand when Radcliffe passed suddenly.

The disbelief ratcheted higher with every step into a simmering anger just below the surface. And really, it was a sense of betrayal that felt like Groundhog Day. Yet another institution dragging him before some finger-wagging committee that—

A gentle hand at his shoulder pulled him out of his stewing.

"Silas, I thought I might have a brief word."

It was Victor. Silas didn't really care for his "brief word." But rounding a bend at a T-junction, he nodded him onward anyway. "Sure thing. What word?"

"Well, the one that explains my vote earlier this evening."

Silas's breath caught in his chest at the mention of the dagger to his back. "Oh, that..." was all he could manage.

Victor leaned in closer as they hustled forward. "I understand if you are irritated with my decision not to join the other three in putting to rest this Weiss business. Hurt and betrayed, even."

Silas kept his head down, eyes locked on the black linoleum floor throwing up squeaks with every pound of his rubber boots. Didn't say a word. Didn't much want to.

"You have to understand, Silas," he continued, "there are forces within the Order that are trying to dismantle the very good work you are doing."

That caught his attention.

"Forces?"

Victor chuckled. "I realize I sound like a bargain-bin conspiracy thriller novel, as you are fond of saying, but I had to abstain in order to let the process continue to work itself out."

"What process?"

"The processes of sussing out those who would destroy Master Thaddeus's original work. Which isn't even touching on the work a whole litany of Order Masters have dutifully performed contending for the once-for-all faith. Including Rowen and yourself."

Silas scrunched up his brow and returned his gaze to the linoleum, saying nothing more.

Whispering now, Zarruq added, "As Jesus Christ himself warned, *'Beware of the yeast of the Pharisees.'*"

"You're speaking of hypocrisy, from Weiss and his cronies."

"Indeed. And how their deeds done in darkness may infect and affect the mission of the Order of Thaddeus—fueling their plots against you and our mission."

He recognized the reference to chapter 12 of Luke's Gospel. Sounded troubling. But also vague and undefined. Which Silas hated. Would much rather people speak plainly, but he understood sometimes discretion was required. Especially when sussing out bad apples in the Church.

Rounding the final bend on toward a pair of double doors, Silas knew it didn't matter in the slightest what bureaucratic bull was raging behind closed doors in the bowels of the National Cathedral. All that mattered was whatever development lay beyond those doors out in Turkey, whatever his crew in the field were phoning home to report on.

That, and whatever nonsense Nicky had dragged to his stoop. Which was a whole other ball of ugly Silas didn't even want to think about.

Silas flashed Victor a smile. "I know you've got my back, Victor."

He sighed with a smile and nodded. "Always."

"Whatever you need to do to preserve the Order, I trust your judgment. Let's just hope the rest of Christ's exhortation comes true with your sleuthing work."

"*'Nothing is covered up that will not be uncovered,'*" Victor intoned, quoting the rest of the passage, "*'and nothing secret that will not become known.'*"

"Indeed."

A pair of biometric scanners greeted Silas at the doors: one for his eyes, the other for his palm. Slapping his hand against the one, he put his face near the other, then waited.

A *blurp* sounded as the scanners performed their duty,

though he imagined it was more an aural indicator for the user than anything that worked the gears that would open the doors.

A few seconds later, there was a click, and one of the doors retracted inside the bunker.

Silas took a breath and stepped inside. Time to get to work.

The opened door revealed a space a bit larger than his study, but altogether different.

Dimmed recess lighting around the perimeter shone down upon narrow tables lining the darkened walls commanded by workstations manned by agents dutifully executing on SEPIO orders. A massive screen at one end tracked critical operation updates and news footage from the world's major outlets reporting on items of interest to the Church. At the center of the room, a raised platform with a U-shaped conference table mounted with small screens, swivel chairs, and direct-line phones to operation centers around the world was awaiting his control.

Zoe looked up on his arrival, those baby blue glasses sliding down her face. She pushed them up the bridge of her nose and stood.

Nicky whistled, craning his head with wide eyes. "Crikey, you weren't joshing about with your whole Navy SEALs for Jesus bit. This rivals any MI6 listening post."

Silas took his seat at the center of the dais table. "You can thank Celeste for that."

He frowned at her. "Lilibet would not be pleased."

"Alright, Zoe, what do you have for us?"

Celeste joined him at his right. "Something about their discoveries at the dig site in Turkey, isn't that right?"

"Dig site in Turkey?" asked Nicky, taking a seat himself at the table like he owned the joint.

Irritation rose in Silas at the move, and he almost said something, but he let it go. Had enough on his plate than to get into it with the Brit spook.

Silas explained, "We've been working at uncovering a set of human remains at the border of Iraq based on a tip one of my agents received."

He propped a polished shoe gleaming in the white LED lights on the table. "What kind of specimen?"

"According to Naomi's source," answered Celeste, "the specimen is claimed to reorder our scientific understanding about human evolutionary development."

"Does UNESCO know about this?"

The United Nations Educational, Scientific and Cultural Organization was a specialized agency of the United Nations that promotes world peace and security through international cooperation in education, the sciences, and culture. And they were definitely not consulted.

Silas turned to the man, eyeing the foot before drilling him with shut-up eyes. "No, *Nick*. We didn't. And we're not. Gonna leave it like that, too. I'm sure a man of your professional persuasion can understand the need for discretion, and a bit of subterfuge."

"Right, got it." Nicky slinked back in his seat and withdrew his foot. "Sorry I asked..."

"What's the word, Zoe?"

She leaned over her workstation and clacked away on the keyboard, bringing up a video image on the large main screen.

Looked like a laptop camera view of the main tent covering the dig site, a rough-hewn wooden tabletop with a pencil and paper in view before dropping down into the ground. Bright yellow LED lights from tripod lights arrayed around the space bounced across thick canvas, showing piles of sand and mawing windows of darkness in the ground with dark shadows. Looked like a cemetery had given up the goods to a bunch of grave robbers.

Supposed that was the truth of it, the SEPIO crew having spent the week sussing out the tip looking for bones. Used the cover of a shell corporation looking to exploit mineral mining possibilities to cut through the red tape with the Republic of Turkey. Nothing like dollar signs to grease the gears of government bureaucrats, especially when a stack of Benjamins are slipped under the table.

As they say, it takes money to make money. Especially in the Middle East.

Nothing but the sound of sinking shovels in hardened, packed sand and the *tink-tink-tink* of picks breaking through rocks was heard through the speakers. A hissing bout of static joined in now as the picture fuzzed in and out.

"Zoe..." Silas complained, folding his arms and leaning back in his chair.

"On it." Some more keyboard clattering was joined by Zoe's muffled curses. "As you can imagine, satellite coverage is pretty crappy in those parts. Had to piggy-back on a few commercial providers to make it work—even a government one from a certain Western nation, but don't tell anyone."

Nicky threw Silas a raised brow.

He ignored him, not at all liking outside eyes on their operation. "I don't want to know about it, Zoe. Just bring the feed back to life."

Took a few beats, but it returned, the audio and video clearer and crisper now. He was just glad Zoe worked for them.

Clearing his throat, Silas said, "Hello?"

The screen fuzzed briefly before snapping back to crisp life, the sound of those shovels and picks his only reply.

"Anyone there?" he asked louder. "Torres, Gapinski?"

A large bald head with a sweaty sheen popped up into view down below from one of those mawing graves. Gapinski's familiar face looked this way and that off camera for the voice from above.

"Matthew, it's HQ ringing," Celeste said, finally drawing his attention to the screen.

Gapinski swiped a large, dirty paw against rivulets of sweat running down his forehead. He only succeeded in leaving behind a muddy mess.

"Always something..." he complained, frowning and wiping his hands on his pants before hoisting himself up to the ground and over to the laptop. His white T-shirt was drenched with sweat and plastered to his body, a carpet of dark hair showing through. Could've done without that visual, that's for sure.

"Hey, guys," Gapinski said out of breath, taking one more stab at his forehead but making it worse. "What's shaking?"

"You tell us," Silas said. "What time is it there, anyway?"

"Four, five in the morning. You know Torres, always the early riser."

"Don't I know it. Heard you hit pay dirt over there."

"We hit someone. Or some-*thing*..."

"What's that supposed to mean?"

"I'll let—here."

Gapinski threw up a whistle and hollered for Torres to get her keister to the laptop.

"He's a ripe one, isn't he," Nicky said, propping that foot back up on the table.

Torres came into view before Silas cared enough to do anything about it.

"Good to see you, Naomi," Celeste said. "We've rung to hear about the fruits of your labor."

Silas added, "Sounds like the tip was worth its stack of Benjamins."

Torres nodded. "You could say that. We finished uncovering the male antediluvian skeleton this past night."

Nicky flashed a furrowed brow at Celeste. "Antediluvian?"

"She means pre-flood narrative," replied Silas.

Now he flashed him a frown. "I'm aware, Master Grey, having been raised in the Church of England. Tried my best, but I never did take to religion, I'm afraid. But what is this pre-flood skeletal remains business?"

Heat raced up Silas's neck at the man poking that pointy nose of his in SEPIO business. Went to offer a biting reply when a hand grabbed his knee, and Celeste intervened.

"How about we let Naomi share, hmm? And let's mind our manners, shall we, Nicky? This is no MI6 operation. When you're in this room, Silas drives the cart. You're merely a passenger along for the ride."

One end of Silas's mouth curled upward, and he threw Nick a wink before returning to the screen. Couldn't help but offer a parting jab.

"Alright, Torres. Give it to us."

"As I was saying," she said, "we uncovered the main set of remains in the middle of the night. A middle-aged man who did not appear to die from blunt force trauma."

"So, drowning?"

"Or food poisoning," Nicky said. "Mustn't let our prior convictions get in the way of—"

"Nicky..." Celeste said, drilling him with eyes that meant business.

He folded his arms in a huff. "Carry on..."

"So we have a skeleton," Silas said. "And the dating?"

"Around five thousand years ago."

"Which certainly puts him at the time of the biblical flood."

Torres nodded. "*Exactamente.* But that wasn't the only set of remains."

Gapinski jabbed Torres with his elbow. "Tell him about the alien!"

"Ouch!" she exclaimed, shoving his arm away. "Hold your horses, *muchacho.*"

Silas threw Celeste a sideways glance before landing on Nicky. Who was leaning forward now with elbows on the table.

"Gapinski is right that we have a true *Homo ignotus*. An Unknown Man. But that isn't all."

Torres reached for the laptop and snatched it off the table, the picture jostling a bit. The view changed to a wider shot of the tent floor, the packed dirt ground opened up into a series of pits, dark and hiding their purpose.

"As you can see," she explained, panning the laptop camera across the expanse, "we've made good progress over the week, and the past few hours we've been excavating farther and farther down. Should probably be taking greater care in removing the layers of sediment, but whatever. We were almost there anyway."

"And?" Silas asked.

"And—" Torres spun the laptop around and came into view. She took a beat, then a breath before her face widened into a smile. "There are several more bone fragments. It's a relative mine of human remains! We're documenting it all with plenty of pictures, which we'll send along. But, man...we've got a major find on our hands!"

"Jolly good, Naomi," Celeste said. "Bravo."

Silas nodded. "Yeah, bravo."

"But here's the thing," added Torres. "The other remains are testing far older than the first one we uncovered."

"Human?" asked Celeste. "Similar to the *Homo ignotus* chap you mentioned?"

"Of *Homo* anthropology, yes. But different than the—"

"Alien!" exclaimed Gapinski, popping his head up from behind with interruption. She frowned and shoved him back.

"How much older?" asked Silas, wondering what they had stumbled upon.

"Another hundred *thousand* with one pair, and then another fifty beyond that for another set of bones."

"Is that unusual?"

"Not really. Earlier in the year, a new species of human was discovered in Israel. A new type of early human not known before that had been living alongside *Homo sapiens*. Or so anthropologists have conjectured."

"Speaking of new, you've got to check this!" Gapinski snatched the laptop from Torres. To which she promptly, loudly protested.

He hustled through the mawing graves of ancient bones, jostling the camera once again. Felt like Silas was back in a Ranger helicopter barreling into an operation, the ride was so jumbly.

"Did you hear that?" Nicky leaned back with a satisfied chuckle. "Ancient remains from our ancient ancestors. That should put to rest your silly notions of some intelligent designer and consign Genesis to the trash heap of history. Clearly doesn't tell the true history of human origins. Just look at what you yourselves have discovered!"

Silas smirked. "Not really, Nick."

"Oh, why not?"

"Because historicity isn't really what the creation narrative of Genesis is about."

"It isn't?" Nicky said with shock. "I thought you lot were tied to the hip at the historical preciseness of Genesis 1 and 2. If not historically accurate, not to mention scientifically tenable, then what good is it?"

"You have to understand—"

"Here we go..." Gapinski said with interruption. "Take a gander and try telling me that don't scream alien. If it don't, I don't know what does!"

Took a beat for the camera to digitally adjust its brightness and contrast settings. When it did, the room gasped as one at the image on display.

Lying prone on its back was a specimen that looked human enough. Two arms and two legs, but that's where it ended. A sixth digit was visible on one hand, as long as the others between the thumb and index. All the organs were obviously missing, the soft tissue having decayed millennia ago. But what was entirely obvious and altogether striking was its skull. A portion was missing, cracked and smashed from the point of death or after, but it rose into the shape of a party balloon above its shoulders, narrowing into a small jaw. Clearly would have supported a large brain, and superior mental capacity and intelligence. Didn't look like anything he had seen before.

So who was it?

What was it?

The image suddenly shifted, Torres returning to the screen after having reclaimed her laptop.

"Like I said. We seem to have stumbled across a *Homo ignotus.*"

"Unknown man is right..." Silas whispered, head swirling with possibilities at what SEPIO had discovered—or rather, uncovered.

Nicky stood, adding with his own whisper, "Homo Deus, more like it."

He turned to the British spook, not understanding his meaning. God-man?

"Initial radiocarbon dating puts the bones around the age of our other *muchacho*. DNA is inconclusive though, so that's a—"

"Wait a hot second..." Gapinski said with interruption.

Silas glanced at the screen to find the man casting his view off camera. He stepped behind Torres then from view.

Just as a low-grade hum was thrown up in the distance that sounded like a freight train rumbling their way. It was joined by a whipping wind gusting through the tent and muttered shouts of confusion.

In Silas's experience, none of it sounded good.

Or was a good sign.

Torres followed him with her gaze, looking off camera and twisting up her face.

Until it fell, her eyes going wide with startled shock.

"Silas, we're being in—" The sound cut to nothing and video feed jumbled around.

Then went black.

They were cut off completely from their SEPIO teammates in the field.

With no clue what was going on.

CHAPTER 7
BORDER OF TURKEY AND IRAQ.

S hould have seen it coming from a mile away. A solar system away, given SEPIO's track record. After stumbling across that set of bones from Alien vs. Predator, they should have packed their bags then and there in the middle of the night and hightailed it to that Four Seasons in Istanbul.

But no! Torres had to get her dig on and go rooting around in the unmarked graves of our dead human ancestors, leaving those alien bones to phone home.

And Gapinski had to join her.

Should have stayed in bed, that's what he should have done.

Even with the bugs, the heat, the cramped quarters. On top of the sweaty shirts and shorts and his underoos sticking to his backside. And then the stiff neck and screaming spine, the barking dogs and joints—even with all that he knew he should've sucked it up and flopped to his stomach in that girly cot and just drifted back to dreamland. Let whatever was gonna unfold next unfold.

Because what was coming in hot and heavy up on their backsides was like a bad Steven Spielberg fever dream. Maybe even a bad Chris Carter fever dream—with Fox Mulder and Dana Scully and all the rest from his favorite childhood '90s TV show surely scrambling around not far behind to catch a glimpse what was about to go down.

Because what was coming in hot and heavy up on their backsides surfaced a wicked memory with bad juju from back in his Marine days serving Uncle Sam in Germany. This wasn't supposed to happen again. Not after he'd suppressed his experience with the help of a rock-solid military doc and a yearlong prescription of chlorpromazine that kept him from going all One Flew Over the Cuckoo's Nest!

Yet that wicked wind whipping through the Ringling Bros big top, the canvas flapping to beat the band, and that low-grade hum with the *tick-tick-ticking* of a clock, followed by the *crink-crink-crink* of some windup toy—all of it flashed him back to those woods in no time flat during that middle-of-the-night Christmas romp that would forever change his life.

"*Que diablos...*" Torres muttered with interruption, crouching and craning her neck toward the circus tent's ceiling billowing in the whirlwind.

What the devil is right, sister...

Gapinski joined her on the cold ground, the sand buzzing with the vibrations and the otherworldly hum bearing down on them. The other worker bees had hightailed it at first sign of the crazy. He slumped against a pile of dirt and brought his knees up to his chest.

"This is not happening..." he muttered, closing his eyes and starting to rock slightly.

Wished he could join the rest who'd fled, but he was SEPIO, and head of security. He had a job to do. Whatever that meant in that moment.

And yet...

"This is not happening..." he said on another shaky breath,

disbelieving the turn that sure smacked of familiarity. He swallowed hard, his Adam's apple tripping over itself across his parched throat, then added: "Again!"

"What's not happening?"

"Huh?" Gapinski whipped his head with a start toward the voice.

Torres. Who was facing him with wide, searching eyes.

"You said this is not happening. What's not happening? You know what's going on, *muchacho*?"

She had to raise her voice above the din of chaos descending upon them—literally!

The low-grad hum picked up pace, growing closer and closer.

Same for the wind, the gusty gale blowing fiercer and fiercer.

Heart was strumming a mean beat now. His head joined in the fun with blooming panic, and he could feel his chest constricting in on itself. Like breathing through a straw, it was!

Forget this...

"If you know what's good for you, sister," Gapinski said, "make like a flea and flee!"

Without waiting for his partner, he leaped from his spot and skittered across the sand—

His foot snagged on a cord snaking from that grumbly mumbly generator feeding the tripod lights, sending him face-planting into the sand and snapping the umbilical cord to their power.

Plunging the space into darkness.

"Sonofa—"

As if the hostiles anticipated his cursing, a piercing bright light suddenly flooded the tent from above. Like the flip of a switch, the brilliance of a thousand suns—white and hot and all-consuming. The otherworldly brightness filtered through the canvas tent, casting wicked, inky shadows across the inside. Transforming the environment into a foreign landscape.

Like an alien planet...

A cyclonic wind whipped the structure even more. The twin canvas entrances anchored at either end danced like loose sails, the heavy fabric snapping with wild abandon.

Then a deafening blast of some sort of horn filled the atmosphere. Like the air horn he used to honk at those oddball European football games he'd crash with his fellow American airmen at Ramstein Air Force Base. Only louder and deeper, drilling through his ears and into his skull—into his very soul, even.

Gapinski twisted to his back in the soft, overturned sand and slapped his hands over his ears. He squirmed like a worm and squinted his eyes, thinking that would squeeze away the bassy blast, but it was no use. The racket ratcheted higher, the sound beating against his chest like a KISS concert from back in the day.

Easing his eyes open, it looked like Torres was losing it too. His partner had sunk to her knees behind her own pile of sand, face twisted up and hands pressing in against her own noggin. Could hardly stand the bassy blast, it was so maddening. Until it wasn't.

It stopped as suddenly as it had flared up, the tent quieting down to nothing but the chirping crickets that had plucked his nerves as much as those hissing mosquitos and that useless grumpy generator.

He eased to his all fours and crawled over to Torres, who was leaning against the dirt pile now.

"*Que paso, muchacho?*" Torres squinted and shook her head. "What in the world is going on?"

"Don't know, sister. But I'm getting the feeling we're not alone."

"You think? This has all the markings of—"

"What was that?" Gapinski said, hushing her with a finger pressed against her lips.

He whipped his head toward a pitter patter sound that had invaded their tent, all around. Something subtle, something creepy. Like children running across linoleum, or a dog running through the woods.

Or something much, much worse.

Torres whispered, "What's that sound?"

"You don't want to know..."

She smacked his arm. He almost yelped, but he held it together.

"What was that for?" he hissed.

"What aren't you telling me?" She was crouching now and holding a Sig Sauer. Good idea.

Gapinski knelt to withdraw his own piece wedged at his back, but came up high and dry.

"Sonofa—" he muttered, slumping back to the sand.

Never leave home without cold hard steel, he'd told Silas one fateful operation when he was just starting out with SEPIO. So much for those words of wisdom. Must have left it under his girly cot.

"Well?" Torres hissed again.

He clenched his jaw tight, mulling over whether or not he should spill the beans.

The pitter patter drew closer, all around. The spotlight deluging their tent with the light of a thousand suns cast creepy shadows all around them, the dark figures slinking along and approaching their position.

Instead of confessing, he clenched his eyes. "This isn't happening...This isn't happening..."

"What's not happening? Hoss, give it to me straight, *muchacho!*"

She grabbed his shoulder and gave it a shake, jolting him back to the moment with a start.

He swallowed and went to answer—

When the pitter patter spun on a dime to a clippety-clop. Like a bunch of zebras running for their lives across the plains of Africa!

And the light cut to nothing before an eerie red spread across the tent instead.

"What the..." Gapinski chanced a glance from behind the sandpile, catching nothing but shadows and definitely not children or zebras.

Eyes tried to adjust to the sudden change, but it was a no go. Couldn't see for the life of him who or what was scampering, and where. Or why the sudden shift from what sounded like an invasion seeking something from their circus tent—

Until he heard it. The grunting rumble of something approaching the dig site. Fast, and not just one something.

Slumped with a quivering sigh, he swallowed hard, his mouth tasting of sandpaper and the coppery tang of adrenaline and exhaustion.

"We've got company."

"Again?" Torres complained.

"Of course. It's a SEPIO operation. What did you expect, a cakewalk?"

"But who?"

Gapinski shrugged, trying to catch his breath. "Competition, I'd wager."

"For what?"

"We've got some pretty slick gear courtesy of the Vatican piggybank. So maybe local bandits, mercenaries for hire."

Even to himself, he didn't sound so convincing.

Torres jerked a thumb beyond their dirt pile. "Or treasure hunters. Those bones we uncovered would fetch a pretty penny on the black market. Believe me, I'd know."

You just tell yourself that, sister. Because they're treasure hunters, alright...

She held up her Sig at her chest and flipped away the safety. "Come on. Let's give them a welcome they never—"

A torrent of *rat-a-tat-tats* cut her off, sending Gapinski reaching for his own weapon on instinct before remembering his screwup.

"Always something..." he muttered, rising to a crouch.

Torres joined him then pointed at the back entrance, the opening still flapping like a loose sail. "Sounds like they're coming from the north. Exiting the south entrance should give us the cover we need to get the jump on them."

"In theory..."

"You got a better idea?"

More *rat-a-tat-tats* gave all the word on the matter.

Gapinski took off in an awkward crouch that made him wish he'd cooled it with the Choco-Choco cake snacks. Couldn't believe he still ate those things after the last SEPIO operation nearly made him a quadriplegic, but they were his weakness. Not to mention giving him a spare tire that wasn't an asset when you're running for cover.

He padded across the uneven ground through piles of sand and debris with Torres close behind, winding his way past the open graves that threatened to swallow the pair whole if they weren't careful. A misplaced footstep nearly sent Gapinski into one of them, but he recovered and plodded onward.

Nearly at the back exit now. Could see a sliver of orange racing along the horizon. A promise of the good Lord's new mercies with the rising of a new day—if they made it out of the crazy alive, that is.

Torres cried a painful curse from behind. Gapinski went to spin around to see what the matter was when something else caught his attention. Not a sound or a movement.

A feeling.

His teammate cried out for help now, but Gapinski didn't answer. Couldn't answer, the impulse or compulsion telling him to keep going. Like a tractor beam drawing him outside into the dawning day.

And to the sky...

The red light that had lighted their way suddenly cut to black, which normally would have sent Gapinski skittering for cover at the sudden turn. But he hardly noticed. His gaze was fixed to the tent ceiling without anything registering between the ears.

Could almost sense the object of his desire drawing him to itself on autopilot now, barely registering Torres's pleas for a helping hand. He was entranced—he was in a trance, his steps on autopilot carrying him through the waving canvas flap and beyond into the barren wilderness.

Pushing into the dawning day, first thing his lizard brain sensed was the smell. Like a summer thunderstorm, the sweet and salty scent of rain and atmosphere charged by electric tendrils. Which made all the hairs on his neck and arm stand at attention, followed by a coating of gooseflesh that threw up a wicked itch all over.

Then there was the sound of it all. Not the bassy blast that had brought them to their backsides, but a continued low-grade hum that messed with his ears joined by the grunting rumbles of a pack of pickup trucks with some miles on them. Those newcomers skidded to a stop, followed now by the cackling calls of some wild boys and that *rat-a-tat-tat* call to arms that had activated him and Torres.

But none of it mattered. Didn't pay it any attention because it didn't come close to the sight his peepers glimpsed. Took a second for it to register, his lizard brain not catching the full measure of it all. But once his eyes adjusted, and the expectations of what he expected from the clear nighttime sky weren't met—well, he nearly crapped his pants at the sight connected to a memory from a past he had never wanted to relive.

"Holybamoly, Batman..."

The sky above was still a deep indigo punctuated by a sea of diamonds. The kind most people only see on the internet or History Channel thanks to all the light pollution of modern living. Except smack-dab in the middle, hanging square above their Ringling Bros circus tent was a patchy void of light and life. At first glance, just looked like any old nighttime view. Dark and blank and waiting for the sun to rise.

But Gapinski knew better.

Because where he expected stars—it was like a black hole had opened up above, except not at all a circle. Shaped like a delta stealth bomber, it was. All triangular and angular, and the size of a football field. Soundless, too, but for that blasted low-grade hum that plucked his nerves. Just hovered there without movement, without motion, without intent.

Gapinski slapped a meaty palm against his forehead, the thing wiggling something fierce against his clammy, sweaty brow. Couldn't think of anything else to do with the sight of it all.

This is not happening...Aga—

A sudden *thwump* from stage right drew his attention. Something familiar, something with the ring of combat.

Right before he caught sight of a projectile streaming toward the black void.

And smacking into it with a deafening *KABOOM!!!* that shook the dawning air.

Didn't have time to hit the deck, it came so sudden.

But then he did as a fireball bloomed from the side of—whatever the heck was hovering above their dig site!

The force of the fire and fury slammed into Gapinski's chest before he knew what was what—launching him from his feet and sending even his oversized keister sailing through the air until he was splayed on his backside.

Where his head slammed into a boulder, all angular and halfway submerged in the sand.

But not before a series of crazies flashed before his peepers.

In that split second between the grenade exploding into the side of the black-hole-that-wasn't-a-black-hole and him sailing through the air, Gapinski expected the craft to shatter. Some wing or tail or cockpit to come cracking off and flailing to the ground like his own arms swinging for purchase.

But that's not what happened. Not at all what he saw.

Instead, after the force lifted him off his twinkle-toes, all the colors of the rainbow suddenly spread out from the point of impact. Like watery, wavy rings after dropping a stone in a pond spreading out from where the projectile had struck. And not really water either, but a gelatinous coat. Almost like the coating of a jellyfish, the substance or technology or whatever shielding the craft from the explosive blow.

And then it vanished, the blanket of iridescent colors drawing back into itself like water circling a drain until the black void was back. Triangular and humming and sucking all life and light from the sky.

Only the triangular void didn't remain. It opened up into a red eye at the center, and another piece from somewhere offstage lifted from the ground and zoomed back to the mother ship, fitting back into place like a stray Lego.

As Gapinski completed his aerial pirouette but before his head slammed into that damn boulder, a sudden updraft of wind whipped the sand all around him with the same cyclonic force burned into his memory from almost two decades ago. And that heady scent of rain and electric charge returned, the gusty air picking up pace now along with the low-grade hum that penetrated deep into his chest.

Then it was over.

Just like that.

The red light vanished. The blackened, triangular void of nothingness shrank to a brightening indigo and sea of stars. The wind and hum and thunderstormy scents vanished.

It was gone. It was over.

Again...

So was Gapinski's consciousness.

Lights out in a flash.

CHAPTER 8

The darkness was all-consuming, oddly punctuated by bright and shiny stars exploding one after another in an otherworldly phantasmic show. Reminded Gapinski of that moment in Germany, at that blasted Ramstein Air Force base when he saw the craft that would turn his world upside down—and career.

A night much like the one that had sent him spinning back into that blasted rock sending his world into confusion, all the sounds of the moment—that bassy hum, the *rat-a-tat-tat* weapon fire, the shouts and cries of his crew, those damn mosquitos hissing sweet nothings in his ears—all of it fell silent to a tuning fork ting that gave those pesky insects a run for their money.

Felt like he was floating in air too, a feeling of numbing weightlessness overcoming him. Like his very soul was slipping from his body and sailing into space toward the Great Beyond where Saint Pete was waiting at his pearlies for his oversized keister to meet his Savior.

Until it all snapped back to the moment.

Took a strong hand and an even stronger voice shouting for his name to draw him back to reality's surface—but it worked.

"Gapinski!" a voice suddenly came into a hearing. Faint, then muffled, then much sharper on the second round. "Hoss, *despierta, muchacho.* Wake up!"

Took a firm slap in the face to finally do the job.

"Alright, I'm here!"

Gapinski snapped open his eyes, and instantly regretted it.

Pain exploded at the back of his head. A mauling, ravenous pain that shot straight through his skull and into his brain and bloomed in the middle of his forehead. Thought he would lose those two precious strips of bacon and fluffy goodness of cheesy egg heaven, but he held it together.

For now.

He was lying on his hefty hinny, neck craned forward at an odd angle under a jagged rock that probably accounted for the pain. Sand covered his face and mouth, his tongue and throat chalky and metallic and gritty.

That's right, the explosion of that projectile from those hostiles at that crazy hostile craft!

Vision took a bit to adjust, the stars moving to the periphery of his vision and darkness fading into focus now. Leaning over him was Torres and that guy Jamar he'd spotted in the other pit.

"You alright, bro?" Jamar said, extending a hand.

Gapinski took it, and the man eased him to a sitting position.

"What happened?" asked Torres. "I called for you, but you didn't answer. Didn't respond to nothing. Went all loco crazy on me. Like you were on drugs, or something."

No, not drugs.

The memory of what he glimpsed came crashing back like a bad hangover. The thunderstormy scent. The low-grade hum. The triangular, black-hole void. The projectile explosive that sent him sailing into the air before said triangular, black-hole void went all Star Trek Next Generation.

Gapinski gawped for words, pointing at the sky as his mouth moved up and down without a sound, without a reply, with barely any breath left in his lungs to keep him going.

"*Despierta, muchacho!*" Torres shouted right before she smacked him on the shoulder.

It was enough to drag his brain back to the moment, back to reality after what he had seen.

Which was what? An experimental craft, a—a—

He couldn't bring himself to think about it. Not again. Not after what went down at Ramstein.

Another smack, another frustrated curse in español.

"Stop that!" he yelled.

"Then get with it, *muchacho!*"

He finally looked at her and answered, "You mean you didn't see it?"

"See what?"

"The spacecraft!"

She opened her mouth, looking like she was readying to spout off one of her smart aleck retorts. Instead, she clamped it shut—twisting up her face and flashing Jamar disbelieving eyes.

"Now I know," Torres finally said, "you really did go all *loco en la cabeza*. How hard did you hit that head of yours?"

Heat raced up Gapinski's neck and anger bloomed in his head. But he let it go. Explanations would come at the debrief. They were still in the middle of it.

"That was crazier than a one-legged jackrabbit," was all he moaned, managing to bring himself to his knees.

Right before a lancing pain at the back of his head sent his vision fading to black and stomach doing the Tilt-A-Whirl. Bile reached for the surface, the back of his throat tasting like sour milk.

He staggered to all fours. "I think I'm gonna be sick."

Torres was quick to bring a strong hand under his armpit, bracing him from another tumble.

"You're injured, bro," Jamar said. "The back of your head, it's all bloody."

"Took a tumble, that's all." He shoved off his partner and stood, the pain blooming in his head and threatening to drop him again.

But there was Torres with that hand of hers. He threw her a weak smile. "Thanks, sister. Looks like you're hurt yourself."

He nodded to her right leg, which she was favoring.

"Had a run-in with an excavation pit. The pit scored a number on my ankle, but Jamar helped me back to my feet. I'll be fine."

"Aren't we a sight for sore—"

He was cut off by menacing *rat-a-tat-tat* automatic weapon fire, joined by a chorus of frightful screams.

At first it didn't register, the cray-cray sight he'd glimpsed before sailing through the air still the first order of business to address.

Then it did.

"The crew!" he exclaimed, twisting toward the main encampment. A patchwork of moonlit tents and stick figures running about in the distance faded into view.

But it didn't make a lick of sense. The threat zoomed out of Dodge into the sky. He saw it with his own peepers before his lights went out. At least he thought so. Maybe he really was crazy in the head, like Torres said.

"We've got company," she said as she and Jamar guided him back toward the tent.

"Huh? No, we don't. It left a minute ago. Didn't you see it zoom back into space?"

She looked at him like he was crazy again. Probably was. Then she gave his arm a stronger yank, pulling him to the edge of the tent. She jabbed a finger at the air with closed lips and drilled him with eyes that told him to pay attention.

And he did, following her gesture around the edge. His heart leaped clear into his head like that craft had just scrammed into the heavens.

Three aging, sagging Toyota pickups were anchored at the edge of camp. Men in black—three or four per vehicle—spilled out with raised weapons that meant business.

Spreading out across the dig site!

The dudes that had just shot that projectile at that—that —*thingy!*

"Always something..." Gapinski snorted a laugh. "Although, no surprise, really. A bunch of AK-47-shooting whack jobs rolling up on us just as we uncover the mother lode of all skeletal remains is par for the SEPIO course."

"Suppose you're right," Torres said.

"What's the plan?"

She withdrew her Sig Sauer wedged at her back. "Same as always. Blow things up and hope for the best."

"Except I don't have my weapon."

"What? That's like SEPIO rule *numero uno*. Never leave home—"

"—without cold, hard steel. I know! But I didn't think we were gonna get jumped by ET and Cigarette Smoking Man's henchmen, alright!"

"What are you—"

"Never mind," he said, waving his arms around in frustration. "Besides, between my head injury and your ankle, we're like a bad Groucho Marx bit. I'm worried we'd do more harm than good at this point."

"I don't know what that means, *muchacho*," Torres said, "but where there's a will, there's a way. Besides, I came prepared."

Torres reached down to her boot and withdrew a small pistol. Peashooter, really, but it would work.

"I gotta swipe a page from your play book," he said. She went to hand it over, but he protested. "Give it to Jamar instead."

The man's eyes went large and mouth fell. "What, me? I'm just an analyst!"

"That didn't stop Jack Ryan when the shucky ducky hit the fan, now did it?" Gapinski took the weapon and shoved it in the guy's hand. "Take it. We've got who knows who coming up hot and heavy on our backsides. Maybe two different factions after what went down a hot minute ago, going after something that makes not a lick of sense out under that big top but could be a big deal for the Order—a big deal for the Church."

"You think?" asked Torres.

"Not really sure what I think, but what else would they want? Not our good looks for their fall fashion catalogue, I can tell you that. We find ancient bones that run the gamut of earthling and extraterrestrial and then hours later Muammar Gaddafi brings along his pals for an early morning raid? No way that's a coinkydink."

"Does sound fishy. And does have the stink of a certain ancient religious terrorist network all over it."

He knew exactly what she was driving at. Nous.

Gapinski turned to the young man and planted a heavy hand on his shoulder. "You're SEPIO, so act like it and defend the Order's interests. Which are really the Church's interests."

Jamar clenched his jaw, then clenched the pistol and nodded.

"What about you?" asked Torres. "You can't fight in your condition."

"Watch me." Gapinski winced, bringing a hand to the back of his head at the pain that deflated his self-confident bravado. Not as sticky, but it hurt like a mother. He added with a mutter, "I'll think of something. It makes sense if we split anyway. Take on the hostiles, create a diversion to protect the Order's interests in that pile of dirt."

It was go time, as Silas would say. On the double.

The shouts and screams of protest from the crew put an exclamation point on the urgency of hopping to it.

"I counted ten or twelve hostiles," Torres said.

"Four-to-one odds ain't good," Jamar said on a shaky breath.

No, they weren't. Vegas odds is what they were.

"You play the hand you're dealt in this line of work, pal." Gapinski nodded toward the south entrance to the big-top bonanza. "I'm heading down the center of our dig. Secure the goods, maybe find a pickaxe looking for a fight and hope for the best."

"Suppose that's the SEPIO way," said Torres.

"On a bullet and a prayer. Except in my case just a prayer."

She nodded to Jamar. "What about us?"

"You two head off to help our crew," Gapinski explained. "Run down the outer wall and draw the enemy fire. A few of the other crew members are armed, and hopefully they've hopped to it to defend their teammates, but I don't have to spell it out. We're riding on you two and your bullets on top of my prayers to carry us into the sunrise alive."

Torres frowned and glanced at Jamar, the pair considering the plan.

Not a good one, not in the slightest. But what choice did they have? They had to protect their crew and save their discoveries from theft—or worse, some fundamentalist whack jobs who wanted to destroy any evidence of our human ancestry.

Or ET's existence, for that matter.

Then she nodded and chambered a round. "*Bueno.* Let's get this party started."

Jamar followed suit and nodded.

Gapinski flashed a grin. "I'll meet you both around front and peel off the hostiles from engaging the rest of the crew."

A *pop-pop-pop* from some pistol told him they might already be engaged.

"*Adios, muchacho.*" Torres saluted, then took off with her new partner around the corner, popping off a few *one-two-three* punches of her own joined by some lead from Jamar.

Leaving Gapinski to plunge into the portal of no uncertain doom. Alone and unarmed.

Riding on a prayer that he hoped would spare his backside and save the day.

The *pop-pop-pop* assault from Torres and Jamar was met with a ferocious *rat-a-tat-tat* response that was par for the SEPIO course.

But Gapinski couldn't worry about that now. Torres could handle herself, and Jamar looked like a quick study.

The Ringling Bros circus tent was about as fun as the funhouse that scared the childhood crap out of him down in Georgia way back when. Portal of no uncertain doom was right!

Without that beam of light slicing down from the heavens or those tripod LED lights he'd cut to nothing, the place was dead dark but for two beams slicing through the north entrance from a pair of headlights anchored outside. The rays cast wicked shadows across the vast space, with wavy dark figures dancing along the ground and high against the canvas structure. Poltergeists on puppet strings, they were. Sent a jolting shiver skittering up Gapinski's spine, it gave him the heebie-jeebies so bad!

Place smelled wicked, too. Like a pipe bomb had just gone off inside a gym locker room. Gunpowder and dirt and sweat swirled in a wretched stew, turning his stomach something fierce. It was empty, for now. An eerie silence blanketing the inside as the world raged on outside in *rat-a-tat-tat* and *pop-pop-pop* fits. Wouldn't stay that way for long once the hostiles secured the site from any intervention from the crew.

So Gapinski got to it, hustling through piles of dirt and past wheelbarrows and wooden crates of supplies, minding his steps around the open graves and searching for the only one of those rooms at the Bates Motel that mattered.

Come on, come on...

With those headlights slicing through the darkness and the shadows doing the Melbourne shuffle, he couldn't tell one open pit from the other. Just bounced from one to the next, none of them looking like what he remembered.

Outside, more *rat-a-tat-tats* and *pop-pop-pops* flared up. Sent a prayer up to the good Lord above that Torres and Jamar would hold the fort while he searched for his alien in a grave haystack that—

"Wait a minute..."

Gapinski caught sight of the generator he'd tripped over that sent their world plunging into darkness. Which meant that *Homo ignoramus*, or whatever it was, was just around the corner.

He hustled over to the silent hunk of junk. Must've run out of gas. Sure enough, there was the pit. Squatting down for a look-see, he could see the original bones Torres had unearthed planted in the middle, with the giant set of bones—large head, narrow jaw, and six-digit hands—resting alongside it in sweet repose.

Twisting around, he scanned the vast space for hostiles. None yet, that he could see. But he knew it wouldn't be long before—

An angry *rat-a-tat-tat* sliced through the still air, the ground spitting up sand from the automatic weapon fire.

"Sonofa—"

Another *rat-a-tat-tat* sent him dropping to his knees behind the generator. When it flared with sparking protest from another spray of bullets clinking into the metal, he dove for the well.

Landing hard next to the skull looking like an oversized butternut squash that was not of this world!

Coming face to face with the thing of nightmares—his nightmares!—spread a tingly blanket of gooseflesh across his body and sent all his hairs standing at attention.

Boots crunching across the ground above brought him back to the moment, and he knew what he needed to do to keep the memory alive and give SEPIO something to work with. Give *himself* something to work with, even, if he had any shot at getting down to the bottom of what had surfaced—both in the Turkish ground and in his noggin.

Shuffling to all fours, he lunged for the sixth digit curled in on that hand and quickly cracked the bone off at the joint, or whatever the heck it was.

"Can't imagine you'll need that now will—"

"*Halt! Nicht bewegen!*" a voice growled, up top from behind.

Gapinski startled at the voice before dread flooded his veins.

Game over.

Always something...

CHAPTER 9

Gapinski froze, his appendages spread out all catawampus like a game of Twister.

Both knees were planted firmly in the soft sand, a rock or something jammed up and good in his right kneecap. One hand was next to the oversized skull from some '90s alien contact documentary, while the other hovered over that sixth digit.

There was that voice again: "*Nicht bewegen!*"

Growly and guttural and sounding like the dude had just finished a plate of overcooked Brussels sprouts.

Always something is right!

Except...

What the heck was a German doing way out on the borderland of Iraq and Turkey?

Expected the same Islamic jihadi whack jobs from SEPIO operations of yor, given their proximity to the Middle East. Not the Germans. Didn't make the slightest sense.

But since he was unarmed, Gapinski obeyed.

Stuffing the bone in his boot, he eased to his feet and turned around, arms raised.

"*Herkommen!*" a short, squat fellow with a bad case of

midlife acne commanded, waving around an assault rifle that put Kalashnikov to shame. A Heckler & Koch, by the look of it, inspired by the Sturmgewehr 44 from back in the WWII days. Not something to be trifled with, that's for sure.

"Yeah, yeah, hold your horses," Gapinski grumbled, climbing up the rickety wood ladder and ambling over to the lad.

"What were you doing down there?" the hostile asked.

"Ahh, so you are sprechen ingles."

The man narrowed his eyes then motioned with his rifle. "Step aside."

Gapinski took a beat, then another, not wanting to give up his ground. But when the man raised his H&K he complied, inching away from the pit's edge.

The German kept his aim and took a step, then another, leaning over the side for a gander. Only problem for Herr Buttface was that his look-see threw off his center of gravity.

And his aim.

Was simple mathematics, which Gapinski sucked at to high heaven. But what he was good at was billiards. The kind with cues and sticks, blocks of blue chalk and pitchers of Coors. Simple arithmetic, really, which wasn't gonna serve Herr Buttface.

In one *ha-ya* motion, Gapinski leaned back and offered a wicked sidekick to the German's backside.

But not before the dude pinched off an angry reply of lead that sailed past Gapinski and into a sandpile, just as he knew it would.

Gotta love billiards math when it counts!

A quick-thinking rejoinder kick to the German's arm sent the weapon sailing before the German went alley-ooping face-first into the pit.

Gapinski hustled after the H&K and scooped it up, then peered over the side.

Dude was sprawled in the sand, unmoving.

He frowned and shook his head. "They don't recruit 'em like they used to, that's for sure."

But how the heck was he going to secure these bones with—

A scything slice of high-beam lights bouncing his way cut off his strategizing. Followed by a strafing spray of bullets across the sandy ground that sent him dancing on twinkle toes for cover!

Gapinski rolled to the ground out of sight behind a pile of sand and kept going, the Toyota coming in hot and heavy and waving those headlights around like lightsabers.

Slumping down into a shallow grave not touched in days, he peeked out for a look-see as the Toyota emptied. Right at the main pit with the golden goose.

The bones!

One man threw crates to the ground, another slid them below. Two stood guard until the one whack job he'd whacked a moment ago came stumbling up the wooden ladder to join them.

Those Germans were tougher than he thought.

And definitely coming for their skeleton gold.

Not on your life, pal—

The tent suddenly echoed with automatic weapon fire and the ground around him began to dance.

"Sonofa—"

He slumped into another shallow grave and played dead, sucking in his generous gut and praying the headlights didn't shine off his eight-ball head and give away his position.

The H&Ks kept at it, doling out more *rat-a-tat-tats* than he'd had in a long time. And that was saying something, given all the SEPIO crazy he'd faced the past few years!

But he couldn't stay that way forever.

So, he crossed himself—which was weird, because he was

Southern Baptist, but it felt right—and then threw up a livid *rat-a-tat-tat* reply before rolling back to the surface. Jutting out his elbows, he crawled across the ground, keeping to the shadows while bullets sent up sandy retorts from all around.

Soon he hustled his way back out the south entrance. Breathed a sigh of relief, but knew the operation wasn't through. Not by a long shot. Because damned if he'd let those whack jobs off with the golden goose sitting in that big-top bonanza! He'd cook their gander, is what he'd do!

Launching to his feet, he hustled along the outer wall back toward the front to catch 'em with their pants hanging around their ankles when they came back to the surface.

The sky was brightening now, the sun peeking over the horizon and clearing the heavens of those brilliant diamond stars. Camp was clear, too. Neither the Order crew nor whack job terrorists were scampering about. Didn't know what that meant, but he had to trust Torres and their new recruit to get the job done.

Because his job was left unfinished.

A whipping gust threw up all sorts of sand, making it hard to see what was what and snapping the canvas with familiarity.

Shielding his face, Gapinski rounded the front of the tent, padding across the open ground.

And came face to face with a hostile outside one of the other Toyotas holding something that looked oddly like an M320 grenade launcher!

So he wasn't crazy. That was the guy who'd shot at the–the–*flying thingy!*

Except now he was raising it in his direction, ready to sink a 40 mm canister of high-explosive crazy straight up his keister.

Without a thought, his veteran jarhead brain snapping into gear, Gapinski raised his own weapon and fired the H&K until it clicked empty.

Sinking *one-two* shots straight into the John's kisser.

"Nice shot!" he congratulated himself.

Just as the last remaining neurological impulses in the dude's noggin sent a signal to his arms to let loose his grenade launcher!

Thwump went the weapon, sending a ball of ugly sailing toward the Ringling Bros circus tent. Shot went wide and wild, but it landed with a thud smack-dab next to the canvas structure.

Sonofa—

Then exploded in a phantasmic ball of fury that sent gouts of sand mushrooming and fiery tendrils sailing into the tent.

The burning shrapnel instantly caught it on fire.

With those mystery bones still inside!

"Always something..."

Didn't take long before fingering flames raced across the fabric walls and scaled the roof, an inferno of arms and legs gripping the big top with destructive purpose.

Thing was gonna drop real fast, with the bones and hostiles inside. With any hope they'd be trapped and killed, then he and Torres could retrieve the goods.

"Gapinski!" a voice shouted from behind.

He spun around. Torres and Jamar were hoofing it his way.

"You're alive!" he said, the sounds of the raging fire like a freight train now.

Torres drew up quick and scoffed. "You doubted me, *amigo*?"

"Naw, sister. I was talking about our resident analyst."

Jamar joined her. "Gee, thanks for the vote of confidence, bro."

Gapinski smacked his shoulder. "Only playing. Did you get our peeps to safety?"

"Thanks to Jamar's quick draw," Torres said, jerking a finger at their newest recruit. "All crew members are accounted for and safely gathered on the other side of that ridgeline."

A crashing sound cut off any reply.

Back at the big top.

One side had slumped into a terrible fiery palsy, while the rest began to teeter under the inferno.

"That thing's gonna blow real quick!"

"With our bones inside *el casa de fuego!*"

"That ain't the only thing inside."

"Whatcha mean?" asked Jamar.

"A truck full of hostiles," explained Gapinski, "ponied up to the dig and started emptying crates in the graves bearing those cray-cray bones we found."

"*Dios mío...*" Torres slapped a hand on her head. "What are we going to do?"

A revving engine was her reply. Deep inside the big top, joined by a spray of weapon fire.

"Hit the deck!" Gapinski cried, sending the three of them scrambling for cover.

They dove behind one of their old-school Mercedes G Wagons on loan from the Turkish government, moored with two blown tires. Guess that meant their deposit was blown. Silas wasn't gonna like—

The Toyota bucket of bolts burst from the tent's mouth like a bat out of hell, reversing in a panic and flying past their position on a cloud of dust. Truck bed was piled high with black cases and a pair of hostiles letting it rip.

And someone else.

The Jap pickup skidded to a halt, and Gapinski got a better look.

Some geezer perched in the front passenger seat smoking a Camel. Didn't know him from Adam. Although...a curious whiff of cloves smacked of something familiar.

Old guy looked real familiar, but he couldn't put a finger on it. The hair and glasses. The rectangular face and broad forehead with a chock of silver hair chilling under one of those old-school brimmed black hats. The beady little down-turned eyes above the straight nose and small cheeks. Even the pink and white polka dot pocket square poking out of its perch against the charcoal suite struck him as familiar.

But Gapinski couldn't place it for the life of him, his brain still a bowl full of mush from taking one to the back of the head. So, he did the next best thing.

He whipped out his phone and snapped his mug. *One-two-three-four* shots of the man in the cab.

Just as another truck from around the tent took off, tearing toward the front loaded down with a bed full of whack jobs, whoever they were. They sent up a flair of *rat-a-tat-tats* but weren't making any effort. More for show, probably prepping for an exit.

Didn't mean Gapinski wouldn't pick up the slack.

He took off after the grenade launcher from the John he'd dropped. Reached it just as the newcomer was meeting up with the Toyota from the circus tent.

Diving for the weapon, he snatched it from the sand and twisted around for a shot. Still one left strapped on the side. He slid it into place.

A shuddering crash put an exclamation point on the urgency. The whole Ringling Bros big top slumped into a pile of charred tent poles and singed canvas.

Clenching his jaw, he took aim and sent a care package sailing at the pair of roadrunners.

Just as the Jap pickup with the geezer threw it into *Drive* on unsteady feet, the tires kicking up gouts of sand before it drove off into the rising sun.

Leaving the other Toyota to eat the grenade sailing in from the heavens. And eat it did.

The projectile landed hard in the bed, sending the hostiles scrambling for a quick exit.

But not quick enough.

The thing went off and splintered the Jap pickup in half, flaming pieces of steel and burning rubber flying high into the early morning sky brightening with the rising sun. Bodies went this way and that. Some on fire; all most certainly dead as doornails.

Leaving him and Torres to sort through the mess.

Torres's familiar *"Dios mío..."* cry of exasperation floated above the din of the encampment trying to pick itself up by its bootstraps. From behind, standing in the remains of that Ringling Bros circus tent.

Thing had gone up like a puff of smoke, the fire from the explosion ripping through the canvas in no time flat. Equipment was surely toast, too. Good thing he had a satellite phone and an uplink back at his tent to HQ to get those photos back home—but still...

Gapinski sauntered over to Torres, who was kneeling now as she waded through the debris for surviving artifacts. He put a hand on her back; she flinched but didn't stop.

"Anything left?" he asked.

"Nada. Those bastards took it all. Everything we had spent the week uncovering. Even *Homo ignotus!*"

His face widened into a grin, satisfied they scored at least one win.

"Not everything."

Torres twisted around for a look at Gapinski's outstretched hand holding a souvenir.

Took her a beat, then another. But her face widened into delightful recognition. She stood with a squeal and snatched the bone fragment from his paw.

"Is this what I think it is?"

"You got it, sister. ETs sixth digit."

Spinning it around in her hand, her face widened into a drunken grin. As if some precious family heirloom had been recovered from a fire.

He said, "Between this and the pictures we took earlier, hopefully we can make sense of all the crazy."

"Hopefully."

"But first things first."

As Torres looked up, Gapinski motioned toward the burning husk of one of those Toyotas. Scattered at the wheels were bodies. Some charred from the explosion, some dead but recognizable.

The smell was real bad. Like a backyard barbecue, though with the stank of spoiled beef.

"I think I'm gonna be sick..." Jamar stumbled off, probably to hurl.

But Gapinski knew they had work to do.

He walked up to one of the hostiles and knelt at his head. Covering his mouth with one hand and yanking down the shirt collar with the other, he revealed a familiar sight.

"Well, you know what this means," Torres said.

"Roger, roger."

"And you know what we need to do."

He frowned. "SEPIO phone home."

She nodded, saying nothing more.

Silas ain't gonna like this one bit.

CHAPTER 10

WASHINGTON NATIONAL
CATHEDRAL.

S ilas paced SEPIO command center nursing his third
cup of coffee. Black, of course. None of that hippy sugar
and cream crap the kids sully up their brew with these
days. Must be a generational thing. Man, did he sound like
Dad, or what?

He took another swig, a slight tremor taking hold of his
hand. Probably from all the caffeine at that hour. Not half bad,
either. From one of those newfangled Nespresso single-serve
coffee capsules he'd bought for the break room down the hall.
A real nice unit, too, costing a few hundred bucks plus all the
capsules the crew went through each day keeping track of
threats against the Church and SEPIO operations contending
for the faith across the world.

Surely giving Weiss fodder for his case against Silas's
management of the Order of Thaddeus.

Had to give it to himself. He was more than adept at slitting
his own throat. Happened at Princeton. Almost happened with
the Rangers. Now it seemed like he'd handed Weiss his head on
a platter that would lead to his firing.

But not yet, not quite. Which meant he still had a job to do.

First order of business was getting back in touch with

Gapinski and Torres and the rest of his crew. '*I will never leave a fallen comrade to fall into the hands of the enemy*' was drilled into every Army Ranger, something he took as gospel and took with him into his command of the Order and SEPIO special-ops unit.

Second leg of this night's operation was figuring out what kind of dead animal had been brought to their doorstep. Had to be careful not to complain too loudly, given he figured the Holy Spirit was behind every operation that came their way. But an MI6 agent with some clandestine subgroup, emerging from the shadows of some Dupont French bistro, seeking Celeste's help with some off-the-books operation—getting to the bottom of UFOs and aliens? That's what Christ's Spirit brought their way?

He trusted the Lord's providential intervention to use the Order to contend for the once-for-all faith and all...but—man, did he work in mysterious ways!

That wasn't even touching on the fact good ol' Nicky McGrath and Celeste Bourne had been partners—in more ways than one, it seemed. How long had their relationship lasted? How deep had it gone? Did she still have feelings for the guy? Seemed cozy enough. Would something be rekindled in the heat of this new operation?

Draining his brew, Silas set the cup down on a desk and switched back the way he came, hustling past the large screen still black with worrisome unknowns. He glanced at the Seiko clenched to his wrist and muttered a curse.

Over two hours now and nothing. Not a peep or a signal from the field. Last they knew, Torres had led her team to uncover a number of human bones that seemed to span the timeline of human development. According to the science story, that is. Had never put much stock in the way the Enlightenment sketched humanity's evolution, trusting the way the Church's story had always spoken of our unique creation more than the science one.

Certainly put Silas at odds with his Princeton colleagues, even some within Christianity who wanted to accommodate the Bible to science. Not that he discounted what science offered; not at all. And not that he thought the Bible was offering a scientific account of creation; it wasn't. For him, when God's Word said *'God created humankind in his image, in the image of God he created them; male and female he created them,'* backed by Jesus and Paul—well, then he tended to put his chips on the Bible's testimony of things. Had put his stock in that testimony for all his Christian life.

But now...with these other bones uncovered from what looked like other lines or generations or ancestors up the human family tree, mixed with more recent versions, or whatever, of the *Homo sapiens* line—well, that brick in his faith was beginning to falter.

And not only for that reason.

Because something else that Gapinski said had bugged him. Something about a different set of bones. A set of remains that came from some tall man with an enlarged head—and six fingers. Didn't know what to make of it at first. There was a kernel of a story that had surfaced noodling over the discovery, which sent him searching Scripture. What he found was weird.

It was from 1 Chronicles, chapter 20. Still recalled the words as he switched back the way he came.

> *Again there was war at Gath, where there was a*
> *man of great size, who had six fingers on each*
> *hand, and six toes on each foot, twenty-four in*
> *number; he also was descended from the giants.*
> *When he taunted Israel, Jonathan son of Shimea,*
> *David's brother, killed him. These were*
> *descended from the giants in Gath; they fell by*
> *the hand of David and his servants.*

Six fingers. On a man of great size. A giant...

From some initial research, he saw the original word for those men of great size was *Rapha*, connected to the Rephaim who were a warrior clan of giants. Didn't have time to research it further, but it sounded mighty close to what they had uncovered alongside the other human remains.

What any of it meant was as clear as the mud he'd been downing the past few hours. But with that feed cut after Gapinski and Torres were startled by something going on at their end of things, and knowing the way these sorts of things tended to trend with SEPIO, on top of the rodent carcass Nicky had brought to their doorstep, or the Holy Spirit, or whatever—all of it was adding up to one massive train wreck that Weiss would surely love nothing more than to use to kick his backside to the curb.

A hand jolted him from his ruminations. It was Celeste, bearing another mug of Nespresso.

"If you're not careful, love, you're liable to wear a trench in the floor of our newly renovated ops center."

Silas smiled and took the mug. "Thanks, but I should probably take it easy. A fourth cup at this hour will put me in a catatonic state." He put out a hand, the tremor looking like it had worsened, though now he wasn't sure if it was because of the caffeine or operation jitters. He clenched it and brought it to his side and took a sip anyway.

"Oy! I best take that back." She did and took a swig of her own, twisting up her face and setting the mug next to an analyst wading through spreadsheets of data. "How you Yanks stomach this swill is beyond me."

He chuckled and brought his hands to his face and rubbed it, a bone-weariness washing over him now as the minutes continued their march into oblivion.

"I'm sure everything is alright," she said, nodding toward

the empty screen. "Torres and Gapinski are the best there is. They can hold their own with whatever has transpired."

"I know. But the 'whatever' is what has me worried."

The screen above suddenly crackled to life, followed by a deafening static that made them both jump.

Silas threw his hands on his ears and spun around. "Zoe..."

"Already on it, chief." Zoe killed the volume just as two familiar faces appeared on the screen.

Torres and Gapinski.

Silas sighed with relief. The pair looked alive enough, if not battered. Was sure there was a story to that one. Looked like early morning there, too, the sun hanging in a clear sky seven hours ahead of DC's own dawning hour. Pink and orange light painted a line of tents behind them. What he wouldn't give for just a few hours in one of those puppies. Just a cot and a mosquito net to keep the critters away.

That could wait; it'd have to. It was go time. On the double.

Celeste said, "Aren't you a sight for sore eyes! We've been worried—" she stopped short and scrunched up her brow. "Is that smoke? And where is the bloomin' circus tent that commanded the dig site center?"

Gapinski frowned. "Yeah, about that..."

"What the heck happened over there?" asked Silas, taking his seat at the center of the U-shaped table.

"I saw a UFO!" Gapinski announced in a rush, throwing off the whole equilibrium in the room. Like one of those record scratches in those '90s sitcoms.

"Excuse me?" was all that Silas could manage.

"A UFO?" Celeste said, one end of her mouth curling upward. "What are you playing at, Matthew? We don't have time for games."

Torres smirked. "Don't listen to him. He hit his head pretty hard."

"No, I didn't!" Gapinski protested. "Well, yeah, I did. But

that was after the triangle-shaped thingy swooped in all *Flight of the Navigator*."

"Gapinski..." Silas said, putting out a staying hand and not at all knowing what to do with that info bomb, especially with Nicky's crazy proposition. "Slow down, brother. Take it from the top."

Clearing his throat, Gapinski reported everything that had gone down in Turkey—from the crazy beam of white light and the hovering something "that sucked up all life and light," in his words; to the incoming hostiles riding in on Toyota pickups and the grenade attack launched at the hovering something; and then the other attacks on the dig site and the missing skeletons, all of them stolen by the hostiles.

"My God..." Nicky exclaimed. "How could you be so daft!"

"*Perdóneme*," Torres said, "and who are you?"

Gapinski snorted a laugh. "Some British dude with too much hair product..."

Celeste suppressed a grin and gestured to the MI6 agent. "Naomi, Matthew, meet Nicholas McGrath."

"Nicky, here," explained Silas, "is an MI6 agent we stumbled across before you rang earlier."

"MI6?" Torres said with a start.

"Quite the story with that one, our own backsides almost getting handed to us on the same platter it sounds like you all almost wound up on. But we'll get to that later."

"How do you like that?" Gapinski said. "Our very own Daniel Craig. Hey, slip another shrimp on the barbie for us while we're away, would ya?" he said in his best faux British accent.

Celeste moaned and shook her head sitting next to Silas now.

"What'd I say?"

"Good try, mate," Nicky said, sliding into a chair next to Celeste, face straight and set with annoyance. "A perfectly pedestrian, if not cliché attempt at a bit of *Australian* slang in a royally wretched accent not of this world. I'm British, by the way."

Crimson rose to his cheeks in embarrassment. "Oh. My bad..."

"Let's focus, please," Silas said. "Glad you're OK, and no one on our side got hurt or worse. But who were these hostiles that rode in on—it was Toyota pickups, isn't that right?"

Gapinski nodded. "That's right. Three of them loaded down with a dozen whack jobs."

"Sounds like local militia," said Celeste. "Perhaps come for the skeletal remains to sell on the black market?"

The pair on the large screen turned toward one another.

"Not exactly..." said Torres.

She spun the camera around with a herky-jerky jostle before easing it down for a viewing. Clear as that rising sun was the telltale sign of the Order's ancient enemy. And Silas's own personal nemesis.

A familiar tattoo came into view. Two intersecting lines. The vertical ends bent down and to the left, the horizontal ends bent inward. Like a cross, but demonic to the core. A phoenix, rising to consume the Church—which was ironic, since it was often an early symbol for resurrection among the earliest Christians.

Celeste groaned, crossing her arms and giving her head a shake. "I reckon that settles it then."

Silas nodded, crossing his arms as well. "Sure does."

"What settles what?" asked Nicky. "That isn't any marking I've ever seen."

"And you wouldn't, Nick." Annoyance flashed between his ears. More from lack of sleep and the urgency of the mission, but the man was a guest and was treading on his turf. And Silas didn't like it.

The man turned to Celeste. "What's his meaning?"

"Nous," she answered, pointing to the screen. "That's who that marking belongs to."

"Was there any doubt?" asked Gapinski. "We uncover the mother lode of bones that answers all our burning questions about the meaning of life and human existence, and we're surprised they rolled up all Johnny on the spot?"

"I suppose not," Silas said. "My brother does have a way with appearances."

"Damn straight. No offense or anything."

"Excuse me, but did you say Nous?" Nicky asked.

Silas leaned back and turned to him. "That's right."

"Greek for 'mind,' isn't it? Or 'reason.'"

Celeste threw him a smile. "Look at you, Nicky."

"Divine reason, actually," Silas answered. "Its origin is in Neoplatonism, stretching back to the early days of the Church. It has gone by many names over the ages. The 'mind's eye,' the 'inner consciousness' or 'inner knowledge.' It is considered to be the original divine principle, the eye of reason for comprehending the divine, leading to higher knowledge and salvation."

Nicky snorted a dismissive laugh. "Stuff and nonsense is what it sounds like. The ravings of that chap who cashed in on some conspiratorial love child the Church was suppressing for centuries."

That annoyance flashed again, and Silas could feel it creeping into his fists.

"Well, it isn't. It's a very real threat to not only our world, but also our very souls. This esoteric self-salvation through inner, divine knowledge has been a nemesis to the Church stretching back to the earliest days of her existence. The earliest heresies were gnostic in origin, teaching that salvation was reserved for a certain select few who could reach spiritual enlightenment and progress and push the human race forward—threatening the teachings of the Church. Nous was behind it all."

"So what?"

"Nicky," Celeste said, turning to him to engage now, "Nous isn't some low-brow, bargain-bin thriller from Kindle's rubbish bin. It poses the gravest of threats. Not merely for Christianity, but also the world at large."

He heaved a sigh and settled back in his chair. "Alright, I'll play along. How so?"

"It's teachings for one thing, peddling cultic stuff and nonsense that could destabilize society."

Silas added, "Nous and its various manifestations have all subscribed to *gnostikos*, the central kernel of gnostic teaching, beginning with the basic assumption of the divinity of the individual. The God-within, a God-consciousness that every person bears to greater or lesser degrees. Each person is a God-in-hiding, as they espouse. There is no sovereign deity, but lesser spirit-deities."

Nicky looked off, seeming to consider this. "Sounds like Friedrich Nietzsche's *Übermensch*. The superman the collective humanity was destined to become."

"Not superman," Silas corrected. "Overman."

Celeste suppressed a grin. "Well, you're both right. The *Übermensch* of the German philosopher you mentioned, Nicky, or overman, is the essential aim of the Nousati. In fact, some of the highest-ranking Nazi officers were members of Nous. Joseph Goebbels and even Hitler himself were Nousati. Heinrich Himmler was a Grand Master."

"The Nazis?" Nicky exclaimed. "Good Lord! Have you got Indiana Jones hiding out in these parts?" He spun around for dramatic effect, searching the room.

Silas rolled his eyes with a huff. "We're serious, *Nick*. Gnosticism and occultism are closely aligned. Pursuit of spiritual power through ritual magic is a constant theme throughout the history of Nous."

"And you're saying this Nous entity is somehow involved in this belief system?"

"Exactly. Nous is the organizational manifestation of this ancient worldview. An organization that has lain hidden within the shadows of history, waging war against the Church. Until recent years, that is."

Nicky replied, "That's the entity you're saying swiped our alien remains?"

Silas thought it was interesting he zeroed in on the larger skeleton with the sixth digit Gapinski had gone on about, but he let it go.

Instead, he simply nodded. "Yes, Nous."

"Why haven't I heard about this group? Like I mentioned, those markings and certainly none of this conspiratorial nonsense straight from a low-brow, bargain-bin thriller from Kindle's rubbish bin, as you suggested, Celeste—" he paused to throw her a wink; she flashed a smile and pushed a stray lock of hair behind an ear. "I'm one of the senior-ranking agents with MI6 and foremost experts on foreign terrorist entities in Her Majesty's government, and none of this has ever registered on my radar."

Silas laughed; couldn't help it. "Apparently not as foremost as you or Her Majesty's government might imagine…"

Anger flashed across Nicky's face at the slight. Celeste intervened before he could react.

"The Order has been keeping track of Nous for quite some time, trying to keep it at bay to preserve and contend for the faith. The bulk of our business is keeping Nous from destroying Christianity—and the world, for that matter."

"Destroying Christianity, the *world*?" Now Nicky laughed. "If I didn't know you better, Celeste, I would check you into Bedlam if I thought it would bring you back to your senses!"

"I'm being serious, Nicky. There's a militancy about Nous that has always threatened the Church and the faith. In the past, Nous struck at the heart of Christian ideas by perpetuating an alternative version to the established orthodoxy."

"I seem to recall that Dan Brown fellow making a quid or two with a conspiracy about such nonsense."

"Now that we're all on the same page..." Silas returned to the screen. "What else can you tell us about what happened?"

"It's like I explained," Gapinski said. "A well-placed rocket-propelled grenade—"

"Well-placed grenade?" Torres laughed. "Yeah, right."

"As I was saying..." He jabbed an arm into her side. "The grenade decimated the Jap pickup and a few Nous whack jobs along the way. Then the geezer in the other pickup took off with our goods."

"What geezer?" asked Silas.

Nicky coughed and winced. "Not entirely politically correct, don't you think?"

"Anyway, what about it? Who was it?"

Gapinski shrugged. "Don't know. Just some dude in a top hat. Something about him looked familiar, though."

Silas leaned forward. "It wasn't my brother, was it?"

"Don't think so. Like I said, geezer."

He nodded, wondering what it meant. "Well, what about the other hostiles? Sounded like there were a bunch you took out."

"Sure. What about 'em?"

"Well, did you give them a once-over to confirm their identities?"

"Uhh, we confirmed one Nous hostile but wanted to check in pronto." Gapinski's face fell, and he threw up a sheepish grin. Until he brightened and added, "*Then* we were planning to do the identification drill. You know, live for your viewing pleasure."

Torres smirked. "Yeah, right."

"Shut up..." he muttered, swinging the camera around to one of the bodies.

Gapinski walked to it and kicked it over, then Torres knelt and yanked back the neck.

Nothing.

Wrists, though, showed the familiar intersecting lines bent at all four ends.

Another Nousati agent.

Torres shuffled over to another body, Gapinski trailing her with the herky-jerky laptop camera. She yanked at the wrists, but found nothing. Then she did the same at the neck.

"*Espera un minuto...*" She motioned for Gapinski, pointing at her discovery.

"Huh, would you look at that," Gapinski said, the picture autofocusing and showcasing a very different set of ink.

A small tattoo, but not the familiar intersecting bent lines.

This one looked more like a man. A cubist interpretation with a boxy body and triangular legs, arms poking out from the shoulder with a triangle neck and a circular head bisected by a horizontal line through the center.

Celeste craned forward. "That's not Nous."

"Nope." Silas sighed and leaned back, recognizing it with dread. "It sure ain't."

"Wait...I remember that from a year ago. Theoti, right?"

He nodded. "Church of the Theotites. The new upstart religious terrorist sect giving Nous a run for their money. A new kid on the block that almost cooked Nous's gander—and the Church's, if I recall."

"Brothers in arms, more like it," Celeste said.

"You think? Last go around they were major competitors."

"And now in cahoots with Nous."

"No way. My brother was kidnapped by their leader—what's his face?"

"Sha, I believe. Of that Theoti outfit."

"That's right. In cahoots with those Markus Braun and Noland Rotberg characters."

"Excuse me," Nicky interrupted, "but isn't that Braun fellow the founder of that social media juggernaut WeNet and WeShare, and the like?"

Celeste nodded. "That he is."

Silas said, "But what are their men doing alongside my brother's?"

"Like Celeste said," added Gapinski. "In cahoots."

He put a hand to his chin and rubbed it. "You think?"

"A lot can change in a year."

Celeste said, "Especially when it comes to undermining the Christian faith."

Silas went silent, considering the turn while Gapinski and Torres confirmed two more Nous agents and two more Theoti were among the dead. The SEPIO confirmed kill count was more than usual. Not a stat Silas was interested in sharing with Weiss, that's for sure. Even Victor, given his equivocation.

"What do you make of this *idiota*?"

Gapinski spun the camera around to find Torres standing at the head of some silver hair. Unusual for Nous to employ someone that old—a geezer, as Gapinski had said. Had to imagine Theoti was also more into younger blood for its muscle.

"Who's that?" he asked.

Celeste said, "Looks well past his fighting prime, whoever he is."

Silas asked, "Who do you got there?"

Neither of the agents answered. Kneeling down, Torres pulled back the man's sleeve up to the shoulder. A faded tattoo was anchored to his bicep. Looked about as old as the man Gapinski said he'd glimpsed in the Toyota.

Except...

Staring back at them was a wicked skull with a sagging

beretta planted on its head. Flanking his ears, an origami design looking like a pair of wings jutted up on both sides.

Gapinski sucked in a startled breath. "I know that tat..."

"You do?" asked Silas. "What is it?"

"A buddy of mine at Ramstein Air Force base had one plastered to his own left upper arm."

"Air Force? I thought you were a Marine."

"The few, the proud," Gapinski muttered, scratching his head with furrowed brow. Shaking it, he continued, "Some leatherneck up the COC loaned me out to our German base for a stint as part of an inter-branch team coordinating our operation in Iraq."

"So, what is it?"

"Air Force Security Forces."

Nicky smacked the table and gestured widely. For a moment, Silas had forgotten he was still in the room.

"What did I tell you, hmm? The US Air Force sends one of its own to reclaim an alien skeleton."

"Nous, Theoti, and the USAF walk into a bar..." quipped Gapinski.

About the long and short of it.

Celeste turned to Silas. "What is the American military doing in bed with religious terrorists bent on the Church's destruction?"

"Wrong question, my dear," Nicky said.

"And what's the right one?" Silas asked.

"Not what, *why*. Because, by the look of it, they are canoodling from here to Sunday. Especially given the UFO sighting and alien remains."

"*Alleged*," Celeste said.

"I know who to call," Gapinski said with interruption.

"Ghostbusters?" Nicky himself quipped.

Celeste threw him a frown. "Who's that, mate?"

"Doctor Georgina Anderson. A parapsychologist with the

FBI specializing in these sorts of things. Saw Doc Gina a decade ago for—"

He stopped short, a look of horror crossing his face.

"Saw her?" Silas asked, brow furrowed with confusion. "About what?"

Gapinski closed his eyes and sighed. "About my experience with unidentified aerial phenomenon. Not just today, but years ago. Back at Ramstein in Germany."

The room clearly didn't know what to do with that truth bomb. Another one of those record scratch scenes, the HVAC hum the only soundtrack to their debrief.

Making a fist, he tapped the top of it with two fingers. "Hello....This thing on?"

"UFO?" Silas managed.

"As in, unidentified flying object?" Celeste said.

"Unidentified aerial phenomenon, actually," Gapinski corrected, "but yeah. Something like that."

"*Dios mio...*" Torres whispered.

"Let me get this straight," Nicky began. "A UAP comes swooping in from the heavens, to what end isn't entirely clear. Only to be chased off with a rocket-propelled grenade from a group of hostiles riding in on Japanese-made trucks, who then swipe a set of mystery remains. Does that cover it?"

"That about covers it," Torres said.

"Which means two actors on this stage," Celeste said. "Those who have been historically arrayed against the Church, joined by perhaps a rogue US agency—and then some unknown group."

"Precisely," Nicky said. "Only remaining question is, what are their aims?"

Enough was enough. Time to sort through this nonsense.

"Come home," Silas said. "Both of you. I'll send an extraction team for the other SEPIO agents and to clean up. Given what just went down, what we know so far and with what our new friend with British intelligence brought us into—it looks like we're in the thick of it."

Gapinski crossed his arms and sighed. "Again…"

Now he sighed. Damn straight.

Again, is right.

CHAPTER 11
WELWELSBERG CASTLE, GERMANY.

Sebastian Grey closed his eyes and tipped his head back with pleasure. His heart thudded expectantly in his chest even as his pulse raced into the gilded ceremonial vial resting on the cherry hardwood desk, the reed protruding from his arm carefully channeling his lifeblood out of his body and into a rising pool of crimson at the bottom.

Thunder rumbled overhead as rain slapped against the windows overlooking the quaint German town below his castle. A literal one, too, with a storied history. A pagan one that served his purposes. Especially the ones that evening.

Breathing in deeply, he caught the tendrils of woodsmoke escaping the crackling fire warming his chamber of cut stone chilled by the autumn air. It was joined by old wood and pulp, the heavenly scents of the walnut bookcases that lined his study filled with tomes containing wisdom from across the human spectrum. Ancient revelation-knowledge accumulated over the centuries he had been leveraging in his quest to build the Republic of Heaven.

The project had begun under the direction of his predecessor, Rudolf Borg, his mentor, before his untimely death. He envisioned this Republic of Heaven, as Borg had called it, as a movement to transcend the confines of the Church's vision for God's Kingdom. Governed not by the whims of a self-centered, self-indulgent, needy Bearded Being in the sky. Instead, the enlightened ones would grab reality by the horns and transcend it to greater heights of purpose. Rising to a higher consciousness, becoming like the gods!

That's where the Church had gotten it wrong all these ages. The entire human experience has been one of constantly emerging from what we have been into what we can become, embodied by the new vision of the Republic Borg had begun to outline, where we humans decided for ourselves what was right and good, true and beautiful—not some petulant Spaghetti Monster in the sky or the ravings of pedophile priests and Protestant patriarchs.

And Sebastian aimed to make that vision, that movement a reality, inaugurating it that night with the help of a few new frenemies. Enemies turned allies for the mutual purpose of subverting Christianity and giving humanity a new reason to exist.

One found in the heavens. Literally...

A pleasurable sigh escaped him, both from the exhumation of his lifeblood and at the anticipation rising inside at what it would bring.

The air seemed to hum with agreement as his blood continued dripping out, readying him for his offering to the Universe. Sebastian strummed his fingers on the hardwood desk in sync with his heart beating his blood into the sacred vessel. Even the room lined by dark hardwood seemed to glow brighter in the presence of his act of letting.

His tongue began tingling now with anticipation as the ceremonial vial filled, desire welling within his belly for what would come next, down below in the bowels of his sanctum, the climax to his reappearing after his hiatus.

And the reemergence of the Ones who had been destroyed so long ago, yet visited in other forms from time to time.

He slouched back in his large leather chair resting securely in his study in the castle fortress he had called home for the past few years after having risen to *Nous Magnum Magister.* Grand Master of Nous, the ancient enemy of the Church.

Rain smacked with continued assault against the panes of glass that separated him from the herd milling about outside. The sheeple still bowing down before that pitiful false prophet who died like a dog those many centuries ago.

He could still hear the peals of church bells clanging away through the weathery onslaught, their thunderous tones grating against his consciousness like nails on a chalkboard.

Until another crack of thunder overhead intervened.

That's more like it...

As the fire crackled and popped away, he reveled in the comforts of his new life: the wood shelving lining the study; the array of books containing knowledge, both accepted and arcane, from all corners of the globe; the tribal artifacts used for sacrifices from lands that died out far too soon; the athame ceremonial blade still dripping with his blood. All of it gifted him by the former Grand Master of Nous, Rudolf Borg. The one killed by his brother, Silas Grey.

Sebastian snapped open his eyes, his head feeling suddenly faint. He eyed the gilded vial and startled. The thing was nearly filled to the brim! No wonder he was feeling it, a goodly amount of the crimson liquid having been let from his arm.

Grasping the slender stem with his thumb and forefinger, Sebastian pulled the long end from his arm, the centimeter worth stuck inside his vein sliding out easily. Blood seeped from the hole in his arm, but he left it. It also collected at the end of the reed, that quickening stirring again.

He dropped his jaw with lustful hunger and pressed of the bloodied end against his tongue. The coppery sensation of pennies sent an instant jolt of orgasmic delight through every nerve ending in his mouth. He sucked at the reed, his lifeblood slowly sapping into his mouth like a straw. His skin rippled with goose pimples at the amplified coppery taste compounded by the salty scent, his head growing dizzy again.

Then he set the slender stem on his desk. Mustn't get too greedy. Soon he would have his fill, and so would the others.

A chime rang from the other side of the study, its echo clear as the bell inside that vintage wooden Howard Miller grandfather clock.

The hour is nigh...

Rumbling thunder in the distance brought him back to the moment, desire welling within from the weight and pleasure of what was to come. And his attention now turned to a box resting next to the gold vial filled with his life force.

Only the box was filled with something far greater, containing the DNA of something ancient, something not of this world.

Sebastian slid the heavy mahogany case toward him, his stomach quickening again with anticipation. It was long and narrow, taking up nearly half the size of his desk.

Nearly missed their window of opportunity to capture the relic, the rogue agency swooping in to intercept the remains— literally. Had it not been for his new partners, Nous would have been denied.

He would have been denied!

Thankfully, the Universe had intervened, opening the portal into arcane revelation-insight leading to humanity's next evolutionary jump. But knowing another actor was bent on suppression increased the stakes and urgent timing.

Sebastian opened the lid on quiet hinges and peered inside.

Resting upon a pillow of crimson silk shimmering in the firelight was a bone. One of the best sources of DNA from decomposed remains. Even after the flesh is long gone, DNA can often be obtained from demineralized bone. And he was staring at the bone of one set of remains with the richest deposits of DNA for harvesting.

The femur thighbone. The longest and largest bone, typically measuring around eighteen inches, a quarter of one's full height.

This one was forty inches long—making its master nine feet tall!

A religious passage flashed through his mind, one he had been loath to read but had read just the same after his research had uncovered the ancient revelation—from the Bible of all places, the Book of Numbers, chapter 13. A report from some Jewish spies scoping out their next conquest, one that sent them quaking in their boots.

Their leader wasn't having any of their whining, but the spies insisted they couldn't *'go up against this people, for they are stronger than we.'* Why? Here was the kicker that had sent Sebastian on his hunt:

> *"The land that we have gone through as spies is a land that devours its inhabitants; and all the people that we saw in it are of great size. There we saw the Nephilim (the Anakites come from the Nephilim); and to ourselves we seemed like grasshoppers, and so we seemed to them."*

All the people that we saw in it are of great size...
Like the nine-foot giant belonging to that femur.

A shiver ratcheted up Sebastian's spine at the thought of the Being this bone had belonged to. At what it meant.

For the world, for Nous, for him...

The rest were stored elsewhere for safekeeping, missing a finger from a hand that had probably been eaten long ago. But no matter. What they would extract from this bone and the others would be more than enough to execute an operation that would finally usher in the Republic of Heaven—a realm populated by a race of supermen!

He had gone to great lengths to find this set of remains. A mole, nestled secretly within the Order that his brother Silas commanded, had supplied the final coordinates to a dig site in Turkey. Someone right under his nose who had been feeding him intel—for a price. Its dividends would more than pay for the six figures wired to that offshore account.

Snatching the box and vial of blood, Sebastian went to a panel on a blank wall that disguised what was below. Pressing his hand against the device, it pulsed blue before flashing green. The wall shuddered before revealing a stairwell that stretched downward.

On toward destiny.

The floor felt cold under Sebastian's bare feet as he slowly descended the stone stairway of his sanctum, earth and stone, mold and must mixing with delight. He had always had a certain fascination with the elemental, the earthen, believing as his spiritual ancestors did that there was a lifeblood that permeated all things, binding them together in divinity.

That One is all, and all is One.

Combined with the best insights of modern science and arcane knowledge, he brought that principle of universal divinity to bear on Nous, leveraging the insights of shamanic sages who tapped the Universal Force—binding them together in order to bind together the world faiths into a new manifestation that would usher in the universal human ideal of peace, prosperity, and progress.

To usher in the next evolutionary manifestation of humanity itself.

Homo Deus.

The God-Man.

Only one thing stood in the way: the Christian claim that

Jesus himself was God. Was singularly divine, the Absolute Principle above all others. The Son of God who was unequal in glory, majesty, dominion, and authority.

Except Sebastian knew better. Had read better than all the others, discovering hidden revelation of a past race of gods who had walked Earth, commingling with humanity in order to produce an advanced race of beings to rule the world and supplant the reign of God.

Forging a true Republic of Heaven.

Still the largest religion in the world, Christianity and its claims regarding human nature and Jesus' singular divinity posed a unique problem for Nous. Claims he intimately understood, having been an ardent believer until those fateful teenage years.

Luckily for him, he had come into possession of something that would bring the faith to its knees—and would become possessed by a force greater than anyone could possibly conceive, evolving into his destiny.

He savored the term Homo Deus, that ache returning to his belly.

God-Man was right!

And he would be the first beneficiary of his experimental research. Of the elemental ceremony taking place down below in short order.

Thunder rumbled as Sebastian continued his descent, LED lights along the base of the stairwell wall lighting his way to the chamber below. The wind howled now as a mixture of rain and heavy, wet snow beat against the thick, interlocking stones of the ancient castle, a violent reflection of the nature of what was about to take place below the legendary, rebuilt heart of Nous.

A sanctum that had born remarkable fruit one other time before, but had been cut off too early by an invading army to have any effect upon humanity.

Originally built in the seventeenth century, it later became the central headquarters of the German SS and central command for Heinrich Himmler. Though it had become a sort of museum and youth hostel post-WWII, the estate had been acquired by the former Grand Master of Nous several decades ago—before his unfortunate demise.

The stuff of legends that man was, Rudolf Borg, the one who had reactivated the enemy of the Church stretching back to its founding, transforming the castle and the alt-spiritual Nous organization into his own needs: a nerve center of spiritual enlightenment and war.

One end of Sebastian's mouth curled upward, the gentle touch of the man upon his shoulders and the mentoring hand that had caressed his ego and guided his own ascension still warming his soul.

Bless the Universe he had the foresight to train his successor in the ways of Nous, ironically a twin to a Master of the Order of Thaddeus, Silas Grey. What they had started together would pave the way for a new, rising, finalizing force that would finally eliminate the Christians, the Church.

The Christ, even!

If only Borg were still alive to see its fruit...

Reaching the bottom, Sebastian made for the ceremonial chamber, but stopped when he reached a statue.

Bird-Man Thoth, the ancient Egyptian god of wisdom.

The ancient Egyptians regarded Thoth as One, self-begotten and self-produced Being, crediting him as the author of science and religion, philosophy and magic. His power was unlimited and unrivaled by all other gods. He was the true author of every work of every branch of knowledge.

Human and divine.

"*You know all that is hidden under the heavenly vault,*" Sebastian intoned, bowing his head reverently before the stone effigy as he quoted from the mystical sayings surrounding the god. "*Now, that which has been hidden shall be revealed.'* And it shall be mine," he finished, clenching his fist with resolve.

Lightning flashed behind him through the windows up the stairwell, illuminating the god of knowledge in flickering white light. Looking much like the towering being of his dreams of late. His nightmares brought on by the revelation he had stumbled across and the primeval rituals he had partaken of.

A few seconds later, thunder rumbled in the distance, bringing Sebastian out of his trance. He stiffened with purpose and continued down the darkly lit hallway, striding forth to meet the gathered men, their voices carrying toward him now. His new partners.

Noland Rotberg and that insufferable Sha character, head of the Church of the Theotites, Theoti, the newest kids on the subversive spiritual block. And the German with the top hat and intriguing past.

Strike that.

The German with the top hat and deliciously beguiling and all-together captivating past Sebastian wouldn't have believed to be even remotely authentic had he not seen the bona fides up close and personal. His birth certificate, the immigration records of his father, the classified files with that paper clip still attached at the upper-left corner.

All of them were waiting for him to arrive with the gift he had secreted away to Nous's headquarters for safekeeping. Still disbelieving he was assembling in the same room with the handlebar mustachioed man and the hairless, olive-skinned boss of the new mystery sect.

A year ago, when the two sides were locked in a deathmatch to take credit for subverting and supplanting the Church, the two organizations had come to something of an agreement. Sebastian and Sha had agreed their aims were mutual, they just came at it from different sides of the same coin.

Nous was looking to use science and nature to subvert and

destroy Christianity, trusting in both modern wisdom and arcane revelation-knowledge reflected by the ancients to destroy the Church. Theoti was more interested in using ancient spiritual knowledge gleaned from the great spiritual, shamanic traditions to bring the Church to heel.

Either way, whether through science or spirituality, killing the God of Christianity and pissing on the ashes of its burnt body was their mutual aim. So, the two joined together to destroy Christianity and carry humanity into its true birthright —the Homo Deus.

And Sebastian bore the two things that would pave the way...

Nearing the heavy walnut door leading into the chamber, a quote from the German prophet Friedrich Nietzsche came to mind. *'God is dead. God remains dead. And we have killed him.'*

Not quite. He was like the cat with nine lives, stubbornly persistent. What Sebastian wanted, and what he suspected Sha and Rotberg wanted as well, was to take credit for the final death blow.

'Is not the greatness of this deed too great for us?' Nietzsche's madman went on, *'Must we ourselves not become gods simply to appear worthy of it? There has never been a greater deed; and whoever is born after us---for the sake of this deed he will belong to a higher history than all history hitherto.'*

Exactly. Sebastian belonged to a higher history, becoming like the gods!

Literally. Transformed from the inside out.

With the help of the equipment and the rite waiting inside those double doors.

CHAPTER 12
WASHINGTON, DC.

S ilas emerged from his mid-afternoon nap and sat up on his well-worn leather couch, tossing off the knit blanket and yanking his arm around for a look at the time.

Just past dinner, his Seiko said. A rumbly grumble from his stomach agreed. Same with his head, an ache at the center from low blood sugar telling him he needed food.

He stretched out the muscle tension along his spine and took in a deep breath before letting out a yawn, the dueling scents of woodsmoke and stale pizza turning that rumbly stomach sour now. Both seemed good at the time, but not a good combo at first wake.

The fire he'd made before taking a snooze had died down to embers, and the pizza slices he'd swiped from the Order mess hall looked just as bad the first go around. He'd needed the snack after leading SEPIO through the night to extract Gapinski and Torres from the dig site and get them on a chartered jet back to DC. Hadn't eaten anything all morning and by the time he thought about it, pizza was on the menu for lunch.

Not the hand-tossed kind, mind you, with tangy pizza sauce and artichokes; a four-cheese blend of parmesan, asiago, fontina, and provolone; maybe some black olives and Roma tomatoes with some fresh chopped basil to top it all off. Nope. None of that.

He was stuck with the Lunch Lady kind from his '90s childhood. Nothing but a square slab of undercooked dough the size of poster board—same taste, same texture. Runny tomato paste more fitting NASA than SEPIO layered the dough, with a tissue-thin sheet of white plasticy shreds posing as mozzarella. All he needed was a side of corn and mushy pears bobbing in clear sugary slime with a small carton of chocolate milk to complete the package.

Thank the Lord for whiskey and peanuts instead!

But now, with that mess hall closed down for the day, leftover Lunch Lady pizza was all he had.

Silas spun his legs around and planted his bare feet on the soft Persian rug and shivered. He'd ditched his suit and silk noose for dark jeans and a well-worn Led Zeppelin T-shirt from back in the day, but now wished he'd at least kept the jacket. Eyeing the leftover slice, he held his nose, then held his breath, and brought it in for a bite.

Yep. Every bit as plasticy as the first go around.

But it was something. And after the twenty-four hours they'd had, Lunch Lady pizza was about all he had going for him.

Chowing through the slice, he swallowed his last bite hard and sauntered to the mini bar in search of that whiskey and peanuts again. What a day.

Between being stalked by an MI6 agent looking like Mr. Bean to being chased by the feds and then assaulting one of them with a frying pan, and then his crew being assaulted by Nous and Theoti combined, along with what looked like a branch of the US military—forget the whisky, time to break out the vodka and rum!

But that could wait. They were in the thick of it, and he needed a clear head. What exactly they were in the middle of was yet to be determined. Still too many unknowns, though he prayed the picture became clearer soon.

Because the fog of war was a royal pain in the backside, as he'd learned firsthand doing Uncle Sam's bidding in Iraq. When the scorching days in the desert were long, the operations freighted with fraught dread, and solutions weren't on the horizon.

Reaching for a Nespresso capsule instead of whisky, an earthy coffee blend with hints of ash and tobacco he'd come to like, he startled at the sound of his heavy wood study door opening with a thud.

"Hey, did you hear the one about a priest, a pastor, and a rabbi walking into a bar?" a voice thundered from behind, too chipper for Silas at that hour after hardly any sleep.

Gapinski led the way, followed by Torres, Celeste, and her old partner Nicky.

"What is this, some kind of joke?" Torres said.

"Exactly!"

Took a beat, but the group moaned as one. Too corny, even for Gapinski.

Silas slid the capsule inside the Nespresso and punched a button for it to do its thing.

"Silas, my man!" Gapinski said, sauntering over. "That jet you sent over was the stuff of Bennifer and Brangelina—"

He stopped short and twisted up his face. "Yikes! You could use a comb, man." Tilting his head back, he took a sniff and winced. "And a shower."

"Gee, thanks. Nice to see you too. See if I ever send a Learjet again. Next time you're flying coach."

Gapinski grinned and opened his arms. "Just messin' with ya, pal. Bring her in."

They clasped hands and embraced. "Glad you made it out alive, brother. But—" Silas pulled back and winced himself at the sharp scent of body odor. "You could use a shower yourself. Oof!"

He scoffed. "I'd like to see you live in the desert for a week with nothing but a bush shower and baby powder."

"How about living in the desert for two months with nothing but a sponge and bucket?"

Gapinski shuddered. "Eww, no..."

Silas grabbed his coffee and slumped into one of the oversized leather chairs at the center of the room. The others joined after having taken a break for the afternoon while Gapinski and Torres flew home, all of them looking about as weary as him. Supposed he should have made a whole pot of brew.

Once Gapinski and Torres were safely in the air, Silas had told the others in the SEPIO ops center to get some shuteye. The pair had a twelve-hour trip ahead of them, and there wasn't any use standing around until they could debrief and plot their next moves.

Nicky McGrath had to get back to his embassy anyhow and confer with his British pals about their mission's unexpected turn. Celeste didn't give him a word either way on his original ask, the one to lend a helping hand to her former place of employ, wanting to hear more about it all later in the day.

Silas wasn't thrilled about that one, not at all liking or trusting the spook. But, given what had just gone down in Turkey, with Gapinski's weird story about some unidentified flying object on top of the odd set of bones that did look like a leftover prop from *Close Encounters of the Third Kind*, and then the conspiracy the MI6 agent suggested could have bearing on the Church—Silas was open to a conversation.

"I've taken the liberty," Nicky announced, "of assembling a dossier for your reading pleasure." He slapped a thick manilla envelope marked UNCLASSIFIED in large red letters on the center glass table with a smack.

Celeste picked it up. She'd changed into jeans and a sweat-shirt. Which was disappointing, given all the crazy. Still wished she was in that fine blue dress of hers.

"What's this?"

"Everything you need to know to bring you up to speed on our operation."

Silas blew across his mug and scoffed. "Yours, not ours. We're not on any *operation*, Nick."

As she opened the dossier, Celeste threw him a familiar sideways frown that told him he should back off.

He took a swig and shifted in his seat. "Why don't you give us the Twitter version before we commit to anything."

Gapinski said, "Before the TLDR—"

"TLDR?" Torres said with a raised brow.

"Yeah. Too long, didn't read. It's what all the cool kids are saying these days."

"*Ai yai yai...*"

"Anywho, could you fill us in on who this spook is from across the pond?"

"He's my former MI6 partner," Celeste explained. "He, shall I say, tracked us down to partner with an operation that has the potential to wreak havoc with the world."

"What kind of havoc?" asked Torres.

"Nothing short," answered Nicky, "of social and political disruption the likes of which this world has never seen before."

Gapinski snorted a laugh. "Oh, is that all..."

"I do wonder," said Celeste, "what sort of social disruption you are playing at, Nicky."

Silas finished another swig of coffee, his headache easing some and those earthy coffee notes joined by the caffeine a balm for his exhaustion. "Agreed. Movies and shows about UFOs and ETs have been with us as long as I can remember. Have to imagine the public has been conditioned to accept such nonsense as fiction."

"But that's precisely the point, isn't it!" exclaimed Nicky.

"Our Western world has indeed been conditioned, as you say, to embrace the existence of UFOs and extraterrestrials the past thirty-some years through powerful media that has led to powerful social effects with disastrous consequences."

He paused, taking a breath and heaving a sigh. As if the weight of the world were on his shoulders. He continued, "And, based on recent intelligence obtained by MI6, the prospect of a resurgence in such beliefs is nigh."

The room settled into a quiet contemplation at the revelation. Silas was troubled by the man's sudden shift in mood.

"I can see why you and your government might be troubled." He settled back and glanced at Celeste, who nodded him onward. "Like Gapinski said, why don't you give us the short version of what's in that packet."

Nicky scooted to the edge of his seat and nodded. "Much of contemporary reconnaissance regarding UFO sightings or UAP—"

"I'm sorry, UAP?"

"Unidentified aerial phenomenon," Gapinski answered. "It's the more official terminology for all the crazy flying around up there."

Nicky nodded. "The chap's right. And crazy is right, but also very much real and very much documented in what was known as the COMETA Report."

"What's this report?" asked Celeste. "I'm unfamiliar."

"An extraordinary study by former high-ranking French officials documenting the existence of unidentified flying objects. The investigative committee considered the veracity of the sightings and how they might impact national security, if anything at all."

Silas asked, "And what did they find?"

"Long and short of it was that five percent of the sightings could not be explained by anything earthly. Not military exercises from secret bunkers, not natural phenomenon like plane-

146 | J. A. BOUMA

tary movements or meteors crashing into Earth. These objects were tracked by pilots and radar, some even photographed. Every single event shared similar characteristics. The objects reached stupendous speeds and accelerations. The UAPs made sharp, split-second, angular turns on a dime. And they could cycle down to a standstill in midair, seemingly defying physics!"

Sounded about right to Silas. He recalled that wackadoodle childhood evening show *Unsolved Mysteries*. With that dude— Schnieder, or Stack, or Spelling, or some other—in a trench coat playacting like a hard-boiled detective, walking through a darkened soundstage surrounded by fog and white lights and going on about such things. But all this nonsense about sightings and abductions...it was all too hard to believe.

"These weren't kooks, mind you," Nicky went on. "These officials, reporting on verified sightings, were generals and former heads of the French version of NASA. Heads of government agencies and chiefs of police."

Celeste said, "Seasoned officers and scientists, then."

"Precisely. And France wasn't the only one making these claims. I already spoke of British efforts at chronicling the phenomenon through Project Condign, but the same was true of Brazil and Portugal, Chile and Peru—"

"And America," said Gapinski.

Silas was surprised he was clearly dialed into the phenomenon. Seemed weird, even for Gapinski.

Nicky nodded. "In fact, the consensus from the report was that the American government was positively coy about what it possessed. Here, let me—"

Rummaging through the file, he found something and read aloud:

"I don't think a powerful country like America finds it acceptable to acknowledge that something strange can fly over and the country can't clear the skies of it. Another problem can be panic, created by people imagining that their military can't protect them...We are convinced that some governments don't say all they know about the subject, and I mean, of course, the States."

Gapinski smirked. "Sounds like the French."

"Regardless, it is true, isn't it?" Nicky tossed the file back to the table. "The US government sure has its own secretive programs looking into the matter, on top of the more public-facing ones."

"Project Blue Book, wasn't that right?"

Definitely dialed in. Which Silas supposed made sense if he had some sort of experience, as he mentioned—whatever that was. Something he'd have to get at soon, because secrets in the middle of an operation always ended in disaster.

"That's right. After the Roswell incident—"

"By Roswell," said Silas, "you mean the famous downed weather balloon?"

Nicky snorted a laugh. "The famous downed weather balloon..." Another snort, another laugh. "Sure. Right. Whatever you Yanks tell yourselves to sleep better at night. At any rate, the US Air Force set up a detailed study of UFO phenomenon in 1948 that eventually became Project Blue Book in the early 1950s. It received citizen reports, investigated their supposed sightings, and tried to offer explanations to the media and the public. Or explain them away, more like it!"

"What do you mean by that?"

"In reality, Blue Book was largely a public relations

campaign to debunk and discredit UFO sightings. Even though the Air Force accumulated thousands of reports and files—12,000 or so with over 700 of the accounts unidentifiable—despite all that, they shut down the program in 1970. Completely shuttered the official investigations without copping to having found anything of substance. Or so they said."

Now Gapinski snorted a laugh. "It didn't end, though, did it?"

"Alongside this Department of Defense agency," Nicky continued, "was another effort launched by the CIA. In January 1953, they assembled a scientific advisory panel, chaired by H. P. Robertson. This chap was a specialist in physics and weapons systems, and these scientific experts met during a four-day closed-door session."

"To do what?" asked Celeste.

"To reduce public interest in the subject matter, that is what! The collective American psyche was gripped by reports of flying saucers, and the government was saturated by hundreds of such reports. So, in the words of the Robertson Panel, they recommended that 'the national security agencies take immediate steps to strip the Unidentified Flying Objects of the special status they have been given and the aura of mystery they have unfortunately acquired.'"

Silas asked, "How would they accomplish this if the subject matter—the sightings, the experiences, the...abductions—if UFOs were so widely seen, how would the government put the genie back in the bottle?"

"Two ways: training and debunking."

"Meaning?"

"Meaning, they would train the public through education on how to identify known objects in the sky, so that they would not be misidentified as UFOs. Weather balloons, sky lanterns, birds reflecting the sun, planetary movements, and so on and so forth. The media was then leveraged to debunk such reports. Television, motion picture, newspapers—they were all in on it."

Torres scoffed. "Sounds like domestic propaganda to me."

"Precisely!" Nicky replied. "In the parlance of that orange-hair president of yours: fake news. The panel advocated the use of psychologists, advertising executives, amateur astronomers. Even Disney was brought into the loop by leveraging popular cartoons to reduce enthusiasm in UFOs and belief in their phenomenon. Walter Cronkite, too, America's voice of reason."

"Old iron pants was a tool of the feds?" asked Gapinski.

Silas turned to him with a raised brow. "Old iron pants?"

He shrugged. "His nickname. I'm a fanboy, alright. So sue me! But to see him used as a propaganda mouthpiece..."

"It didn't stop there, either," Nicky went on. "They also urged that civilian groups studying UFOs should be carefully monitored and watched by domestic surveillance agencies, given their great influence on mass thinking if widespread sightings should occur. All in the interest of national security, of course."

Silas smirked. "Not like we haven't heard that before."

"Fixed within the public discourse, then, was the taboo and outright ban against taking UFOs seriously. Until 2017, when the whole lid was blown clear off the intelligence industrial complex and Uncle Sam's drawers were left flapping in the wind!"

"Lovely image you conjured up there, Nicky," Celeste said. "I do seem to recall something about a continued program deep in the bowels of the military."

Nicky snorted a laugh. "Deep in the bowels is right! So deep that buried in the Department of Defense's billion-dollar military budget, twenty-two million of it was secretly spent on a secretive program that continued investigating UAPs behind double-locked doors for years."

"Oh, yeah," Gapinski said. "The Advanced Aerospace

Threat Identification Program, I believe."

He nodded. "The Pentagon had always maintained they had given up on such investigations and only begrudgingly acknowledged its existence after the *New York Times* blew the whistle."

Silas understood all too well how that sort of nonsense happened in the DoD. The American public would go ape if they knew half the stuff their hard-earned tax dollars were spent on. But UFOs, in the 21st century? Seemed pretty out there, even for the Pentagon!

"What is noteworthy," Nicky continued, "is that the funding was procured by a Nevada Senator and given to his pal, Robert Bigelow."

"Why do I know that name?" Gapinski said.

"If you were involved in the Air Force at any level, then you'd recognize that he is the chairperson of one of the foremost military contract corporations. The bloke is an ardent believer in UFOs and alien life, and he was allocated most of the funds to hire subcontractors and procure research with the express intent of leveraging the advanced UFO technology to create military hardware."

Silas drained his coffee. "Now that is bargain-bin conspiracy thriller nonsense, if I ever heard it!"

"Hardly. An employee of Bigelow Aerospace blew the whistle on a program within the corporation that labors at reverse engineering something recovered that was not man-made, something not of this world that was recovered years ago. He has suggested another aerospace contractor, Aether Aerospace, is in possession of extraterrestrial technology that are remnants of unknown origin—with agencies inside the government seeking to leverage this technology for their own ends."

"And what ends are those?"

Nicky shrugged. "Toward what end do all those who seek to

leverage mysteries and secrets stoking public fear?"

"Power," replied Celeste.

He nodded. "What better way to gain or maintain power than to stoke terror into the hearts of the global community with the arrival of beings from another world bearing technology capable of destroying humanity. That isn't even touching on the actual technology procured from such entities that could be used in gaining the upper hand in nationalistic pursuits of global hegemony. Both China and Russia, along with America, are said to have in their possession such technology."

The revelation settled hard within the room, the HVAC hum the only soundtrack for their quiet contemplation. But what were they supposed to do about it? Had nothing to go on but this dossier of historiography from a British spook.

Except...

"Gapinski," Silas finally said, "you took a number of pictures of the dig site, isn't that right?"

He held up his phone and gave it a shake. "Sure did, chief."

"Not much to go on, but maybe you snapped something useful."

He got to work initiating the streaming function that connected his phone to the massive television display anchored above the fireplace. Then he started cycling through the images he had taken of the dig site.

Began with the initial findings, the one set of antediluvian bones, then the other alien-looking ones before the remains Torres had claimed were older, the various *Homo* lines mixing in a way that added a weird dimension to things. Took some shots of the hostiles, but not the one he claimed was hovering above the dig site. Just the three Toyota pickups and black-clad men running about. Then the images of the familiar tattoos, the two from the religious terrorist organizations and the military security force.

Silas leaned back and brought a hand to his chin. "So Nous, Theoti, and the US Air Force roll up into an Order dig site."

Gapinski smirked. "I already made that joke, chief. Doesn't have the same ring as the one I was sharing on our way in but—"

"And a Nazi war criminal..." Nicky suddenly stood, taking hesitant steps toward the screen and staring at it with wide eyes.

"That's not how the funny works, silly."

Silas followed the MI6 agent's gaze to one of Gapinski's photos still on the screen.

There was an older gentleman dressed to the nines from the '50s, complete with a top hat and pocket square and smoking a Camel.

Could definitely go for one of those right then...

"Who's that?" he asked.

Gapinski answered, "The old dude I was telling you about. Came rolling up with the rest of them before it all went kablooie. Real familiar, he was."

Nicky snapped his head to Gapinski. "For heaven's sake, why?"

He shrugged. "Not sure."

The agent shook his head and let it go. "Regardless, he should be dead, not sitting in a rusted-out Japanese pickup truck!"

Silas startled. "Dead?"

"That's right."

Celeste asked, "Nicky, who is that? What aren't you telling us?"

"Hans Kammler is his name. A ruthless General Lieutenant who architected Auschwitz's expansion and efficiency."

"Nice resume," Torres quipped.

"He also directed a special projects outfit for an institute that sought arcane knowledge and ancient technology to harness for the Nazi war machine, believing secret miracle weapons shrouded within this ancient arcanum would turn the tide of the Second World War."

"What sorts of weapons?"

"Everything from guided weapons and atomic energy to death rays and anti-gravity devices."

Celeste put up a hand. "Excuse me, but did you say death rays?"

"And anti-gravity devices?" asked Silas.

"Like UFOs?" added Gapinski, staring at the picture he'd taken.

Nicky threw him a glance, saying nothing. He returned to the image, shaking his head in disbelief. "As far as the world is concerned, this man is supposed to be dead."

"And yet," Silas gestured at the screen, "there he is."

"Who, by the way," said Celeste, "would have to be carrying over a hundred years on him."

"Like I said, geezer," Gapinski quipped.

"Operation Paperclip..." Nicky whispered, trailing off.

"Operation whatchamacallit?"

The man startled, turning to him. "I said, Operation Paperclip."

Silas shook his head. "I'm not familiar."

"Neither am I," said Celeste.

Nicky returned to his seat, looking white and unsure of himself. Silas didn't know whether to laugh inside with glee at the sight or cringe in fear at how unnerved the man looked. What did he know?

"Operation Paperclip," he explained, swallowing hard before continuing, "was a secret intelligence program of the United States government that helped secret away over sixteen hundred scientists, engineers, and technicians from the German army into America's own military and scientific apparatuses."

Silas said, "Are you suggesting America took Nazis into our own government programs?"

"Precisely. It was a way to get technological knowledge from the Nazi war criminals. And mark my words, most if not every single one of those bloody buggers were war criminals!"

This was too much. Silas was never one to idolize America. He understood Uncle Sam had its share of issues. Nation building being a prime recent example. But this…secret military technology, procured by Nazis through a secret program sanctioned by the Deep State? Did not compute. Not in the slightest!

"But what was the point of it?" wondered Celeste.

Nicky continued, "Truman didn't want Nazi war criminals on US soil, but he also didn't want them falling into the hands of the Soviets. You have to remember, while the two nations were allies in the war against Germany, they weren't best mates. Given the clear ideological differences, it was the beginning of what would turn into, shall I say, frosty relations stretching on for decades."

"But how did they make it work?" asked Torres. "That takes some *muy grande cajones* to smuggle Nazis across the US border."

Gapinski snorted a laugh. "And apparently Uncle Same was the coyote!"

"Officers would pull the files," Nicky explained, "of scientists and other military officers who were valuable to the United States and signal their worth with a paperclip on top. They cleaned up their record, gave them a new history, and *voila*! Ready-made worker bees in the military industrial complex and race to beat the Soviets. Wernher von Braun was one such fellow who rose through the ranks in NASA as the second in command."

"Are you kidding me?" exclaimed Silas. "You're telling me a Nazi ran our space program."

"Precisely! Von Braun was a war criminal with direct involvement in the German V-2 slave labor project, and a man who only escaped justice thanks to Operation Paperclip because of his experiential value with rocketry."

Silas turned to Gapinski. "You said you yourself had an experience with this sort of phenomenon. This UFO technology, or whatever."

He opened his mouth to answer, then shut it and simply nodded.

"And that you knew someone to call. Someone we should speak with about what you saw." He nodded to Nicky. "About what our new friend has been going on about."

"That's right. Gina Anderson."

"Who is she?" asked Celeste.

"A parapsychologist with the FBI."

Still wondered why Gapinski had seen a parapsychologist, and what it meant for his connection to this operation—whatever it was. But Silas let it go.

"I'd say it's time to get the show on the road."

"So, we're in this then?" asked Celeste. "With MI6?"

He heaved a breath, hesitating to commit but nodding. "Except not for MI6. For SEPIO. For the Church. Whatever it might mean."

She smiled. "That's all I ask."

Not sure if he was ready for SEPIO to saddle up again, but Silas knew they didn't have a choice.

CHAPTER 13

QUANTICO, VIRGINIA.

Thunder rumbled overhead from a thick canopy of billowy charcoal clouds engorged with more promised rain. The SEPIO trio had already had their fair share of cats and dogs flopping down from the heavens on the drive down from DC earlier that morning. Now more was coming?

About the long and short of how their past twenty-four hours had gone—and what was to come.

Gapinski eased their Mercedes SUV into the Marine Corps Base in Quantico, Virginia, sloshing through puddles underneath a billboard that announced their arrival. *Crossroads of the Marine Corps* the sign read above.

A memory flashed from when he'd rumbled underneath those welcoming words as a pimply faced, barely graduated high school graduate. Nearly wet his pants when Grandpappy had dropped him off for basic training before he shipped out to Parris Island, but he'd stuck with it. Didn't have a choice. Jim George would've skinned his hide with his bare hands if he'd bailed!

He pulled up to the gate manned by a brunette who looked like she could skewer him in no time flat. That was new, a nice addition to the base. Would have made Marine life much more bearable had the brass integrated members of the female persuasion at the turn of the century.

Gapinski handed over his and his teammates' IDs, explaining they had an appointment with Dr. Georgina Anderson—him, Silas, and Celeste. Torres had stayed behind to sulk about the stolen remains and get a read on where they'd gone. So far, what she'd discovered about the finger bone he'd swiped was nutso.

Something half human, half—something else! A hybrid combining the building blocks of DNA with some other weird compound.

Something not of this world...

The jarhead with a ponytail snatched the IDs with skeptical, assessing eyes then got on the horn to verify his story.

Truth be told, it wasn't an appointment, per se. More a hidey ho from an old patient. He'd pulled some strings by leveraging the Order's connection with the Vatican to get through and book a meet-and-greet he'd prayed to God would never have to be repeated.

Waiting for the Marine to confirm their appointment, he ran the memory from nearly two decades ago back through the ol' noggin. He sighed again, racing a hand across his bald head and regretting the move when he reached the back of his head.

He winced. From the painful blow back in Turkey, but also from a distant memory.

Gapinski knew darn well why he'd opened his yapper.

Because what had happened to him way back when had almost cost him his faith. His life, even—for a second time in a decade. And if that Brit Nicky was onto something with his intel, if there really was a conspiracy to control the population with stories of UAPs and aliens visiting from distant planets, and all of it was somehow mixing together in a stew of scientific confusion about human origins and identity, with wackadoodle spiritual terrorists involved—well, then he'd stop at nothing to get to the bottom of it all.

Because his own experience with the paranormal in those woods outside of Ramstein had turned his whole world upside down. Everything he thought he knew about his place in the world, not to mention humanity's place in the world, and about the goodness of God's good creation, his image bearers—even God himself as the biggest cheese, the most intelligent and powerful being in the universe...All of it had been flipped upside down that fateful night!

And laying his peepers on those bones in the middle of that desert in Turkey, right there alongside those other ones, Noah's sons or whatever and the other human ancestors—it was enough to send him spiraling down into another schizophrenia fit.

Just like last time...

A horn from behind jolted him back to the moment, as well as the stern eyes from the young buck jarhead shaking his and his crew's IDs in his face.

Gapinski snatched them and nodded to the grunt.

Another horn, joined by firm instructions to get a move on, sent him jolting forward.

"Yeah, yeah, yeah," he muttered, rolling his window up. "Don't get your skivvies in a bunch."

Winding through the Marine base on toward the FBI Academy, a twinkly ring from some cellphone in the back flared up.

Silas twisted around from the passenger's side to Celeste. "Who's that?"

Celeste showed him. He frowned and muttered, "Nick the Slick."

Gapinski said, "What, your old lover got you on speed dial or something?"

"*Gapinski!*" the pair bellowed.

"What?"

"He wasn't my old lover," she said, voice edged with defense. "Well, I suppose we did date a time or two."

"That's what they all say..."

She smacked him on the shoulder; he yelped.

"At any rate, should I answer it?"

Silas twisted back to the front. "Why is he calling?"

"He could have answers for us, not to mention our next maneuvers for our operation."

"I'm calling the shots, not Nick."

"It's Nicholas—"

"I thought it was Nicky," clarified Gapinski.

"Gapinski!" the pair bellowed again.

He huffed and returned to his driving.

"As I was saying..." Celeste continued. "It's his operation, not ours. We were brought on board as a courtesy."

Silas snorted a laugh. "More like to save his backside..."

Now he got a smack, followed by the familiar yelp.

"Great, now it went to voicemail," she complained. "What should I do, oh *Master*?"

He waved a dismissive hand. "Whatever you think is best, *dear*."

There was a long, painful pause. So painful Gapinski was readying to get another smack for not even doing anything.

"Fine." She sighed and stuffed the phone in her pocket.

A lover's spat already, only a few hours in? This was going to be a long day...

Rain that had been held at bay joined another rumble of thunder above, the heavy drops skidding down the windshield in snaking rivulets. Of course. And him without his umbrella.

The base hadn't changed a wink since he'd seen Gina the last time in that padded room for that thing he'd rather soon forget. Winding past naked trees that had shed their leaves weeks ago, he made for the large compound of '70s-era concrete eyesores that made up the FBI's special agent training

HQ. A large parking lot sat across from the main entrance. He parked and they hoofed it to the main desk.

After signing in and getting their visitor passes, Gapinski led them to Doc Gina's office on the fourth floor. Knew the route by heart after hoofing it himself those many months.

"Man, if you've seen one fed building," Silas said, craning around for a look-see, "you've seen them all."

Gapinski snorted a laugh. "Ain't that the truth. Although, looks like they've added some foliage from the last time I was here." Sad attempts at decorating the joint with big potted plants lined the hallway. At least it was something to add a bit of life to all the utilitarian drab.

"Cinder blocks and pale paint." Celeste *tsked* and shook her head. "About the long and short of Yankish tastes, I reckon."

"As if the SIS building is anything to write home about. Looks like it belongs in the Wizard of Oz, with its blocky pale walls looking weirdly like a Mayan temple, capped by those weird emerald hats!"

Silas winced with a chuckle. "Ooh, you better watch yourself, partner. She knows where you live and work."

Celeste hummed an agreement. "I'd listen to the man if I were you, Matthew."

Gapinski swallowed hard and hustled faster, minding his Ps and Qs.

Another twinkly ring was thrown up from Celeste's pocket trudging up the stairwell.

Silas threw her a frown but said nothing. She ignored him and the phone.

Gapinski leaned over to Celeste. "Lover boy—erm...our illustrious Daniel Craig, I presume?"

Now she threw him a frown. "Crack on with your mouth shut, Matthew, if you know what's good for you."

He hustled up the stairwell, taking the stairs by twos.

Because he definitely did know what was good for him. Get out from the middle of that one!

Reaching the fourth floor, he let himself into Gina's wing of things. "Here we go..."

The door led into a large open-floor office area with low-rise cubicles and fluorescent lighting that shouldn't be OSHA approved. Hated the way its white lighting made him look pastier than he really was. Government-issued lemmings in dark suites and white shirts clacked away at computers and yakked away on phones.

Gina's office was at the back corner, a nice little closed-door joint that looked out across a forest and smelled like the view, with a comfy leather couch he stretched out on during their sessions. Still recalled every one of the divots and shapes and colors of those ceiling tiles all those years later after staring them down for weeks in therapy.

Gapinski smiled, smelling the familiar piney comfort from there and making for that corner office through the gauntlet of cubes.

It was always a little weird lying down and baring his soul to someone who was just a few years older than him. She'd been fresh out of graduate school and hired into the FBI only a few months before their first therapy session. Her graduate work with survivors of cult ritual abuse had turned heads and earned her a spot on a domestic terrorism task force. After his... incident, she'd gotten loaned out to the Marine Corps to run interference.

A familiar laugh, high and heady, floated above the cubicles. Sending his heart soaring and weakening his confidence. What would she think seeing him like this all these years later?

And then he saw her, chatting it up with some colleagues just outside her door. Up ahead was a tall woman with striking red hair, a white mug cradled in one hand he knew was filled with peppermint tea.

Something inside Gapinski jumped at the sight. The jumbly bundle of nerves, yes, but it was more than that. Joy washed over him. Like reconnecting with a childhood friend after a few decades. Didn't expect that in the slightest. But supposed reconnecting with his military-issued shrink made sense, given all they'd gone through together.

Given all she'd helped him work through.

Gapinski heaved a shaky breath, clenching his hands into fists for stability, then put on a smile.

Sauntering over, he called out to her, "What's up, doc?"

Gina wore a nice-fitting blue blazer with matching skirt, legs still as smokin' as the last time he'd admired them their last session. A modest gold necklace ringed her neck with a tiny cross anchored at the center. One of the reasons he'd taken to her way back when, appreciating the way she broadcasted her Christian faith in such a subtle, yet public, way.

The woman spun around, her face twisting up with confusion until falling with recognition. Glossy crimson lips stretched into a disbelieving smile.

"Matty G?" she exclaimed, then raced over to him.

Went to throw his arms around her, but she stopped short and took a step back.

That's right! Not the touching kind of gal.

Instead, he grinned and waved.

Silas suppressed a smile and threw Celeste a grin, mouthing *Matty G?* She shrugged and patted her heart, as if knowing there was a level of intimacy between the pair.

He blushed at the thought and show of affection, but welcomed it just the same.

She threw up a wave of her own with a disbelieving smile.

"Uh, surprise!" Gapinski waved jazz hands and offered a chuckle.

"Surprise is right! What on earth are you doing here?" She

craned for a view over his shoulders at Silas and Celeste. "And who are they?"

"Umm, well...some friends. Do you have somewhere we can talk?"

She threw Gapinski assessing eyes before gesturing toward the back corner. "Why don't you step into my office. For old times' sake."

It was just as he remembered it. Spacious, warm, smelling of pine and cedar.

Gina had always struck him as more of a girly girl, expecting rose petal and lavender Yankee Candle Co. scented candles. Definitely not the lumberjack chic ones a brawny dude might light up when he needed to add a bit of feng shui to his digs after a long day's work. But there it still was, the scent as heavenly as ever. As was that leather couch anchored at the back next to a window overlooking a forest of trees still clinging to their dignity at the tail-end of fall.

Gapinski flopped down onto it, kicking up his heels on the armrest and throwing his hands behind his head. He'd mastered the art of the confessional pose after weeks spilling his guts. Technically, Gina was a crime fighter. But her doctorate in clinical psychology on top of the one in forensic psychology had made her suited to lend a helping hand to the military when they came calling. And calling they did when several jarheads had encountered that flying thingy not of this world way back when.

Including Gapinski.

Staring at the ceiling, his mouth widened into a smile. "You kept my mark."

Settling into her therapist chair with her mug, Gina followed his gaze and laughed. "Couldn't very well erase my most memorable client, now could I?"

"He has that effect on most people," Silas said, slapping his feet from the armrest. "Make some room, would you?"

"What mark is that, Matthew?" Celeste asked, searching the ceiling.

Gina answered, "The one where he sent a fountain pen sailing clear through the ceiling tile. My favorite, too. A graduation gift. Never did retrieve it."

Gapinski sat up, his neck warming. He rubbed it. "Yeah, sorry about that…"

She laughed again and put an affectionate hand on his knee. "Fond memories, those weeks were…"

Now she seemed to redden, running a hand through her ginger hair and crossing a leg.

"As welcome of a surprise your visit is, Matty, what's the meaning of this unexpected interruption?"

Gapinski handed it over to Silas with a nod. Better to let the chief deal with unpacking the cray-cray. Could get interesting.

Silas nodded and cleared his throat. "Doctor Anderson—"

"Please, Gina is fine."

"Alright, Gina. My name is Silas Grey. I'm the Master of a religious order called the Order of Thaddeus. This is Celeste Bourne, director of operations for a special project called SEPIO. You already know Matt, who's also part of the Order."

A giggle slipped through Gina's widening lips. "I'm sorry, but did you say Matty is part of a religious order? What, like the Franciscans, or something—monkish robes, celibacy, vows of silence, the whole nine yards?"

She laughed again, throaty and from her belly.

Gapinski frowned. "Geesh, don't act so surprised."

Then her face fell. "Oh, you're serious. Sorry about that." She straightened her skirt and pushed a stray lock of hair behind an ear. "I suppose a lot has happened in the past seventeen years since we last saw each other."

He brightened at the pleasant memories from before that seventeen-year gap.

"Anyway, sorry. You were saying something about some Order—Silas, is that right?"

Silas nodded. "The Order of Thaddeus."

"Never heard of it."

He went into his normal spiel, sketching the lay of the Order land for Gina.

She tilted her head and hummed at the end. "I can appreciate that. I've often wondered what's to become of our faith in the face of rising criticism—more from inside the Church than outside, with all these exvangelicals and prosurgent nut jobs running around deconstructing Christianity to a nub of its former self."

Gapinski leaned over to his teammates. "She's one of us."

"Ahh, a fellow believer," said Celeste. "What denomination?"

"Charismatic Catholic."

"So tambourines and dancing," Gapinski said, "on top of the smells and bells."

"Don't forget speaking in tongues," Gina added. "The whole charismatic nine yards."

Silas said, "In high school, I visited a parish in the Catholic charismatic renewal. Enjoyed the experience. More engaging than my own traditional parish. Then again, I was never good at sitting still in those wooden pews during Mass."

"I was brought up Anglican," said Celeste. "Though my parents were more free-range believers, preferring to express their faith outside the confines of denominational, ecclesial strictures."

"My Grandpappy was a Southern Baptist preacher," added Gapinski. "So definitely no dancing or tongues for me."

Gina smiled, crossing her leg over the other and sipping from her mug. "As fascinating as this is, I imagine you didn't come here to compare denominational credentials."

Silas cleared his throat. "No, we didn't. We came for your help."

She glanced at Gapinski. "My help? In what way?"

"Two words," Gapinski answered. "UFOs and aliens."

"I see..." Gina brought a hand to her chin. A tell showing she was intrigued.

Silas continued, "An MI6 agent solicited our help with—"

"Wait a sec," Gina interrupted. "You were contacted by a foreign intelligence agent operating on US soil?"

His eyes flashed wide with recognition at his slip-up. As an FBI agent, Gina would be compelled to report the incident. Gapinski worried this would be the end of the line for them. She was a by-the-books agent all the way.

"He was a former partner of mine," explained Celeste, "seeking my help with a case involving a government agency on the brink of exposing a vast conspiracy to hide from the American public the existence of UFOs."

"We already know they exist," Gina said. "Don't you read the news?"

"Yes, but the added layer is the revelation of extraterrestrial biological entities having made contact."

Now she made a fist and tapped the top of it like a microphone. "Paging the '90s. I think they want their government conspiracy TV show back."

"She's serious, Gina," Gapinski said. "Now, I don't know the MI6 end of things, but I do know that my backend almost got a Disney fast pass to the front of Saint Pete's pearlies."

She startled. "What?"

He explained what happened at the Order dig site, with a special emphasis on the cray-cray alien bones. The big head, the long body, the sixth finger!

"A sixth digit, you say?" she asked, bringing that hand down from her chin.

"Does that mean anything to you?" asked Silas.

She didn't answer, instead asking, "What is it you believe I can do for you?"

He shrugged. "You tell us. Gapinski here says you're a parapsychologist."

"That's right, with specialties in cultic phenomenon."

"He also said you helped him with—" He stopped short and glanced Gapinski's way.

He nodded him onward. "It's alright. She helped me gather up my marbles after I'd lost it."

"I wasn't going to say that. I understand you oversaw Matt's therapy after some sort of UFO or UAP or whatever they're called—some aerial encounter."

"It was more than an aerial encounter, wasn't it—" Now Gina stopped short, muttering to herself and shaking her head.

Heat flashed up Gapinski's neck, and his head rang with a klaxon clang of warning bells at letting the proverbial cat slip from the proverbial bag.

"I'm so sorry, Matty. I cannot believe I just violated my profession's cardinal rule..."

Silas and Celeste both eyed one another with what he'd expected. Hence the ixnay on the lienay bductionay!

Or at least the *something* encounter...

Suddenly, Gapinski realized the room had wound down to zero. Nothing but the HVAC hum and rain rapping an MC Hammer beat on the windows.

So he cleared his throat and eased around on the couch to face them.

"Yeah, so about that Ramstein encounter."

"The one with the UFO," said Silas.

"Righto."

"Sounds like there's more to the story."

"You could say that..."

"One that should probably wait," said Celeste. "Wouldn't want to waste any more of the good doctor's time, hmm?"

"Not a waste," Gina replied. "Not at all. And if your—shall, we say, new friend from across the pond is on to something... well, then Matty's experience those years ago could be relevant."

Silas glanced at Gapinski. "Really, how so?"

Now Gina glanced his way before getting up from her seat and padding to the door. She drew a curtain across the window and locked it.

Returning to her seat, she scooted her chair closer and said lowly, "Couldn't prove it at the time, but I had always felt Matty's experience—all of the airmen, really—smacked closer to MK-Ultra than anything paranormal."

Silas furrowed his brow. "MK-Ultra?"

"The code name given to a project designed and executed by the CIA."

"What kind of project?" asked Celeste.

"Experiments on human subjects for two decades that were wholly illegal, using hallucinogenic drugs for mind control, information gathering, and psychological torture."

"And here I thought the West fought a war to lay to rest such barbarism."

"Remarkably," Gina went on, "some of the names uncovered in the congressional hearings—scientists and government agents and whatnot—show up in some of the alien abduction stories and events."

"What?" exclaimed Silas. "You mean the same people, the ones from the US intelligence community who ran MK-Ultra—they were identified by abductees?"

"Exactly. Which makes sense, given the nature of the project was to experiment with false memories. Apparently, it worked. Government agents succeeded at implanting false memories of alien abductions."

"Hold on, the US government is responsible for false memory implantation?" Celeste asked with disbelief.

Gapinski craned around the office. "I don't know, Gina. You might want to mind your Ps and Qs. This place could be bugged!"

She laughed. "It isn't a state secret, exactly. Or it was until Congress discovered the program by happenstance, one with mind manipulation and programming as the end result. Most evidence for the program was destroyed, except for nineteen or so boxes. They were missed in the original purge, which was the only reason we know about it."

Silas smirked and shook his head. "Never underestimate the feds' ability to mess up their own operation."

Gina took a sip of tea and shifted in her seat. "Several clinical and experimental trials have demonstrated the creation of pseudo-memories that subjects have subsequently come to believe as truthful depictions of reality."

"Fascinating..."

"Frankly, I wouldn't be surprised in the slightest if there were still a program funded by the Defense Department where subjects are treated with hypnosis, drugs, and other special effects to program them into believing that they are in contact with higher, alien intelligences."

Celeste leaned forward. "Do you possess such knowledge, doctor?"

She put up a staying hand. "Only a conjecture. But it wouldn't surprise me if somewhere in the bowels of the Pentagon there has been a secret public relations effort put on by the government with the hopes of acclimating the public to the reality of alien life-forms. We already know they basically continued Project Blue Book after it was said to expire, the program investigating UFOs. Why not a similar program for aliens themselves?"

A faint buzz grabbed everyone's attention.

Silas pulled out his phone and startled. "Hold that thought..."

Gapinski threw Gina a glance; she threw him a wink. Almost made him want to be her patient again, though that sounded a bit kinky. The whole doc-patient fantasy had always struck him as creepy anyway.

Shaking away the thought, he confessed his dirty mind to the good Lord above and asked, "What's up, chief?"

He showed his phone to Celeste, who frowned. "Trouble is what."

Gapinski sighed. Always something...

CHAPTER 14

Nicky McGrath plucked every one of Silas's nerves.

Had been since he'd laid eyes on him back in that French bistro. Or rather, since Nick had laid those green bromance eyes on him, all come hither and all. Turned out those eyes were for Celeste, not him. Which plucked those nerves to high heaven!

Something about the Daniel Craig wannabe—Gapinski sure hit the nail on the head with that one—none of him sat right. Maybe it was the accent, all highfalutin and better-than. Maybe it was the man's swagger, him trying to own the SEPIO ops center and take control of the operation that still made not a lick of sense.

Sure, he was the one who had invited the Order into the mess, dragging the dead mouse to their doorstep, but whatever. Didn't like it one bit, especially the fact a foreign agent was operating on US soil and trying to rope his veteran backside into some hair-brained operation from the spooks across the pond. Silas still bled red, white, and blue when push came to shove.

But he knew it was more than that. If he was honest with himself, that is.

Never had been the jealous type. Or so he thought. Because since learning Nicky and Celeste had been partners, and then had some sort of romantic entanglement, whatever that was— well, let's just say the part of his lizard brain that had wooed Wilma Flintstone from going after Barney Rubble back in the Stone Age was rearing its ugly head.

Maybe it was because he was usually the heartbreaker, ending relationships early before they could get any sort of ground effect, that cushion of air beneath a plane just before things got real good and lift-off was achieved. Figured it was better to end things early than suffer his own heartbreak. Probably something to do with his childhood, never staying in one place long enough to make any real friends or learn how to keep them.

The psychoanalysis could wait. Maybe Doc Gina could help.

All that mattered, in that moment, was that Nicky had texted him. Probably after trying to reach Celeste and not getting through. How he managed getting his unlisted number, he didn't want to know. Another one of those nerve-plucking maneuvers he'd have to deal with.

True to form, the text was as cryptic as one would expect from an MI6 agent:

3333 MIB Silver

Guessing it's why Nicky had been trying to get Celeste on the horn. Silas regretted making a fuss about it now. Kicking himself for it, really, given the implications of the text.

The self-flagellation could wait.

Because all that mattered, in that moment, was doing something about what Nicky had texted him, given he had a pretty good idea of what it meant.

Having spent time with the British military during his

time in Iraq, and making good friends with one of them, Eli Denton, Silas had learned a thing or two about security codes.

That first one, the quadruple three, indicated a security threat. The added *Silver* was interesting. A more American variety, a code that indicated a weapon or hostage situation. And MIB was self-explanatory.

Men in black.

As in, the feds.

Like the ones who had rolled up on their backsides when this whole blasted thing began a few days ago in that blasted French bistro.

All Silas had wanted was to decompress from Weiss's shellacking and throw back a few G&Ts. Even help Celeste pick out a few things for their wedding that always seemed that much farther away. Yeah, right. No cigar on both fronts.

Such was life in the Order...

Didn't take a genius in algebra to do the math. They were in danger. Probably by the feds themselves. And on a military base of all places!

Par for the SEPIO course, it was.

"What kind of trouble?" Gina asked.

Gapinski shook his head. "The SEPIO kind, I'd wager."

She took a sip of tea, as if the world were right. Much like those violinists on the Titanic who kept playing as the ship was sinking. She said, "Hope it's nothing serious."

He snorted a laugh. "My guess is the entire US military has surrounded the building and is waiting with a platoon of jarheads just outside your office door with M16s aimed for our heads—amiright, chief?"

Silas stood, shoving the phone in his pocket. "Something like that."

"What?" she exclaimed, nearly spilling her tea. "What's this about? Matthew, what have you gotten me into?"

Gapinski opened his mouth to answer, gawping for words, until he looked to Silas with eyes seeking help.

He went to answer when a shrilly ring cut him off.

A landline from Gina's desk.

She stood to answer it.

"No! Leave it there." Silas put out a staying hand and hustled to intercept her, reaching around her desk first while she stood on the opposite side—the phone between them, waiting for either to make a move.

"Does the name Stein mean anything?" he asked, glancing at the caller ID.

"That's agent Stein. My boss."

"Even more reason to leave it."

She let it ring, for now, but asked, "You never answered me. What's this about?"

The phone cut to silence, the call ending and Stein moving on.

On to plot his next move, Silas figured.

Until the man didn't, the phone striking back up its insisting song again with Stein's name emblazoned across the caller ID.

"Just got a text from Nicky," Silas explained, leaning over the phone. "Says we've got hostile company on the way. Armed company. The men in black variety."

"Always something..." Gapinski complained, standing along with Celeste.

Gina folded her arms and threw him a not-so-happy glare. "You mean the foreign intelligence officer operating on US soil?"

"We don't have time to go into it. We need to move. Betting your boss is trying to extract you first. Get you out of harm's way before the boys in blue—"

"Don't you mean men in black?" Gapinski said. "Or worse,

the boys in forest green cammies. We're on a base full of them jarhead types after all."

Silas's heart sank at the realization, but he shook the feeling away. "Either way, we don't got long before whoever is making plans to come storming in here does just that. Hence the innocuous phone call. Last thing the feds would want is a hostage situation on their hands." He quickly added, "Which isn't at all our intent!"

"Gina, is there an exit nearby?" asked Celeste. "A way for us to make our escape?"

The woman froze, eyes wide and mouth hanging open as if in a question.

Silas could feel the gears turning even as the phone kept ringing. Her gaze, a bit vacant and far-off, didn't bode well, but he understood it. She was a fed, and if the men in black were after these three newcomers, then she had an obligation to defend America's interests—whatever they might be.

"Hey, doc," Gapinski said. She turned to him; he smiled. "You trust me, right?"

That seemed to shake her loose. She swallowed hard and blinked twice, one hand rising to that ginger hair of hers and beginning to twist it absentmindedly. Pulled a single hair out, too, before returning to the tick.

But she nodded. "Implicitly."

Gapinski nodded. "Then can you listen to Silas? For me?"

Another nod before turning back to him for direction.

Silas eased in a grateful breath. So far, so good.

"Guessing we don't have much time, and Celeste is right. Is there an exit nearby? Somewhere we can escape?"

She nodded. "A fire exit just around the corner. Leads to the underground parking garage."

"That's perfect! Do you have a car?"

"Yes..."

"With a spacious trunk?"

"Enough for three?" Gapinski asked, nodding with understanding.

Celeste eyed Gapinski. "Plus..."

"A minivan, actually," Gina answered.

Gapinski raised a brow. "Didn't take you for a grocery-getter type."

She shrugged. "It gets decent gas mileage. Plus, it's got tinted windows and a bangin' sound system."

"Alright, I'll give you a pass on the grocery-getter."

"I don't understand. What's your interest with this UFO and alien business that they would come after you?"

"*Our* interest," Silas said, waving a hand at all of them. "No way it's a coincidence that we come seeking your help understanding the alien abduction phenomenon and UFO sightings —and then we get warned about hostiles coming up on our six. Government agents ready to put a kibosh on our little pow-wow."

"No coinkydink there!" said Gapinski.

Gina threw her hands up and shook her head. "I can't be party to this! It's one thing to let you leave. It's a whole other thing to give you my car."

"Drive us, actually," Silas clarified.

"Even worse!"

Silas ran a frustrated hand through his hair. They didn't have time for this.

The phone struck up another song and dance. One he imagined would be the last before all hell broke loose.

"Look, we still need your help. Now more than ever."

Those eyes went wide again, along with that mouth. And then more hair twirling before she plucked another red strand.

Silas came from around the desk now. He said lowly, "Doctor Anderson—"

"Please, Gina," she said, her gaze still far off.

He nodded. "Right, sorry. Gina, you said it yourself, right

before I got this text from Nicky. You said you wouldn't be surprised if all of this nonsense about ETs and UFOs is a government-orchestrated conspiracy."

She nodded, saying nothing more.

"Something about getting the American public ginned up to the idea of alien life-forms after stringing the public along on the UFO front."

Her eyes met Silas's, something seeming to register in them.

The phone suddenly cut off its mournful cry. And she hustled around her desk, kneeling and opening what looked like a safe.

After a few seconds, Gina stood with two handguns. A Glock 19M and a smaller Ruger. She pulled out her own Glock hidden at her hips beneath her coat. Surprised she didn't pull it on them then and there. She still might.

But then she did something unexpected. She handed the Glock to Silas and Ruger to Gapinski.

"If this goes sideways, I'm your hostage. You clocked me and forced me against my will."

Gina grabbed her own weapon by the muzzle and swiped it against the side of her head. Hard, too, and totally out of nowhere. A bit violent but also ballsy. Silas had to give her credit for the show, and her trust in them.

A cut opened up at her hairline and blood began to drip from the wound. She staggered a step and looked like she might go down, but she shook her head and handed over her weapon to Celeste.

She nodded and took it. "Right. We best be getting on with it."

Silas was already at the door, parting the curtain and slowly unlocking the door.

Room looked clear. No clattering keyboards, no humming phone conversations, no loitering and jawing it up at the water cooler. Just what he'd suspected. They'd cleared the deck to reel in the sharks.

Not good...

But no sign of any MIBs, or fatigue-clad jarheads, so at least they had that going for them.

So far.

Gripping his Glock—not his first weapon of choice, but he had to leave his Beretta home—Silas eased open the door and took a step outside, his boots sinking into the surprisingly plush Berber carpet. Must be a recent upgrade, a whiff of wooly new-carpet smell confirming it.

Heart was strumming a mean beat now as he padded farther out, giving the others room to make the exit. Breath was picking up pace and head began swimming with the cognitive dissonance of packing heat in a federal building.

What was he going to do if men in black really did start piling in across the empty office? Open fire, kill a fed? All for Nicky McGrath's hair-brained conspiracy about aliens and flying saucers?

He scanned the vast space of cubicles and coffee makers and fluorescent lights, spotting not a single agent. No one, nada.

Which meant things were about to get real. Real soon.

Celeste tapped his shoulder and nodded toward the corner. Gina was already at the emergency stairwell and ushering Gapinski inside. She went to meet them and Silas followed.

Getting to the door just as a noise caught his attention.

From behind and down at the far end beyond the maze of cubes.

He spun around and eased the door closed, looking through the slit while his stomach sank to that fresh Berber.

Men in black, weapons extended and weaving through the bureaucratic detritus.

And not in black suits but black body armor, with full head-gear and FBI emblazoned across their chests in bright yellow.

Not good...

Shutting the door, a soft echoey *click* sounding like clanging pots and pans, Silas motioned for the others to move.

"We've got company..."

"The notorious MIB?" Gapinski asked.

He nodded, taking the stairs by twos as the others shuffled ever downward. Didn't take long before they were passing Level 1 down past the Basement and then on to Parking.

Surprisingly, meeting no resistance.

Silas crossed himself on instinct, thanking the good Lord for their traveling mercies.

So far...

Gina burst through the door into the parking garage, the clangy echo far louder than Silas cared for.

He glanced behind, worried the feds on the fourth floor would hear all the racket and their cover would be blown.

A few beats ticked by. Still nothing.

Looked good to go.

Silas spun back to join his crew. "Go, go, go!" he urged, Gina tearing down the concrete with Gapinski at her side.

A Honda Odyssey shrouded in shadows came into view several cars down.

Right as tires squealed toward them from behind!

Gina and Gapinski twisted around for a viewing. Celeste didn't wait for the visual, instead darting between a Civic and Camry. So much for Made in America pride from the feds.

Silas joined her, crouching at the driver's side door and bringing his weapon up for action.

Just as white lights sliced through the dimmed darkness, the high beams growing more intense as the car approached.

Couldn't tell how many, but it sounded big.

Like one of those Chevy Suburbans that had planted its hindquarters outside that French bistro.

More light, more tires on cement, more revving of an engine.

And then it flashed by. Not a Suburban, but some Ford knockoff. It kept going, too, disappearing from view.

Silas exhaled a breath he didn't realize he was holding, easing to a stand and stepping back into the parking garage.

Celeste joined, as did Gapinski and Gina.

"That was a close one," Gina said.

"Yeah, I thought our gander was cooked for sure," Gapinski agreed on a shaky breath.

Silas swallowed hard and hustled past the pair. "Let's get the heck out of here."

"Don't have to tell me twice."

Gina jogged past him and directed them to her van. Grey and bulky and tinted, like she said. Not an ideal getaway vehicle, but it would do the job.

Silas opened the hatchback trunk, the door easing open with automation. "Hop in."

"Do I have to?" Gapinski complained.

"Not if you don't mind bending over for lost soap in a federal Supermax prison."

His eyes flashed wide before the man climbed inside.

"Good choice."

The sliding door was already open. Celeste climbed in first, then Silas.

When a shrilly *bring-bring-bring* sliced through the carpark with a wicked echo.

His phone!

Muttering a curse, Silas silenced his device still wedged in his pocket while yanking on the door handle. The sliding door had other plans, the automatic door gliding to a close without his say-so. What would the world do without progressive tech?

Gapinski popped his head above the headrest from the trunk. "Impeccable timing, chief."

"Who is it?" Celeste asked in a whispered rush.

Silas pulled out the phone and frowned. "Nicky McGrath..."

Gina brought the grocery-getter to life just as the door finally came in for a landing. He answered the call.

"Not exactly the best time for a chit-chat, Nick."

"Ahh, so you're alive," Nicky cooed. "I was beginning to have my doubts."

"Gee, thanks."

Gina eased out of the parking space and pressed the Odyssey forward.

"You're welcome, by the way," the British spook went on. "And if you're on your way, I must apologize. You're cleverer than I gave you credit for, given you interpreted my coded text."

Silas smirked and shook his head. "Thanks for the vote of confidence, and—" He couldn't believe he was saying it, but— "thanks for the tip. We're leaving the carpark now."

"Crikey, still?" Nicky exclaimed.

"It's not like you gave us much notice!"

"Was I right? The feds are on to you, aren't they."

"You were right. Floor cleared out and then the men in black came storming in."

Nicky smirked. "I'd like to see how you got yourself out of that sticky wicket."

"Literally just slipped down an emergency stairwell."

"What? I ought to try that next time..."

Gina interrupted, "We're coming up on the Academy checkpoint."

"I've got to go," Silas whispered.

"Wait! I'm motoring my way to—"

He ended the call and stuffed the phone back in his pocket, then bent low in the well, wedged between the driver's seat and rear bucket seats.

The darkened van suddenly tipped back before brightening. Must be ascending back to the surface. He threw Celeste a glance, and the pair shared a moment.

Here we go...

Silas went to throw up a prayer but felt foolish that the Lord would help them evade law enforcement. Although, he figured it was for a good cause, so he prayed he would help them escape, or at least stay the feds' hand.

And bring their backsides to safety!

Squealing brakes told him they'd reached the checkpoint, the sound not giving him much confidence for the road ahead.

The minivan's momentum slowed, and Silas unfurled from his crouch enough to see personnel in fatigues waiting for the car to approach. Didn't much look it over, and only seemed to give Gina a passing glance. And yet—

Moment of truth...

Eyes closed and curling back in on himself to make himself as small as possible, Silas held his breath and ticked off the seconds. Used an old Rangers trick he'd developed to keep his head in the game and cleared of panic. Because the thought of being arrested and dragged to some CIA black site for interrogation, or getting into a shootout and ending up dead—well, it was enough to send his pulse soaring again and worry blooming.

999, 998, 997, 996...

The van stopped, and Gina rolled down her window.

990, 989, 988, 987...

Muffled words were exchanged and then a laugh from Gina. Playful, even flirtatious.

976, 975, 974, 973...

Then it was over. The van picked up speed, and the engine whirled into overdrive, the scents of dead leaves and woodsmoke riding into the car on a whipping breeze through the window before it was closed.

The car eased a collective sigh of relief, Silas and Celeste unfurling from their huddled hiding place and Gapinski popping up from the back. Sky was still dark, still foreboding, which looked and felt about right given the stakes.

Gina flipped on some music for the winding drive to the final checkpoint. Some hark plunking a weird tune with an alto really going at it.

"You bought a minivan with a bangin' sound system for opera?" Gapinski said.

Gina eyed him from the rearview mirror. "Got a problem with that, Matty G?"

"No, ma'am..."

"When it comes to music," Silas said, arching his back to stretch out the ache, "never question a woman's judgment."

"When it comes to anything," Celeste added with a wry grin, "never question a woman's judgment."

He smiled back and nodded. "That too."

Gina raced through winding roads carrying them back to that large sign hanging over the main entrance. One exit down, one more to go.

Seemed like only a beat later and she threw up an "Uh oh..." before slamming on the brakes. Which threw up another wicked squawk along with a bit of grinding this time around, joined by squealing tires that meant nothing good.

Silas snapped his head to the front. And sucked in a panicked breath.

Uh-oh was right!

Place was swarming with those familiar black Suburbans, their reds and blues like toddlers flinging paint across the ground and towering barren trees. A dozen of those jarhead cammies were milling about too, bearing stern faces and even sterner M16s—the men and women clearly waiting for something.

For them.

CHAPTER 15

Time froze, the moment calcifying into a vacuum of ticking time as the two parties at either end of the boulevard faced off to assess what was going down.

Reminded Silas of a near miss in downtown Fallujah. He and Colton and a few other buddies under his command had hit up one of the local bars. This was weeks after much of the brutal fighting had wound down to zero, but there were pockets of Republican Guard soldiers still roaming around, not willing to admit defeat.

He'd heard about the local watering hole from Major Pepper of all people, his CO. Boy, was the man a lonely heart, on account of that bark and bite and bald head of his, on top of his general pain-in-the-assery. But Silas had to give him credit when he knew him and his boys needed a night off. Recommended the hole-in-the-wall and told him to take a few hours.

So he did, him and his boys, enjoying kebabs of char-grilled meat on metal sticks, spiced rice wrapped in grape leaves, and bowls of cooked rice with spices and carrots, beans, and grilled nuts. His favorite was *mezguuf*, skewers of seasoned fresh carp grilled to perfection. All of it washed down with some local brew that wasn't half bad. It was just what the doc ordered, and surprisingly what the Major ordered. One of the few times he was grateful for his mandates.

Trouble came on the way back.

Parked a few blocks down from the bar, and on the final leg, a group of five men were lumbering down the block. Silas immediately sensed trouble.

It wasn't just that a group of people were heading their way. Passed plenty of couples and families and kids. It was the way they raised their heads and slowed their gate upon recognition. The hardening of faces and exchanging of glances, the whispered Arabic and clenched fists. All of it suggested they knew who him and his boys were.

The enemy. And they were ready to do something about it.

Much like what was going on a klick down the road at the final checkpoint. Two groups facing off, waiting to see what was what.

And who would blink first.

Just like before, back in Fallujah, he swiped a page from Kenny Rogers's playbook. Sometimes you hold your ground as much as your cards. Then there are those times you fold 'em and walk away, or just plain throw them up in the air and run.

That was one of those times, the one back in Fallujah.

Silas and his boys had backed up the way they came. They were unarmed and on leave, and not at all interested in creating an international incident. But the quintet couldn't leave them well enough alone, the men tearing after them with raised fists and wielding bats, the familiar *Amrikiun* slang for Uncle Sam's errand boys shouted with rage in a way that signaled they meant business.

He didn't wait around long enough to find out what that business was, him and Colton and the rest hightailing it out of there. Didn't have a clue where they were or where they were going. The group bobbed and weaved through unfamiliar streets of beige stone buildings all looking the same, past nighttime strollers and street venders to get out of Dodge. Managed to hustle back to the car and lose the knuckleheads, but it was a close call. Too close, one the Major didn't hear tale of, that's for sure.

As they say, history doesn't repeat itself, it rhymes. And now the boys and girls in camo were recapitulating the interested looks and exchanged glances from Fallujah, the whispered words and clenched weapons that told Silas they were in trouble.

Now they were stepping aside for the black Suburbans, the beasts easing through the gate and assembling in a line—

And making their way toward their position. Slow and steady, with a few men hanging out the side—doors open and weapons drawn.

At them!

"Gina..." Silas said. "Now would be a good time to get us the heck out of here."

She didn't say anything. Just sat there, eyes wide and mouth open with indecision.

Gapinski added, "Uh, doc, I'm not of the opinion orange is the new black. A jumpsuit in that shade would clash with my skin tone!"

Others joined the Suburbans, and now they were shouting orders for them to exit the vehicle.

"Silas, what do we do?" Celeste whispered.

Gapinski answered, "We need to back this puppy up and get out of Dodge, is what!"

"I can't," Gina said on a shaky breath. "My father would kill me."

Didn't know what in the slightest that meant. Whatever it did seemed to be paralyzing the agent into inaction. In the heat of battle, with a dozen feds closing in on their twelve.

Not good...

Silas edged to the middle between the pair of seats up

front. "Then let me take over." He gestured to the passenger's seat, adding, "Slide over and let me drive, alright? We got you into this mess. It should be our responsibility to get you out of it."

That tick returned, the twirling of her ginger hair as she stared forward right before she plucked a strand and startled, as if the act had helped her come to a decision in the heat of the moment.

Gina unbuckled and gave up the controls, sliding and slumping into the passenger's seat.

"I am so dead..." she muttered, a hand returning to that twirl.

Not if Silas could help it.

He threw the minivan into reverse. "Hold on..."

Pressing a bracing arm against the passenger's seat, he whipped his head around and floored it. Didn't even bother with the speedometer, the engine blowing past second and third gears in no time flat as he sped back down the drive. Was surprised how much skip the van had in its step. Just hoped he didn't crash.

"I must say," Celeste said, "I didn't know Honda had it in them."

"I got an upgrade for a turbo boost," Gina said, then twisted around for a look. "Egads! I'm in so much trouble right now."

Gapinski snorted a laugh. "Yeah, you can pretty well kiss your career goodbye, doc."

Silas chanced a glance out front, not at all liking what he was seeing.

Three SUVs had slowed to regroup, the feds scrambling to mount their ponies and arm up to take down the threat.

Them!

Giving him a widow to right the ship.

"Hold on..."

Slamming on the brakes, he twisted the steering wheel. The

centripetal forces whipped the Honda around its pivot point, throwing Celeste and Gapinski around the cabin.

"Oy, love!" Celeste shouted, smacking into the side window.

Another thud at the ceiling rang, followed by Gapinski's familiar "Sonofa—"

"Sorry!" Silas said, throwing the minivan into *Drive.*

"Dude, warn us next time you go all Jack Bauer on us!"

"I said hold on..."

Celeste winced, rubbing her forehead. "You better hop to whatever it is you're planning, love. Because even with the turbo-charged engine, the feds are gaining on us!"

Silas glanced in the rear-view mirror. A wave of black SUVs sporting whirling reds and blues up top crested toward them, their sirens blaring and their intercepting intent clear.

Didn't have to tell him twice.

Silas floored it, the van lurching forward on uncertain feet but gaining ground real quick.

Thunder rumbled overhead and a canopy of dark, low-hanging clouds promised nothing good. A wall of naked trees kept Silas on course racing through the Marine base. But he was flying blind, and now those clouds were making good on their promise, large drops slamming into the windshield.

He shook his head in frustration. "Where the hell are we going?"

"Stay straight ahead," Gina said, pointing with one finger while the other twirled those red locks of hers.

"But where does it take—"

The shrilly *bring-bring-bring* of Silas's phone cut him off. He muttered a curse and retrieved it. Without looking at its face, he handed the device behind him.

"I believe it's for you, dear."

Celeste took it with a huff, then answered the call. "Nicky, we're having a bit of a go of things at the moment. The American military, on top of the federal investigative arm, apparently have it out for us. Perhaps—"

She was cut off, an irritated MI6 agent jawing it up through the squawk box from where Silas sat. He glanced back at her while she listened, her face creasing with worry.

Signaling nothing good...

Those rain clouds were really cranking it out now. Large rain drops smacked into the windshield like bloated hornets, the downpour assaulting them in kamikaze splats and picking up speed—making it difficult to see and drive across the slick pavement.

He flipped the wipers to full-on flap and glanced at the speedometer. The ticker was cresting past 60 mph and aiming straight for the red zone of terror. But none of it mattered if they ended up wrapped around one of those streaking trees!

Celeste tapped his shoulder. "Right. Nicky says he's up ahead."

"On base?" exclaimed Silas. "How'd he—"

Gunfire erupted from behind, cutting off a reply. A menacing *rat-a-tat-tat* followed by *pop-pop-pops* that clanged against the Odyssey's metal hide—with several bullets sinking into its backside.

"They're shooting at us?" Gina exclaimed, twisting around for a look.

"Not you, us," Gapinski answered, gesturing from him to Celeste and Silas. "Us us."

"Remember—" Silas said, weaving from one side of the road to the other, the back end fishtailing a bit on the return trip.

"Keep her steady, love," said Celeste.

Gapinski snorted. "If the bullets don't kill us, Silas's driving will."

Silas wiped his brow then turned to Gina. "Just remember, if this thing goes south, we took you hostage. Got it?"

She quickly nodded.

Another round of menacing *rat-a-tat-tat* and *pop-pop-pops* kept Silas on his toes. His evasive maneuvers seemed to be working well enough.

Until the rear window burst!

One-two bullets punched through, sending blunted shards of the tinted tempered glass scattering inside.

The first sank into the console, shattering an iPad-style display and cutting off that opera nonsense. So much for the soundtrack to their featured film!

The other punched clear through the front windshield, leaving behind a whistling sound followed by dribbling rain.

Gapinski threw up a shriek and scampered into the bucket seat next to Celeste. She joined him in a proper British cussing. Even Gina got in on the action, making even the hardened Iraqi veteran Silas blush at her expletives.

"Everyone alright?" Silas shouted behind, jerking the wheel again while giving the engine some more high-octane love.

"Been better," Gapinski groaned.

"I should've stayed in bed," Gina added, head between her knees.

"Bloody hell," exclaimed Celeste, "what's the plan to extract us from this mess of things?"

Silas smirked. "I thought Nick would've come riding in on his white Shetland Pony by now."

"Oh, come off of it, love. If it wasn't for Nicky, our bloomin' backsides would be sitting in the brig as we speak!"

"If it wasn't for your former lover, our bloomin' backsides would be sitting back at HQ!"

"Is that what this is about?"

"Uh, guys..." Gapinski said.

Silas ignored him, cursing himself before correcting himself. "Partner. I meant partner."

She sputtered her lips and laughed. "Oh, no you didn't!

Your Shakespearean jealousy would be comical if it wasn't rearing its ugly head in the heat of battle and liable to get us all killed!"

"Shakespearean jealousy my ass!"

"If you spared one second getting your head out of that ass of yours, you would have learned my former *partner* is waiting to extract us up ahead."

"Uh, guys..." Gapinski said again, louder, more insistent.

Silas spun toward him, as did Celeste, the pair shouting *"What?"*

"Egads!" Gina shouted, pointing up ahead and to the left.

"What she said!" Gapinski shouted.

Silas returned to the road, righting their ship back to the right lane and scanning the landscape for signs of danger.

Took a beat, then he saw it.

Egads was right.

Two more bogies at their nine were flying toward their route from stage left. Not Suburbans. Marine light tactical vehicles. The A2 series Humvees, green and really cranking it. Plumes of rainwater billowing behind them as they raced to intercept their target.

Them!

"Always something..." complained Gapinski.

Celeste leaned forward. "Love, I do believe those lorries aren't planning to stop any time soon."

No, no they weren't.

"A broadside to our kisser, is what they're planning," Gapinski said in agreement.

Silas gripped the steering wheel and did the only thing he could do.

He floored it.

The pedal sank into the floor, goosing the engine just enough to set it sailing faster. But...

It was gonna be close.

Real close.

Rain was really coming down now, too, those liquid hornets making it impossible to make sense of the road and playing havoc with their paws clamoring for purchase on the slick road. Making adjustments to the steering wheel felt like they were riding on a bed of air. Silas feared any evasive maneuvers would send their ride hydroplaning into those naked trees standing at attention from the sidelines.

But he held his breath and pressed forward anyway, those two intercepting Humvees drawing closer while the Suburbans at their six gave them no other options.

Could really use that opera music right about now!

White knuckled and lungs screaming for oxygen, Silas continued holding his course and breath, waiting for either bad-luck snake eyes or a lucky roll of the dice.

"I hope you know what you're doing, chief," Gapinski said.

"Steady on, love," Celeste added. "Steady on..."

Gina just sat there twirling her ginger locks again. Looked like she was muttering a prayer, too. Not a bad idea.

The distance from the intersection was narrowing.

Moment of truth...

A deuce or lucky seven?

Speeding past the side road, he chanced a glance out his window—making contact with mean-looking grunts sporting fatigues, sunglasses, and military-issued hair. A second longer and he would've been eating their grill.

Instead, he sailed past.

Just as the lead Suburban from the trio chasing them from the checkpoint plowed into his intercepting comrade.

It was a real doozy of an accident, too. Crunching metal, squealing tires, exploding glass and airbags—the whole nine yards.

"Boom!" Gapinski shouted, twisting back for a look-see. "Score one for the good guys."

Gina groaned, burying her head in her hands.

"Bravo, love!" Celeste grabbed his shoulder. "Never doubted your ability to save the day."

Silas heaved in a relieved breath, swallowing hard and sighing with relief.

Then he chuckled, shaking his head. "Like I said. Never underestimate the feds' ability to mess up their own operation."

She laughed. "Apparently you Yanks are bigger screw-ups than our Box 500 domestic security agents!"

"Not so fast, Batman and Robin." Gina pointed out back. "Looks like one managed to survive."

"Always something..." growled Gapinski.

And now they were shooting. And not the half-assed *pop-pop-pops*, either. Livid *rat-a-tat-tats* clattered and clanged and pinged off the Odyssey's body. They weren't messing around! Too bad for Gina's pimped-out ride.

"What are we going to do?" Gina asked, voice surprisingly calm given the circumstances. Though perhaps her calm demeanor had something to do with that tick of hers, one hand still twirling away while another plucked a single red hair.

Silas sailed, "Celeste, didn't you say lover boy—erm, your former partner..." he glanced behind to find a frowning fiancé. Not good. "Sorry. Anyway, didn't you say Nicky was on the horn, something about coming in to rescue us?"

"That's what I was trying to tell you before you got your bloomin' knickers in a twist!"

He deserved that.

She took a breath and raked a frustrated hand through her hair. Edging toward the middle console up front, she held out her smartphone with the map app already drawn up.

"Right, he's apparently parked off a service road just outside the boundaries to the base."

"I know that road," Gina said. "Joplin Road, isn't it?"

"Correct."

"Off base, that's for sure."

"Where is it?" Silas said, straining to look at the map app.

Celeste pointed to a blue pulsing orb at the end of a winding blue-brick road.

"That's like five miles away!"

"Three and a half, actually."

Silas scoffed. He glanced behind and gave a flick of his wrist to the steering wheel, the van banking into the left lane. Then he goosed the engine some more, cresting seventy now and easing back into the right lane again.

The feds followed him with every wrist flick, gaining on them and answering with another round of weapon fire.

"Gapinski, you still armed?" he asked.

"Yeah…" his partner said, a brow raised with suspicion.

"Then I'd suggest you make use of our obliterated rear window if you want to see another day."

Gapinski glanced at Celeste for confirmation. "What, like shoot the feds?"

"Can't," Gina said.

"Why not?" asked Silas.

"It violates 18 US Code, section 1114, actually," Clearing her throat, she continued, "*Whoever kills or attempts to kill any officer or employee of the United States or of any agency in any branch of the United States Government (including any member of the uniformed services) while such officer or employee is engaged in or on account of the performance of official duties, or—*"

"I get the idea, sister!" exclaimed Gapinski.

Another *rat-a-tat-tat* followed up with an unexpected *pop-pop-pop* put an exclamation point on the urgency.

"You don't need to kill them," Silas said. He turned to Gina. "Or attempt to kill them. Just throw them off our trail long enough to get us to safer ground."

"And where is that?"

"That damn blue dot!"

Could tell Gapinski didn't know what to do. Silas kept at his routine, bobbing and weaving through the slick road, the naked trees funneling them ever farther into the Marine base property. Even as more bullets sailed past into those naked trees and sank into their backside. One wrong shot and their tires would shred.

Or worse.

"Oy, there it is!" Celeste tapped him on the shoulder and pointed ahead.

Rounding a bend, the road opened up for a half mile before bending sharply left. But to the right there was a gravel turnoff, a clump of trees still clinging to their leafy dignity, a high chain-link fence, and another road that curved the opposite direction.

"I assume that's our—"

A sudden jolt from the rear sent Silas's head smacking into the steering wheel. Pain lanced across his face and blood bloomed at his nose. The others shouted, and the horn threw up a honk at the sudden bang along with a hideous crunch from the back.

Didn't take a genius to know what had happened. Wiping his nose on his sleeve, one glance in the rear-view mirror confirmed it.

Their new friends had plowed into their backside and were coming in hot and heavy for a second helping.

Not if Silas could help it.

Time to go for broke.

CHAPTER 16

S ilas punched it, the pedal sinking into the floor with acceleratory intent.

Wasn't nearly enough to evade the incoming bogie.

The Suburban smashed into their rear, pulled back, then let her rip again.

Sending the Honda weaving across the slick pavement on uncertain legs.

"You alright, love?" Celeste asked.

He wiped his nose again, wincing at the pain. "I'm fine. But it'd sure be nice if you gave us some covering fire, Gapinski."

Gina offered, "18 US Code, section 1114, says—"

"I don't give a damn what US Code whatever says!" Silas growled. "Not when the feds are hunting us down like animals."

"Fugitives, more like it..."

He let it go. She was right, but they were so close to escape. And if the government went to such lengths to shut them down and shut them up—a trio of monks, basically, who were seeking answers to questions about public knowledge—then what were they onto?

Almost there, almost to freedom...

Another smack at the back nearly sent them off course, the back end wobbling and trunk door flying open from the impact.

Dead leaves and the faint traces of woodsmoke riding in on a cold breath flooded inside. A hissing noise from the eight tires pounding the wet pavement made it hard to concentrate. Now they were really exposed. One clear shot would end their escape real quick.

But they were close. Just a few more—

A *pop-pop-pop* sent Silas crouching, worried it was aimed his way.

But the sound was closer. And inside, not out.

He chanced a glance behind, seeing Gapinski taking aim and punching off another *one-two-three* shots.

Just as their fed tail began leaning to the right on wobbly feet.

"Egads!" Gina exclaimed before twisting that hair of hers again.

"Nice shot!" he said, hope surging even as they surged toward their off ramp.

"Can't say I advocate lobbing shots at bobbies," Celeste said, "especially the federal variety, but cracking good shot anyhow!"

The Suburban fell behind, and Silas eased up a bit to bring their bird in for an emergency landing.

"Hold on!"

"You've been saying that this whole trip!" Gina complained. "That your go-to line when the shiznit hits the fan, or what?"

He went to reply but chuckled instead. "Something like that. And maybe buckle up is more like it."

"Safety first."

The crew took his cues to heart, three clicks sounding off in rapid succession and Silas following suit.

"Alright, here we go!"

And go they went.

Silas floored it, then twisted the wheel at just the right moment, sending the Honda banking clear into the high fence topped with barbed wire. Wouldn't stop a pack of moose interested in a new habitat, let alone an escaping Odyssey, but that's the feds for you.

The minivan crashed through the chain-linked fence, like a knife through butter sailing to freedom with ease.

Until a massive oak side-swiped the entire length of the driver's side, throwing up a hideous crunch.

Gina moaned, burying her head in her hands. The others held steady, bracing themselves for whatever came next.

Which was a good thing on both counts, because a berm with attitude was waiting for them, a two-story hill that meant business anchored directly ahead.

It also meant airborne. Silas worried they wouldn't even make it that far, the Honda's snout getting stuck in the packed earth.

But nature proved him wrong.

Didn't get the physics of it all, but tires gained purchase and the incline did the rest—sending the Honda ramping up the dang thing and sailing through the air toward Joplin Road where a silver foreign ride was idling on the shoulder, hot exhaust puffing out the back with impatience in the crisp fall afternoon.

Until it started tipping, banking Gapinski's way. And then down the engine's way.

"Hold on!" Silas said, bracing himself against his armrests.

The impact came sooner than the movies make such soaring flights out to be. The nose crashed with a hideous crunch, the front end accordioning before the van toppled to its right side.

Airbags instantly deployed all around the van as it fell, cushioning the blow to their faces and bodies, which did the job. A reminder to grab a Honda next time he was in the market for a new car.

Pain bloomed at Silas's face and blood seeped from his nose again. Appreciated the safety feature, but that'd leave a mark.

He shook it off and unclipped his belt. "Everyone alright?"

"Been better," Gapinski moaned, unlatching his belt and falling with a thud against the wet black pavement, shattered glass crunching under him.

Celeste shook her head and winced, bringing a hand to a cut at her forehead. "Just a surface wound. I'll live."

She was still harnessed into her seat belt and struggling to get out. Looked stuck.

Silas went to help when he noticed Gina leaning against the deflated airbag on the road. Still, unmoving.

"Gina, you alright?"

Nothing.

Just what they needed.

He went to unlatch his belt when he ran into Celeste's problem. Stuck.

A bolt of lightning lanced across the sky, bright and blue, thunder clapping an instant later along with the inevitable downpour. Rain picked up real quick along with a whipping wind, the water seeping through cracks in the windshield and broken side windows. They needed to get out, and fast.

Silas jammed the release button again, but got no love. He tugged against the belt, but it didn't budge.

"Here, try this." Gapinski reached around and sliced the nylon strap at the shoulder, having already done the same for Celeste.

It gave, and he quickly unwound the belt from around his waist then climbed over to Gina.

She didn't look good. There was a gash at the side of her head and blood running down her face. Eyes were closed and mouth open. Thankfully, Silas felt a faint breath, but she was out cold.

"Gina..." he said, gently smacking her cheeks. "Come on, Doctor Anderson, we've got to go."

Her eyes fluttered open. "Happy birthday, baby Jesus," she moaned, eyes batting again and chest heaving a breath. "Egads, my head hurts."

Celeste appeared over his shoulder. "She going to be alright?"

"I think so."

Gapinski was opening the side door where Celeste had been seated, which was now the top hatch for their escape.

Gina sat forward and winced, slumping back into her seat.

"Easy does it, Gina," Silas said, unlatching her seat belt and getting it out of her way.

She met Silas's gaze. "Who are you, cutie?"

He blushed and smiled. "Silas Grey, remember? Matt Gapinski brought us by, along with Celeste Bourne."

Now she moaned. "You kidnapped me." Then she glanced around. "Hey, this is my ride."

"Blame the feds..."

Gapinski hoisted himself up on the top of the van and helped Celeste climb out to join him.

"We've gotta go, chief," he called down. "I'm afraid this thing might blow!"

Panic threatened to settle in now at the turn. Not only from the accident but the whole shazam, the chase and the FBI and military pursuit. What a mess it was.

"Can you move?" Silas asked Gina.

She sat forward and winced again, but nodded.

Silas wrapped an arm around her neck and helped her out of her seat. He climbed out from the front of the cabin to give her room. Gina made it to all fours, a good sign, before following him into the back.

Gapinski and Celeste helped Silas out and then grabbed Gina by both hands and brought her out as well. Soon, all eight feet were on solid ground and hustling to Nicky for escape.

The Honda looked like a beached whale with its face smashed in. Steam hissed from the front end, and fuel was running down the pavement. One stray spark would set it ablaze. Now sirens echoed in the near distance, livid and searching. Wouldn't be long before they arrived, and they were hauled off to the brig or some CIA black site.

Not good.

"About time you showed up!" Nicky shouted from his vehicle, the man sporting a black turtleneck now and holding a Burberry umbrella.

Heat ran up Silas's neck as he helped Gina along. Plucked his every last nerve, that man did.

Hobbling across the pavement, she glanced at her ride. "You do realize you owe me a new minivan, right?"

"Don't worry, the Order's good for it." Gapinski grabbed Silas's shoulder. "Ain't that right, chief?"

Silas nodded, saying nothing. Yet another unaccounted expense that would surely give Weiss more fodder. That wasn't even counting their own ride they had abandoned in the Academy parking lot. Thankfully, it was untraceable, but still...

How he was going to explain that to the board—how their operation contact, who just happened to be an FBI agent, lent them her ride after they left theirs, while running from a squad of marines and Suburbans full of men in black—now that would take some finessing.

But he couldn't think about that now. Didn't want to think about that now.

Nicky folded his umbrella and gestured to his vehicle. "Don't lallygag. Pile in, would you?"

"Don't have to tell me twice," Gina said, climbing into the back.

Gapinski smirked, following her. "An Audi? Gotta love the Brits..."

"Beggars can't be choosers, Matthew," Celeste said, sliding next to him and closing the door.

Sirens were growing closer now, and it sounded like a chopper could be closing in, the bassy thwapping of its blades all the encouragement Silas needed to hop to it.

He scrambled around the front and slid into the front passenger's seat.

"Punch it!"

"Your wish is my command..." Nicky threw the Audi into *Drive* and let its turbocharged V-6 engine do its thing.

They sped north, the trees flashing by now and rain smacking the windshield. But they'd made it. They were free. Not unscathed, but alive to live another day.

And fight another fight.

Nicky raced onward. "Maybe now you will believe me when I tell you there is a vast conspiracy at the highest levels of government seeking to suppress any knowledge of first contact between humanity and intelligent life-forms, hmm?"

Gapinski raised a hand. "I'm sold."

Silas went to bite back a reply, but thought against it. What was the point? Besides, the guy did save their backsides, had to give him credit for that one. And he'd been working on trying to produce more of the fruits of the Spirit. Peace, kindness, gentleness, and all the rest. Opening his big mouth would set him back a pace or two.

Instead, he went with, "Just drive and get us the heck out of here."

There was another reason he kept his mouth shut. A tremor in his hand, along with his heart hammering in his head and shaky breathing were physical tells of what was going on inside.

Deep down he knew Nicky was right. The circumstantial

evidence was adding up to some sort of suppression by forces bigger than himself, bigger than the Order of Thaddeus. Forces arrayed against any disclosure of craft and intelligence not of this world.

But why? Who could give a rat's backside why the Order was poking around the FBI asking questions that were basically in the public domain anyway?

Only thing he could figure was there was something to it all. Something to the reports of unidentifiable crafts piloted by alien beings—something to the reports of contact with such beings, abductions by them even.

He swallowed hard, staring through the rain-streaked window out into the countryside laid to waste by colder temperatures.

What did that mean for the Church, first contact and all? What about for the Christian faith, the Church's teaching surrounding the uniqueness of humanity—teachings about the uniqueness of God, even?

More troubling yet: What did first contact mean for humanity?

Silas wasn't sure he was ready for the answers.

––––––

NICKY PUSHED THE LIMITS ON HIS AUDI AS MUCH AS HE FELT comfortable. The crew rode in silence, nursing their wounds with a medical kit the MI6 spook had stowed away in the glove box.

When Silas felt they had driven far enough, he suggested they pull off and regroup at a Cracker Barrel he spotted. The others questioned his wisdom with the feds hunting them, all except Gapinski who was happier than a clam to get his paws on a Country Boy Breakfast.

"Think about it," Silas said. "An MI6 spook, an FBI agent,

and three Christian religious order agents just sitting in an American restaurant chain in broad daylight. No way would the feds think to look for us there."

"Doesn't have quite the ring of a John le Carré novel to it," Nicky said, "but the chap does have a point."

He sat back with a satisfied grin as Nicky pulled into the parking lot, sandwiching their Audi between a Ford F-150 and an aging, sagging Cutlass Ciera, both from another century that felt right.

Climbing out, the scent of burning wood hung heavy in the parking lot, along with grilled meat and something sugary. Stomach rumbled something fierce on their march across the parking lot and his head felt faint now with hunger.

They took a table in the corner flanking a bay of windows and within darting distance of an emergency exit. No way would they be caught flatfooted again.

After the waitress took their orders, drinks soon arrived. Food would take longer, which gave them a chance to recount the last few hours to Nicky. Gina was reluctant, casting an understandably skeptical eye at the MI6 agent. But after what just went down, with the full force of the US government bearing down on her, she quickly warmed to him.

After the travelogue, Nicky sipped his Lipton and shook his head. "Crikey, that explains a lot."

"Explains what?" asked Silas, downing a swig of his black brew that wasn't half bad.

"SIS has been following a series of UAP waves the past night."

"UAP waves?"

Another Lipton sip, followed by a grimace, before explaining, "Over the course of the last seventy years or so, there have been these waves of unidentified aerial phenomenon concentrated in specific locals. One of the more famous was the Berlin wave, where some hundred-forty-plus sightings were reported on a single night in late November 1989."

Silas settled back with his coffee. "Over a hundred? By, what, crackpots and wackos?"

Nicky frowned. "Not if you consider Belgian police officers and military personnel, including high-ranking colonels, amongst the crackpots and wackos. And that's not even touching upon the many civilians who also witnessed the phenomenon, which was then repeated a few weeks later in December."

He threw back some brew, feeling sufficiently chided. "Well, what did this—wave of...well, aerial phenomenon look like?"

"Triangular crafts with three flashing lights, then another red one at the center that some reported as detaching and reattaching, along with a low humming noise."

Gapinski sucked in a startled breath. "That exact same UFO is what I saw in Turkey!"

Celeste shushed him. "Oy, mate, keep your voice down!"

A few of the locals glanced their way. One farmer jerked a thumb and muttered something to his friend across the table behind a raised coffee mug.

Nicky edged closer to the table. "Did it exhibit the telltale flight characteristics, with sudden high speeds and changes in direction on a dime?"

Gapinski shook his head. "Couldn't tell exactly. It was dark. But it did get out of Dodge real quick after the grenade exploded on its backside."

"At any rate, such waves were also common in America as well. In July 1952, there were significant sightings logged over the US capital. Numerous witnesses reported UFOs over the Capitol Building specifically and the White House. Jets were scrambled, but the UAPs outmaneuvered them, up to eleven *thousand* kilometers per hour."

Gapinski said, "Uh, translate that for us Americans, por

favor?"

"Suffice it to say, Matthew," answered Celeste, "that is bloomin' fast."

"And these historic waves," Nick said, "they are back. The past few days."

"But none of this matters if we cannot retrieve those bones, does it? Torres said the DNA was inconclusive, yet it tested at a similar age to the other specimens. They hold proof that something not of this world might have visited us."

Gina asked, "What do you mean, what bones?"

Just then, a pair of servers arrived with their food. And lots of it. Mounds of meat and eggs and all manner of Southern comfort. Smelled amazing, like Dad used to make on Sunday mornings before Mass. When the servers left, the five famished agents dove into their respective plates of Cracker Barrel goodness.

Wielding her burger, the FBI agent circled back to her question, wondering what Celeste was referencing.

"A giant with six fingers, is what!" Gapinski replied. "And a massive head. Can't forget about that. Something straight out of *The X-Files*, it was."

"I have a lead on that as well," Nicky said.

"Really, what lead?" asked Celeste.

"Our hunch in MI6 is that the program within the Department of Defense goes beyond mere UAP development and stretches deep into more biological interests."

"Aliens, you're saying," Gina said, stuffing a handful of fries in her mouth.

"Precisely. When you reported on the attack in Turkey, I put out some feelers to our SIS posts in the region and managed to secure a tail number."

"Identifying an airplane?" asked Celeste. "Where to?"

"A private airstrip in Germany."

"Well, that's encouraging," Silas said. Sort of pained him to acknowledge it, but he added, "And I appreciate the effort, Nicky."

Nicky nodded with a slight grin. "My pleasure."

"Although, I wonder what use they are to us. So, we find some bones—"

"*Alien* bones," Gapinski exclaimed with a mouthful full of grits.

Eliciting a shush from the whole table.

"Alien bones, then," Silas said lowly, "or whatever they are."

"And don't forget the others," added Celeste.

"What others?" asked Gina.

"Several more skeletons found alongside the alien remains or whatever. Ones that were decidedly *human*. Or rather, humanoid."

Silas explained, "Several of the other specimens were dated hundreds of thousands of years before an antediluvian singular one."

Gina raised a brow. "Antediluvian? As in, what, Noah's bones?"

He chuckled. "Something like that."

"You've got yourselves a real mystery on your hands."

"That we do. What we don't have are any answers to any of it. What it means, especially when it comes to what we're concerned with."

"And what is that?"

"Preserving and contending for the Christian faith."

"I might be able to help you on that front."

"In what way?"

Gina bit into her burger, chewing and seeming to mull over her words.

Swallowing, she answered, "There's a guy I know. Another scholar who might be able to help."

"And who might that be?" asked Celeste.

"A professor at a seminary in Grand Rapids, Michigan.

Elijah Fox."

Silas threw Gapinski a glance. "It wouldn't happen to be Grand River Theological Seminary, would it?"

"It is. Are you familiar?"

"Familiar enough." The memory of Gapinski collapsing at the university on their last operation was still fresh. Definitely didn't want a repeat.

"I'm a bit surprised by your suggestion," Celeste said. "I can't imagine many seminary professors are interested in such phenomena. What is this professor's experience in the matter?"

"His experience in the matter is my own experience in the matter." She paused, taking a beat and a breath, then added, "Eli was my partner for a few years, the pair of us having come through the Academy together and working on cases dealing with domestic terrorism, especially the cultic kind with an emphasis on UFO and contactee cults, as well as the paranormal."

"Sounds interesting enough," Silas said. "But why him specifically, for this operation?"

"Not only does he have the professional experience, he also has the academic kind."

"How so?"

"He's been sharing with me research he has been doing into the biblical connection between UFOs and the alien abduction phenomenon, finding the deeper supernatural meaning to the seemingly natural occurrences."

"I'm sold," Gapinski said, finishing off his sirloin steak.

"The man sure sounds competent enough," Celeste said, turning to Silas. "And we could certainly use an experienced hand from a familiar place."

Silas agreed. The mission was a weird melding of government operations and spiritual mystery that didn't sit right. What better than to have a former fed who also had the theological insight to help them wade through all the mess?

"Can you make the connection for us?" he asked.

Gina nodded. "I can and I will, but I should warn you. Eli can be a bit...much."

"What does that mean?"

"Don't get me wrong. He's a genius and a wonderful person. It was a spitting shame the way he left the FBI..." She trailed off, her gaze falling to the floor.

Looked like there was a story there, but he let it go. Probably should poke and prod more, but they were desperate for answers. Poking and prodding often led to no place good.

Chewing a bite of burger, she offered, "Autism Spectrum Disorder. That's the other variable you need to know."

"He has autism?" asked Celeste.

"No, he's autistic," she said with an edge. "I am as well, actually. But I've...well, let's just say I've been able to find better management of the peculiarities of living as an autistic person."

Silas settled back in his chair with his coffee to consider this. Colton had been on the spectrum, as they say. Though he wondered what Gina would say about that characterization now. Relocation was always a challenge, the change in his environment messing with his head. Fellas would razz him for his peculiar fixations on rattling off the stats of this vehicle specification or that armament velocity. Didn't talk about it much because it didn't seem to affect him all that much.

He finally said, "I think it's worth paying the professor a visit."

"I think it's worth *you* paying him a visit," Nicky said.

"What do you mean?"

"I reckon you and that rather gargantuan fellow along with the FBI agent—"

"Hey, who are you calling gargantuan?" Gapinski protested, mopping up his gravy with one remaining biscuit.

Nicky raised a brow, eyeing his plate. "As I was saying...At any rate, I can't imagine you need more than a few agents meeting your professor asset, whilst I and Celeste go searching for our mystery bones."

Silas opened his mouth to protest but took a swig of coffee instead. Didn't like it in the slightest splitting up the crew. Especially didn't care for Slick Nick gallivanting across the globe with his fiancé. But he trusted Celeste. Always had, always would. And she did have a good point earlier. Those bones were part of the picture, as foggy as it was. If they had a lead on them, then it was probably worth pursuing.

Nicky threw Celeste a grin. "Like old times, ain't that right, mate?"

She blushed and pushed a lock of hair behind an ear. Heat ran up Silas's neck with irritation. Better not be like those last times.

Silas went to respond when Celeste intervened. "From where I sit, you don't have enough to go on, Nicky. Besides—" She gestured to Silas and Gapinski with her tea mug. "We're a team. We stick together. For now. Get us something more concrete to work on, then we'll talk about partnering again."

Nicky frowned and slumped in his chair. "Suit yourself..."

Silas suppressed a satisfied grin. Turning to Gina, he said, "At any rate, you good to personally make the introduction for me and the rest with your professor friend? Care to make a trip to Michigan?"

She shrugged. "Might as well, now that I'm on the lam, having broken twenty-three sections of the US Code, not to mention umpteen points and subpoints of the rules and regulations on FBI behavior and conduct."

Gapinski shoved a final scoop of grits in his mouth and smirked. "You're our hostage, remember?"

"Suppose it's for a good cause."

Silas hoped she was right, because they were all on the lam.

And in the middle of a government conspiracy worthy of its own season of *The X-Files*.

CHAPTER 17

GRAND RAPIDS, MICHIGAN.

Grand River Theological Seminary looked about like it did the last time Silas had visited. Only less leaves and far colder.

At least the sky was clear, an autumnal sun hung low and pressing against the horizon, throwing up all sorts of shadows that made Silas long for mulled wine and a roaring fire. Perhaps stretch out with one of those John le Carré espionage yarns Nicky had mentioned. He shook away the thought of quiet comforts. Especially the thought of Nicky.

The MI6 agent had tried coaxing Celeste again to help him do his job. Silas thought the joker just wanted to make a move on his fiancé, but she played it cool and demurred, insisting she had to stay the course with the Order's own operation to make sense of the crazy. The agent trotted off back to the British Embassy alone to debrief with his fellow spooks on their findings.

For her part, Gina tried contacting their next asset but never got through. His assistant said he had an evening class that day, and they were happy to connect afterwards. So off they flew, hoping Elijah Fox held some answers, on a buck and a prayer.

The SEPIO way.

Swaying clusters of naked trees and piles of brown leaves along a long entrance drive blew on a frigid gust as they rolled into the parking lot. Just in time to catch the professor after his early evening biblical theology class. Silas just hoped the man had answers, because he was at a loss.

Gapinski parked the Ford Excursion near the entrance and everyone got out.

"Man, doesn't this take you back?" he said as he sauntered to the front door.

"Take me back?" Silas said. "You were the one passed out in the hallway."

"I wasn't passed out! Just paralyzed."

Celeste added, "Shows you what snacking on Choco-Choco cupcakes will do to you."

"In more ways than one..." Torres said, coming up from behind.

"I heard that!" Gapinski complained.

"Matty," Gina said, coming to his side, "what's this about passing out, about paralysis?"

"Just a day in the life of SEPIO."

"Glad I joined the team..."

Silas reached the entrance and threw her a smile. "And we're glad you joined us."

"Hope Eli can be of some help."

He opened the door for his crew and guest, totally agreeing. Hoped the good Lord above and the good professor could offer some answers as well.

The main seminary building was as functional on the inside as it was on the outside—gray cinderblock walls, punctuated by plush couches and table-and-chair setups for group studies that tried to imbue the stale atmosphere with a dose of Starbucks ambiance. Your typical '70s-era utilitarian box that smelled like it too—old wood and the dampness of a basement masked only by the dueling scents of new carpet and coffee.

Passing a table of students working on their Hebrew vocabulary, and even more studying—or cramming for tomorrow, as was probably the case—a tinge of longing rose within Silas for what he had left behind. What he was forced to leave behind after he was sacked from Princeton University, in many ways thanks to the Order of Thaddeus.

Those were the days—for a time. He wondered if his fondness for the past would ever wane. Part of him hoped it wouldn't. But he also knew the Lord had good days ahead for him. Maybe letting go of what had been was best in order to fully embrace the present, and the future.

Several classrooms down a long corridor leading to the administrative wing were still in session. Silas could see Calvin VanDyke waving his arms around, their other professor asset who had helped them last go around. He wondered how the man's former student, Peter Daniel Young, was doing, the pastor from Mill Creek Junction who was yet another asset who had helped them solve a mysterious power being peddled earlier in the year by charismatic grifters selling nothing but deadly hope. Maybe they could catch up over drinks with the good pastor on their way through town.

Making a loop looking for Elijah Fox, Silas had to stop himself, a word he'd used—not once, not twice, but three times —surprising him.

Asset. Sounded like his days back in Iraq using the locals to suss out Donald Rumsfeld's deck of cards, the fifty-two most wanted Iraqi officials. These were people with lives that could be disrupted by his calls for help. Needed to remember that. Never wanted to take advantage of them or put them in harm's way.

Celeste whistled from the other end of the common area. "This way, love."

She motioned to a set of heavy wood double doors as the others slipped inside.

"If you were asked the question," Elijah said upon entrance, clearly in the middle of a lecture, "'What does it mean to be human?' what would you say?"

Silas joined his teammates in the back row of the vast space. Looked like a theater, a large stage commanding the front and the wood-paneled room of pine lined by noise dampening panels. The sights and smells reminded Silas of his days back at Princeton. The warm bodies and warm drinks crammed inside the lecture hall. The old wood and carpet, the old paint and plaster. The half-dazed and half-awake students slouching in sweatpants and oversized hoodies.

This crowd was a far cry from those on Silas's old stomping grounds. Lots of collared shirts and ties, skirts and blouses, along with some jeans and hoodies. Mostly a professional crowd training to be counselors and pastors and teachers, many for a second start to their career.

The professor didn't seem to notice their arrival, the man letting his question hang and the students considering it. Silas smiled to himself. Like any good professor.

After a few more beats, Elijah continued, "A Harvard social scientist sure tried to give an answer. In his book, *Our Post-Human Future*, Francis Fukuyama argued against the drive toward bettering the human race through prescription drugs, genetic engineering, and life-enhancing methods common in twenty-first century Western culture. The reason? Because of an inherent dignity to humanity he called 'The Factor X.'"

He made air quotes and snickered to himself. A young guy, maybe mid-thirties, with an olive complexion and a nest of dark curly hair. Thick black glasses framed a long face above a hooked nose. If Silas wasn't mistaken, the man looked Jewish. Which was interesting, the man teaching the Bible at a Christian seminary.

"Everyone on the planet possesses an X factor that separates us from the rest of creation and gives us an inherent worth and dignity. In his words—" Elijah closed his eyes and tipped back his head, quoting, "*'there is something unique about the human race that entitles every member of the species to a higher moral status than the rest of the natural world.'*"

Another snicker before a hand went to his glasses for an adjustment.

"Here is a non-religious social scientist attempting to defend the dignity of humans apart from God, while appealing to some random, chance-induced genetic occurrence in human development. Bringing the human race one step farther up on the evolutionary ladder just past eating our own poo. Talking monkeys, if you will."

The room laughed at the characterization, Gapinski chief among them. Talking monkeys. An interesting way to characterize human evolution, that's for sure.

Elijah started pacing now, the man bobbing on the balls of his feet, as if ready to spring into the air with a bundle of pent-up energy.

"So, I have more rights than my backyard tree or dog Zoe because of some random biological 'qualitative leap,' as he says, in my distant ancestors' development? For real?"

The man stopped at one end of the room, doing something with his fingers, pressing them together, one after another, before pivoting back toward the other end of the room. Same spring to his steps, the professor really into his material.

"For this humanist," Elijah continued, "Factor X is not a spiritual or religious or theistic idea—certainly not a Christian one. It is a genetic and biological quality that was inserted into humanity at some point during the evolutionary process from ape to human."

He stopped back at his lectern, returning to his notes.

"According to God's Story in the Holy Scriptures, we are

unique because of our connection to our Creator, because he created us in his image. The great Protestant Reformer John Calvin voices this vintage Christian belief well."

Silas squirmed at the mention of the Reformed theologian. Probably his childhood Catholic rearing its head!

"While others have related the concept of the Image of God to human superiority to animals, Calvin believed our human identity was directly connected to God himself. He says humanity was made to participate in *'the divine wisdom, right-eousness, power, holiness, and truth'* because we were crafted after the Creator of the universe himself. Humans aren't unique and special because of our highly honed intelligence or advanced socialization. We are worth something far greater because we've been crafted after God himself."

Elijah paused, closing his eyes and taking a breath. His mouth widened into a grin and chest rose with the intake of a deep breath.

"Stop for a moment. Let that sink in. You've been created in God's image!"

Another pause, an even wider grin and deeper breath. As if he were taking in the grandeur of his own teaching, and delighting in it.

"Go call your best friend and tell them, 'You're made in God's image. You're God's crowning achievement!'" The professor snapped open his eyes and drilled his students. "Seriously, do it! Whip out those fancy-schmancy phone thingies of yours and call someone who needs this word."

Without hesitating, the room complied, as if it were the most natural of things to randomly give someone a call and remind them of the Imago Dei. Probably had encountered the teaching tool a time or two. An odd pedagogical tactic, that's for sure, but one that brought a smile to Silas's face.

Gina laughed, her voice getting lost in the cacophony of calls. "That's Eli for you. Ever the showman."

"The man sure knows how to work a room," said Celeste. "And wholly unexpected. Certainly confounds my expectations of people with autism."

"Autistic people," she corrected, her face falling before a thin smile rose to her lips. "I think you'll find much of what you expect from us will be confounded."

Celeste threw Silas a glance that looked like a mixture between panicked and perturbed. He cleared his throat and shifted in his seat.

"I, for one, appreciate his use of vintage Christianity language. A man after my own heart, and the Order's."

That smile returned to Gina's face. "Yes, a plumb line through his work he's been developing the past few years."

"Interesting..."

The calls died down and Elijah resumed teaching.

Adjusting his glasses, he said, "Maybe you've never thought of your human identity in this way before, that you are a Statue of God. Maybe you've never thought of your neighbor or boss or in-laws that way before. But that's who we are. Stunning. Breathtaking. No words!"

He leaned against the lectern now, eyes passing across the students with silence.

"Does this realization, that you have been formed and patterned after God himself, stir something inside of you? Is there an emotion or thought or *ah-ha* moment that wells up within you?"

Elijah's voice drew quiet now, contemplative. "It does for me. It reminds me that I am immensely important, valuable, cherished. By the Creator of the universe!"

He swallowed hard, and if Silas wasn't mistaken, the professor's eyes began to glisten.

"I didn't just simply happen. I am not a more advanced version in a long line of other creatures. I am not a talking monkey."

Another hard swallow and now a sniffle. As if the revelation was a deeply personal one.

"Neither is my server at On the Border and Starbucks, my bookseller at Barnes & Noble and garbage collector, or physician and dentist. And neither are you. You are not a creative, productive bundle of cells and sparking neurotransmitters."

His voice was above a whisper now, a microphone doing all the heavy lifting.

"I am an Image of God, a Statue made in God's likeness. So are you."

The room hung in silent contemplation at those words.

I am an Image of God, a Statue made in God's likeness. So are you. Silas couldn't help but smile at the truth of those words. Even his own eyes glistened at the reminder.

"But what does this mean?" Elijah continued, his voice rising again. "That we are patterned after God in our personhood and purpose? Unfortunately, the sand in our hourglass has run out. So long."

And with that, Elijah packed up his notes and strode down the center aisle, ignoring his students—including Silas and his crew seated at the back near the door, even Gina.

The professor either didn't see them or ignored their presence, pushing through the door.

Leaving Silas without a clue what to do next.

CHAPTER 18

The rest of the room seemed to take Elijah Fox's abrupt departure in strides, as if it were a normal feature of his classes.

Silas couldn't understand it, not in the slightest. Part of the joy of professoring was the back and forth between his students, which mostly happened after class. Had fond memories of sparing with certain ones who thought the latest takedown argument generated on Reddit would be the clincher to proving Christianity wrong, and Professor Grey a moron. Luckily for both, the Spirit of the Lord was wiser and more enlightening than the zeitgeist of fringe internet discussion boards.

"You'll have to excuse Eli," Gina said. "Sometimes he misses cues."

Gapinski snorted a laugh. "Like the ones where long-lost friends are sitting in the back row of his seminary class?"

"Like that one. He's not one to socialize anyhow."

"That surprises me," Celeste said. "He seemed so personable and open during his lecture."

Gina shrugged. "Like I said. Much of what you expect from us autistic folks will be confounded."

Silas threw her questioning eyes. "Now what?"

She stood. "Go after him."

He did as she said, leading his crew through the doors and out into the common area. But Elijah wasn't around.

Gapinski and Torres wandered to the exit, looking into the darkening evening for the professor, but came up dry.

"Perhaps he went to his office," Celeste said.

Silas said, "I think I remember how to get there."

He hustled past the smaller lecture rooms, their doors opening now and students emerging from class. Up ahead was a long vanilla hallway bathed in awful fluorescent lighting, leading to a number of windowed doors peering into book-lined offices. Took some doing, but they found an office with a gold ELIJAH FOX placard anchored to the wall, second from the end, next to VanDykes's.

The door was closed, so Silas knocked.

A muffled "Enter" was thrown up from inside.

He did as he was told, leading the others into a cramped space that barely fit the visiting group. It overlooked a large pond, where the set sun cast a waning palette of burnt oranges and brilliant pinks across its waters. The undergraduate campus across the way was lit by white lampposts.

The office was orderly, no piles of books or folders spilling papers strewn about. A far cry from Silas's days at Princeton.

Smelled of juniper and cedar, the piney, earthy scent filling the room from a lit candle at the center of a small meeting table in the corner. Elijah's thick black glasses rested atop a clean desk, papers stacked neatly, unlike his own. Music played softly from a vintage record player anchored between bookcases. One of those all-in-one wood contraptions with built-in speakers. Not his idea of hi-fidelity listening, but Silas gave him points for trying. Especially for the Jimmy Smith throwback, the organist really going at it on the Hammond. The album Root Down, if he got it right.

Where he'd had a Mr. Coffee in his Princeton office, one of those newfangled Nespresso machines sat in the corner. A clean mug was perched beneath its nozzle, ready to go at a moment's notice. Silas took a step toward it, eyeing the emblem. A coat of arms depicting gold lions on a red background, a white cross anchored at the center. He immediately recognized it. The University of Cambridge. Interesting school of choice for an American.

Elijah had his back to them. He was hunched over a laptop overlooking the lake shimmering silver now under the gaze of an emerging full harvest moon.

Clattering away without acknowledging them, he offered, "Office hours are between two and four every other day. Without exception. See you tomorrow. Give the door a yank on your way out. It sticks."

Silas threw wide eyes to Gina. The man was blunt and to the point. Sure didn't mess around. Which was a bit comical, though could get old real quick.

Gina cleared her throat. "How about you make an exception for an old partner."

Elijah's head snapped up, then he spun around and gasped.

Standing, he exclaimed, "Oh my cheeps! Gina colada?"

He said it like the Caribbean coconut rum drink Silas's father loved.

She laughed. "The one and only."

He darted from around his desk and came right up to his former partner, though the two didn't embrace. Instead, they both waved a hand, the motion synchronized and almost touching, but not quite. Looked like a greeting they had practiced, and perhaps honed, over time.

A little odd, but whatever. Time to get to it. It was go time.

Silas cleared his throat, which brought Elijah's head snapping toward him, putting a spring in that nest of black curls' step.

"Who are you?" he asked.

"Silas Grey." He gestured to his crew. "This is—"

"Office hours are between two and four every other day," Elijah interrupted, then added: "Without exception. See you tomorrow. Give the door—"

"A yank on our way out. Yes, I know. Apparently it sticks."

"Eli," Gina said, "these are some new friends of mine."

He gave SEPIO an assessing eye. "They aren't government men, are they?"

"Not anymore, partner," Gapinski said.

She explained, "They are with a religious order trying to make sense of somethings I thought you might be able to shed some light upon."

Elijah said nothing, those eyes searching SEPIO again with probing silence.

"I see you studied at Cambridge," Silas said, trying to connect with the man.

"Ah, a Cantabrigian," Celeste said. "I'm an Oxonian, myself."

"Oof," Elijah said with a grimace. "Oxford? Too bad."

She threw Silas wide eyes, clearly not knowing what to do with the slight. Had to suppress a smile at Celeste being rendered speechless.

Silas went with it: "Gina says you're a person with autism—"

"Autistic person," Elijah corrected.

"Isn't that what I said?"

"Nope."

"Umm, alright..."

"So, what are you," asked Gapinski, "some sort of savant or something?"

"Nope. That's a common misconception. Only point five percent of autistic people are savant. I'm not one of them. I suck at math. And playing the piano."

Gina chuckled. "Eli's being modest. He does have an eidetic memory, so he might as well be a savant."

Celeste said, "An asset to any government agency, I reckon."

Elijah nodded. "I was..."

The man trailed off, looking off at the ceiling. Silas wasn't sure if that was just his normal posture, or if there was something deeper there he wasn't sharing.

"Well, my best friend was autistic," Silas said, making a second stab at connecting.

"Good for him." Elijah raised a brow. "Wait, you said *was*? What happened to him?"

"He died during service. We served together in Iraq with the Rangers."

"Sucks for him."

Again, blunt and to the point. Uncomfortably so.

"Why don't we have a seat," Gina offered, dragging one of three chairs over to Elijah's desk.

"Help yourself," he said, scurrying back to his chair.

Torres and Gapinski slid the other two to join her while Silas and Celeste remained standing.

"You might find it interesting," Gina said, turning to Silas, "that Eli here is Jewish. Or was. Ethnically, anyway."

Elijah nodded. "A Messianic Jew, yes."

"I'm Jewish," Torres added.

His eyes snapped to her, sizing her up. "No, you're not."

"Uhh...*sí lo soy.*"

"Nope. *No, no eres.*"

Guy spoke Spanish, and he was challenging Torres. Real interesting...

"Well, half," Torres continued. "*Mi mama* was an Israeli and *mi papa* was Mexican."

"Then you're not Jewish. You're Mexican with Jewish ancest—"

Gina brought a hand to Elijah's desk, rapping on it gently

with her knuckles, which seemed to snap him out of his groove. She chuckled nervously and cut off any further argument from the man.

"Eli, I'm sure we should let Ms. Torres define herself as she understands herself. Lord knows we understand what that's like—" She threw halting eyes at him and added, "given how the neurotypical world has tried to define our own existence."

Elijah fell silent, his eyes going to a stack of papers arranged neatly on his desk before searching the room.

Man sure was blunt, to the point. Honest to a fault, too. Which Silas wasn't sure if he appreciated yet. Again, could get old real quick. But there was something about the young man that seemed genuine. On the surface, the back and forth seemed overly caustic, hostile even. Like he was challenging every conversation partner to a duel. But there was an earnestness to his tone that signaled he meant well. That he was probing and prodding to reach the right answer, the exact one. Almost like a tick, like he wasn't satisfied unless the world was precisely defined. Unless he himself could precisely define it. Professor was a good gig for him, and an agent of the FBI.

SEPIO, even...

Could get interesting, that's for sure.

"Messianic's interesting," Gapinski said.

Now those eyes swung in his direction. "How so?"

Gapinski's eyes suddenly went large. Like a big spotlight of interrogation had just switched on above his head. Supposed that was about the truth of it.

He swallowed, answering, "Uhh, because you're a prof at a Christian seminary."

"So? What's your point?"

"Well, Messianic. That means that you're looking for the Messiah, don't it?"

"Found."

"I don't—"

"It means I've found the Messiah. Yeshua Hamashiach."

"What's that? Yiddish."

"It's Hebrew," Silas said, intervening in a clear misunderstanding. "It means Jesus Christ is the Messiah. Messianic Jews believe their people's expectations—ethnic and religious—have been fulfilled in the coming of Jesus Christ."

Gapinski nodded. "Ahh, gotcha. My bad."

Silas frowned, getting impatient with the meet-and-greet. Time to move things along.

Clearing his throat, he said, "Agent Anderson—"

"Please, Gina," the FBI agent said.

"Alright then. Gina here says you've had an interest in unidentified flying objects."

Elijah put up a hand. "No. In unidentified aerial phenomenon."

"Oh, that's right. UAPs they're called these days. In any event, she said you two made up a two-person task force studying UFO cults."

"That's right."

Celeste asked, "What sort of interest do you carry?"

"My interest lies in the questions aliens and UAPs conjure. Not only their existential questions, but the supernatural ones."

"Such as?"

"What is humanity? Who put us here? Who is God? Maybe the God we think of is really a superior alien being."

Silas widened his stance. Good questions.

He asked, "So for you UFOs and—"

"UAPs," Elijah corrected.

His neck flashed hot, but he let it go.

"Right. For you, UAPs and aliens are spiritual matters."

Elijah cocked his head to the side. "You could say that. There is a major intersection between aliens and UAPs and biblical theology. The unseen world on full display, angels and demons, gods and God himself interacting."

"Gods?" Gapinski wondered with a raised brow. "As in, plural?"

"Of course. What else would I mean?"

"His work at the Bureau," explained Gina, "touched on this supernatural intersection. Specifically alien encounters and the UAP phenom but also more broadly, how it manifested in ways the government might be interested in. Serial killers, cultic ritual abuse, animal sacrifices, and what not."

Celeste said, "Can't imagine the American government was too keen on exploring such notions. I imagine they much more prefer naturalistic explanations to the bedlam plaguing their country than anything touching on the demonic."

"Nope," Elijah answered. "They weren't."

Again, seemed to be more to the story there, but Silas let it go.

Instead, he asked, "So what is this interest you have in UF—" He stopped himself before another blunder. "I mean, why are you interested in UAPs and purported abduction stories?"

He shrugged. "Some people like vintage cars or collecting baseball cards. I'm into alien contactee conferences."

Torres smirked. "Some hobby."

"It's also professional."

"So, in your professional opinion," Torres asked, "are there UFOs?" Elijah went to correct her when she put up a staying hand. "Save it, *muchacho*. I am meaning ETs and flying crafts, the kind us lay people talk about."

"Most definitely."

"Which?"

"Both."

He said it so matter-of-factly that it took Silas by surprise. A seminary professor, suggesting UFOs and ETs were real. Did not compute.

"By UFO sightings, as you suggest," Elijah went on, "I mean seeing things that are not identifiable. Could be experimental aircraft. There is a long history in the US of such a thing. But some still defy explanation because of their shape, speed, and way that they come apart and then reassemble. Which gets into the spirit realm."

"Can you elaborate on that more?" asked Celeste.

He went to answer when a *bring-bring-bring* filled the room, joined by a buzzing and the Macarena.

"Silence!" Elijah exclaimed.

Silas quickly complied, silencing his phone. He glanced at Torres as she did the same, and chuckled. "Macarena, huh?"

"Don't look at me!" she protested. "Los del Rio are *muy loco* in my book."

"That would be me," Gapinski said with a sheepish grin, raising his hand as the song flared up again.

"Silence!" Elijah said, eyes wide and fist pounding on the desk with insistence.

He fumbled with his phone but managed to cut it off before the final dance move.

But not before glancing at who was calling.

"Zoe calling you all as well?" Gapinski asked.

"*Si*," said Torres.

Celeste nodded. "Right, HQ was ringing me as well."

"And me," Silas said.

"Smells like trouble," Gapinski growled.

Silas went to answer when their phones buzzed with interruption in unison. Not a phone call. A text message. In all-caps, four-exclamation panic.

> *CHECK THE NEWS. FIRST CONTACT IS LIVE*
> *ON CNN!!!!*

"First contact?" Gapinski asked, twisting up his face.

"Oh my cheeps..." Elijah said, bringing a hand to his mouth.

All eyes snapped to him for an answer.

Which he gave with a shrug. "They must have arrived."

"Who, Eli?" Gina asked.

Another shrug. "Who else? The Nephilim."

Silas was familiar enough with the ancient biblical term, but the others clearly weren't, giving the professor nothing but blank stares.

He clarified, "Extraterrestrial biological entities, Old Testament style."

"Always something," Gapinski growled.

Silas couldn't have said it better himself.

CHAPTER 19
WELWELSBERG CASTLE, GERMANY.

Sebastian Grey was awakened by the scent of cinnamon and cloves. Which was odd. Not only because he should be unconscious right then. But also because he shouldn't have been able to smell anything at all given the confines of the experimental chamber.

It was only after rising back to consciousness—that sweet scent compounded by whispered conversations, a gentle breeze skating across his skin and chilling his flesh—that he understood the full measure of things.

He blinked, glimpsing the vaulted chamber of stone and the symbol anchored at the center of the ceiling glinting in the candle light. An ancient one that had given rise to the arcane revelation-insight he had been testing the past twenty-four hours.

Except...

Reality snapped with full recognition now.

He was lying at the bottom of a glass tube the size of his Washington, DC, bathtub. The liquid had been completely drained from the hydrochamber that had served as a cocoon for his transformation.

For his rebirthing into a new creation. Where he sloughed

off the old shell of his former earthly existence and put on the new celestial one. A gift from the Universe's caretakers, forged through modern science and ancient remains.

But why was he awake in the first place? Something wasn't right.

He sat up, the wretched scent of cinnamon and cloves stronger now. But he paid it no mind. What mattered was what had happened, and whether the process had begun or had been cut short.

He regarded his body, toned arms and legs, a flat stomach sporting a six-pack most men his age would die for. His skin was pasty white and wrinkled. He looked positively pruney, like any old bath skin!

Flexing his fingers and examining his arms and legs, one end of his mouth curled upward. No, not the typical bath skin...

Yes...It's happening!

Bringing his hands to his head, he had further confirmation, his hair having completely fallen out and an unexpected but delightful pair of growths sending his heart soaring toward the heavens.

Ironies of ironies!

"Ahh, the man is coming back to the land of the living."

Sebastian was shaken from his self-examination. He snapped his head toward the echoey sound, and frowned.

The friend with the top hat from across the pond stepped from the shadows, pulling a drag off that hideous habit of his.

"*Hallo Herr Grey.* It is good to be seeing that you are still being alive."

He threw the German American cold, narrowed eyes. Why the hell was he awake and talking to that ingrate!

"Get me out of here," Sebastian growled. He reached an arm toward the man seeking assistance, and he went to go to his knees—

But slipped and crashed back to the glass hydrochamber

bottom, biting his lower lip. He cursed, sucking at it. His tongue danced with the taste of pennies. Nirvana...

"*Achtgeben, Herr Grey,*" the man said. "Be taking care of yourself. The serum is leaving you wobbly."

Brawny men in black shuffled from off-side to lend a hand. Sebastian was loath to accept it, but his head was spinning, every limb was weak and heavy laden.

They helped him out of the hydrochamber and to the cold stone floor.

The German American regarded his nakedness with searching eyes, taking a drag from that cancer stick of his and grinning at the sight. Whether from a pleasure that appreciated his appearance or the progress of his transformation, it wasn't clear.

One of the grunts draped a thick white robe around him.

He stood tall before the man. Taller than he had been just a day ago, Sebastian towering now and a newfound strength coursing through him.

"What is the meaning of this?"

"We were worrying the process would be too damaging." He sucked at his cancer stick and blew a cloudy stench, gesturing around the chamber. "Especially after the others were having issues."

Sebastian followed his gesture, finding empty hydrochambers among the several still filled with subjects.

Nodding, he asked, "Is the transformation complete?"

"Not...yet. But soon, very soon, *Herr Grey*. Besides, there are being bigger things that we are to be discussing."

"Such as."

"It appears our competition is continuing its assault against our aims."

"What?" Sebastian exclaimed, eyes going wide and weakness returning to his limbs.

But he held steady. The past few days had been nothing but

a bundle of stress keeping the warring powers in check. What a wonder their competition was still bent on perpetuating the myth of UFOs and alien intelligence among the public—or so those sheeple thought.

Of course, he and his new friends understood the matter otherwise…

"Should we be worried?"

"Nein," the man answered, his one good arm still holding the cancer stick waving Sebastian off, throwing up a trail if cinnamony smoke.

Sebastian flared his nostrils at the continued stench, but let it go.

"For heaven's sake, why not?"

Another drag before answering: "Because, *Herr Grey,* their interests are only in being to perpetuate the hysteria to preserve the illusion of control and power. We are wishing to actually break open the mythology surrounding the occurrences."

"Is everything in place, then?"

One final drag before the man flicked the butt to the stone floor, sparks flittering about before his black boot snuffed them to nothing.

"That is what I was wanting to talk with you about."

He put an arm around Sebastian, the wool of his coat sleeve scratching his bare neck, and then he told him what came next.

All irritation left him, replaced by a quickening in his belly that spread a grin across his permanently pruned face.

The world was not ready.

Neither was his brother.

CHAPTER 20

Gapinski thought he was going to crap his pants. Like, for real. His whirly twirly stomach was doing cartwheels, and his lower innards were going all watery at the mention of first contact.

"This isn't happening..." he muttered, his disbelief compounded by rising dread at the truth of the matter threatening his bowels to go footloose and fancy-free.

But he held it together, literally squeezing his momma-given baby bottom like there was no tomorrow as a fresh wave of the shimmy-shakes roiled him something fierce, the anxiety of the breaking news connected to a distant memory he never wanted to relive again ratcheting his heart rate and lungs to beat the band.

And stirring up his innards into a sloshy, mushy stew that threatened his tighty-whities!

Because, having picked up the professor's lingo at a group meeting in Germany after Uncle Sam shipped him back to his post when Doc Gina got his head back on straight—he knew exactly what first contact meant.

And it was nothing good.

Apparently, the term was some fancy-shmancy anthropological one, meant as the first meeting between two human communities—like those Pilgrims rolling up on the shores of the American natives. Only that's not what his pals meant by it. Not in the slightest.

First contact, the real one that mattered most, was the first meeting between humans and ET. More Elliott Taylor stumbling upon the wrinkly dude with the glowing finger in a cornfield, and less William Bradford of the Plymouth Colony having a sit-down with Samoset of the Wampanoag Nation.

And CNN was broadcasting some exclusive on the end of human existence as we knew it! Or at least our pride of place in the universe.

"You got a TV in this study of yours?" Silas asked, searching the joint.

"Nope," Elijah replied, swiveling in his chair around to his computer. "The interwebs will have to do."

Silas and Celeste leaned over the professor's desk as he brought up cnn.com. Gapinski held his ground, having no interest in the slightest engaging the nonsense breaking news he feared wasn't nonsense at all. Between that flying triangle and those hella-crazy giant bones he and Torres had unearthed, he'd seen all he needed to know it wasn't nonsense.

First contact was right...

"You alright?"

The voice startled him, as did a gentle hand on his arm, the dam below threatening to break at another roiling wave crashing into his innards.

It was Gina. Her eyes were wide and probing, locked onto him with concern. The kind he remembered from back in the day when he would spend an hour every morning for four weeks sprawled on her couch getting the lowdown on how messed up he was from his Marine-issued shrink.

Gapinski glanced at Silas and Celeste craning over Elijah's

desk. No, no he wasn't alright. But he wouldn't let on after Torres had suggested what he'd seen was all in his head.

Because it wasn't. None of it was. Not now, not back then.

And it looked like he wasn't alone.

"There we go..." Elijah announced.

The webpage showed a wide shot of a brightly lit news studio fresh off a commercial break. It was studded with America's colors and massive LCD panels. The main camera swooped in for a close-up of a dutiful-looking Kai Renolds, the mainstay of The Most Trusted Name in News. Though Gapinski thought the motto's claim was as laughable as Fair and Balanced, but whatever.

Regardless, this was it. Showtime for ET during prime time.

"If you're just joining us," the well-makuped anchor began, dark brown hair slicked back and glistening under too many klieg lights to count, face stoic with a set jaw and earnest eyes, "this is a CNN breaking news report with Mara Mitchell standing by at a field in southwest Ohio."

Torres asked, "What's in southwest Ohio?"

"Corn," answered Elijah, face glued to the computer monitor.

She smirked. "That's newsworthy?"

Silas answered, "Looks like we're about to find out."

Gapinski folded his arms and leaned back, furrowing his brow with confusion, and concern. That Kai dude looked scared, his eyes wide and forehead creased, even with all that pancake plastered to his face and those lights and CGI tech making him a decade younger. And did he detect a hint of a sweaty sheen at his brow. Was like the dude had seen a ghost or something.

Or reports of alien first contact...

"Isn't that right, Mara?" Kai said, shaking him back to the moment.

An equally well-makuped woman, hair blond and blown,

lips glistening maroon, appeared on an 80-inch screen mounted next to the CNN anchor.

"That's right, Kai," the familiar and sexy Mara Mitchell said, smiling and nodding with enthusiasm. Made Gapinski a bit hot under the collar, and he hoped no one noticed. "We're coming to you live from a field outside Dayton, Ohio. You can see behind me a swarm of emergency vehicles tending to the victims of what can only be described as something ripped from the pages of an Isaac Asimov science fiction story, or even a Stephen King horror novel."

Kai cleared his throat, shifting in his seat and wiping a line of sweat from his brow.

Silas said, "It's weird to see such a seasoned veteran so shaken like this."

"And unnerving," Celeste agreed.

"News must be *muy malo*," Torres added.

Elijah nodded. "And *muy loco*."

Torres turned to him with a raised brow, but said nothing.

"And why is that?" the male news anchor continued. "What do you have for us in the heart of the Buckeye State?"

The woman gripped her mic and nodded. "A few hours ago, a local deer hunter stumbled upon eight people lying prone in the cornfield behind me." She gestured toward the open space crowded with emergency vehicles, lights whirling and twirling something fierce. Checking a yellow notepad bound by a spiral at the top, she continued, "According to his report, the eight men and women were unconscious and arrayed in a circle, feet pointed toward the center."

Elijah hummed. "Eight. That's interesting."

"Why is that?" asked Silas.

"Because the number eight is connected to the planet Mercury, which is said to relate to messaging and communication relays from the Divine, especially the interplanetary kind in paganism."

"A wealth of information, our new prof friend is..." Gapinski said.

"Sounds ritualistic, doesn't it?" said Gina.

"I'd say," Celeste agreed.

"Local witnesses from the farmhouse," Mara went on, "reported seeing intense lights and a humming sound coming from this part of their property. In fact, it was the lights that drew the original hunter to the field. The man expected to shoot a prize-winning head of antlers at the peak of deer-hunting season. Instead, he was in for a frightening surprise."

Kai asked, "How did the man describe what he saw?"

"I'd like to let him tell it in his own words. We have him standing by."

Mara gestured off camera, and a tall, burly man with a mullet the size of Gapinski's childhood pet ferret ambled over. The deer hunter threw the camera a sheepish grin and eyes that looked about like the ones those deer would toss head-lights from late-night drivers.

Shoving her microphone toward the hunter, Mara asked, "As the first person at the scene of the crime, what did you see? What did you think?"

"Thought they was dead, I did!" The man identified as John Deere—not kidding, only on CNN—was wearing a woodland hunting parka and a bright orange vest, like he'd stumbled out of the woods then and there.

"But they weren't, were they?"

"Naw, ma'am. Just dazed, I guess. And right confused. When I jiggled one of the ladies' feet—you know, to see if she was livin' or passed—she startled awake and screamed like a banshee!"

"Understandable, given the circumstances."

"Suppose so, ma'am. But it was the way she backed up on hands and feet. Pointing at me and claiming I was one of them."

"One of them?" Mara Mitchell asked, leaning in with squinted eyes.

The hunter nodded. "The ones that probed her."

"Probed?" Her eyes snapped wide with surprise. "She said that?"

"Yuppers. Then she screamed again, going on about abductions this and gray giants that."

The man took off his hunter's cap and raked a shaking hand through wispy silver hair at the memory.

"Tried to 'splain myself, that I was just a humble hunter. That I had no part to play in what had happened to her. Definitely not the probin' part."

John Deere pointed an insisting finger at Mara before addressing the camera, then rinsed and repeated his nervous cap maneuver. All the while the reporter nodded earnestly with a creased brow, silently waiting for more.

"Anywho, then the others awakened from their own drunken stupor, or high, or whatever. Figured 'twas the shrooms up along the riverbank that did 'em in. But I couldn't make heads or tails of how they got way out there. Where their cars went throwing up all those lights. T'what drew me to 'em in the first place."

"Unreal..." Silas said, giving his head a shake.

Gapinski nodded, a familiar fear ratcheting up his spine and a cold dread spreading through his veins. The chief didn't know the half of it.

Had suppressed most of what he himself experienced with the thanks of Doc Gina. But now, with this news report of lights and abductions, and then this hunter's testimony, this John Deere fella—all of it was enough to give Gapinski's bowels another round of the shimmy-shakes!

"Let's talk about those lights," Mara said, angling the conversation along. "What did you see, exactly?"

The hunter heaved a shrug. "Just what I said. Bright lights, big and bold and white. Thought the second coming of our Lord Jesus Christ 'twas upon us! The low-grade hum told me 'twas somethin' else, though."

"Like what?"

Another heaving shrug. "Dunno. By the time I arrived, the lights had cut to nothin' and the sound was gone, too. Nothing left behind but those eight bodies. And a smell."

"A smell?" asked Mara, brow furrowed.

Gapinski sucked in a startled breath, the mention of the leftover scent connected to a memory flashing to the surface.

"Smell..." he muttered as another fresh wave of cold dread washed over him.

The hunter grunted an affirmative. "Like my son's dead pet lizard, is what it was! And something burning, like burnt toast. Along with the smell of a summer storm thrown into the mix."

The website suddenly threw up a commercial, the ticker counting down to the end of some newfangled prescription drug that was supposed to help with anxiety disorders.

What Gapinski wouldn't give for a dose of that right about now!

"Impeccable timing," said Elijah sitting back.

Torres smirked. "Suppose even CNN's gotta make a buck."

"And what better way than during a breaking story about aliens."

"Did that testimony strike you as oddly specific?" asked Celeste. "The one about burnt toast and summer storms?"

Silas chuckled. "And don't forget dead lizards."

Gapinski closed his eyes, the memories of that fateful night in Germany flooding back to the surface.

The *smells* of that fateful night in Germany flooding back to the surface.

The static charge from lightning, like a summer storm. The charred scent of—not necessarily burnt toast, but of burnt something. He'd thought it was gunpowder at the time, but burnt toast would work too.

Last but not least: dead lizards. Nailed that one right on the money.

The commercial ended, and the webpage reloaded to Mara Mitchell mid-interview. A young chick with long, matted hair wearing a white gown was huddled under a dark blanket. An older couple gathered around her on either side. Probably her parents.

Six or seven more were resting on the ground behind her. Probably her abductee compadres, everyone wearing the same white matching gowns. Almost like the getups patients wear at hospitals.

"...the most magnificent experience I had ever had! Not at all like the movies make it out to be!"

"You reckon," Celeste said, "this woman is one of the eight people that hunter stumbled across?"

"You're speaking of your abduction," Mara said, face pinched and earnest. "As you've claimed."

Elijah said, "There's your answer."

The chick went on, "And you know what was the most enlightening? They explained my faith to me in ways my church never had before!"

That got the room's attention, every one of the five craning closer to the laptop for a viewing. Even Gapinski perked up.

"You're a Christian?" Mara asked.

The woman nodded, her face bright and wide. Which was super odd for Gapinski. Not at all his reaction to his own experience with ET!

She said, "They are the ones who brought Jesus Christ to Earth two-thousand years ago, man! They gave us to humanity to offer us an example of love, don't you see? They said we weren't ready to accept their gift, which is why the people of Earth crucified him. Why, they gave him a royal kick in the rear and told him to get the hell out of here! We couldn't stand his message of love."

"She sounds high," said Elijah.

Silas leaned in closer. "Sounds like something, alright."

Gapinski shifted and brought a hand to his chin, a tremor jiggling his jaw. Knew she wasn't high, just coming down from the abduction experience.

"They told me he ain't coming back, no siree," she went on. "The man Jesus they sent the first time was taken back to the mother ship that he travels on. We saw him and were standing right in his midst! He is only a Prince of this part of the universe, but soon they will send another to bring the same message."

"And what message is that?" asked Mara, leaning in with interest.

"Love, man. Love is love is love! I just hope we're ready to receive it this time. Otherwise, we're screwed."

"When should we expect this...message, as you put it?"

The chick's face fell, and her head whipped towards the camera—her eyes giving Gapinski's bowels a fresh dose of the shimmy-shakes!

"Two days," she said. "Two days."

"That's oddly specific," Silas said.

Celeste added, "And quite the ticking clock."

Gapinski swallowed hard. That it was.

Mara thanked the woman and stepped to the side, the camera following her.

The reporter turned to the camera. "What's remarkable about this story is that it isn't the only one emerging from across the world."

"She's right," Elijah said. "WeShare is blowing up."

He turned around his mobile device. The others leaned in for a viewing.

"Hashtag FirstContact is trending."

"What's a hashtag?" asked Gapinski.

Torres turned to him. "Where've you been the last decade, Hoss?"

Silas snorted a laugh. "Yeah, all the cool kids are using the user-generated tags to share topics on those crazy microblogging sites."

"Like WeShare."

"Well, I'm not cool enough, alright," exclaimed Gapinski. "So sue me!"

The room quieted. He reddened from the outburst.

"Sorry. Just feeling under it after all that's happened."

Doc Gina squeezed his arm, throwing him a reassuring smile.

"Right, what's WeShare saying?" asked Celeste.

Head down into his own device, Silas answered, "There's a whole mess of these—whatever they are happening across the world."

"China, Italy, Ukraine," Torres muttered, staring at her own phone. "Even *mi ciudad Puerto Vallarta* from childhood!"

"We've got grainy images with the same hashtag," Silas went on, "Photos and videos showing lights bobbing in the sky."

"Oy, check this out," exclaimed Celeste. "There are even still shots of the men and women in similar circles as the one the hunter came across as well. Eight of them. Similarly arrayed."

Silas asked, "The same one from southwestern Ohio?"

She shook her head. "This image is geotagged in California."

"Egads!" Gina suddenly cried.

"What's wrong?"

"Well, now—this is crazy..."

"Doc..." Gapinski said. "Don't hold out on us."

She held up her phone for all to see.

Silas and Celeste craned for a look. Gapinski squinted,

catching sight of something far worse than those Heaven's Gate wannabes!

Egads was right! Hashtag FirstContact wasn't the only kid on the WeShare trending block. Joining it was another one just as cray-cray.

#TheTruthIsMe.

Celeste twisted up her face. "The truth is me?"

Silas chuckled and nodded knowingly. "That's pretty clever."

"I don't follow. What sort of stuff and nonsense is that gibberish?"

"Yeah, me neither," said Torres.

Gapinski said, "You know, a play off of '*The truth is out there*' slogan."

"What's that?"

"Only the greatest slogan of the greatest television series from the '90s!"

Silas nodded. "Yeah, it is. Though it did go weird at the turn of the century."

Gapinski shrugged. "What didn't?"

"What are you going on about?" asked Celeste.

Gina answered, "They're talking about *The X-Files*. Which isn't important. What is are the testimonials."

"Of what?"

"Of abductions. #TheTruthIsMe lists hundreds of people being paralyzed by visitors in the night who watched them in their sleep and spoke to them telepathically."

"Giants, with six fingers?" Gapinski whispered on a shaky breath, more to himself than anything, the memory now burning bright within.

Gina glanced at him and nodded, sending his bowels whirling and twirling again.

"Metal tables, probes," Silas said, scrolling through his own device. "Even claims of impregnation by alien-hybrid beings."

Celeste shook her head, one hand covering her mouth while her other scrolled on like the chief. "This is unreal!"

"Hold up..." Gina stood, leaning toward the laptop.

Elijah spun around, everyone joining him at following Gina's gaze.

Which landed on a black live-stream newsfeed. As if the connection had been yanked.

"Try reloading the page," Silas suggested.

"Alright, Captain Obvious," Elijah complained, hitting COMMAND-R every few seconds. "What do you think I've been doing?"

Page loaded fine. The live-stream video did not.

Celeste folded her arms. "I can't imagine something like this happens often. Unless..."

Gapinski finished the thought: "Unless the shiznit has hit the ET fan?"

She turned to him and nodded.

The seconds ticked by as the room waited for word from the Most Trusted Name in News to gather up their marbles.

"Looks like we're back." Elijah pointed to the laptop screen. "Or the feed is, anyway."

"And it doesn't look good..." Gapinski said lowly.

Kai Renolds was back, sweating to beat the band and eyes bugging out, earnest as ever.

"...with another breaking news story. It appears—" the man stopped short, a well-tanned hand wiping his brow. "Just...roll the film," he instructed someone off-stage.

The video faded to a shaky camera ducking behind a pickup truck. Authorities were running this way and that in an empty field covered with fog, news camera lights aimed at nothing but flattened cornstalks, with people screaming and crying and carrying on like they'd been left behind at the second coming of Christ!

Now it swung to a frazzled Mara Mitchell.

"Something...unexpected has just happened," she reported on a shaky breath, brow creased and mouth hanging open in a question.

She swallowed hard and whipped her head back and forth, that brow still creased and that mouth flapping in the breeze. Searching for what, the good Lord only knew.

"My money is on a cable re-run," said Elijah.

Torres asked, "What's that supposed to mean?"

"He means," Gapinski replied, "they returned."

Before she could ask what he meant, Mara returned.

"We have been witness to—" More brow furrowing, more mouth flapping, more head whipping back and forth. Until she landed on: "—a close encounter of the third kind!"

Elijah snorted a laugh. "How original."

Celeste shushed him as Mara continued with a rushed report.

"An electromagnetic anomaly cut short our broadcast. But we did manage to capture some shaky footage. What you are about to watch is the first known broadcast-quality capturing of a UFO."

"UAP!" exclaimed Elijah.

There it was. Broadcasting for all the world to see.

A triangular craft the size of a small house ringed by pulsing blue-and-green lights swooped down behind an oblivious reporting Mara. It hovered just above the ground in the field lit only by news-crew lights, white lights flooding from underneath with a low-grad hum. Then a number of shouts and screams before the camera fizzed out.

Mara returned, swallowing and catching her breath. "The most disturbing part is that in the intervening minutes between our camera briefly malfunctioning before finding restored power—what we can only attribute to the...to the craft. After it retreated, the group of rescued men and women were no where to be found."

Another swallow, another set of panicked breaths before saying gravely: "The eight had simply vanished."

Couldn't bring herself to say *abducted*, but it was certainly implied.

Silas shook his head. "This doesn't make any sense. We're to believe some UF—erm, I mean UAP..."

"See, you can be taught," Elijah quipped.

He frowned but continued, "So these civilians get off-loaded by some craft in the middle of an Ohio cornfield in the dead of night, only to get picked up again when the cameras are rolling?"

Celeste said, "Does sound rather dodgy, doesn't it?"

Elijah replied, "Not if this UAP report is an entirely new one."

"You're meaning some competitor to the original, aren't you?"

"That, or the original UAP crew left a probe up someone's—"

"We get it, Eli!" Gina groaned.

"But that's insane!" Silas said. "Two competing UAP forces vying for abductees?"

"Wasn't that an *X-Files* subplot?" asked Gina.

Torres added, "That's exactly what happened in Turkey!"

Silas brought a hand to his head, rubbing at his temple with worry.

Gapinski slumped in his chair, burying his head in his hands. "This isn't happening...Again."

"What's not happening again?"

"Huh?" He snapped his head back, finding Silas staring at him with the same concerned eyes as Gina. "Oh, was that out loud?"

"Matthew, what are you going on about?" asked Celeste.

"Nothing..." he said, glancing at the laptop, Mara continuing her panicked reporting.

She followed his gaze. "What is it you've been keeping from us, this encounter you said you endured?"

"I said, it's nothing!" Gapinski snapped with more bite than he intended. Last thing he needed was his teammates finger-pointing at him with mockery, questioning his sanity.

He sighed, running a hand across his clammy, bald head. "Sorry, Celeste. Didn't mean to bite your head off."

She rested a hand on his shoulder. "No worries, mate. Just concerned about you, given how traumatic your past experience sounds."

Torres snorted a laugh. "Concerned he's due for a med adjustment, more like it!"

He glared at her with narrow eyes. Her eyes went wide, and she frowned. "*Lo siento, amigo.* I was only joking, but...I'm sorry."

Waving her off, he stretched out in his chair, mulling over what to make of it all. And how to talk about his own personal experience with it.

"You know, Matty," added Gina, "sometimes the best thing we can do when the crazy train rolls into town is to share our own story. Sometimes it helps. Us and others."

Gapinski glanced at her, meeting her eyes and catching a slight nod.

He closed his eyes and sighed. Last thing he wanted to do was drop his drawers for all the world to see. Especially his SEPIO peeps.

But...what the heck? The crazy train had certainly rolled into town! Perhaps the good Lord would use his past to help them make sense of it the present.

So, he swallowed hard, his Adam's apple tripping over itself on a dry throat. Then took a deep breath and dove into his experience.

One he vowed never to tell again.

Or relive.

CHAPTER 21

RAMSTEIN AIR BASE, GERMANY.
CHRISTMAS 2007.

"Last one to the 18th Hole is a rotten wiener schnitzel!" I shouted, huffing and puffing across the fairway down Woodland Golf Course.

A bitter breeze bit at my baby face, chapping my lips and stinging my eyes. Dang, it was cold in these parts! My Southern blood was definitely not made for this German soil. But the scent of woodsmoke riding in on Nature's breath, joined by pine and grass and dead foliage made up for the cold.

As did the fact we were just half an hour outside Christmas. Thought I even caught the jingle-jangles of some sleigh and huffy-puffy grunts of eight reindeer taxiing Saint Nick across the globe.

Nope. Just me trying to outrun my fellow Ramstein comrades, a wreath lined with bells I'd swiped from the door leaving the Pizza Gallerie in a half-drunken stupor throwing up the jingle-jangles. Scratched something fierce, its needles nicking into my neck, but the piney scent more than made up for it.

It was Christmas Eve, and me and the boys had a night to ourselves with a twelve pack and all the time in the world.

"Gapinski, you couldn't outrun Bigfoot if it was chasing your ass. Let alone me!"

It was Tommy Harris, sprinting past in that utility uniform the airmen sported on base, the beige and green colors almost making him blend into the trees nude from winter. Supposed that was sort of the point. But why airmen donned those threads, and in the dead of winter in the middle of Deutschland was beyond me.

Joey Nederveld threw up one of those laughs of his, deep and from the belly and echoing through the crisp winter air, hiking up his arms and coming up from behind as well.

He reached for the twelve pack of hefeweizen. "Maybe I should take those off your hands, Gapinski. Lighten the load."

"Not on your mama's life, son."

"My mama's dead."

I startled, nearly dropping the beer. "Oh, my bad."

Nederveld slapped my back and threw up another one of his belly laughs.

"Just jokin', my man!"

He laughed again and took off, leaving me steaming in my own utility uniform and wishing I'd gone back to the barracks. But Harris and Nederveld were about the only friends I had at Ramstein Air Base. A marine loaned out to the largest tactical fighter wing in the Air Force responsible for pounding Saddam Hussein's empire back to the Babylonian Stone Age wasn't exactly welcomed with open arms. Sort of a kumbaya go-between the Air Force and Marines, but that didn't much matter to the fellas. So, when the pair invited me to a celebratory night of Christmas Eve pizza and booze, and then a toast to Christmas at midnight on the 18th Hole, I couldn't refuse.

Harris twisted back and shouted. "Don't leave your wiener schnitzel flappin' in the German Christmas breeze, Gapinski! Hop to it, son!"

There was Nederveld's belly laugh again, joined by Harris's nasally cackle that kicked my backside into gear.

So I hiked up my lederhosen and raced to catch up, what little hair I still had left on my mid-twenties head doing jack squat against the frigid wind racing through the fairway.

Shaved a kilo off my big-boned frame, but finally made it to the 18th huffing and puffing billowing breaths behind.

"It's cold as a mama's stare out here!" I complained, slumping down on the frozen ground still cut short.

View was amazing, though, clouds creeping across an otherwise clear sky with a million diamonds strewn across it. Reminded me of summer nights back home. Back before the world went sour after those damn Islamic whack jobs sent those planes into the Twin Towers and America went to war. Back before I'd joined the Marines and found myself sprawled out on a German golf course in the dead of winter. Never in a million years would my Southern noggin have thunked that cray-cray scenario up.

Catching my breath, I wrenched the wreath off from my neck and tossed it to the frozen green. Then I rolled over to grab a beer—

When Harris saddled up beside me. "I'll take those..."

He swiped the twelve pack before I could intercept.

"Come on!" I protested, scrambling from the frosted ground, but slipping back to my hiney.

The fellas roared with laughter, the soft cha-cu sound of a 12-ounce can of Deutschland's finest snapping to life, followed by dripping foam. Then another, Nederveld joining Harris in the fun.

"At least toss me a cold one, would you?"

"Think fast, Gapinski." Nederveld bent back and drew his arm into a quarterback throw.

Letting one of the cans rip. It sailed high before plummeting back to the green.

I scrambled up from the frosted ground, springing to my feet, hiking back up my lederhosen, and leaping for the interception.

Catching the can with one hand before landing back to the ground, my feet slipping and flipping to my backside again.

Tweedle Dumb and Tweedle Dumber let her rip again, the pair nearly choking on their hefeweizen. Hoped they did.

Easing to a sit, I cracked open my own can and threw back a swig. Ahh, heaven. Sweet and fruity with notes of banana and clove. The bubbles tickled my nose and I nearly sneezed, but I held it together.

"What do you suppose those are?" Nederveld threw back a swig and gestured.

Following his gaze, I raised my can to my lips.

And froze.

White lights were zipping along the treeline down the way, rising and falling at odd angles and speeds, then just sort of hovering above the forest. Another breeze flared up, carrying with it the woodsmoke and pine from earlier and sending all the hairs rising on my body. Though, that might have been because of the freaky-deaky sighting of those lights.

Clouds were coming in heavier now, blown in by that wind and obscuring the spectacle, so it was hard to make out exactly, but— whatever it was, 'twas real strange.

Maybe even Mulder and Scully strange...

No, that couldn't be right. I chuckled and shook my head.

"Maybe it's a sortie," I said, throwing back another swig.

Harris scoffed. "A sortie? Aircraft deployed from base to engage some hostile enemy? What, like Liechtenstein?"

"Uh...yeah?"

Nederveld threw up one of his laughs again. "Have you learned nothing during your time on base, Gapinski?"

"Laugh it up, fuzzball," I muttered, filling my mouth with beer as heat ran up my neck in embarrassment.

He was right. I'd learned nothing in the months I'd been on base. Just a dumb Southern hick who barely made it through high school and basic by the skin of my chinny-chin-chin.

Throwing back a swig, I added, "Then it's some exercise or patrol, I don't know!"

Harris cracked another can. "It's Christmas, dumbass. We ain't got flyover exercises tonight. Not this late, anyway."

"Good point..."

Draining my beer, I cracked open another can myself and watched the show. Wasn't just one white light either. There were three of 'em, and a red one joining those ones at the center. Moving in sync, too, like some choreographed dance, bobbing and weaving through the sky.

Strangest part was how quiet it was. No roar of jet engines or sonic booms you'd expect from flyovers coming from the base. Maybe the mosquito wings, as I liked to call them, on account of the appearance of the Air Force insignia—maybe they were testing out some newfangled stealth bomber. Who knew?

What I did know, and what those hairs standing at attention across my body seemed to sense, was that it was wicked—

The lights swirling above suddenly plummeted to the ground, disappearing behind the treeline up the way.

—weird...

"Holybamoly, Batman!" I yelled with a start.

"Did you see that?" Harris said, tossing his can to the ground and springing to his knees.

Nederveld bolted to his feet. "Looked like it crashed or something."

We sat and stood and knelt, still and silent as could be. Listening, discerning, intuiting what the hey-ho-day we'd just witnessed.

Finally, Harris joined Nederveld, then started off. "Come on, we need to check this out."

Nederveld agreed and off they went.

I went to protest, but they quickly disappeared through the woods beyond the 18th Hole.

Draining my second can, I stood, stumbled forward on well-lubricated feet, but chased after them. "Always something..."

Scraggly branches grabbed for my face as I hoofed after them, having not a clue where we were going but heading in the general direction of those lights. The clouds rolling in above didn't help matters, dowsing the moon's light and dimming the world to a creepy

ABC Afterschool Special specially designed to scare the living bejeebus into kiddos and their parents about the dangers of free-range childrearing. Latchkey kids they called 'em back in my day. Been there, done that, got the sippy cup to prove it!

A root sent me stumbling to the ground, face planting into a patch of snow.

"Sonofa—"

Mouth and nose filled with leaves, needles, dirt—at least I hoped it was dirt!

Not my idea of Christmas fun, that's for sure!

I staggered to my feet and stumbled off, groping my way through the forest again and making for the light that had grown in brightness.

"Fellas..." I called out. "Harris? Nederveld? You there?"

Didn't take long before the fellas up ahead were silhouetted in a freaky glow that sent another bout of adrenaline keeping those hairs ramrod straight.

What was going on? Couldn't believe my eyes and feared we had a possible downed aircraft, on Christmas of all days. A shiver ratcheted up my spine at the next thought.

Or something far worse...

Then I chuckled, shaking my head. "No way in a Chris Carter fever dream!"

Watched too many episodes of The X-Files as a teenybopper, that's for sure! Nope. The truth was not out there, in that part of Germany.

At least I hoped.

Took some doing, but I caught up to the fellas, who were standing at the top of a hill, all silhouetted by the glow of whatever had sailed into Earth.

When I ponied over near the suspected crash site, the fellas spun around and put out their hands.

"I think we should scram," Harris said.

"Yes, scram. Good idea," Nederveld said in agreement.

I twisted up my face in confusion. "Whatcha talking about? We've got a crash-landed something. We gotta see if anyone's hurt, if anyone needs—"

"Whatever it is, it didn't crash," said Harris, glancing across his shoulder.

I tried following his gaze, but it was a no go. Couldn't quite see the landing site from where I was.

"What do you mean?" I asked.

"What I mean is—" He turned back, then said, "It landed, it didn't crash."

I frowned, pushing past them. "Let me see for myself..."

Ground was moist from patches of melting snow, my feet slipping and sliding on leaves and moss and rocks, the smell of dead foliage thrown up alongside that woodsmoke again. Feet were cold and wet sloshing around in my boots. What I wouldn't give to curl up with an Agatha Christie novel and a pint of Christmas ale right about—

"Hold the stein..."

Couldn't believe my peepers. Was certain I hadn't had too much to drink. Us Gapinskis could hold our liquor. Definitely our weizenbier.

But this...what was staring me in the kisser made me seriously rethink that assumption.

I looked again, and realized Harris was right. We weren't dealing with a plane crash or anything else we'd ever had to respond to before.

There was a bright light coming off from this weird object on the forest ground. Was throwing up some equally weird noises, too. A low-grade hum with the tick-tick-ticking of a clock, followed by the crink-crink-crink of some windup toy.

Nederveld and Harris ended up deciding to go check it out. I wasn't down with the bro plan, but after I made a stink about *making sure nobody was hurt, I relented and we hoofed it on the double down to the clearing.*

As we approached the LZ, a silhouetted triangular craft came more fully into view. Something like ten feet on each side and six or seven feet high. It was shrouded in this cray-cray weird fog rolling in through the clearing in the woods. Couldn't tell if it was coming from the craft or some odd weather pattern, but the cloud settled down around the craft.

We stood at the top of a berm surrounded by pine trees, not believing our eyes. Felt like Lucy Pevensie when she shoved through that wardrobe and through those trees the first time she stumbled into Narnia. Totally unreal...

"Not too large, is it?" Harris whispered.

Nederveld added, "And nothing I've ever seen before, that's for sure!"

"You're right about one thing," I said, the pine and woodsmoke grounding me firmly in reality while my head swam with disbelief.

"What's that?" asked Harris.

"The thing didn't crash. Look at it, fully intact and just sitting there in that small patch of land right there in the woods."

Heart felt like it was doing the conga line as we crept toward the craft. Had to have been some newfangled stealth fighter tech from Ramstein. But something deep down in my innards told me something different.

"What the hell is wrong with this thing."

Looked over to find Harris whacking his radio against his thigh. None of us left home without our lifeline back home to base. Was regulations when on leave, even on Christmas.

"What's wrong?" I asked.

"Can't communicate with the base worth nothing. Look——" He held up his radio, the yellow display all garbled.

Took out my radio from a side pocket for my own look-see.

Same bad story on my end too.

"All three radio frequencies," Nederveld added, "command, security, law enforcement—you name it, all are breaking up in crackly static. Listen."

The man engaged his radio, but no go on that front. Just crackly static, like he said.

I asked, "So you're telling me we're without a line back to base?"

"Should we turn back?" Harris swallowed hard, face white and sheeny with sweat. Chuckled to myself at the sight, then felt bad about it. Never one to finger-point at a man while he's down. But with all Harris's bravado, almost made an exception.

"Good idea," Nederveld replied with a nod. "Try and relay some emergency radio transmission back to central security back on base."

The fellas turned to leave when I shouted: "Look!"

Fog was clearing, revealing the full measure of all the crazy.

At first I was confused by what I was seeing. Didn't have a clue, not one bit of understanding. Truly unbelievable, it was!

Then fear rose in my head, threatening to overtake me. But I smacked a hand against my cheeks—literally, once, then twice—and I said I had to keep focused and see it through.

A million thoughts were running all at once, though. Was this a threat to the base—to us three, even? Was it a threat to humanity itself? And where was Will Smith's Captain Hiller when you needed him at a time like that?

Wanted to throw up my hands and scream for sweet baby Jesus to take me away. But I held it together. Knew I had to determine what the heck this thing was, and if it threatened the base and town.

So I stepped out and started down the hill—

Falling on my backside and tumbling down in a rolling mess of arms and legs and lederhosen!

More dead leaves and pine needles and what I hoped was dirt jammed up my nose and in my mouth. Before I knew it, I was face to face with the triangular-shaped craft!

Almost crapped my pants, then and there, but I held it together—squeezing those baby bottom cheeks together and standing as my airmen pals came down after me.

That woodsy breeze blew more of the fog away, revealing blue and yellow lights swirling around the exterior. Looked like it was part of the surface of the craft itself, the thing was lit up like a Christmas tree!

And now it smelled like a thunderstorm, the air around us was so electrically charged. Could feel it on our clothes and skin, it was racing across our hair. Like static electricity, when you race across carpet in wool socks and it dances across your skin, or you rub a balloon across your head and all your hairs stand on end. For those of us who still have air, at least.

Probably the weirdest thing of it all was there was no sound to it. Not a peep or a hum coming from the craft. Now granted, I was a Marine. But I'd been around jets the last several months. Except nothing in all those months, not my training or my experience, prepared me for what we saw. The craft was no type of plane I'd ever seen before. In the movies, maybe. The X-Files for sure. But not at Ramstein!

After about ten minutes or so standing with our beer steins and wiener schnitzels just looking at the thing, Harris suggested the craft wasn't hostile.

"Agree on that one," said Nederveld.

"Let's check it out further," I said, disbelieving my own ears at the suggestion. But by now I was curious what the heck we had on our hands.

Wasn't sure about the security protocols to follow, so Harris took the lead in completing a thorough on-site investigation, including a full physical exam of the craft.

We each slowly walked around the craft, sizing it up and down, noting its lights and angular three corners, the smooth charcoal skin that still flickered with those blue and yellow lights. Was totally overwhelmed by it all. Thought I would crap my pants, then and there, it was so out of this world.

Literally...

Nederveld whipped out his phone and snapped some low-grade

photos, Harris jotted some notes in a little notepad of his.

I just kept walking around the dang thing, soaking up all I could, astonishment and awe overwhelming me. Oddly, all fear had evaporated. What I felt was like nothing I had ever known before. A high higher than the ganja the boys and I toked on from time to time.

The oddest thing of it that I noted were symbols etched into the craft on one side. All the size of my hands. Pictorial in design, the largest was a triangle centered in the middle of the others, with some circles and lines. Put my hand on the craft, and sure enough, they were etched right into the skin. Was real warm to the touch, too, and smooth like glass. But it had the quality of metal to it, and I felt a tingly voltage running through my hand and moving up through my arm.

Now that nearly made me crap my pants!

What came next actually did. Well, not crap, but I did pee a little.

You would too if the Independence Day spaceship started jumping and jiving!

Had to have been an hour of us checking out the craft, when a white light underneath began to ratchet up with intensity. Along with those odd tick-tick-ticking and crink-crink-crink noises.

The fellas and I scrammed like it was nobody's business! Ran straight up the berm and into the pine trees to take up a defensive position away from the craft.

Then it lifted from the ground. No noise or air disturbance. Just levitated and maneuvered through the trees.

Right before it shot off into the heavens at an unbelievable rate of speed. It was gone before I could blink!

That's when I knew it, deep down. We all did.

Whatever it was we'd set our peepers on, the craft or spaceship or whatever—its technology was far, far above what we could ever engineer.

After it shot off into the sky, I felt utterly alone, even though Harris and Nederveld were standing on either side. Felt small, too. Real small. Because I realized that it was 100 percent certain us

Homo sapiens weren't the coolest kids on the planetary block. Not in the slightest.

After returning to base, we went straight to our CO and unloaded everything we'd set our peepers to.

But that's not all that happened.

That's not the end of the story.

CHAPTER 22
GRAND RAPIDS. PRESENT DAY.

This was unreal...

Silas didn't know what to make of it all. Sure, Gapinski could be a little much. Even spun tales that weren't always the most believable, like the one about skydiving with Bette Midler.

But this was a whole other level of crazy that seemed too farfetched to not be true.

Why would he make something like that up, witnessing a UFO up close and personal? Didn't make sense in the slightest, none of it.

Between this breaking news report from Kai Renolds and Mara Mitchel coming out of Ohio to the hashtag trends on WeShare broadcasting personal experiences of not only UFO sightings but abductions, on top of this story from one of his own—it was all making his head spin something fierce.

Silas had half a mind to just let Weiss win, to pack up and start that gig he'd dreamed about. Set up his sailboat repair shop down in the Florida Keys, a bucket of Coronas and bowl of limes anchored at his side, white sand between his toes and palm trees swaying overhead in a warm breeze kicking up the dueling scents of salt and fish and coconut—the whole nine yards.

Why not? Certainly earned a life of anonymity repairing cranky old coots' rigs after his tours fighting for freedom on top of however many operations fighting for the Church. Ten, twelve? Lost track around the time modern-day Templars rose to fight for the faith. Now that was a trip and a half. Right up there with WeShare hashtags of first contact!

But he knew better. Was bred to never give up and never back down. He had Dad to thank for that.

So back into the fray of things he'd go. Weiss's consequences be damned.

"Crack on, Matthew," Celeste said, snapping Silas back to the moment. "Don't leave us bloomin' hanging!"

"Yeah, Hoss," added Torres. "What happened next?"

Gapinski ran a hand across his head glistening with sweat and shifted in his seat. Made sense. Not sure he would've fared any better under the gun for a story like that.

"Well, that night I went back. Alone, before dawn."

"You went back into the woods?" Silas said, "Back to where you found what looked like an alien spacecraft—all by yourself, without any backup?"

Gapinski nodded.

"Ballsy," said Elijah.

He smiled. That it was. Had to give the man that.

"Go on, Matthew," Celeste said again, "what happened next?"

He eased in a deep breath and closed his eyes, as if reliving the experience. "It was back."

"What, the spacecraft?"

"That's right."

"So, let me see if I got this right," Silas said. "You discovered strange lights in the forest on the other side of a golf course off-base. Three of you did, on Christmas Eve after a night of pizza and beer and general off-base shenanigans at the 18th Hole. You go into the forest to investigate, where you discover a strange triangular craft sitting right there in the middle of a clearing. About ten feet on each side, with multiple lights. Then it rapidly maneuvered up into the sky and quickly left the area. Sound about right?"

"Good TLDR, chief."

Again, unreal.

"What happened next?" asked Celeste.

"What she said." Silas jerked a thumb at his fiancé.

"Well, we were debriefed by the CO," Gapinski explained, "and then advised to return to the landing site in daylight to look for physical evidence. But I wanted to go first to make sure I wasn't delusional."

"Makes sense."

"So, I went back to the golf course to find my way back to the landing site. When I got there, I came across all of these broken branches scattered about."

"Broken branches?" Torres said, brow furrowed.

Silas asked, "Like something had come in for a landing, you mean?"

Gapinski nodded. "But there was more."

"What more?" Celeste asked on a shaky breath.

Hadn't recalled seeing her like that before, shaken like that. Last time was a few years ago when she'd had an encounter with the Devil himself. Wondered if she saw shades of her story in Gapinski's.

Running a hand across his head again, he continued, "There was a hole in the tree canopy above and broken branches, like I said. Even abrasions on the sides of trees facing the landing site and these scorch marks, some on the ground too, the grass and weeds and what not. Most important were three indentations in the ground."

Celeste gasped. "The marks left by the UFO, isn't that right?"

"Righto. The landing gear in the three corners of the triangle thingy. Was sorta relieved to find proof that what I'd seen had really happened. Was beginning to think I'd gone all crazy!"

"No doubt about it."

Torres snorted a laugh. "Yeah, your encounter with ET explains a thing or two."

He flashed her a frown and narrowed his eyes but didn't offer a response.

For Torres's part, she immediately understood she'd stepped over the line and apologized. Gapinski blew it off, but you could tell it had been a hard time for him. Had probably been in shock with what he'd witnessed. All of it had weighed heavy on him. Probably still did.

"So you went back to the site," Silas said. "Anything else happen? Anything else you saw?"

"That's right. I went to the site where that—that *something* had touched down and found the three indentations. Two or three inches deep and a foot across in diameter on the ground in a triangular pattern. Had brought along a Geiger counter, too. One of those radiation readers by that German scientist."

Celeste leaned forward with interest. "And?"

"And I discovered mild radiation. But while taking the readings, I noticed a bright red-orange oval object with a black center in the forest. Reminded me of an eye and appeared like it was blinking. Maneuvered real strange, too. Horizontally, through the trees with some vertical movements thrown into the mix, zigzagging around the trunks as if under intelligent control."

He swallowed hard, wiping his head clean again.

"Then it started coming my way. Was brighter than it had

been, growing larger and larger. Then pieces of it started shooting off!"

"Pieces shot off from it?" exclaimed Celeste.

"No doubt about it. It was some cray-cray shiznit!"

"Oh my cheeps..." said Elijah.

Torres pointed to him. "What he said."

"I scrammed back into the forest on the fastest twinkle-toes I could muster!" Gapinski explained. "Ran like a madman on a mission back to the 18th Hole but also scared crapless at what I might find. Finally reached the clearing, and there it was. The light. When I approached it, the orange glow suddenly cut to nothing in no time flat. Then it went off silently down the fairway. Just watched in amazement for a minute or two, standing there panting like a dog trying to catch my breath. But I followed it to the 17th Hole."

He paused, catching his breath, then added, "Suddenly, the object exploded into five white lights that quickly disappeared."

"Exploded?" asked Torres.

"That's right."

"What did you do?" wondered Celeste.

"I ran down the fairway and looked for anything it might have left behind, residue or burn marks, but found nothing. But then I spotted several objects with multiple red, green, and blue lights in the northern sky, which changed in shape from elliptical to round and moved rapidly at sharp angles. Saw several more to the south and—"

Another pause, another breath catch. Then: "Well, one approached my position at this cray-cray speed, and then just skidded to a stop, right above me."

Silas furrowed his brow. "It stopped overhead?"

He closed his eyes and took a breath, then nodded. "Then it sent down a concentrated white beam—a small, dense pencil-like shaft of light, like something out of a movie. Lit up the ground all around me."

"What did you do?" asked Celeste.

Gapinski shrugged. "Just stood there, paralyzed. Couldn't move worth nothing. Wondered whether it was some cosmic signal, some divine communication—or if I was gonna die, then and there. Didn't have a freakin' clue."

One more breath, joined by another hand across the scalp.

"Then it happened," he said in a whisper.

Silas leaned forward. "What happened?"

"My head exploded in starlight, and I blacked out."

"You blacked out, *muchacho*?" asked Torres. "Like when I found you in Turkey?"

"Something like that. By the time I came to, the beam had switched off, and the object zoomed back up into the sky."

"Just like that?" Elijah said.

"Just like that."

He leaned back in his chair. "Interesting..."

Celeste asked, "But what happened to you, Matthew?"

Torres smirked. "Yeah, Hoss, were you abducted or what?"

Anger flashed across his face, and crimson rose to his cheeks. "Something like that. Most of what happened is pretty foggy. I do know several hours had passed."

Silas said, "How's that?"

"My watch froze at half-past three. Forty minutes after I'd gone back out to check the forest. But when I came to, the sun was beginning to rise."

"Golly..." said Celeste. "Some sort of electromagnetic anomaly?"

Gapinski nodded and rubbed his face. "All I know is, I had a wicked headache, like I'd downed a bottle of Grandpappy's moonshine. I also remember a weird smell."

"A smell?" Silas said.

Gapinski nodded. "Like when my pet lizard died a horrible death of starvation."

Torres raised a brow. "You starved your pet lizard?"

"Forgot to feed him for a week. He kicked the bucket somewhere inside the walls of our family double-wide. Boy, did it stink up the joint! The tangy smell of a Port-a-John and sour beef standing outside for too long."

"Could do without the visual, Hoss!"

"Anyway, point is, I remember this rancid smell from when it all went down in Germany. But then there was this almost sweet smell to it all."

"Sweet and rancid?" asked Silas.

"Cloves mixed with bleach. Or maybe antiseptic, like rubbing alcohol."

"Like the deck of a ship?"

"Or an operating room?" said Celeste solemnly.

That idea sent a shiver through Silas, Gapinski saying nothing more.

"Well, what about the cloves?" he asked.

Gapinski shrugged. "Not sure, but it was like something I smoked as a kid."

Silas nodded with a smile. "Djarum Blacks, right?"

"That's right!"

"Aren't those illegal now?" Torres asked.

"And for good reason!" said Celeste, drilling Silas with unapproving eyes. Not a fan of his fag puffing habits, as she had put it.

"Oh, yeah, almost forgot," Gapinski went on, rubbing the back of his neck. "There was a wicked scar at the base of my skull."

"A scar?" asked Silas. "What for?"

He shrugged. "Not sure. All I know is, it was there when I woke up from all the crazy. It wasn't there before. Hurt like a mother, too."

Everyone leaned back in their chairs, silence filling the void at the revelation.

Made sense. Because as Silas had thought from the beginning of this whole ordeal, and Gapinski copping to his own experience with it all—

This was unreal…

"Obviously," Gapinski went on, "this experience is not something I ever wanted to speak about. Not with you all, not with no one. No offense or anything."

"I reckon not," Celeste said.

Silas wondered, "How much did the United States government really know about the Ramstein incident? I mean, I understand you told your CO, as any grunt would."

"Right, but did they take it seriously?"

"Did they go beyond your own testimony and—well, investigate the UFO?"

"UAP," Elijah corrected.

"That too."

Gapinski answered, "I'm pretty sure agents from the Air Force's major investigative service were on the base and secretly investigated the case in the days following."

"The Office of Special Investigations," Silas said, "isn't that right?"

"Righto."

"Wait a minute!" Torres exclaimed. "Isn't that the guy we saw with that tat back in Turkey?"

"Naw, that was the Security Forces Squadron. OSI is different, but they do work together in partnership to keep US bases secure and check out any suspicious activity."

"Like flying saucers?"

He cocked his head to the side, mulling that over. "I'd imagine you're right."

"Still, I'd say that is quite the connection," Celeste said, "with what transpired in Turkey. Do you know what came of it all? What the OSI or Security Forces found?"

Gapinski shook his head. "Not really. But as you can imagine, the incident had everyone nervous. The high-ranking muckety-mucks wanted to stay out of it, and the OSI didn't want anyone involved that they couldn't control. Even got interrogated myself."

That was news to Silas, Gapinski coming under the high-command gun like that during his service. "You got the overhead spotlight treatment?"

"Me and Harris and Nederveld. All three of us did. Didn't offer much, the three of us pretty well in shock at the time. OSI told us not to talk about any of it or our careers would be toast."

Gapinski lowered his head, looked like in shame. Whether from the experience itself or covering it up, Silas couldn't tell. Either way, he felt bad for the guy. What a thing to carry.

"If I could interject," said Gina. "We later discovered sodium pentothal, what you would call a truth serum—it was used with some form of brainwashing or hypnosis when administered during these interrogations."

"Golly!" exclaimed Celeste, turning to Gapinski. "Your government pumped you with a cocktail of truth-telling drugs?"

He shrugged, sitting in silence.

"The whole ordeal," Gina went on, "had damaging, lasting effects on the men involved. I oversaw their psychological treatment when the DoD sent them my way. They didn't know what I discovered. It was all classified top secret."

"Nearly lost my marbles." He stiffened, adding, "Would've, too, had Doc Gina here not fixed me up right and good."

She grinned. "You're too kind, Matty."

The pair exchanged a silent moment, the two clearly having bonded way back when.

Gina went on, "From what I gathered during my involvement, repression by the OSI, using such pharmacological means, is not uncommon in the military, but nobody involved will ever admit that."

Silas glanced at Gapinski. "You're speaking of a government cover-up, using drugs to—what, erase Matt's mind?"

"Exactly. Not only that, the witnesses seemed to have been exposed to high doses of radiation from the landed object. The other two have health problems to this day."

Gapinski's jaw dropped, and he regarded her with wide, surprised eyes. "You've kept tabs on Harris and Nederveld?"

"They've Facebooked me from time to time, yes."

"How are they?"

"Coping."

He snorted a laugh. "Hear that." Shaking his head, he continued, "Still have no idea what I saw that night. Gut tells me UFO, but maybe just some new toy in Uncle Sam's toy box. Either way, it was something beyond our technology, judging from the speed of the objects, the way they moved and the angles they turned. Without a doubt, they were under intelligent control. And whatever happened to me when that light went on and my lights went out…"

He paused, taking a breath and swallowing hard. "I don't know what, but part of my brain was shut off. And I'm glad it was."

The room settled into a contemplative silence.

Silas didn't have a clue what to make of it all. Too unreal for words.

As a kid, he'd had a fascination with space. Dad had gotten him a telescope for Christmas when he was twelve while still in Guam, and he'd dreamed of escaping to distant planets on a rocket ship cobbled together from cinder blocks and corrugated metal he'd found cast aside during an Army building project. Was even caught up in the '90s fascination with UFOs and alien cover-up stories as a teenager thanks to *The X-Files*.

He grew out of it all during his post-9/11 military service, the massive changes roiling the world keeping him focused on this planet. During graduate studies in theology and Church history, he'd wondered whether the Lord had created other intelligent life across the vastness of his universe. His reading of Scripture and theological studies told him no.

But now, with these stories coming from Ohio and bubbling to the surface across social media—Gapinski's own stories of witnessing some flying object, a UFO or UAP, or whatever, on top of what sounded eerily like an abduction...

It was all too unreal.

Breaking the silence, Silas asked Elijah, "So what say you, professor?"

"About what?" Elijah asked.

He frowned. "Whether the Lions have a chance at the Super Bowl this year."

"Have they ever had a chance at the Super Bowl since the '90s?"

"Elijah," Gina said, laying her hand on the desk, "I think he means to hear your opinion about the subject matter. What you think about Gapinski's story, and what we've been seeing on the internet."

"Right, professor," Celeste added. "Is there anything to these rumors—" she stopped short, turning to Gapinski and smiling before continuing, "—and genuine experiences of the paranormal? I guess I am interested in what Silas was getting at. What do you think about the phenomenon? After all, it is why we came all this way."

Elijah shrugged. "That's easy. Of course UAPs and aliens exist."

CHAPTER 23

Silas didn't expect that response. Not from a Messianic Jewish professor at an evangelical Protestant seminary. Didn't expect it in the slightest.

Shifting in his seat, he asked, "What do you mean by that?"

Elijah leaned back in his chair and looked at the ceiling. "Christians too easily write off people with UAP alien stories— even Christians who have them!"

He snapped his eyes back to Silas, then regarded Celeste and Torres. "You yourselves heard from one of your own. Yet you've written him off as a wackadoodle nut job."

Now Celeste shifted. "I'm not so sure about that..."

Torres did the same and smirked. "Yeah, you don't know us. We were just razzing Gapinski, here."

Elijah smirked. "Really? There was no sarcasm whatsoever in your question about whether the man was abducted by little green men?"

She slouched a little and reddened a shade. "Maybe just a little."

Interesting observation. And here Silas assumed people with autism, or autistic people, or whatever PC term was correct—here he thought they were socially awkward and unaware. Supposed Gina was right. Their type did confound his expectations.

"How about we agree," he said, trying to bring the conversation back to the task at hand, "that we're all a little thrown by these events. Not least of which is one of our own getting wrapped up in them all."

Silas turned to Gapinski. "I believe you, brother. As unreal as it all sounds...I believe you."

One end of Gapinski's mouth curled upward, and he nodded. Even breathed a sigh, as if one person believing him had relieved him of a decade of silent shame. Supposed that was the truth of any of our lived traumatic experiences. Only takes one believer to set things right.

Celeste put a hand on his shoulder, giving it a squeeze. "As do I, Matthew."

"Yeah, me too, Hoss," Torres added. "And sorry for the snark earlier."

"No worries," Gapinski said with a chuckle. "Not sure I'd believe me either. Sounds too cray-cray to be true. Even coming from me!"

They all shared a laugh at that one.

"Let's get back to it, Elijah," Silas said. "Because Gina's right. We came for your expertise in this area, as a biblical scholar. What's your take on it all?"

He shrugged. "Like I said, I believe they're real."

"But in what way?"

"People who have witnessed unidentified aerial phenomenon or have had abductee or contactee experiences genuinely have questions and are seeking answers. Not just nonbelievers but genuine Christians, too. In fact, there's an entire church in Puerto Rico that claims to be filled with people who have been abducted. These are fellow brothers and sisters in Christ who claim to have been visited by aliens—taken even!"

"So, you're saying, professor," said Celeste, "that these are genuine spacecrafts piloted by aliens?"

"Nope. I didn't say that."

"You said UAPs and aliens are bloomin' real!"

"Nope. I said they *exist!*"

She scoffed. "Stuff and nonsense..."

Elijah seemed to shrink back in his chair, his face going white and eyes going wide. Didn't know what was going on, but Silas wondered whether confrontation wasn't the man's forte.

Intervening, Silas said, "I think what Celeste means to say is that, if you aren't suggesting these UFOs—"

"UAPs," Elijah said, perking back up at the correction. "They're unidentified aerial phenomenon. UAPs, not UFOs."

"Alright, UAPs, then. Simply put, what are they? The one from Roswell, the waves over Belgium and DC, as we've been told?"

"I believe the flying saucers people have identified are experimental aircraft based on Nazi designs."

Silas glanced at Celeste. There was that connection again.

She offered, "You're speaking of Operation Paperclip."

Elijah snapped his attention at her and smiled. "Wow. You're more in the know than I expected."

Her mouth fell, as if opening for a question. Then snapped shut.

Probably best.

"What sorts of designs?" asked Silas, moving it along.

He shrugged. "Designs like wingless delta shapes. Which is how these UAPs—or UFOs in your layman's terms—are described. Triangles."

"Definitely what I saw in Germany," Gapinski confirmed. "And Turkey for that matter."

"Think of it," Elijah continued, "If the public had learned the Nazis were working at Roswell after just winning World War II, they would go ballistic!"

"So aliens were a convenient cover story," reasoned Celeste, "to hide the fact Nazi scientists were lending their scientific acumen to the American military industrial complex."

"And later space race," added Torres. "Don't forget that von Braun guy headed up NASA."

"That's bloomin' right!"

"So it was all misdirection," Silas said, the pieces coming together. "To steer the public's attention away from what the government was doing when their experimental aircraft were discovered."

"Be that as it may," said Celeste, "this doesn't answer the other side to the phenomenological coin."

"And what's that?" Gapinski asked.

"The existence of aliens. Real or not."

"I'll get to that," Elijah said, "First, recognize how incredibly evil and wicked these experiences are. Abductees feel chosen, part of something special. They identify with their so-called abductors, the aliens, in a way that's far more sympathetic than normal."

"Sounds like Stockholm syndrome," said Celeste.

"Astute observation."

Gapinski twisted up his face in confusion. "Stockholm whatchamacallit?"

Gina laughed. "It's a mental syndrome whereby victims of abduction, not necessarily alien, or people held hostage against their will, identify with their captors. So in the case of alien contactees or abductees, such abductors are viewed as helpful messengers sent to help humanity, not to hurt us."

Silas asked, "Then what's their objective?"

"More importantly," added Celeste, "what do abductees claim is their objective?"

Gina shifted and crossed a leg, one side of her skirt riding a bit too high. Silas saw Gapinski steal a glance, looking like he didn't mind one bit. Until he caught his glance, the man offering an impish grin and looking a bit hot and bothered.

"Time is running out," the agent explained, jolting Gapinski from his gawking and refocusing Silas. "That's the objective. Or rather, the message."

Celeste asked, "What does that bloomin' mean, time is running out? For whom?"

"For our planet, for humanity. And the aliens are said to be giving us humans a little more time to change, because we are close to destroying everything. They are making sure we do not destroy the planet because we are special. They want to save Earth. They are worried about what we are doing and they want to help us clean it up. They gave messages to abductors to take better care of the planet. They want to save the planet because Earth is special, and they are giving us time and a message to change. Or so abductees claim."

Silas smirked. "Sounds like your run-of-the-mill doomsday cult."

Celeste added, "With a pinch of radical environmentalism thrown into the mixture."

"There is that, certainly," Gina went on, "but much of the messaging is about their benevolence through gift giving."

"Gift giving?"

"It is said that the visiting alien beings will give us technology. Military, yes, but also healing. Abductees claim our alien visitors are masters of genetics, so they can alter and eliminate most of our diseases. They want to help us not pollute our planet. Again, more of the environmentalism messaging, but their aim is to heal us, especially in preparation for a higher consciousness from their gifts."

"So, the long and short of abductee alien confessions," Silas said, "is that these...visitors, or whatever—they're not a military threat to countries but our helpers, our messengers."

Gina nodded. "Even though many of the so-called UFO

sightings have taken place around military facilities, they claim no military threat. Instead, it is about making contact in order to aid in human evolution and increase our human consciousness, all so that humanity globally will live a better way."

"And our increased consciousness," added Celeste, "will lead to a more peaceful, loving, and hospitable global community, am I right?"

"Exactly."

Gapinski snorted a laugh. "Sounds like the perfect John Lennon iTunes hit."

Gina laughed. "Pretty much."

There went that leg again, this time sliding underneath her. And there went that crimson blooming in Gapinski's cheeks. The man was twitterpated, that's for sure!

Silas said, "I can see the spiritual connection with all this talk of higher consciousness, and these visitations or communications or whatever happening at that level."

"Speaking of which." Celeste asked, "Gina, you mentioned earlier a demonic, spiritual dimension to all of this."

She nodded. "Most definitely."

"Is that the FBI's official stance?" asked Silas.

"Most certainly not."

They shared a laugh.

"My clinical, as well as professional, criminal opinion is that much of what passes off as alien abduction is really cultic in nature. And my Christian convictions tell me it is demonic."

"Sounds about right, but what makes you personally and professionally say that?"

Gina answered, "For instance, two friends of mine have delivered people from the trauma of abduction experiences by confronting the residual memories and lingering fears in a spiritual angle in the name of Jesus Christ."

"Almost like an exorcism?"

She nodded. "Somewhat."

Celeste visibly shivered. "Goodness. Certainly gets at the sinister nature of the beings said to come from other planets, but instead they sound quite like our own. Demons and what not."

Silas added, "It sounds like the messaging that abductees get is inherently anti-Christian."

Gina nodded. "That's exactly right. Jesus is said to be nothing special. He was selected as humanity's alien messenger. In fact, Jesus is one of the aliens! You heard that same messaging parroted by the woman in the news report."

"Jacques Vallée," explained Elijah, "is a prime contactee researcher who noted the sinister spiritual element messaging. Messaging never directed at other religions but only Christ in Christianity."

Dread grew in the pit of Silas's stomach. Had not a clue of the nature of the UFO and alien abduction phenomenon, for one. But to hear it put in these starkly Christian terms—starkly spiritual terms, where the Devil seemed to be at the controls of the spacecrafts, and his demon minions acted as his stage hands. It was all too unreal.

"John Mack," Elijah went on, "was a Harvard researcher and psychology professor who spent much of his professional career delving into the dark side of alien abduction stories. He helped put together an MIT conference in 1982, and one of the papers connected alien abductee stories with satanic ritual abuse."

"Golly..." said Celeste, bringing her arms close around her chest.

Silas understood why. The mention of such abuse probably brought up her own past with the occult.

Gina explained, "Remarkably, or perhaps unremarkably if you're dialed into such phenomenon, there are touch points with what has happened to abductees regarding their narratives of capture and experiences with abduction and also Luciferian rituals—something like twenty plus similarities."

"Such as?" asked Silas.

"All of it will be familiar if you've ever watched *The X-Files* or other such alien conspiracy media. Everything from the use of metal tables to wounds on the body and probes used by little green men in unmentionable places."

Gapinski shuddered. "I think we can let our noggins extrapolate on that one."

"Even unsettling messaging with birthing hybrid children."

"Hybrid child birthing?" Celeste asked, shaking her head with furrowed brow.

Gina nodded. "Women are convinced they are carrying a hybrid child. In the case of alien abductees, something part alien and human. And in the case of satanic ritual abuse, the anti-Christ himself, or even a beastish, divine alien meant to do good things and help humanity reach their full potential."

"Certainly sounds like a connection between the two."

"Again, there is this messaging regarding being chosen and special. Very shamanistic, actually, tuning you into the realities of the universe to take humanity a message of salvation, given to a select few."

"So, you're saying," Silas said, shifting on his feet and trying to get his head around it all, "that part of these...abduction experiences, I suppose you'd call them, whoever is doing the abducting—these experiences seem to have a deeply spiritual element to them all. Demonic even, satanic."

"The abductors," Gina explained, "want abductees to believe that God hates them and Satan is the true authority. There is also an element where demonic forces act upon people directly. Again, there have been cases where people have been addressed with the name of Christ and it all stops— the memories, the abductions themselves, the feeling of harboring a hybrid alien child. Signifying a clear demonic element to it all."

"Having had my own run-ins with the Devil," Celeste said, "I can see where you would suggest such experiences are more spiritual."

Elijah turned to her. "You were abducted by aliens?"

"No, but I might as well have been. For me, it was a Ouija board and seances."

"That's spiritually dangerous. And stupid."

She laughed, pushing a stray lock of hair behind an ear. "Yes, I'm aware, mate. 'Twas by the grace of God I didn't reap any further produce from the demonic fields I had been tilling. Nothing like the trauma of what these abductees sound like."

Silas marveled at his fiancé. More gracious than he would have been. And there was that bluntness again. Understood Elijah wasn't trying to be a prick. Just came off that way. But again, he could also appreciate his no-nonsense air about him. Said what he thought and let it be that. Could respect it. Could even use someone like that at the Order of Thaddeus to shake things up.

Now there was a thought.

"At any rate," Gina went on, "during the course of our FBI assignment, Elijah and I came across several dozen cases of people who purported to have been abducted by aliens and reported them as nasty creatures—huge reptilian creatures that were the stuff of nightmares."

"Did you say huge?" Gapinski said, flashing wide eyes at Silas. "How huge?"

"Interviewees described them as eight or nine feet tall."

"Just like those bones we discovered in Turkey!"

Silas nodded. Interesting connection.

"Some of the others reported to us that they believed the Grays, as many within the abductee community call them, some of the beings they encountered seemed to them like bio-bots."

"Bio-bots?" asked Celeste, brow furrowed with confusion.

Gina nodded. "Beings created in their own image and likeness, so to speak."

"What, like mankind was said to have been created in the image and likeness of God, according to Genesis chapter 1?"

"You're catching on. But these intelligent beings were not of the chapter 1 variety. More like chapter 6, according to Elijah's theories."

"Intelligent beings?" Silas scoffed, muttering under his breath. "Are you kidding me?"

Elijah snapped his attention toward him. "I understand most Christians are uncomfortable with the idea that there are other intelligent beings somewhere in the universe outside of our terrestrial body. Even such distinguished scholars as yourself, Master Grey."

"Obviously, *muchacho*," Torres said. "Because I never read nothing about no aliens in the Bible."

Elijah turned his attention to Torres now. "Have you read anything about gravity or toilet paper or internal combustion engines in the Bible?"

Her eyes flashed wide, then she glanced at Silas. Like a deer in headlights asking for help.

"The point is," he continued, "Anti-alien is the position taken by biblical absence. Which is a pretty poor argument, given lots of things are real and not mentioned in the Bible."

"Like gravity and cars and toilet paper," Silas said. "I get what you're saying, but it seems like quite the leap to assume aliens exist simply because the Bible doesn't speak about them."

"Nope."

"Nope what?"

"Nope. It isn't."

Heat flashed up Silas's neck. This was getting irritating.

He leaned back and crossed his arms. "Care to explain?"

"Because the Bible *does* speak about them."

It was one of those proverbial record scratch moments, where the room winds down to a confused silence wondering whether it heard someone right.

"Como say what, doc?" asked Gapinski.

"Hoss's spanglish is *muy horrible*," Torres said, jerking a thumb his way, "but I'm with him. *De qué estás hablando, muchacho?*"

"What I'm talking about, *muchacha*, are the sons of God in Genesis 6. The divine beings who copulated with female humans, who then birthed the Nephilim."

"*Quién?*"

"The warriors of renown..." Silas said, recognizing the obscure passage. Had never considered it in the light of that conversation before, and it made his head spin with possibilities.

"As in *muy loco* hybrids," Torres added, "like the *muy loco* DNA we recovered in that *muy loco* finger?"

Elijah answered, "I don't know about any *muy loco* finger, but bingo. Supernatural heavenly beings produced divine-human hybrids."

The room squirmed at the revelation.

"A moment ago, Gina," Celeste said, "you said these intelligent beings were not of the chapter 1 variety in Genesis, but rather more like those of Genesis 6. Something to do with a theory you yourself have concerning the matter, Professor Fox. Is this what you mean by the Bible speaking of aliens?"

"Not aliens, per se," Elijah explained. "The sons of God, the spiritual beings serving on Yahweh's divine council, who tried to raise up an elite group of humans on Earth. A Homo Deus, if you will."

"God-Men," Silas said.

He nodded. "They were to be a great civilization, and you find similar resonance with the alien abduction stories. Where alien-human hybrids are supposed to be raised up to bring humanity into their fullest self. The alien visitations are a catalyst leading to our ultimate destiny of being more than human."

"And it is thought," said Celeste, "that technologically advanced aliens have built civilization, then."

"The sons of God of Genesis 6 sound like aliens and claim extraterrestrial parentage of the men of renown. It is thought that they and their offspring created the pyramids and Stonehenge. Though this is a more extreme position than I am willing to take."

"This is unbelievable," Silas muttered under his breath.

Elijah shrugged. "That's the problem with most modern Christians. They can't conceive of the world being home to more than the triune God, angels, Satan, and demons."

Silas replied, "In my line of work, those are the main actors."

"Granted, but that's not the full story. The world is also inhabited by other gods."

"Don't you mean idols?" asked Gapinski.

"Nope. If I meant idols, I would have said idols."

"Sorry I asked..."

"I think what Gapinski is getting at," said Silas with intervention, "is what do you mean by other gods? Like Zeus and Krishna?"

"The gods of the nations. The ones assigned to them after Genesis 11 as territorial spiritual beings. These were not demons and definitely not merely idols. In fact, they were superior to demons and definitely not at all mere blocks of wood or carved stone statues."

"Then what are they?" asked Torres. "Like ghosts or something?"

Elijah tilted his head and looked off. "That's a good way of putting it, yes. Spiritual beings of all sorts can appear visibly and even physically. They can communicate with people in the world in which they had once been part of."

"Reminds me of the medium at Endor that King Saul consulted," Silas said. "When he spoke to Samuel from the dead."

"Good call. Biblical writers all believed divine beings could eat, drink, fight, and—and here's the germane point to our discussion—they could also produce offspring with humans."

"Eww," Gapinski said with a shudder.

"I must say," said Celeste, "this doesn't sound like any Christian teaching I've ever heard of. Although, my parents were more of the free-range Christian variety, so perhaps I missed something along the childhood catechism way."

"If you read the Old Testament for what it says," Elijah continued, "rather than what we assume it says, no one should miss it, free range or not. It clearly assumes that other gods exist."

"Suppose the Ten Commandments' first command does."

Silas quoted from Exodus 20, *"You shall have no other gods before me."*

Elijah smiled. "Precisely my point."

"Clearly it meant to deny the existence of other gods besides Yahweh."

"Nope. Clearly it does *not* say they do not exist. It is an explicit command not to worship what *does* exist. The Book of Deuteronomy makes it more explicit in chapters 4 and 32 when God divided up the nations—a clear reference to the story about the Tower of Babel in Genesis 11. What does God's Word say Yahweh did? He chose Israel from among those nations as his own possession, placing the other nations under the authority of the sons of God."

"What about Israel's religious creed?" asked Silas.

"What about it?"

He went to answer but was intercepted.

"*Hear O Israel: The Lord is our God, the Lord alone,*" Elijah quoted, "Israel's creed, as you said—all it says is something about *Israel's* God. It doesn't deny the existence of others. Israel's faith was distinct from other god-worship in ancient times because of its claims about their God. That Yahweh, the personal name of Israel's god, was an *elohim*, and that no other *elohim* was Yahweh. They never would or could be. He was totally unique among the other gods."

Silas said, "But that flies in the face of everything we know about the monotheism of Israel, not to mention Christianity!"

Elijah shook his head. "Not if you have a piss-poor understanding of monotheism, which is actually a 17th-century term imposed on an ancient culture."

Piss-poor understanding? Who did this guy think he was, anyhow?

He took a breath, running an irritated hand through his hair. "The term denies that there are any gods but one god, you know that. Mono, one. Theism, god. One god. Any freshman Comparative Religion 101 course teaches that."

"Except Israel's faith doesn't fit neatly into this old view. They believed in many gods. But they also believed in only one Yahweh, who was superior to all other gods and their Creator. These other gods were meant to serve on Yahweh's divine council."

Silas's head was spinning. This understanding of the unseen realm, the ordered universe of God and the rest totally blew apart his categories.

And his theology.

Not to mention a decade of theological training and professional teaching!

"This was the research I was telling you about," Gina said, shaking him loose from his reeling.

He cleared his throat. "Interesting research—and *theories*, professor." Silas shook his head and crossed his arms. "I've never heard of this interpretation of Scripture before."

"That's because you're a doctrinal theologian," Elijah said, "and I'm a *biblical* theologian. And Jewish. Well, Messianic. Even then, early Church Fathers, like Clement of Alexandria and Ambrose of Milan, believed the sons of God and their offspring to be spiritual beings."

Silas took a pause, and a breath. Felt himself hot under the collar and a little embarrassed at his ignorance. Didn't want to spout off and come across as a complete jackass.

"I don't understand how this relates to our mission at hand, with UFOs—"

"UAPs. Unidentified—"

"Aerial phenomenon. I know, doc. But what does any of this have to do with such phenomenon and so-called alien abductions. Gapinski's, the others?"

Elijah went to answer when a shrilly *bring-bring-bring* sliced through the office. Followed by the familiar buzzing of an incoming text.

And something else.

Something bassy, something thwapping in the near distance.

Something very, very familiar.

"Silas, love!" Celeste held up her phone, eyes wide and jaw set.

The room seemed to bend toward it as one, squinting to read the message emblazoned across the screen in all caps.

Gapinski sighed and shook his head, "Sonofa—"

"Run?" Elijah said with interruption, reading the text with furrowed brow. "From what?"

Gina stood. "Our former employer, that's what."

CHAPTER 24

Choppers had been the bane of Silas's existence back in Iraq. Ironically, they were more so this side of civilian life, given all the SEPIO nonsense that had sent those thwapping buzzards his way.

Hated flying in them, for one. Hated flying, period. Was why he went into the Army and not the Air Force. Dad had always said, if God had wanted people to swim, he would've given them fins and gills. More so: Had the good Lord wanted people to fly, he would've given them wings.

Damn straight.

So, when he was called up to the Rangers, and he found out jumping in and out choppers were part of the gig, he almost said "Thanks, but no thanks!" Didn't, but his hatred of flying, really born through childhood fear of it being shuttled from place to place as a boy, was enough to keep him from joining the elite ranks of Uncle Sam's Black Knights.

But that wasn't all of it.

The way they kicked up gouts of dust, spreading it far and wide, was a real pain in the backside. Got into every nook and cranny of his gear and personal effects in the barracks. Not to mention all of *his* nooks and crannies—nostrils, ears, eyes, mouth. Blech!

Then there was the sound. The relentless bassy thwapping that irritated the snot out of him, grumbling like a garbage disposal with a fork stuck down its gullet. In the thick of Operation Iraqi Freedom, those birds were coming in and out for what felt like every minute of the day, shuttling soldiers around and coming in for supply reloads. A conveyor belt of fork-infested garbage disposals for weeks on end. Nearly drove him crazy from it all!

Yes, sir, Silas knew choppers like the back of his hand. Thorns in his side with long memories.

So, with that sound in the distance gaining a head of steam —no doubt about it, that was a chopper coming in hot and heavy on their position.

And not one of those lame Huey utility birds, either. But a Black Hawk from the Army surplus store. The kind the feds used to round up domestic terrorists or bust bagmen smuggling narcotics across the US-Mexico border.

The kind still on the hunt for three Order special-ops agents and one FBI agent on the lam! Or Nous or Theoti, he supposed. The Air Force even, given it looked like their Security Forces agency was in the mix.

Either way, whoever it was, however they found them—it wasn't go time but scram time. For the second time in as many days.

Par for the SEPIO course, that's for sure.

Silas bolted to his feet and went to the window overlooking the pond anchoring the center of the college campus. Couldn't tell where it was coming in from. But by the sound of it, they didn't have much time. And no doubt about it, that chopper wouldn't be the only piece of hardware coming in hot and heavy on their position.

Celeste joined him. "Nicky McGrath is saving our bloomin'

bums for a second go of things with the US government, I reckon."

He smirked. "Our MI6 hero."

"Does the FBI even use helicopters?" Gapinski asked. "I thought Suburbans were their ride of choice."

"The Tactical Helicopter Unit," answered Elijah, "a subunit of the Tactical Aviation Unit, uses military-converted tactical Sikorsky UH-60 Black Hawks and tactically enhanced Bell 412s and Bell 407s."

"Good to know…"

Silas spun from the window and headed for the door. "Which means we've got maybe five minutes to get the heck out of Dodge before—"

"I can't," protested Elijah. "I have a dentist appointment in the morning."

He did a double take. "What?"

"I have a dentist appointment in the morning. And I have a buttload of work to finish up before the night is out."

Gapinski snorted a laugh. "Tell that to Uncle Same, doc!"

Silas opened the office door and glanced out into the hallway.

Coast was clear for now, the final set of evening classes still going on. That all-quiet-on-the-Western-Front vibe would change real quick, real soon.

He shut the door and turned to Elijah. "You're not going to have any teeth to get cleaned if you don't get moving!"

"Nope." The professor spun back around to his computer and started clacking away. As if no one else was in the room, without a care in the world.

What was with this guy?

"Torres and I will clear the building," Gapinski volunteered, "while you deal with McMurphy here."

"Good idea." The pair left as Silas shuffled to Elijah's desk to talk some sense into the man.

He planted both hands on the cleared surface and leaned toward the back of Elijah's head. "We don't have time for this, professor! Any minute now, hostiles will be—"

A gentle hand rested on his arm. It was Gina.

"Let me..."

Silas nodded and backed off in an irritated huff as Gina inched around the desk to speak with Elijah.

Hopefully, she could talk some sense into the man. Otherwise, they'd have to ditch his backside and save their own.

Yet he sensed Elijah could blow this case wide open with his biblical knowledge. Something rang true about his comments on the sons of God. Comments that connected to what Silas had recalled earlier in the operation about the Nephilim.

What they had to do with UFOs and aliens, he hadn't a clue. Just hoped Elijah did. Otherwise, they wouldn't have a chance in—

"*I. Have. Work. To. Do!*" Elijah shouted.

Hot Hades...

Silas cringed at the outburst, but figured the outburst was something to do with his autism. Didn't know much about it, but he did know high-stress situations could often trigger such responses, especially when his brain was dialed into a task or a decision that wouldn't let him go. His friend Colton back in Iraq struggled with that.

Yet the clock was running down to zero. If Gina didn't convince him to get with the program, he'd have no choice but to bail and go it alone with his crew.

Celeste came up to his side. "He's a ripe one, isn't he?"

Silas grunted an agreement, saying nothing more for fear of saying too much.

"Do you trust him?" she asked lowly. "Are you sure he and his...disorder, disability, whatever you call an autistic person—

do you reckon it's manageable under high-stress circumstances?"

He didn't have a clue. But he was beginning to think this was a mistake relying on someone who was so unreliable.

Yanking his sleeve back, Silas checked the Seiko watch that had kept him on task most of his life. Cluing him to the fact time was up, on top of those bassy thwapping blades nearly overhead now.

It was go time.

With or without Doc Fox.

The office door burst open, muffled voices laced with panic flooding behind Gapinski and Torres.

"We're under attack!" Gapinski panted, doubling over and resting his palms on his knees.

Celeste smirked. "You're a sharp one."

"No, he's right," said Torres. "Something's been flying low, circling the campus and buzzing this building before darting back into the sky. Almost like it's scoping out our position for..."

She trailed off, not able to finish what Silas knew she meant.

For an attack.

The word sent a shudder ratcheting up his spine.

"Torres and I got peeps moving on out," Gapinski explained, "but we've got to hustle. Bad juju in those skies, there is. Bad juju."

"Right, brilliant, Matthew." Celeste turned to Gina and Elijah. "I reckon it's about time we get on with it. Come along, professor. Time to go."

"She's right, Eli," Gina said. "The rest of the faculty and students are evacuating, and who knows what's about to happen."

Elijah didn't move. He transfixed his eyes ahead, his gaze vacant and far-off. Then he started something peculiar. His fingers, running through some sort of tick.

Thumb to index finger, thumb to middle, thumb to ring finger, thumb to pinky. Then rinse and repeat.

Just sat that way for near a minute as that bird above buzzed the seminary building again, keeping his fingers strumming from one to the next. Same as from the lecture.

They didn't have time for this!

Silas went to coax the doc into leaving, but the professor sprang to his feet.

Coming out from around his desk, Elijah joined Gina. "As long as I don't miss my dentist appointment."

He smirked. "Don't bet on it, doc..."

Gapinski and Torres led the charge out the door with Celeste following. Silas held back to make sure the other two joined them, which they did.

The faculty wing of the seminary building was clear, with doors left open in the rush to escape. The waning muffled, confused cries in the commons area led them back down the vanilla hallways, where doors to vacant classrooms were similarly left open. Inside, laptops and books, notebooks and pens, even satchels and purses were left behind.

The last of the students were hustling out the glass entrance doors when the SEPIO crew and their two former FBI assets rolled up. Silas ushered them out into the chilly fall night, the sky cloudy and air feeling wet on top of familiar fall scents.

Autumn was his favorite season, and that Midwestern night reminded him why. Just wished he could enjoy it with a mug of hot cider and a sugar and cinnamon cake donut. Mouth was watering just thinking about the tart apple flavor and sweet spice, but no go on all the above.

Because there were those chopper blades again. Somewhere above the low-hanging, heavy autumn clouds. Bassier, thwappier, and way too close for comfort.

Hustling out into the parking lot crowding with way too

many people and slick from a misting rain, Silas spun around for a look.

Faint light sliced through the canopy above shrouding the aerial craft from view with eerie waves of white. Would be a full harvest moon, he figured it, if those clouds weren't in the way. That sound like a garbage disposal with a fork down its gullet was all around, just above the shroud and coming at them again.

Then he spotted it. Dipping below the cloudy canopy and making a run toward the seminary building from across campus.

He pointed at the buzzard. "There's that chopper of yours."

Gapinski spun toward the direction of his gesture.

And gasped.

"That's not just any chopper, chief. That's an Apache!"

"What?"

Celeste said, "Isn't that one of your Yankish attack helicopters?"

"An American twin-turboshaft attack helicopter, actually," Elijah corrected, "with a tailwheel-type landing gear arrangement and a tandem cockpit for a crew of two that features a targeting and night-vision systems package mounted—"

"Thanks, Wikipedia," Gapinski interrupted, "If that thing is armed, we're short on time!"

"Armed?" said Torres, then laughed. "You've been reading too much Clive Cussler, *muchacho*."

The man crossed himself. "May he rest in peace..."

Celeste turned to Silas. "Why would the US government send a bloomin' military helo armed with missiles to intercept us at a Protestant seminary?"

"For the same reason it sent our colleagues joined by the Marines to intercept us at the FBI Academy."

It was Gina, looking into the sky while twirling those ginger locks of hers. She plucked a single hair and let it fall to the pavement.

Then spun around to answer Celeste. "To shut us down."

"What dog crap stuck to your shoe," said Elijah, those fingers going at it again, "did you drag into my study?"

A hissing rush from behind rising from the din of that damn thwapping chopper caught Silas's attention.

Twisting back, he caught sight of a tubular projectile, a faint contrail spinning out from its backside.

Right before it sank into the seminary building's side—at the back, where the faculty offices were, the ones they had just been sitting in.

And exploded with a menacing, phantasmic show of fire and fury.

The rush of heat and force from the blast sent Silas staggering backward. But he held fast.

Grand River Theological Seminary—now that was another story!

A fireball bloomed from its wounded side. One of those mushrooms of orange and red and yellow that reminded Silas of a Jiffy Pop. The aluminum foil expanding as the popcorn popped on his childhood stove, Sebastian and Dad looking on —but in fast motion, it all happening within seconds in a way that takes your breath away in the movies but leaves you ducking for cover in real life.

Especially since bricks and glass and aluminum roofing fell all around them, the fallout thudding into cars and clattering along the pavement and hitting bystanders.

The crowd screamed and threw their hands over their heads, running with panic from the inferno engulfing the '70s-era monstrosity. Acrid black smoke billowed from the gaping wound across the parking lot on an unfortunate wind that only made the blaze more intense.

Wished he hadn't been so hard on the thing, so snooty,

given it was toast. But regret and remorse could wait. They still needed to make it out of the attack alive.

Celeste said, "I reckon Weiss isn't going to like this turn of things."

Silas's gut sank to the wet black pavement glowing a menacing orange. "No, I reckon not."

"Look!" Torres shouted.

A line of vehicles emerged through the smoke at the end of the long drive, coming in hot and heavy at the other end of the parking lot.

Three black SUVs. Suburbans. And zero mystery who was riding up on their backsides.

"Always something..." growled Gapinski.

"How the bloody hell did the feds locate us?" Celeste asked.

"And twice in the same number of days?"

"Can't be a coincidence."

"No coinkydink there!"

Silas clenched his jaw. No, no there wasn't.

Same bad story, same bad channel.

SEPIO versus the feds.

Now with a group of civilians in the crosshairs.

Could it possibly get any worse?

CHAPTER 25

S ilas withdrew his Beretta from his back. Figuring out
how they found themselves in the same mess could
wait. Staying out of federal custody was all that
mattered.

And surviving, given the firepower the incoming hostiles
were packing.

"You armed?" he shouted to no one in particular.

Three rounds were chambered in rapid succession, the
familiar metal clang both surprising and heartening.

Celeste, Gapinski, and Torres each clenched their Sig
Sauers. Ready, willing, and able.

Gapinski raised a brow. "You really had to ask?"

"Sig Sauers?" Elijah laughed and withdrew a weapon of his
own from his ankle. "I much prefer Heckler & Koch's VP9. With
its cold hammer forged polygonal bore and reinforced polymer
frame, carrying nineteen 9mm rounds—"

"Save it for the other side of success, Wikipedia," Silas interrupted, finding Gapinski's nickname to be apropos.

Gina brought out her own weapon, another H&K pistol,
chambering a round and nodding her go-ahead. Apparently
these two played by the same playbook—and SEPIO's.

Never leave home without cold, hard steel, as Silas had been warned early in his tenure with the Order.

Which was a good thing for what came next.

The three bogies braked hard, their tires throwing up a squealing exclamation point before throwing open their doors.

And men in black with long black rifles jumped out. Three groups of four or five. All suited up with armor and helmets. The big dogs, in other words, putting Uncle Sam's post-9/11 militarized policing dollars to good use.

With their night scopes painting big red targets on each of their backs.

"I count fifteen," said Celeste.

Silas nodded. "Same. More than two-to-one odds."

"Not Vegas bad, at least," quipped Torres.

"But still not good. Especially with that bird still flying overhead."

"And armed to the teeth!" groaned Gapinski.

He frowned. And that.

"Sonofa—"

Rat-a-tat-tat weapon fire cut off Gapinski and sent the SEPIO quartet plus two diving for cover. Then more: *rat-a-tat-tat, rat-a-tat-tat, rat-a-tat-tat.*

All of the bullets went high and wide, arcing overhead rather than thudding into the smattering of vehicles moored to the pavement.

Or worse, taking down the smattering of seminary students fleeing for their lives.

Which told Silas it was mostly for show. Wanted to let the crowd know who was boss and gain immediate control of ground zero.

At least for now.

For their part, the two former FBI agents weren't having anything of it. They immediately engaged. Like a switch was flipped to autopilot inside their heads.

They hustled to an aging, sagging cherry-red Crown Vic a few cars over, each taking one end and opening up on the hostiles. Didn't even think about it. Just engaged.

Which was Silas's kind of pair.

And it was successful in throwing off the hostiles' equilibrium. Didn't see that coming from the look of it, the weapon fire faltering and the clumps of men—or women, as the case may be; he certainly had an equal opportunity opinion when it came to the gender makeup of hostiles in the 21st century. Whoever they were, they were scattering for their own cover as Gina and Elijah unloaded.

Score one for the good guys! They needed it after the baddies obliterated the seminary in one fell swoop.

Whoever they were.

Gina popped off a *one-two-three* shot, then spun back to Silas. "We need to get these civilians to safer ground."

"Right," Celeste said, joining her at her side and firing off her own triplet. "Got one."

Elijah groaned. "Title 18 of the US Code section 1114 states, *'Whoever kills or attempts to kill any officer or employee of the United States or of any agency in—'*"

"*We know,*" the SEPIO agents said as one.

A barrage of rounds sank into the Crown Vic, sending the six crouching for cover.

"Except—" Torres twisted to offer a *one-two-three* reply. "—we don't know these are government agents."

"That's true," said Elijah. "Section 3109 of the same code states, *'The officer may break open any outer or inner door or window of a house, or any part of a house, or anything therein, to execute a search warrant, if, after notice of his authority and purpose, he is refused admittance or when necessary to liberate himself or a person aiding him in the execution of the warrant.'*"

Celeste said, "Except we're not in any bloomin' house!"

Another barrage put an exclamation point on that fact of the matter.

"Law enforcement officers," explained Gina, "must identify themselves and announce their purpose before using force."

"Knock and announce," Silas said, tossing a few *pop-pop-pop* shots over the Crown Vic's bow to keep the feds on their toes.

"That's right," said Elijah. "A clear violation of federal law."

Torres snorted a laugh. "Yeah, right. Tell that to the boys coming at us at eleven, twelve, and one!"

"Or gals," said Gapinski, joining Silas with some back-up *pop-pop-pops* of his own. "I think by now we've been able to dispense with silly modern notions of gender roles when hostiles are slinging lead left and right!"

"Suppose you're right."

"They didn't announce themselves, either," Elijah went on, ignoring the pair, "so their fate is in their own hands."

He stood and fired his H&K. *Pop-pop-pop. Pop-pop-pop.*

Then sank to his knees behind the Crown Vic. "Got one. And I'm writing my congressman for their clear violation of US law."

Gina added, "They're also not wearing any identifying markers."

Silas said, "I didn't see any yellow FBI letters emblazoned across their chests, did you?"

"No, I didn't."

Elijah huffed. "Something else to put in my letter!"

"Right," said Celeste. "Which makes me think this isn't the US government."

"Or at least any overt operation," said Silas. "No reason why the Air Force isn't working through another agency."

"Nope," Elijah said, shaking his head. "The Posse Comitatus Act prevents the US military from engaging on US soil to enforce federal policies."

"Ha!" Gapinski snorted a laugh. "As if that ever stopped

Uncle Sam from flexing its muscles through other agencies. Helloooo. Ever heard of Waco?"

More *rat-a-tat-tat* weapon fire flared up, followed by screams and shouts of injury.

"Guess not..."

Silas muttered a curse between a clenched jaw. They were stuck behind a Ford reject while the hostiles gained the upper hand with a pack of civilians in the way. Some clearly going down in the melee.

Their melee, with them as targets, not these poor pastors-in-training.

Time to change direction. But how?

"This isn't working," Silas grumbled. Standing, he emptied his Beretta at the hostiles in frustration.

Two flipped backward with injury. Thought he caught geysers of blood blooming from their necks, too. A small consolation for the attack, but not what he'd had in mind flying to the Midwest.

He let slip another curse before letting the magazine fall to the pavement, sinking to his knees along with it.

Just as a fresh barrage of bullets clattered off the only thing standing between them and death.

Glass shattered now, and the Crown Vic sank in a hiss of air. Wouldn't be long before a bullet or two caught the gas tank in the kisser.

Then all bets were off.

"I've got an idea." Gapinski gestured to the pond at the center of campus. "How about you and me draw them to that puddle over yonder."

Silas followed his gesture. "What, the lake?"

"Nope. Not a lake," corrected Elijah. "It's a pond."

"What's your plan?" asked Celeste, ignoring the man.

"We need to get these civilians out of here," Gapinski went on. "But to do that, we need a diversion."

"A diversion?" said Gina. "I think 24 wants its Jack Bauer back."

He turned to her with a grin. "You a fan, Doc Gina?"

She winked. "Don't you know it."

"Oh, I do..."

Silas rolled his eyes. "How about we wait to revel in our shared television dramas until after we've successfully navigated our way out of this one, alright?"

Gapinski cleared his throat. "Sorry, chief..."

"Now, this plan of yours. What of it?"

"Plan is, I'll jump in our Excursion and make a mad dash down that road running past the water." He pointed to a service road that jutted off the seminary parking lot lined with barren trees and white-lit streetlamps. It wound around the lake or pond, or whatever, off into the undergrad campus. "They'll think we're making an escape, see, but in their pursuit, I'll 'crash'—"

He threw up air quotes at the side of his head for emphasis. Which made the whole cockamamie plan sound even more cockamamie.

"But not really crash, see," Gapinski went on. "Just make it look like they've got us good to Sunday. I'll scram into the water, dive down deep—real deep and pull a Michael Phelps, swimming like a madman to the other side."

"What the heck are we doing," Torres said, folding her arms, "while you're getting your MacGyver on?"

"Jack Bauer," Gina corrected.

"You and Celeste are shepherding the shepherds over here —" Gapinski yanked a thumb behind at all the seminarians crouched and crying behind. "Silas will watch my six from the dorm anchored to the backside of the baseball field, just in case of any funny business. Then we'll rendezvous at the pitcher's mound at the center of the field, or around those parts."

He gestured to a massive sports complex flanking the

service road, the baseball park dark and shuttered until the next game. Where most undergrads featured a football stadium to draw in the masses—and massive alumni checks—apparently this one thought America's pastime was where it was at.

Was a good rallying point, given its central location, and it did offer a nice walled-in base to respond to anything that might come after them.

But Silas didn't like how exposed they'd be from the air with that chopper somewhere up in the clouds. Hadn't seen hide nor hair of it since it launched its hellfire missile at the seminary, just its continued garbled fork-infested garbage disposal racket. The thought of it swooping down from the sky to intercept them—or worse, finish them off...

Seemed like a disaster waiting to happen. But Gapinski was right. They needed to get the civilians to safety, needed a diversion to draw the hostiles off. The Excursion was reachable, with a little firepower backup. So maybe his plan could work.

"Can you manage getting off to it?" asked Celeste, popping off a *one-two* shot, then another *three-four* follow-up.

To which the hostiles answered with their own *rat-a-tat-tat* rejoinder.

Gapinski nodded. "You give me covering fire, I'll make it."

Another *pop-pop-pop* from Celeste, joined by the same from Elijah and Gina, gave Silas time to mull it over.

He said, "Seems overly complicated to me. But it's not the worst plan SEPIO's had, I suppose."

Gapinski grinned with pride. "Saw it in a movie once."

Silas turned to him. "A movie?"

He held his grin and wiggled his brows as if he'd invented sliced bread itself.

"Well, did they live to see another day?"

He frowned. "Not sure. The wifi signal cut out before I could finish streaming it." Shaking his head, Gapinski slapped his back. "Don't worry. I'm a pro at this sort of thing."

"Because of some B-level streamer movie you saw on a bad internet connection?"

"It'll work, chief. Trust me."

The continued bassy thwap of the chopper blades some-where overhead, compounded by the raging fire at their backs and frightened screams of students racing for safety, reminded him they didn't have much to go on. A buck and a prayer was about it.

The SEPIO way...

Gapinski put a hand on Silas's shoulder. "I can do this."

Silas looked him in the eyes, hesitating a beat but nodding him onward.

He grinned and nodded back then looked to the other four. "You give me covering fire. When I get the show on the road— literally, peddling our Ford to the lake—then you let up and get the civilians to safety. Got it?"

They nodded, though their muttered agreements told Silas they didn't necessarily agree. Gapinski was a good troop and could handle himself, but this was a whole other level of engagement SEPIO hadn't had before, let alone him.

A government entity was bearing down on their backsides —for the second time—civilians were in harm's way and an attack helicopter had just blown up a seminary building! That wasn't even touching on the fact purported alien remains had been uncovered in some Turkish desert, sparking this whole nonsense to begin with. And now ET was trending on WeShare on top of one of his lieutenants having a close encounter of his own kind back in the day—all of it threatening how the Church had understood our human identity as the Imago Dei, bearing God's image, as well as God's own place among other intelligent life-forms.

Silas hoped the man could deliver. Because if he couldn't... more was at stake than making it out alive.

"You ready?" Gapinski said, drawing him back to the moment.

A barrage of *rat-a-tat-tat* automatic weapon fire put an exclamation point on the fact of the matter, sending the SEPIO team crouching further behind the Crown Vic and throwing up another wave of frightful protest from the civilians.

"Right, let's do this," Celeste said, weapon at the ready.

"I'm ready, too." Torres held up her Sig with a nod. "*Vamos, muchacho.*"

Silas glanced at the two newcomers, who he'd expected to have defaulted to their ticks by now. The twirling of hair and the rapping of fingers against one another.

Instead, their faces were set as flint and weapons drawn for action, looking like the FBI professionals they had been and nodding Gapinski onward. Felt bad about his assumptions—which they surely were confounding.

Silas drew in a breath and drew closer to the front bumper, Beretta raised and a fresh magazine ready to unload.

"Like Celeste said, let's do this."

The others scrambled for a shot, the hostiles holding their positions at the other end and looking like they were assembling for their own raid.

Whoever they were, whatever they were planning.

Now or never.

CHAPTER 26

"On my fire," Silas said, taking aim at one of the men hoping to even things up a bit before everything hit the fan.

Felt guilty when time came to use such violence during the line of SEPIO duty, taking a life for the Church's cause and all. But the way he figured, he was defending life from the injustice of murder more than taking it. Same line he'd fed himself during his Rangers days when cynicism at the country's cause began throwing up the same guilt.

Prayed the good Lord understood.

Silas crossed himself on instinct, for good measure, then opened fire.

Downing his target and jolting the hostiles into activation.

Along with the rest of his crew, who began their own *pop-pop-pop* volleys.

Giving Gapinski a window to hop to it.

The man bent low and hustled across the slick pavement, bullets skipping across his path from *one-two-three* punches setting sail from the hostiles' position.

But he never faltered. Just kept hustling on those twinkle-toes of his to their ride still anchored near the smoldering seminary building. Surprised the thing survived, but the Ford lived up to its build-tough name.

Sidling up to the Excursion, Gapinski threw open the front passenger's door and slipped inside to the driver's seat. Took a beat, but soon the beast roared to life.

Throwing off the entire equilibrium of the melee.

The hostiles clearly didn't know what to do, where to shoot.

For their part, Silas and his SEPIO crew didn't make it any easier, the five remaining agents continuing their assault as best they could under the same conditions.

Which gave their teammate enough of a window to floor it up onto the walkway and front lawn strewn with blown bricks and broken glass, taking a hard right and rumbling back down to the parking lot on toward destiny.

Which in turn activated the hostiles into making their own vehicular maneuvers. The Suburbans instantly sparked to life, and men piled back inside before pealing after their comrade.

"Hold your fire!" Silas commanded. Didn't want to let on they weren't on that Ford pony as it sped away.

Avoiding the incoming Suburban trio, the SEPIO crew hustled around the front end of the Crown Vic as the hostiles raced by. From open windows, they threw up *rat-a-tat-tats* in sweeping arcs out front and at their position for good measure, but received not a single reply from Silas and his crew.

Once they cleared, Celeste and Torres led Elijah and Gina to rounding up the student civilians while Silas padded toward the confrontation down the road. He raced to the dormitory anchored at one end of the baseball diamond butting the lake.

Just as, right on cue, the Excursion veered off the road straight for the lake. Helped he got a blow-out from a well-placed shot from the pursuing hostiles, but it looked convincing enough.

And sure enough, the bulky SUV launched itself over the

pond and landed in the water with a splash worthy of that 24 TV show Gina had referenced earlier.

It sank into its murky depths. And fast.

The massive vehicle's nose dipped toward the bottom, taking the rest of it with it into the pond's murky depths.

Panic seized Silas's chest, his heart ratcheting up and lungs searching for air with the thought Gapinski was being dragged down with the SUV. He gripped his Beretta and raised it, every nerve fiber wanting to spring into action and take down the hostiles to save his friend. Held his fire, but he wanted to open up on the bastards who had driven the man into the water in the first place.

For their part, the Suburbans held their position anchored at the lake's edge. Just idled there, watching the show from inside their own SUVs without movement, without response. No doubt watching for signs of life and ready to pounce.

He glanced behind to see his other teammates executing the other part of the operation, Celeste leading a large group of the adult students off the property into an adjoining field with Torres making up the rear, while Gina and Elijah offered triage for the injured.

Snapping back to the lake, the seconds ticked by.

Silas gripped his Beretta harder, holding his fire but getting close to the trigger point.

"Come on, Gapinski. Come on..."

Without training, most people can manage to hold their breaths underwater for ninety seconds before needing to take a breath. Longer with the kind of training Silas and Gapinski had in the military. But that was some time ago, for them both.

He glanced down at the Seiko clinging to his wrist and cursed. Three minutes past now. Would be a stretch for the big guy to go much longer without needing a breath.

A frigid breeze struck a whistling tune through the campus, carrying along with it the familiar scents of fall. Woodsmoke, dead leaves, crisp pine. The seconds continued their death march as he stood still. Waiting, intuiting, discerning whether Gapinski was—

A faint splash echoed his way. Down the road, past the dormitory, at the lake's edge.

He stepped out from his perch and craned toward the sound. Could have been a goose coming in for a landing, for all he knew. Wasn't loud enough to attract the hostiles' attention, and was probably nothing more than a toad tucking himself in for the night.

But the sound kept hope alive as an indication that—

"Gapinski's alive..."

Silas heaved a relieved breath as he caught sight of a dark figure scrambling through the cattails waving gently in the breeze. Feared the movement would cost him, that it was too dramatic. But as the man slinked away into the shadows, and surely toward the baseball diamond according to the plan, the Suburbans remained planted at the feet of the lake, their Excursion now completely immersed underwater.

Yet another strike against Silas's record with Weiss, who would surely use it to bury him as another sign of reckless disregard.

Screw him. All that mattered was Gapinski was safe. So were the civilians and the rest of his crew.

Satisfied, Silas slunk back behind the dormitory, letting the hostiles content themselves with their wild goose chase at the pond.

Except...

They didn't take the bait. Now they were peeling off. One by one, the three Suburbans spun around and disengaged. Brakes squawking and tires squealing before their white lights sliced across the grass and road and engines roared with pursuing intent. And they headed for—

The baseball diamond!

One after another, the black menaces sped off down the road leading to the sports complex down the way, rounding toward the entrance at the other end.

It was like they knew where Gapinski and his crew had headed, and they weren't letting up until they had him.

But how? They hadn't communicated on open channels about the plan. Only SEPIO and Gapinski knew what was what.

Not only that, it was like they were after him or something. Almost like they were tracking him down. Like some sort of stray animal with one of those subcutaneous chips he'd gotten his cat Barnabas when he brought the feline back to the States.

Hustling faster, he chuckled. That didn't make a lick of sense. What would anyone want with—

He stopped short, literally winding his pace down to zero as he approached the bleachers flanking the pond.

A wind gusted from behind, sending crunchy, dead leaves skittering past and all the hairs rising to attention.

Are you kidding me?

The events of the past few days flashed by.

The craft Gapinski said he saw coming in hot and heavy above him. Right before it was blown of course—literally by a rocket-propelled grenade.

Then the hostiles, the feds or whatever, homing in on their position at the FBI Academy. Which had never made a lick of sense.

Unless they were searching for something. Tracking something down.

A stray...

But how?

Then he had it. His lungs drawing in a startled breath at the possibility that was quickly sharpening into a distinct probability.

Gapinski had mentioned waking up from his initial—

encounter, or whatever it was. The one way back in that forest at Ramstein on Christmas. With the triangular craft, and the beam of light that sliced down from above. The one where he woke up with the wicked headache and the memory of spices.

And the ache at the back of his neck. Where he found a scar.

Had Gapinski been tagged? The back of his neck embedded with a chip to track him down when the time came?

And was ET calling for his stray?

Not possible. Flat not possible...

Something zoomed overhead. Something bassy, something humming. Didn't see it. Felt it. A wind racing by as some object above disturbed the surrounding air that didn't seem at all connected to anything substantive, anything he could catch a glimpse of.

Until he did.

A—something fell from the sky and disappeared behind the bleachers. All shadows and curved angles, making sharp maneuvers he had never seen from any aircraft during his military service.

Silas's heart galloped forward something fierce on faltering legs, his head pounding with a rush of blood and bowels churning with watery dread.

"Are you kidding me..."

Except it wasn't a joke. It was real. His reality. All of theirs.

Including Gapinski's.

"Gapinski..." Silas whispered on a shaky breath.

The thought of his partner on the other side of the divide with that thing, that craft coming in for a landing, sent him into action.

"*Gapinski!*" he yelled now, bolting through the bleacher scaffolding and making for the massive dugout that stood between him and his teammate.

'I will never leave a fallen comrade to fall into the hands of the enemy.'

The Ranger's creed had been his lifeblood for almost a decade of service. It still stood as a standard for the way he lived his life. Especially with his tenure at the Order of Thaddeus, first as a SEPIO agent and then as Master.

And no way in hell would he let his lieutenant, his friend and confidant in the Order and in the faith, fall to those spawns of Satan, or whatever the heck Elijah would categorize them as.

Only way in was up and over the massive concrete structure straight ahead that flanked the pitcher's mound.

Scrambling over the player's dugout, he saw it.

Or rather, them!

At the center of the field was the craft. Hovering above the ground six or eight feet, unmoving and still.

What he could only describe as a UFO. Damn Elijah's and Nicky's UAP nonsense description. This was a UFO, plain and simple. Something straight out of some Steven Spielberg or Chris Carter fever dream, as Gapinski had said.

A sleek delta-shaped craft. Triangular. Almost like a stealth bomber, but thicker and larger. Its skin was almost translucent, the surrounding green grass and brown dirt, even the dark brown brick dormitories and silver bleachers almost blending into the craft itself.

And there was no sound to it. No whirling of jet engines or hum. Just a low-grade bassy vibration to the air, penetrating his chest with a rattle. Nothing at all like the thwapping chopper blades from earlier. Nothing seemed man-made.

Next to the craft was Gapinski. Lying prone, stiff, unmoving.

And approaching him were three—beings! Gigantic and broad-shouldered. Shadows shrouded them, so Silas couldn't get a good look at who or what they were. But his gut told him everything he needed to know.

First contact...

Or in Gapinski's case, second contact!

No way would he let those bastards touch his teammate—his friend!

Silas went to dart from his perch when a light sliced through the park.

Bright and hot and blinding.

Right before a harsh mechanical humming spread across the open plain. And some weird *tick-tick-ticking*, like a clock, followed by the *crink-crink-crink* of some windup toy.

Then a pressure bloomed in his head. A vibrating, painful pressure that stopped him in his tracks with his hands thrown against the sides of his head and jaw clenched with teeth-aching agony. Felt like he would topple, vertigo overcoming him and causing imbalance, and retch from the topsy-turvy pain.

Reminded him of the Havana syndrome he'd heard about. Electromagnetic microwaves aimed at US embassies by some foreign nation, followed by a vibrating pressure that sparked waves of headache and nausea and imbalance.

Then it stopped. As sudden as it came on. No more pressure, no more pain. No more imbalance or blinding light.

And no more Gapinski.

He was gone!

His body vanished along with the three giant bastards clomping toward his position.

And now the triangle—the UFO...it was rising from the ground on a bed of humming air.

He ran for the pitcher's mound, aiming for the craft with his Beretta and not caring a lick about the hostiles arrayed outside. Let them attack. Silas didn't care. All he wanted was to reach his friend before it was too late.

Squealing tires from behind and the absence of any hostile intervention told him he had nothing to worry about, the hostiles apparently doing their duty.

Standing guard while the real firepower came for what they were looking for.

Because that's exactly what it seemed like.

And now that they got the goods, they—whoever *they* were, which was not at all clear—were quickly ascending into the sky, disappearing into the billowing canopy above.

A crackling snap of lightning streaked across the divide, tendrils of purply blue electric charge slicing through the clouds. Followed by a deafening clap of thunder that sent Silas staggering in his pursuit.

Whether from a thunderstorm about to rain down the funk or the craft having launched out into the upper atmosphere, Silas wasn't sure.

What he was sure of was that Gapinski was the target. More than a probability at that point.

What it meant, he didn't have a clue.

"GAPINSKI!" Silas screamed, craning his neck toward the heavens in a useless search for his crewmate.

"GAPINSKI!!!"

Reaching the pitcher's mound, he slumped to his knees, staring into the nighttime void from hell.

CHAPTER 27
WELWELSBERG CASTLE, GERMANY.

S ebastian Grey finished lighting the final candle when he received word "the package is secure." And by *package*, the underling meant another of the abductees from the past few decades.

But it had been a close one, those competing factions within the government still using their own knowledge against them to thwart their efforts at securing the Great Unveiling. Competition had always been at the heart of the American democratic project, the competing ambitions and impulses of mankind meant to check and balance one another. Prime among them, the military industrial complex.

From the start of the American misadventure leveraging Nazi science and technology, various factions had vied to gain and maintain their own power over their knowledge—both modern and arcane. From intelligence agencies to law enforcement on toward every military branch and their contracting partners—they all tried to deny what was undeniable.

And contain it.

That had been the headache Nous and Theoti had been dealing with, along with the Security Forces of his German American friend. Not only securing the ancient artifacts bearing the final piece to the DNA-puzzle used to replicate the Universe's offspring. But also rounding up those who had been used to further the State's myth and reserved for the Great Unveiling—when the full nature of the Universe would be revealed.

The venerable American cosmologist, Carl Sagan, was right: "It is the responsibility of scientists never to suppress knowledge, no matter how awkward that knowledge is, no matter how it may bother those in power; we are not smart enough to decide which pieces of knowledge are permissible, and which are not."

Same for pesky politicians without a backbone!

Except knowledge of this nature was too great, too uncontainable. If it wasn't the Americans, it would be one of the other nations that had been divided among the Universe's sons. For too long, they had sought to suppress the full measure of that power. Both technological and existential, craft and creation.

Flying object and intelligent alien...

Of course, it made sense, Uncle Sam doing its damnedest to hide the true nature of the Universe. After all, who could trust a nation-state to protect them when an entire civilization of higher Powers was just around the corner?

Sebastian slipped into a black cloak and knelt in the circle, the dancing flames from thirteen candles playing across the vaulted space of stone and shadows—representing the Wheel of the Year and the perfection of the earthly and heavenly alignment of seasons.

But that wasn't all.

Beneath him was a number far greater. The five-point star.

The Pentacle, representing the four natural elements—earth, water, fire, air—and spirit.

Uniting both natural and supernatural.

Both man and God.

And no one would thwart his efforts at making the marriage

complete. Not least within his own person. He was so close he could taste it! The silence and waiting welling up within now and ready to burst.

For good measure, Sebastian flicked his tongue with satisfaction, the muscle having gone through its own transformation along with his flesh. His gratification came in part from his foresight to partner with the one who held the last secret to the Power that would reveal all.

That would raise humanity up to its final evolutionary rung, grasping the full knowledge of its creative power. After all, knowledge *is* power, they say.

No, no, no! Power is *knowledge*, making use of revelation-insight to bend reality to the will of mankind. That's what our original ancestors understood, guided by the stars.

It was time for humanity to reclaim that divine right, once and for all.

To take its place among the gods—to *be* like the gods, with an intimate, unadulterated awareness of all they themselves knew and beheld.

With Sebastian firmly at center of that sphere of power.

A shudder rumbled through the chamber, more a force acting upon his very atoms than an aural intimation of what had arrived.

The static charge of a thousand thunderstorms quickly filled the chamber, along with the tart scent of a zoo.

The reptile exhibit, of course.

The shadows themselves swelled with the Presence that would reveal all.

A jolting bolt of excitement and anticipation rushed through Sebastian's veins. He pulled the dark cloak tighter as an orgasmic grin spread across his face.

The time had come to complete his metamorphosis.

To take *his* place among the gods.

Showtime...

CHAPTER 28

MILL CREEK JUNCTION, MICHIGAN.

W*hat a night...*
Silas stretched out on a well-worn tan cloth couch in a cramped space lit by a single banker's lamp on a CEO-style desk. A few bookshelves lined one wall with two brown herringbone wingback chairs in front of the desk next to the complementary tan couch along one wall where he'd been mulling next moves.

The office belonged to a small-town pastor, Peter Daniel Young. Pastor of a Baptist church in neighboring Mill Creek Junction. Silas figured no one would think to track down an old Catholic religious order holed up in the pastoral office of an Independent Baptist church in some sleepy farming town.

That was the hope, anyway.

After everything went down at the seminary, and with no SEPIO outpost to return to in that part of the country, Celeste suggested they connect with an old asset who had helped the Order earlier in the year. Peter had been instrumental in helping them break open a case centered around a bunch of charismatic hucksters who had rolled into his town and roiled the world. Peter was more than willing to help, offering his church office as a home base to continue their operation.

Letting rip a wide-mouth yawn and rubbing the weariness from his face, Silas glanced around the space, and smirked. Place smelled not much different than the church he grew up in, memories of his Falls Church parish rising to the surface. Mold and mildew, old wood and stale Folgers. Same for the basement carpet and nave hard-back pews and potlucks of his childhood '60s-era church. Funny how Christian houses of worship smelled the same, no matter the denomination.

Silas simply sat. Didn't move, felt like he wasn't even breathing. Still disbelieved everything that went down at Grand River Theological Seminary.

Celeste and Torres had found Silas still at the pitcher's mound. Not so much in a catatonic state as he was in a disbelieving state. His teammate had been taken. His right-hand man snatched from him, before his very eyes.

By something straight out of *Close Encounters of the Third Kind*!

By *somethings*...

Not only was he beside himself that Gapinski had been taken. He was beside himself that he had *let* his partner get taken out from underneath his nose. The whole thing totally blew apart his categories of both the seen and unseen realms. Categories about what was earthly and heavenly, natural and supernatural.

Terrestrial and extraterrestrial.

Knew he didn't get a good enough of a look at who—or what—had taken his teammate. But with what he saw hovering at center field, and what he had witnessed happen to Gapinski —the man prone and unmoving, levitated above the ground, and those...*beings*, or whatever, taking him away. All of it had sent him reeling.

Had sent his faith reeling!

It wasn't even that he never kept the door open for the possibility of alien life-forms somewhere out there, in outer space. The universe was certainly vast enough for something to exist elsewhere, and he had a robust enough of a doctrine of creation and the Creator to assume God could have crafted such beings anywhere he wanted.

It was that the thought had never even entered his mind. He was much more earthly minded in his theology, much more tangible and concrete in the way he thought about his faith. How it manifested itself in the world, how it connected to life's daily grind.

And yet, what he had seen was seriously messing with his faith. Or rather, how he compartmentalized it, leaving little room for the unseen realm that seemed to be breaking more into the seen realm in greater measure.

For the Order of Thaddeus's part, he had never sensed much of a focus on that part of reality either. Contending for the once-for-all faith was more about battling flesh-and-blood bad actors threatening the faith—both inside and outside the Church.

Given the sort of power rising to the surface of late, he might have to do something about that. Maybe concoct another project, alongside SEPIO, to address the very real threat that formed the Church's real struggle. The one 'against the cosmic powers of this present darkness,' as Paul taught in the Book of Ephesians, chapter 6. Perhaps the Order should be taking a stand against them as much as the flesh-and-blood threats from Nous, from Theoti, from his very brother even.

First things first was getting Gapinski back and figuring out what the heck was going on with these UFO and ET sightings. Only silver lining to all the darkness on that front was Nicky, of all people. Celeste had asked the MI6 spook to work back channels through British intelligence and military agencies to possibly get a read on what went down in West Michigan and possibly locate a possible bit of intel that could possibly lead to

Gapinski's whereabouts. The man went to work and would call the minute he found something.

But given all the open possibilities, which was about all they had, he wasn't holding out hope. And it pissed Silas off.

Crossing his arms, he prayed the good Lord would make good on his promise to never leave or forsake his children. Because Gapinski was in a world of trouble, and if anything happened to him—

Lord Jesus Christ, Son of God, please bring our brother home safely...

The door opened and Peter returned with a tray of five mugs and a large silver carafe. Trailing him were his teammates and the newest additions to their motley crew.

"Figured coffee and tea," the pastor said, "was on the menu this late hour."

Silas swung his legs around and nodded with a smile. "Just what the doc ordered. Thanks pastor—erm, Peter. And thanks for lending us your ecclesial digs. For a second time."

He nodded. "No worries. Although, I'm looking forward to getting my honorary SEPIO badge now, after a second round of Navy SEALs for Jesus fun."

"You've got it! Because Lord knows you've earned it."

Setting the tray down on his desk, the pastor handed the one mug of hot water with a tea bag draped across the corner to Celeste, then promptly poured the fresh brew into the other mugs. Surprisingly didn't smell half bad.

Taking a swig of brew, the nutty caramel notes sitting just right, Silas asked, "Any word from Nicky?"

Celeste frowned. "Not yet. I've pestered him enough the past hour that I think I should leave him well enough alone. The man's good at what he does. If there is anyone who can get a read on Gapinski's extraction, it's Nicky. In the meantime, I've also asked Zoe and Abraham to work overtime seeking leads."

He nodded, saying nothing more.

Gina and Elijah settled into the wingback chairs facing Peter's desk, each armed with their own mug of brew. Torres slumped into the couch next to Silas, thanking Peter for her own mug of coffee.

"What I don't understand is—" She paused for a sip, humming with pleasure. "What I don't understand is how the heck these jokers rolled up on us a third time."

"Mole," Elijah offered.

Silas scoffed. "A mole? No way."

"You've got a mole." The man took a sip of brew, saying nothing more.

He threw up another scoff, shaking his head. "Whatever…"

"Elijah does have a point," Celeste said, sitting down between Silas and Torres. "You don't think it really is a mole, do you?"

Silas threw her a frown. "What, at the Order? Inside SEPIO?"

She shrugged. "It is possible."

The thought had certainly crossed his mind. But some double agent, buried inside the Order of Thaddeus, under his watch? No way would he consider it. Flat no way. Especially not with Weiss breathing down his neck. That'd surely be catnip to his witch hunt.

He shook off the thought. "Anything's possible, but—"

"And this seems far more probable than not," Celeste continued with interruption. "Three times we've been found. Tracked, really."

"Tracked…That's a good way of putting it."

"Which doesn't bode well."

"It's the Watchers offspring, I tell you," Elijah said, shaking his head before taking a swig of coffee.

Torres crossed her arms. "What are Watchers, *muchacho*?"

"I'm with Naomi," said Celeste. "I believe you mentioned this earlier. However, I'm uncertain of the meaning. I certainly don't recall such a term as part of my religious upbringing."

"Nope." Elijah laughed. "You wouldn't."

"And why not?"

"Because they're not in any Christian text and certainly not part of ecclesial catechesis. At least not named as such. Although, I suppose there is a mention of the good kind in the Book of Daniel..."

"Again, what are they, *muchacho*?" Torres prodded.

He answered her in what Silas assumed was Spanish.

"How about," Gina said, resting a hand on his arm, "you translate for the uninitiated. Both the Spanish language and the Watchers."

Elijah rolled his eyes. "The Watchers are the sons of God in 1 Enoch."

Gina explained, "This is the research I was telling you about. The reason I brought you all this way to the Midwest."

Silas nodded, recognizing that same language from earlier. Sons of God.

"And what," Celeste asked, "are these sons of God you make mention of, for the second time?"

"They concern the other gods in Psalm 82:6 called the sons of the Most High. Elsewhere they're called the *beney ha-elohim*."

Torres snorted a laugh. "Oh, is that all..."

Celeste nodded. "Naomi is right. What are you going on about?"

"Sorry. The Hebrew is '*the sons of God.*'"

Torres furrowed her brow. "Don't you mean angels?"

"Nope. They are what the text says they are. Gods. They outrank angels. The Hebrew word for *angel* is entirely different."

"Are they demons then?"

"Not exactly. Some are indeed fallen spiritual beings, but they outrank demons as well. The details aren't important."

"What is?" Silas finally asked, eager for the man to get to it.

Elijah snapped his head toward him. "The Book of Genesis, chapter 6."

"Cain and Abel?" Torres asked.

He frowned. "That's Genesis 4. I said Genesis 6."

"Yeah, yeah. Cool your jets. What's it matter?"

He smirked. "It matters because that's where rebellious members of Yahweh's divine council have sex with human women."

"Hold the phone. *Qué dijiste*?"

"I said—"

"I know what you said, *muchacho*. But ain't never heard that one before."

"I agree with Naomi, here," said Celeste. "I'm a bit foggy on the details of this one."

"Here, why don't I..." Silas snatched a well-worn Bible from Peter's desk. A big one with a brown leather cover, pages edged in faded gold and a red ribbon marking the center.

Opening it, he found Genesis 6 and read aloud:

When people began to multiply on the face of the ground, and daughters were born to them, the sons of God saw that they were fair; and they took wives for themselves of all that they chose. Then the Lord said, "My spirit shall not abide in mortals forever, for they are flesh; their days shall be one hundred twenty years." The Nephilim were on the earth in those days—and also afterward—when the sons of God went in to the daughters of humans, who bore children to them. These were the heroes that were of old, warriors of renown.

"I don't like that translation," Elijah said, "but that will do."

"It goes on with the lead-up to humanity's wickedness and Noah finding favor in the sight of the Lord."

"Noah?" Torres said with a start.

Celeste said, "As in the flood narrative?"

Elijah smirked. "You're a quick one?"

Silas couldn't help but suppress a grin. Blunt and said what he thought. Was warming to the fella.

"These opening verses in Genesis 6 launch the Great Flood story," Elijah explained. "In some of the ancient Jewish books that didn't make it into the Bible, like the Book of Enoch, the actors in this story named the sons of God are called Watchers."

He sprang to his feet, bobbing back and forth on his heels with pent up energy. Clearly ready to unleash it on the room. He also started up that tick, his thumb touching each of his fingers before repeating it while he paced.

"What's fascinating about this story in Genesis is that it reflects other kinds of stories that all the other major religions and cultures around the world also possess."

Torres snorted a laugh. "You mean the one about gods mating with women?"

"The Mesopotamians and Greeks," he went on, ignoring her question, "Egyptians and other African tribes, even Native Americans and Asian cultures. Each have a story within their religious and cultural worldview that tells of beings coming down from heaven to mate with women, eventually birthing unusual offspring."

Silas sat back and brought a hand to his chin, intrigued by the thread beginning to connect to what was happening in their world, and what Gina had shared before about abductee stories, especially from women.

"What kind of unusual offspring?" he asked.

Elijah spun on his heels to face him. "These non-Semitic cultures and religions posit divine-human hybrids birthed with the intention to rule over humanity with divine right. These beings breached the established boundaries, falling from their heavenly positions."

The room went silent, but it dawned on Silas what he was getting at.

"You're speaking of these sons of God, aren't you? These ancient people, wherever they were in the world—they mistook the sons of God for some sort of space visitors."

"Aliens!" exclaimed Torres.

Celeste added, "Which would mean—"

Silas stood with interruption. "Which would mean people in our own day could mistake alien visitors for these fallen sons of God!"

Elijah nodded. "Bingo. At least their Watcher-spirit offspring."

"Mind blown." Torres made an exploding motion with her hands at the side of her head, throwing up an explosion sound for good measure.

Silas could relate.

"Because of Hollywood," Gina said, adding to the discussion now, "you'd be hard pressed to find anyone who isn't familiar enough with alien abductee narratives, which frequently speak of sexual contact as part of their alien abduction experience."

"I'm afraid to ask," said Celeste, "but in what way?"

"Sperm harvesting for men, the harvesting of female eggs. Obviously, forced intercourse."

"Which sounds eerily like this part of the Bible." It was Peter, adding his own voice into the mix. Understandably laced with fear.

Elijah shuffled to his chair and plopped down, leaning toward the group. "It also connects to the future when Christ returns."

Now Peter leaned forward, slapping his palms on his desk with a thud. "Huh?"

"I'm with him," said Torres, yanking a thumb his way.

Celeste said, "You're speaking about the end times."

"The apocalypse," added Silas, dread growing in his belly at the connection.

Elijah nodded. "Think about the Gospel of Matthew, chapter 24."

"Not too quick on the Bible-pistol draw there, prof," said Torres.

"*But about that day and hour no one knows,*'" Elijah quoted, eyes closed and head tilted back, "*neither the angels of heaven, nor the Son, but only the Father. For as the days of Noah were, so will be the coming of the Son of Man. For as in those days before the flood they were eating and drinking, marrying and giving in marriage, until the day Noah entered the ark, and they knew nothing until the flood came and swept them all away, so too will be the coming of the Son of Man.*'"

Silas shifted. "Jesus' discourse on the Day of the Lord, and the necessity for watchfulness. To keep awake, to live right, because no one knows when Christ will return."

"And the last thing you want," Torres added, "is to be caught with your pants around your ankles, so to speak."

Elijah frowned. "Interesting visual, but close enough. Yes, that's true. When Jesus' disciples asked him when he was going to come back to Earth, Jesus connected the events leading up to the flood to his second coming. '*For as the days of Noah were, so will be the coming of the Son of Man.*' But not like you might think."

"And what might we think?" asked Silas.

"You said it yourself. You defined those events in moral terms, living right. I can't fault you, because most Christians think Jesus means cultural sinfulness as well."

"But you're saying those events," Celeste said, "those sinful acts, aren't what Jesus was referencing?"

"Nope," said Elijah. "You'll notice Jesus refers to 'marrying and giving in marriage' a verse later."

"Right, what of it?"

"Who is doing the marrying and giving in marriage?"

Silas sighed with irritation. Wasn't accustomed to being schooled like this. Not in the slightest, and not by someone in his thirties. But he let it go. He needed Elijah on his side, and his pride wouldn't accomplish that.

"Why don't you help us out, prof," Silas said instead.

"It's easy. The ones marrying and giving in marriage are the only actors in Genesis 6 leading to the events that trigger the flood."

Torres said, "Who are..."

"The sons of God and the human women."

"You mean the spiritual beings who birthed what you think is ET?"

"Exactly. The Watchers."

"Which means," Celeste said, "the revelation of extraterrestrial biological entities, and their spacecraft technology, could be the harbinger of the apocalypse?"

Elijah turned to her and nodded, taking a swig of coffee and saying nothing more.

"But that can't be right," Silas protested. "The flood was triggered by God's regret for making such rebellious beings—human beings. Not for supernatural beings impregnating human women!"

"Nope."

"Yes."

"Nope."

Silas sighed, bringing a hand to his forehead and rubbing away an ache. This wasn't working. They needed answers. Needed to find Gapinski for one, but also needed clarity about these paranormal experiences. Definitely didn't need sophomoric theories about ET from a thirtysomething Protestant seminary professor!

A *biblical* theology professor, no less, who didn't seem to care a lick about how *historical* theology and *doctrinal* theology had viewed the issue over the course of the Church's eras. From the early fathers to the Medieval scholastics and beyond. Completely disregarded how the historic Church had understood the natural and supernatural worlds!

Which should have made complete sense. After all, Elijah was a Protestant and taught at an evangelical seminary!

Silas grinned to himself at his funny. But then his face dropped at the insult.

He shifted in his seat, guilt washing over him. They were on the same side here. He knew that. And mocking him for being on part of the Church's bench that wasn't always the most historically rooted was lame. Should listen to the man, given his Old Testament experience, and even his Jewishness. He was clearly knowledgeable about the Bible and the deeper, more supernatural worldview of Scripture, as well as the Jewish worldview behind the Hebrew faith that later informed the New Testament.

Which left Silas exposed for what he didn't know. For what he lacked in knowledge about the Bible, about the Jewish worldview that was a backdrop for the Christian faith, about the supernatural realm that could very well be breaking into their natural realm.

As UFOs and ETs...

"What about this sons of God business?" Celeste asked, bringing Silas's attention back to the moment. "Why would a human woman want to have sex with these creatures, anyhow? It makes no bloomin' sense!"

"That's where my research has been taking me," Elijah replied.

"And where is that?" asked Silas, genuinely interested in understanding.

Elijah's eyes flittered up to the ceiling, and his fingers started doing that tick again. Thumb to forefinger, thumb to middle, thumb to ring finger, thumb to pinkie. Then rinse and repeat.

"It's complicated..." he went with, saying nothing more.

"How so?" Silas pressed.

The professor suddenly sprang to his feet and started pacing again. "Look, all I'm trying to get you to understand is that the Bible and other ancient religious texts all inform us that there is a supernatural world that interacts with the natural, human world. Has been from the very beginning of time. Why is that so complicated?"

He was raising his voice and gesturing wildly. "Those supernatural beings, the sons of God, or their offspring rather—they can appear in the flesh, and the Bible makes reference to some of these occasions. Ancient religious texts not included in the Bible suggest they can shape-shift. Enoch says this, as does one of the Nag Hammadi Gnostic texts found in Egypt decades ago that specifically says this is how Genesis 6 happened."

"Eli..." Gina said, grabbing Elijah's attention and gesturing to his seat.

He glanced around and swallowed hard before sliding back into his chair.

"Sorry. Sometimes I can get like this when people press me for answers I don't have and am uncertain about."

Silas nodded, appreciating his honesty. He glanced at Celeste, who took a breath and puffed it out, looking uncertain about the man.

Silas said, "If I may ask, Professor Fox—"

"Elijah," he interrupted. "Or, Eli, if you prefer."

He smiled. "Alright, Elijah, if I may ask, what is it you're uncertain of?"

"The connection between all of this." He swept his arm around the room, but Silas understood he meant all that had been happening. "I know there's something there, I just know it."

"Then let's make the connection." He paused, knowing the truth of the matter. It was out of his hands. He needed this quirky man to help put the pieces together. "Let's get you what you need to make the connections."

"Nope. Can't do it."

He flashed panicked eyes at Celeste. Was it something he said? Had he burned the bridge? Had the man caught his irritation at him and his knowledge?

Taking over, she asked, "Why is that Elijah?"

He shrugged. "What I need is in the Vatican Archives."

Silas grinned, glancing at Celeste with a nod.

"I think we can help you with that."

Elijah brightened, his eyes widening and mouth curling into a grin. "Oh my cheeps. Really?"

He chuckled, but before he could respond, there was a faint buzzing sound in Peter's office. Looked like it was from Celeste's pocket.

She apologized and withdrew her phone. "Hold a minute, it's Nicky."

Celeste answered the call and listened while the MI6 agent spoke, *uhh*-ing and *hmm*-ing until her face brightened and she flashed a thumbs up.

Finally, some good news...

"Brilliant, Nicky!" exclaimed Celeste. "We'll rendezvous at Paderborn Lippstadt and motor on from there. Cheers."

She ended the call and slid the phone in her pocket.

"Sounds like news," said Torres.

"Good news, I hope," Silas said.

Celeste grinned. "The best bloomin' news one could hope for! Nicky reports that his contacts with MI6 flagged the tail numbers of a decommissioned military transport aircraft leaving the area."

Silas slid to the end of the couch. "What plane? Why were they flagged? What was on it?"

"Holy twenty-questions, Batman," Torres said.

"A good chance Gapinski was on it, that's what!" Celeste explained. "Another flight manifest shows the same tail numbers leaving an airfield in the eastern part of Turkey."

"Turkey?"

"The one Nicky mentioned yesterday and wanted my help investigating. That's why the tail number was flagged by MI6."

"Good chance, indeed," Silas said. "And good news."

"The best news!" Torres agreed.

"Which means we've got work to do. Sounds like you're already set to meet up with Nicky, Celeste."

"And me!" Torres raised her hand.

"Fine." Silas nodded to Elijah and Gina. "Care for a trip to Rome?"

"I hate flying," said Elijah.

He sighed, another roadblock thrown up.

"But I'll go."

Silas nodded and prayed the good Lord would make their paths straight.

To rescue Gapinski and get to the bottom of whatever the heck was going on.

And discover what the Church's Archives might say about it...

CHAPTER 29

ROME, ITALY.

Silas finally managed to navigate through the congested Eternal City along the Tiber, the famous dome of Saint Peter's Basilica peeking just above a line of buildings, making for their destination, the reason for climbing into a jet in the dead of night and zooming across the Atlantic.

Archivum Apostolicum Vaticanum.

Better known as the Vatican Archives.

Normally not accessible to the public but only to scholars once they are seventy-five years old, the Order of Thaddeus had a special arrangement with the vault of Church creeds and confessions and papal papers stretching back centuries. They also had made a special connection with one of the curators, Bartholomew Braley. The young American had helped them uncover the Emperor Code and save the Church from the hands of a wicked conspiracy that was definitely on par with bargain-bin ebook thrillers.

Zoe, the intrepid SEPIO operational support guru, had sent two Gulfstreams to the Grand Rapids International Airport to transport two groups to two separate locales: Celeste and Torres to Büren, Germany, to meet up with Nicky and suss out the lead to recover Gapinski and perhaps the bones that had been swiped from their dig; Silas and his new honorary SEPIO agents, former FBI agents Elijah Fox and Gina Anderson, to Rome.

Had been a relatively calm flight, Elijah cashing out with sleeping pills that seemed more like tranquilizers to help him cope with flying. Gina had explained the fear was deeply rooted in childhood trauma, but she didn't get into it. Silas didn't ask, just thankful the man was willing to overcome his fears for the sake of the operation, and the Church. She had joined her former partner in sleeping most of the time while Silas nursed a few too many Glenlivet whiskeys during their ten-hour flight to Rome.

Couldn't help it. The fruity notes of cinnamon, apple, vanilla, and caramel from the 18-year bottle had been a balm for his worries and confusion the puddle-jump over. Worries about what the arrival of ETs meant to his faith; confusion over what his faith said about such intelligent life-forms, if they even existed in the universe.

Silas had understood humanity to be the crowning achievement of God's creative ambition. The "very good" exclamation-point declaration to his creation. We were the ones created in his image and likeness, nothing else. Certainly not aliens! When people look in the mirror and see something far less than the Image of God, something is disastrously wrong.

At some level, this is a deeply mysterious thing to try and describe, that we are made in the image and likeness of God. Theologians, like Silas himself, had often found it elusive. But an insight from the first book had clued him in. Something from Genesis 5:1-3:

> *This is the list of the descendants of Adam. When*
> *God created humankind, he made them in the*
> *likeness of God. Male and female he created*

> *them, and he blessed them and named them*
> *"Humankind" when they were created.*
> *When Adam had lived one hundred thirty years, he*
> *became the father of a son in his likeness,*
> *according to his image, and named him Seth.*

When teaching students in his religion electives at Princeton, Silas had asked them to consider the traits passed along from parent to child—in the same way aspects of God's own traits were "passed" along to Adam and all humanity.

Children reason, make moral choices, and have a conscience. They have emotions, create, form relationships, and communicate with others. Somehow, in some unique way, these aspects actually reflect our Creator.

Those tender moments between spouses or times friends supported you are in some way like the relational dynamics of Father, Son, and Spirit—the Holy Trinity.

The times of rip-roaring laughter around a table at the local pub or coffeehouse after a well-timed punchline in some way reflects the cleverness and wit of God himself.

How you creatively express yourself through music or clothes or quilting or sculpting or decorating or any number of creative things images the Creator.

The rage someone feels in the face of injustice or the deep concern or grief a parent feels for their child or the inner movement of the soul after hearing a moving story—we feel and experience emotion because God himself feels.

Who we are in our humanness somehow, in some way reflects our Creator. As Image Bearers of God, our personhood is patterned after God. The Imago Dei, as it has been called.

Certainly gives a whole new definition to our questions about our meaning and worth. Should also impact how we view the people around us, and ourselves.

Silas continued his trek toward the Vatican, an ache welling within from missing those days teaching those students.

He shook away the memory, and the regret at being fired, the regret at having to give up about the only thing he'd been good at in life—apart from blowing things up and shooting up a nest of bad guys.

Turning into a roundabout, he got to thinking about the other thing that was really chapping his backside about this whole operation.

This business about other gods that Elijah went on about. Probably the most unsettling part, even beyond what all the nonsense from the past few days meant to the meaning of human nature, the nature of our human identity.

Because if Elijah was right, that there were competing gods to Yahweh, as lesser as they might be, and if the Bible had something to say about them—well, what did that mean for the nature of God, the doctrine of God that Silas had studied and pondered and taught for years? What did it mean for the argument Christians had made for centuries in the exclusivity of Jesus Christ, that he alone was the way of salvation—the way to the Father, as he himself voiced in John's Gospel?

From the very beginning, Christians have declared: *'I believe in God the Father, Almighty, Maker of heaven and earth.'* Not little *g* god with a pluralized *s*—not many gods, or sons of God, like Elijah was spouting off.

God.

The only one true God embedded in these ancient words from the Apostles' Creed. A belief that stretched back well before those opening lines to the Church's Creed were penned.

As Paul declared in his first letter to the Church of Corinth, chapter 8:

> *We know that "no idol in the world really exists," and*
> *that "there is no God but one." Indeed, even*

though there may be so-called gods in heaven or
on earth—as in fact there are many gods and
many lords—yet for us there is one God, the
Father, from whom are all things and for whom
we exist, and one Lord, Jesus Christ, through
whom are all things and through whom we exist.

Citing Israel's own theological code declaring 'no God but one,' Paul equated Jesus Christ with the only one true God of Israel.

It's called christological monotheism, Eli—the belief that the one God of the universe is Jesus. So why don't he put that in his pipe and smoke it!

Silas startled, worried he'd muttered his irritation.

He glanced in the rear-view mirror to Elijah, who was looking out at the Eternal City awash in the brilliance of the setting sun.

Closing in on the Archives, Silas recalled that when Paul visited the multi-god city of Athens, he acknowledged their spiritual interests but then declared those gods false and called its worshipers ignorant. And vintage Christians do the same in our own multi-faith world!

Christians join Paul and the rest of the historic Church voices in gently, but honestly, proclaiming 'an idol is nothing at all in the world' and 'there is no God but one.' Not that nonsense about other gods, as lesser as they might be to Yahweh, that Elijah was spouting off!

The Buddha is nothing at all in the world. Same for Krishna and Allah, as much as Zeus and Artemis.

There is no God but Father, Son, and Spirit—co-equal in power, majesty, and glory. Revealed in three persons and possessing one essence. And he is both the Author of our Story and an Actor within it.

As Author he alone is King. He alone is high and lifted up.

He alone is holy. He is distinct and separate from all other things. The only one true God who is outside and above creation. God is not part of creation, he is distinct from it, separate from it. He is not some sort of energy or spark or force that's part of the universe.

Unlike most religious concepts of the gods that are distant and removed from the world, Christians do not worship a distant God. He isn't removed from what happens in life on Earth. No, the Church worships a personal God who is involved with the world. He breaks into our world, he is part of it by being part of the Story of his people at every turn.

God doesn't reveal himself through history and Scripture as some cosmic alien being come to destroy us. No, he shows up time and time again as the God who came to rescue us!

Take the start of Israel's story. God showed up in a burning bush while Moses was tending his flocks on a mountainside. Why? Because he heard the cries of oppression from his people. And he came to do something about it. To rescue them. Then, several hundred years after this story, God showed up again in a small insignificant city while shepherds were tending their flocks outside of Bethlehem. Why? Because he heard the cries of oppression from his people. And he came to do something about it.

As the Gospel of John says, God became flesh and blood and moved into our human neighborhood. He became one of us! God walked around in our world. God experienced everything that life has to offer. He experienced our pain. Our fears. Our hardship and struggle. He understands this life because he *lived* this life.

The absurdity all brought a surprising rise of emotion to Silas. He cleared his throat and blinked his eyes.

What kind of God does that? Chooses to become an actor in the very drama he created, yet spun wildly out of control because of his rebellious creations?

Yet this is who the one true God is. He came to take away our guilt, to pay the price for our sins. To rescue us!

Is *this* the god of Islam?

Is *this* the god of Buddhism?

Is *this* the multi-gods of Hinduism?

The questions haunted Silas as he drove the Black G-Class Mercedes toward the Vatican. Gapinski would be proud, and a bit jealous, the man's ride of choice. Weiss would definitely not be happy, the man blowing a gasket at the needless expense and chalking it up to yet another reason why Silas wasn't fit for the job.

Whatever. He had bigger things to worry about than expense accounts. Like what the Vatican Archives held for the future of the Church, and humanity.

Housed in a fortress-like part of the Holy See, the secretive nature of the Vatican, along with the hidden trove of ecclesiastical documents within, have fanned the flames of speculative fiction and conspiracy theories for decades. The central repository in the Vatican City for all the acts put into effect by the Holy See also contained precious documents stemming from the Church broadly for centuries. Particularly germane to the Catholic branch, the state papers, correspondence, papal account books, are archived within, as well as many other documents which the Church has accumulated over the centuries.

Silas was hoping those other documents would point them in the direction that would shed light on the biblical and theological side to this blasted UFO and alien conspiracy nonsense.

One end of Silas's mouth turned upward at the sight of the basilica looming larger now, a beacon of faith for millions of believers, for what the Church had taught about our human identity and even God's identity—standing the test of time.

Because while he didn't want to admit it, the whole operation had left him feeling uncertain about both beliefs—rocked, even.

He rolled up to a military police checkpoint at the *Via della Conciliazione* with Saint Peter's Square dead ahead, the dome gleaming a brilliant white underneath the glowing moon and a canister of lighting strategically aimed to draw the eye toward the holy place. After a radio check and confirmation of their appointment inside, the MP let them through, this time without the aid of an escort of Vatican gendarmerie. Must be moving up in the world. Perhaps being Order Master carried with it an untapped perk.

He thanked the guard and pulled the Escalade forward down the dark cobblestone road normally bustling with tourists. At that hour, it was completely barren, the five-story brown buildings of various shades almost pressing in against them as they made their way down the long corridor of businesses and apartments guided by the orange glow of lamps mounted high on stone pillars.

He trundled along toward the square before slowing at another military checkpoint guarded by a pair of men dressed in colorful Renaissance-era uniforms striped in red and blue, orange and yellow, necks ringed by white collars and heads fitted with black berets.

The Pontifical Swiss Guard.

Butterflies suddenly fluttered in his stomach, especially after they waved him onward.

The drive in was even quieter than the main roads in Rome outside the Vatican, as if they had entered into a completely other dimension. Looked about like he remembered it from last year, with manicured bushes and lawns, buildings styled in Roman and Baroque and Gothic architecture.

He bypassed a small parking lot adjacent to a six-story building, dipping through a small arched entryway that led inside to a vast courtyard that served as a parking lot for the Archives and other ecclesiastical departments for the Holy See.

Silas parked then turned to his new teammates.

"What do you think?"

Elijah shrugged. "Could use a power wash."

He chuckled. About what he expected from the guy.

"I can't believe I'm here," Gina whispered. "Ever since a girl, I've dreamed about this place."

Silas said, "I hear you. Just wait until you see what's inside. Both above and below ground."

"Below ground?" the pair said with shock.

He led them up a short set of stone stairs, his breath feeling shallow at the excitement of entering into one of the most hallowed, if not secretive, spaces in Christendom—for the second time!

He just hoped beyond those glass doors leading inside were answers.

Because if not...well, the world and the Church were screwed.

CHAPTER 30

Stepping through the heavy glass doors into the vestibule of the Vatican Archives was like stepping through a portal into a world that had held the Church together for centuries. While embroiled in secrecy and conspiracy, the Archives had preserved the most crucial creeds, declarations, and records to safeguard and guide the once-for-all faith entrusted to God's holy people.

Just the place a trio of operatives with the Order of Thaddeus would feel right at home.

Silas's senses were instantly flooded with the smell of aged paper and old furniture and vintage artwork—everything you'd expect in a museum or an archive of the Church's affairs. And that wasn't even touching on the eye candy spread before them like *Willy Wonka and the Chocolate Factory*!

"Oh my cheeps..." Elijah said, craning his neck around in wonder at the sights.

"I hear ya, brother," Silas said.

"Me, too," Gina agreed, voice laden with marvel and wonder, with the same written across her face.

He understood the feeling, his breath now fully taken away by the vast, sparsely lit space, a faint white glow filtering down through large windows above anchored in the finely gilded ceiling. He'd been in some pretty impressive ecclesial buildings before, and this ranked high on the list for capital-I impressive. And this was the second time he had taken in the sights! Still, just as impressive and spiritually suggestive as the first glimpsing.

Stone angels peered down from above, anchored to several archways supported by thirty-foot chocolate marble columns with similar marble tiling the floor in a cream and brown pattern with more of the chocolate marble decorating the walls stretching in all four directions. The gilding continued in abundance around the inner arches and ringed the perimeter of the ceiling, Latin phrases too dark to read etched inside. Biblical figures and other Christian saints made of similar stone rested in alcoves stretching the length of the space in between a series of arches that seemed to run forever.

The group stepped farther inside, their footfalls echoing in the silence of their awe. They reached a small section and stared agape toward the ceiling, an alighted dome painted sky blue with floating angelic beings amidst a cloudy swirl of pinks and yellows and whites mesmerizing them.

"Alright, I confess," said Elijah, "the flight was worth it."

Gina nodded. "I'd say…"

"Even as a Protestant, I can appreciate the sacred space."

"We'll make a convert out of you yet, Eli."

"This just might."

Silas chuckled, understanding the awe that the Protestant seminary professor was feeling. He himself still appreciated the level of beauty and pageantry the Catholic Church brought to the faith, unlike his Protestant brothers and sisters who seemed more interested in fancy lights and fog machines.

Though he agreed that through the blood of Christ we have direct access to the throne of God, as the book of Hebrews teaches, the veil being torn and the gift of grace and mercy dispensed directly to believers by the Spirit—still there was something about the high church churchiness of what he had experienced as a boy that did something for his faith that more low-church varieties couldn't.

Perhaps that's why he enjoyed the Order of Thaddeus's headquarters so much, located in the Episcopal Church building of the Washington National Cathedral, and the Anglican faith itself—Protestant doctrine and Catholic ceremony, the best of both worlds. Though he wasn't all that interested in parsing out folks who embraced Jesus as Lord and Savior. If it was good enough for the Apostle Paul, it was good enough for him—whether high church or low church.

A set of rushing steps jolted the trio from their trance.

Coming toward them from the other side of the building was a tall, trim man in a black cassock, a bright purple sash wrapping his waist and the same color edging the sleeves and neck and buttons in bright piping. The uniform marked him as an upper-level ecclesiastical official. Silas recognized the young man from their first visit.

Bartholomew Braley had a clean face, bright blue eyes, and a chock of dirty-blond hair. A Southerner who had been overly helpful and vital to an operation last go around. Silas just hoped the man could offer a second run on both his generosity and skill.

Reaching them, he smiled and bowed. "Greetings, in the name of the Father, Son, and Holy Ghost."

The Order Master and the two former FBI agents returned the same greeting.

Silas extended his hand; Bartholomew reached in for an embrace. The pair hugged a greeting and offered a few brief words of small talk about the flight over and weather, the latest rumblings about the Pope and other bits of ecclesiastical intrigue.

"I must confess," Bartholomew said, "I was surprised to hear from you a second time."

Silas said, "Well, I was surprised we needed your help a second time."

"Something about aliens and gods?"

He glanced Elijah's way, who was staring off at the ceiling and working through that finger tick of his. Whether the setting or the circumstances were throwing the man, he couldn't tell. Just hoped it didn't get in the way of the operation.

Silas went with: "Something like that."

Bartholomew smiled and bowed. "Regardless, I understand that if the Order is calling upon the Holy See for help, I can trust its urgency. No reason to tarry, how about we get to it."

"Appreciate the help. Lead the way."

Gina grabbed Silas's arm. "This is so exciting!"

He chuckled. "I know the feeling."

"Don't you think, Eli?"

The man shrugged. "It's passable for excitement."

Silas said, "Just wait until we get down below."

Bartholomew shuffled forward toward an ornately decorated bronze door. He withdrew a large ring of bronze keys, searching for the right one in the mess. Finding it, he stuck the key in the lock and turned.

It unlocked with a *click*, and he swung the door open on well-oiled hinges, giving not a squeak or sigh.

Bartholomew motioned for the agents to enter. "In we go..."

"Just like that?" Elijah said, stepping toward the opening. "I expected a far more sophisticated measure of security at the door to the Church's secret archives than a mere bronze key."

He shrugged. "What did you expect? A series of keypads followed by complicated puzzles and booby-trapped corridors?"

"Of course."

Bartholomew slapped him on the back with a chuckle.

"Sounds like you've been reading a few too many conspiracy thrillers."

"I don't read fiction and would never be caught dead reading conspiracy thrillers. Too cliché and pedantic."

Silas chuckled. "Well, you're living one now, brother, so might as well start reading to know what you're in for."

Gina said, "I'm sure we'll have plenty of time for reading when we're through with this. Until then, it might be wise to get to it. Whatever conspiracy is roiling the world isn't waiting, and I suspect the solution is waiting down below."

Silas nodded Bartholomew onward, appreciating the woman's no-nonsense approach to the world. Could use someone like her working for the Order, on top of Elijah. Something to think about, that's for sure.

The man led them down a corridor with walls decorated by the same chocolate marble and the same cream-and-brown tiles stretching its length, joined by saintly statues in memoriam. Same for the ceiling, paved in gilt, with carved angels watching their movements from above. Soon they arrived at another set of bronze doors anchored at the end of a long hallway. This time with the keypad entry Elijah had been expecting.

"Now this makes more sense," he said, eying the device.

Bartholomew withdrew a key fob separate from the ring he had used earlier, waving it at the security device.

With a *click*, the doors unlocked, withdrawing to reveal an elevator.

To which Gina gasped and spun back behind Elijah.

"Egads! What is that thing?"

Silas threw her a furrowed brow. "Uh, an elevator."

"You never told me about an elevator!"

Elijah turned to her. "You'll be fine, Gina colada..."

She sucked in a breath and shook her head. "No, I won't!"

He turned to Bartholomew. "Is there another way into the bowels of the Archives?"

Their guide shook his head. "No, I'm sorry, there ain't."

Gina promptly sat down on the floor. "Then I'm staying put."

Silas ran a frustrated hand through his hair, then leaned toward Elijah and whispered, "What's the problem?"

He turned to him. "Elevatophobia."

"That's a thing?"

"Acrophobia," Gina corrected with eyes closed. She swallowed and added, "compounded by claustrophobia."

Silas muttered a silent curse and turned to Bartholomew for help. He just stood and shrugged. Now he sighed. They didn't have time for this.

But they also didn't need his judgment. Lord knew he had his own foibles, including a mild fear of flying and heights himself. Not as pronounced as these two, and didn't manifest in these sorts of protestations, but he had his own issues. In fact, during his first operation with SEPIO, lingering PTSD had reared its ugly head—resulting in a fatality thanks to him freezing during a firefight that still haunted him.

So he was the last person to judge.

But they were in the middle of an operation, and the clock was ticking. How he would move it along and get Gina back on board—he didn't have a clue. Totally out of his league here.

Elijah knelt and put up a hand in front of her. Not touching her knee or shoulder, nowhere on her body. Just hovered an open palm in front.

"Gina colada, look at me."

Her eyes snapped open, and she flitted them toward the man before landing on his hand. She instantly put up a palm herself. Again, not touching his, but just hovering it over his hand. Like the pair had done the first time they had reconnected at Elijah's office.

Silas recalled something about autistic people having a rough time with touch and personal space. Seemed like the next best thing to make a connection, the intimacy and reassurance of touch reimagined for the pair with their unique situation.

"Remember what you told me," Elijah said, "before we boarded the plane to come here?"

She started twirling her hair now, really going at it before plucking a single strand. She nodded, saying nothing.

"You got this. That's what you said. Haven't been in a plane in years, but you reassured me I could do it. And I did."

Gina let go of her hair and sighed, her face softening with his words.

"You got this, Georgina Anderson."

Silas thought he caught a faint smile at her mouth before she withdrew her hand and stood.

"OK, Eli. But I don't have to like it."

He shook his head. "Nope, you don't."

She walked to the threshold of the open elevator door, took a breath, closed her eyes, and took one giant step inside and stood planted at the center of the elevator.

"I've got this," Gina muttered. "I've got this..."

Silas sighed a breath he didn't know he was holding. That was close. He normally expected external forces to foil their forward movement, not roadblocks on the inside—certainly not the psychological ones.

But the newcomers had overcome their fear for the sake of the operation, if only for a moment. Mad respect for them, that's for sure. And through the power of words where the power of touch was absent. Something else he could learn from the pair who confounded his expectations.

Elijah joined his former FBI partner, shuffling around Gina's side to the back of the carriage and spreading his hands against its walls to brace himself for the descent. No doubt having to overcome a lesser internal threat to his aerophobia. Bartholomew joined them at the controls, and Silas made up the rear at the entrance, nodding at their guide to get to it.

Holding up his key fob again, Bartholomew hit a button and down they went.

His ears popped the farther they descended. Gina's muttering picked up pace, continuing on for all five stories. Whatever got her through.

Then the carriage slowed and eased up with a lurch, and the doors opened to reveal a well-lit hallway of white-washed stone walls, a red runner with golden tassels across a polished walnut floor leading the way through. Modest, unassuming, and entirely discrete. Could have been any number of offices or university corridors strewn across the globe.

"Cheated death once again," Gina muttered, making the familiar sign of the cross.

"Amen and amen," Elijah echoed.

Silas quickly exited to give them space, and the two quickly followed.

The air was sweet and sanitized, temperate and climate-controlled. Which made sense, given the kinds of documents and relics preserved beneath the Vatican Archives.

He just hoped there was something in them that would blow open the conspiracy. Because they were running out of time.

Hustling through the corridor, he glanced at his phone, scrolling through WeShare.

Dang.

More reports coming in on the #TheTruthIsMe topic strand. And no update yet from Celeste on what, if anything, they found in Germany. Probably too early, anyhow. Just as weird was no news from the US government, the President or Homeland Security. Santos was MIA as America made first contact. What was up with that?

"Just down the hall is a room," Bartholomew said. "Same one you used last time when you were investigating the crazy Constantine conspiracy."

Soon they arrived, and Silas followed Bartholomew inside. The other two followed close behind, their gasps and hushed amazement echoing his own the first time he had come.

The workroom looked more like a CIA black-site warehouse, stretching the length of a modest basketball court and nearly another story in height. All the chocolate marble walls and creamy brown tiles from the main level were replaced by the utilitarian white walls and charcoal carpet Silas had grown to loathe from his Ranger days.

A black cage stood in one corner, wires coming out the top with tiny blinking red and blue and white lights behind a mesh fence. A sophisticated server, powering several workstations silently arranged in a neat row on one wall. The far end was anchored by a set of four flat-panel displays arranged as a massive display, like the White House situation room.

The whole environment also reminded Silas of SEPIO headquarters back in DC and their outposts strewn across the globe. Which was impressive, considering the sclerotic nature of the Church that was often a century behind the times. But that wasn't all of it. And not at all what delighted him.

Along the opposite wall and running down the middle were tables piled with ancient manuscripts. Very ancient, by the look of it. And smelling all metalicy and pulpy and musty from age.

Tables stacked with the Church's cache of documents stretching back centuries. Reinforced steel cases of thick glass that meant protective business housed fragile-looking parchments browned with age and scrawled with neat Greek and Latin characters, their pages well preserved. Not surprising, considering the Church had perfected the art of climate control. A few codices bound by stiff leather and smelling of the heavenly hides sat together on one table. One was open, and beautiful hand-drawn marginals ran up and down the page next to the text, bright and colorful flowers and vines and cherubs blowing golden trumpets.

Elijah stepped past Silas. He crossed his arms and gave the room a sweeping gaze. "This will do."

Silas said, "What is it you're looking for?"

"An ancient Jewish manuscript I'll bet is buried somewhere inside."

"Jewish?" Bartholomew said with surprise.

He spun toward the man. "That's right. Something I've been researching that forms the backdrop to the worldview of the early Christians. Something ancient flowing from the same worldview articulated in the Book of Deuteronomy."

Bartholomew waved a hand toward that server anchored in the back corner. "If it's research you need, that mainframe will give you all the power you need. All of the knowledge and wisdom gleaned through the Church's lifetime and contained in the Vatican Archives that is germane to the faith has been fully digitized."

Elijah slapped his hands together and rubbed them with a grin. "Then let's get started."

Walking to the front, the Archives caretaker led the professor to a workstation. Behind it was a massive screen, dormant of any information. Resting on a table was a tablet device. Bartholomew picked it up and handed it to Elijah.

He took it, eyeing it with interest. "What's this?"

"Your portal into the Church's knowledge." Bartholomew tapped the surface, bringing it to life. On its face was a blue background with a search bar anchored at the center. Wholly unassuming and unadorned, but pregnant with possibilities.

"I assume you know how to work a search bar," Silas said, envy growing at the opportunity Elijah had to dive deep down the rabbit hole. He missed those days, most of his minutes now consumed with paperwork and witch hunts led by Weiss.

"Affirmative," Elijah said, already tapping away on a digital keyboard.

The tablet instantly transformed into lines of results.

The professor ran a finger down the list, scrolling as he went and not stopping.

"What are you searching for, Eli?" Gina asked. She was only met with a finger pointed in the air in silence before he went back to it.

Elijah kept at it for what felt like an hour but was only several minutes, refining his search as he went and returning to his results.

Until he suddenly stopped his scrolling and typing.

And threw up a satisfied grin.

"Gotcha."

CHAPTER 31

Not a small amount of envy wound through Silas as the young professor finished up his search, standing back with that satisfied grin on his face. He clearly knew how to leverage technology to further his research aims, something that was a bit out of his league. To his irritating shame.

Back in the day, Silas had been something of a whiz himself, but more because of mastering how to navigate hardbacks and hard-copy evidence to form the backbone of his research endeavors. He'd risen through the academic ranks at Princeton faster than most in his department, and the youngest among the aged professors thanks to those research chops.

And as one of the foremost experts on the emerging field of relicology, the study and research of historic religious relics, Silas had made a name for himself in the field of early Christian religious artifacts and their significance for the Church. Which led him to his own relic passion project, the Shroud of Turin, the cloth believed to be the burial garment of Jesus Christ and the most significant Christian religious artifact.

Which, ironically, had eventually led him to standing in

that very room simmering with envy after his life was blown up —literally, Nous having tried to take him out.

Now this guy, almost a decade younger, was running circles around him on a subject he knew nothing about, using methods that made him feel old. Silas knew he needed to get over himself, but his fatal flaw of envy was rearing its ugly head something fierce.

So he took a breath and threw up a prayer that the Holy Spirit would work to root out that ugly sin that could tank the operation. Not to mention his relationship with Elijah.

To which the Third Person of the Trinity reminded him of a verse from the Book of James on the subject, chapter 3: *'where there is envy and selfish ambition, there will also be disorder and wickedness of every kind.'*

Alright, Lord, hear you loud and clear. Point taken!

Craning over Elijah's shoulder for a viewing, Gina said, "You seemed to know exactly what you were looking for."

"Of course." He turned to Bartholomew. "Your magisterial tech helped matters as well."

The man bowed with a smile, saying nothing but appearing to appreciate the compliment.

"What did you find?" Silas asked, craning over his other shoulder.

The professor cleared his throat and read aloud:

And it came to pass when the sons of men had multiplied that in those days were born unto them beautiful and comely daughters. And the angels, the children of the heaven, saw and lusted after them, and said to one another: "Come, let us choose us wives from among the children of men and beget us children."

And Semjaza, who was their leader, said unto them:

"I fear ye will not indeed agree to do this deed, and I alone shall have to pay the penalty of a great sin."

And they all answered him and said: "Let us all swear an oath, and all bind ourselves by mutual imprecations not to abandon this plan but to do this thing."

Then swear they all together and bound themselves by mutual imprecations upon it. And they were in all two hundred; who descended in the days of Jared on the summit of Mount Hermon, and they called it Mount Hermon, because they had sworn and bound themselves by mutual imprecations upon it.

"That sounds familiar," Gina said, "but I can't place it."

Silas nodded. "I agree. What is it you found? What were you reading?"

"A passage from the Book of Enoch," explained Elijah.

"That's a book you mentioned before," Gina said. "Back in your study."

"And definitely not a book in the Bible," said Silas. "I understand it to be an extra-biblical Jewish source."

Elijah set down the slate device and smiled. "Most believers aren't having much experience with the Book of Enoch. It isn't in the Bible, the Christian Scriptures anyway, but is regarded by our Israelite brethren as Scripture. My people."

"What is this mystery book of yours," asked Gina, "this Book of Enoch?"

"Also understood as 1 Enoch, to separate it from two other works of the same name, it is a pseudepigraphal book."

"A pseudo-what?"

"Not important," he said, waving a dismissive hand. "What is, is that the book is an ancient Hebrew apocalyptic religious text, ascribed by tradition to Enoch."

"The great-grandfather of Noah," said Silas.

"Correct. It contains unique material on the origins of demons and the Nephilim, why some angels fell from heaven, a prophetic exposition of the thousand-year reign of the Messiah, and an expansion on the flood material."

"Sounds like much of what we were talking about earlier," said Gina. "But it's not any book I've ever heard about, that's for sure!"

"And you wouldn't," replied Elijah. "It was written during the Second Temple period of Judaism, most likely during the so-called intertestamental period between Malachi and Matthew. In fact, it would have served as a scriptural backdrop for the New Testament itself."

Silas crossed his arms, frustrated with what seemed like a massive rabbit trail while his partner was missing and rumors of aliens and UFOs, or whatever they were, were bearing down on Earth. Mostly, he just felt out of his league. Elijah clearly knew what he was doing, what he was talking about. Was also far more well-versed in the ancient Hebrew worldview and Old Testament context. Not Silas.

He was a theology guy, and mostly a Christian one. When it came to the Bible, his expertise was more the New Testament than the Old. Even then, his work dealt more with what other people throughout the Church's history said about the Bible than what the Bible itself said. Something he felt exposed about. And something he'd have to fix.

Shifting, he cleared his throat. "I don't understand why we're concerning ourselves with this book. Why is it in the Vatican Archives, anyhow, since the Church hasn't recognized it as Scripture?"

"That isn't entirely true," Bartholomew interjected.

"*It isn't?*" Silas and Gina said together.

Elijah chuckled. "Our illustrious Archives caretaker is

correct. Several early Church Fathers treated 1 Enoch as Scripture. The *Epistle of Barnabas*, a very early letter circulated during the earliest century of the Church, quoted from it as Scripture. Tertullian and Irenaeus, both heavy-hitting theologians, used the same language when referencing 1 Enoch, that it was Scripture."

"Then there's Peter and Jude," said Bartholomew.

Gina raised a brow. "Peter? Like, Peter Peter?"

"And Jude?" said Silas, bringing a hand to his chin.

"Isn't he the one who started your religious order?"

He shifted again and crossed his arms, even more exposed now that he didn't even know the very founder of his order was connected to this mystery book that apparently held the secrets to unlocking this conspiracy. Not good...

"Bingo." Elijah cleared his throat and closed his eyes, then quoted from memory:

> *For if God did not spare angels when they sinned, but sent them to hell, putting them in chains of darkness to be held for judgment; if he did not spare the ancient world when he brought the flood on its ungodly people, but protected Noah, a preacher of righteousness, and seven others.*

"Second Peter, chapter 2," said Bartholomew. "A reference to 1 Enoch."

"Very good, Vatican Archives Man. And now—" He again quoted from memory:

> *Enoch, the seventh from Adam, prophesied about them: "See, the Lord is coming with thousands upon thousands of his holy ones to judge everyone, and to convict all of them of all the ungodly acts they have committed in their ungodliness,*

*and of all the defiant words ungodly sinners have
spoken against him."*

"Jude 14 and 15," Silas said.

"Which directly quotes 1 Enoch," explained Elijah.

"I guess I never caught that before. That even the New Testament writers referenced and quoted from extra-biblical sources."

"Not only that, but the Jewish worldview was largely built around much of what we find in 1 Enoch, as well as several broader themes of the Hebrew Scriptures themselves."

"Let's go back to what you quoted, Eli," Gina said, playing with a lock of her ginger hair. "Because it strikes me as familiar."

"As it should. What I quoted is an expansion of Genesis 6."

He went to quote that portion of Scripture from memory as well when Bartholomew stepped up to the plate instead, saying:

> *When people began to multiply on the face of the
> ground, and daughters were born to them, the
> sons of God saw that they were fair; and they
> took wives for themselves of all that they chose.
> Then the Lord said, "My spirit shall not abide in
> mortals forever, for they are flesh; their days
> shall be one hundred twenty years."*
> *The Nephilim were on the earth in those days—and
> also afterward—when the sons of God went in to
> the daughters of humans, who bore children to
> them. These were the heroes that were of old,
> warriors of renown.*

"Nice work!" Elijah exclaimed, smiling wide and throwing

him a thumbs-up. "Clearly you were trained well in your graduate education."

Silas smirked. "Show off..."

Then he caught himself, heat rising up his neck and blooming in his cheeks.

"I'm sorry," he quickly said, covering for his jerk-face comment, "but what's the point of this?"

Elijah slapped a hand to his forehead. "Oh my cheeps! Forgive my impertinence. I'll move it along. Here, more from Enoch..." He returned to the tablet, reading aloud:

And all the others together with them took unto themselves wives, and they began to go in unto them and to defile themselves with them, and they taught them charms and enchantments, and the cutting of roots, and made them acquainted with plants.

And the wives became pregnant, begetting great giants, and the giants begat Nephilim, who then bore Elioud—growing in accordance with their greatness, who consumed all the labor of men. And when men could no longer sustain them, the giants turned against them and devoured mankind.

"Nephilim..." Silas whispered.

"The giant Fallen Ones, the Watcher-Spirits who tempt humans and draw them away from God."

The professor paused, swiping at the device. "Then another section to connect the dots..."

And Azazel taught men to make swords, and knives, and shields, and breastplates. And there arose much godlessness, and they committed fornication, and they were led astray, and became corrupt in all their ways.

> Semjaza taught enchantments, and root-cuttings,
> Hermani taught the resolving of enchantments,
> Baraqijal taught astrology,
> Kokabel the constellations,
> Ezeqeel the knowledge of the clouds,
> Araqiel the signs of the earth,
> Shamsiel the signs of the sun,
> Sariel the course of the moon.

Another breath, another swipe of the device.

"In this next section," explained Elijah, "after having looked upon the lawlessness raging upon Earth, the angels themselves appealed to Yahweh to intervene." He read aloud:

And they said to the Lord of the ages: "Lord of lords, God of gods, King of kings, and God of the ages...Thou seest what Azazel hath done, who hath taught all unrighteousness on earth and revealed the eternal secrets which were preserved in heaven, which men were striving to learn: And Semjaza, to whom Thou hast given authority to bear rule over his associates. And they have gone to the daughters of men upon the earth, and have slept with the women, and have defiled themselves, and revealed to them all kinds of sins. And the women have borne giants, and the whole earth has thereby been filled with blood and unrighteousness."

Silas sighed, not at all understanding where the man was going with this deep dive into obscure Hebrew-sect nonsense.

Sounded like it added up to a hill of beans! And with Gapinski's life on the line, and the Church's teachings concerning our human identity and nature—the very nature of God himself and his place in the universe...Impatience was plucking his nerves something fierce.

"This is fascinating and all, but what the hell—"

He stopped short, Elijah raising a brow along with Bartholomew.

That heat returned to the back of his neck from embarrassment.

Watch it, Grey...

"Erm—I mean, care to elucidate the nature of how this fascinating information relates to our current operation at hand?"

"I agree with Silas," Gina added. "This passage is from the Book of Enoch, is that right?"

Elijah nodded. "Bingo."

"Well, what's it talking about?"

He fiddled with the Archives tablet again. "One more to bring it all together."

Running his finger down the device, Elijah found his spot and grinned, bouncing back and forth on the balls of his feet with triumph.

"This is the piece I was missing, connecting my research concerning the sons of God and 1 Enoch to my intuitions concerning the Nephilim."

"What is it?"

"An obscure Jewish text connected with the tradition of Enoch, where the ancient prophet addresses the bastard-born giant Watcher-spirits."

Returning to the device, he read:

Why have ye forsaken the high, holy, and eternal heaven, and lain with women, defiling yourselves with the daughters of men and taking to yourselves wives. Why have you acted like the children of earth and begotten giants as your sons?

And now the giants, who are born from both spirit and flesh—they shall be called evil spirits upon Earth, and on Earth shall their dwelling be. Evil spirits have gone forth from their bodies, because they are born from men, and from the holy Watchers is their original creation. They shall be evil spirits on Earth, and evil spirits they shall be called.

And the spirits of the giants afflict, oppress, destroy, attack, do battle, and work destruction upon Earth, causing chaos. These spirits shall rise up against the children of men and against their women, for they have come from them.

Elijah finally set down the tablet. There was that word again.

Watchers.

"You asked what is the meaning of all of this, Master Grey."

Silas nodded. "That's right. Seems like a bunch of ancient Hebrew gobbledygook to me."

He frowned but let the characterization go. "That ancient Hebrew gobbledygook, as you framed it, references the nature of our current predicament!"

"Really, Eli?" Gina's eyes went wide with interest. "How so?"

"The fallen sons of God and their offspring."

Silas startled, his brow crunching with confusion before his face fell. "Fallen sons of God?"

"Bingo. The fallen sons of God, which you heard in the Genesis 6 narrative and from 1 Enoch, then this obscure text."

Silas was getting annoyed with all the Hebrew nonsense that didn't at all seem to connect to the task at hand. Even more annoyed that Elijah wasn't getting to the point!

With a huff, he finally blurted, "Who are they?"

Elijah turned to him. "Why, your aliens, Doctor Grey." Taking a beat, then a breath, he added: "And it appears they mean business."

CHAPTER 32

BÜREN, GERMANY.

The world around Celeste seemed to crackle with an unholy energy perched on the bluff overlooking a massive triangular structure with three round towers connected by massive walls nestled in the valley below. A roiling river with white-cap waves snaked through the small German town past the Renaissance castle that promised to hold answers for their operation.

Thunder rumbled in the distance, a stiff, frigid breeze picking up and sending dried, dead leaves dancing in a whirling dervish that seemed to beckon the Devil himself.

The static charge of a thunderstorm tinged by woodsmoke and those dancing dead leaves filled Celeste's head with a dizzying sense of fall, making her second guess her intuition.

Perhaps that's all it was. Lightning in the stratosphere, the electrostatic discharge from two electrically charged regions in the atmosphere disturbing the peace—her peace.

There it was again.

An energy that seemed to pulsate from the castle down below, sending all of her hairs standing at attention and causing Celeste to bring her arms close around her chest.

Something sinister, something familiar.

Something not of this world.

Reminded her of her past, as haunting and shameful as it was. A power from childhood stemming from a string of experiences that had all started innocently enough, as they often do. With, of all things, a Ouija board during a sleepover at her best mate Hannah's house.

The bitter wind picked up its pace from behind, dried leaves blowing past again along with the heavenly scent of burning wood gusting along with it. She pulled her jacket tighter against her body and kept her arms wrapped around herself for heat, her mind pulsing with memory from that fateful night, and wishing to the Lord Almighty Nicky and Torres would hurry it along.

Celeste and her SEPIO partner had taken the Gulfstream to rendezvous with the MI6 agent at an airfield just outside Büren, Germany. She had wanted to stop over in London and pick up the journey together as a threesome, but Nicky wouldn't have anything of it. Insisted on rendezvousing in Germany, and Celeste picking up more petrol in Spain before continuing on the rest of the journey to Deutschland.

Supposed there was wisdom in his plan, the man not wanting to clue anyone into the fact that MI6 was working with a Christian order on a secret operation with global political ramifications. He eventually picked them up in a Peugeot rental that reminded Celeste why the French would never succeed at anything, where they motored to their lookout point staking out the old German structure that had once been home to the Schutzstaffel.

The Nazi paramilitary organization headed by Heinrich Himmler, known simply as the SS.

For what reason, she could only imagine. And pray— hoping her teammate was indeed inside, and fairing well.

Whatever it was, the sun was setting fast, shrouded by a thick canopy of rain clouds that portended doom whilst her

SEPIO teammate and former partner were rummaging around in the French sedan for equipment to raid the outpost that contained answers.

There was that energy again, an electrified pulse that snapped her back to her past.

Closing her eyes, she could almost feel the smoothness of the old polished Ouija board against her fingers. A vintage thing belonging to Hannah's great granny, made of honey wood with black lettering branded into it, smelling of mothballs and a musty basement.

She had been skeptical of it all, teasing Hannah for her superstitious beliefs. But sure enough, it performed on cue. A Voice, low and growly, spouting garbled gibberish, had sounded in her mate's basement. The same one that would confront her all those years later in the SEPIO operation straight from hell.

She drew her arms in tighter, that frigid breeze returning along with the woodsmoke and static charge.

What she wouldn't give for an evening nestled in front of a fireplace with a popping fire, a mug of spiced wine in one hand, a cozy mystery sporting a female detective lead in the other.

Cracking sticks and swishing brush, followed by some cawing bird sent a frigid fright spreading through her veins.

She spun around to find Nicky hustling up the path. He was bearing a large black bag, followed by Torres with the same.

"About bloomin' time you made it to the precipice, Nicky," Celeste complained, rubbing her arms and dreading the inevitable, given what she sensed deep within their target—some version of the Voice she had encountered more times than she cared.

But she also knew the truth of it, that it was her duty to storm the gates of the castle below to see what lay within. Although it wasn't clear what, other than circumstantial evidence that Gapinski had arrived in the area on the same private jet bearing the same tail numbers that had fled Turkey with their alien bones after the initial raid.

"Sun is slipping fast, so we best get on with it."

Nicky sloughed the bag off his shoulder to the ground. "'Twill be best that way, given our operation and what lies within."

"Let's have a chat about that, shall we? Because you have been mighty coy about our being here."

"Yeah, Double O Spook. Fess up, would ya?" Torres threw her own bag to the ground and turned to Celeste with a wry grin. "That's my name for your old partner."

Nicky rolled his eyes. "How original..."

"As Naomi said, how about you clue us into what you've dragged us halfway around the world to accomplish for Her Majesty's government."

He stepped to the edge of the cliff, the waters churning beneath in white cap waves no doubt stirred by both the fall wind and demonic force beyond its shores.

"Do you know anything about that castle there?"

Celeste joined him, drawing her arms back to her chest. "Not really. Something about some Nazi headquarters."

"Nazis?" Torres exclaimed, coming up to Celeste's other side. "*Dios mío...*"

"Sorry, mate..." Nicky said softly, eyes fixed on the massive weatherworn stone triangular structure. "God isn't anywhere to be found in these parts."

He took a breath, then continued, "At any rate, that castle, Wewelsburg, was home to Himmler's Schutzstaffel, but it was also the headquarters for a number of higher-level operatives working on magical weaponry that would usher in Hitler's infamous Third Reich."

Torres snorted a laugh. "Magical weaponry? What, like flying saucers, Double O Spook?"

He turned to her. "Precisely. Ostensibly developed by

experts in rocketry, the Nazis pursued super aerial crafts that possessed the powers of electrical and electromagnetic disruption. Quite similar to our current pursuits."

She turned back to the structure, lightening fluttering in the near distance reflecting off from the blackened, weatherworn edifice. "Impossible..."

"No, my dear. Very possible. In fact, the ensuing test projects were potentially responsible for the so-called Foo Fighters."

"The American rock band?"

Nicky twisted up his face in confusion. "I haven't a clue about any American *rock band*. They were unidentified flying objects that appeared in the sky during the height of the Second World War, as reported by the Allied air forces."

"And they were developed in that castle," Celeste said, nodding toward the building.

"Among other things. We know that for a stretch of time during the middle of the war, the German Army High Command commenced an investigation into the possibility of atomic disintegration, chain reactions, and anti-gravity machines."

"In other words, nuclear weapons that would turn the tides and lead the Nazis to world domination."

"Precisely."

"So that's where the Man in the High Castle lived..."

Nicky laughed. "Philip Dick. Clever as always, Celeste."

She threw him a weak smile, saying nothing more.

"But that was half a century ago," Torres said. "The Nazis lost the war, Germany paid the price, and they promised to be on their best behavior. What's this got to do with what's been going down the past few days."

"It is germane to our operation because the maxim *you cannot kill an ideology with bullets*—" Nicky swept an arm across the valley toward the castle, "—lived on inside that stone structure."

Celeste creased her brow, following his gesture. Another shiver ratcheting up her spine.

Torres asked, "What are you talking about, *muchacho*?" She nodded toward the castle herself. "What went on in there?"

"R&D into military weapons was only a corollary to a much deeper foundation being hammered and honed within those stone walls. It was also the epicenter of a little known and little researched magical philosophy known as theosophy."

Celeste snapped her head toward the man with recognition. "Theosophy?"

He nodded with a chuckle. "Stuff and nonsense is what it was! Yet it formed the backbone to Himmler's more extracurricular pursuits outside the normal Nazi military channels."

"Theo-whatchamacallit?" Torres asked.

"Theosophy," Celeste said. "I recall Rowen Radcliffe mentioning it in regards to Nous and Rudolf Borg's pursuit of the Holy Grail."

"Oh, yeah. That former wackadoodle Nous Master who tried to clone Jesus."

"Makes sense," Nicky said, "given the legend was part of a panoply of items Himmler and his cronies were pursuing as part of their search for the miracle weapon that would lead the Nazis to ultimate victory."

"Literally, *divine wisdom*," Celeste went on, "it was a pseudo-spiritual movement that formed in the late nineteenth century. Surprisingly, it has stuck around for some time now in the West. Equal parts religious, philosophic, and scientific."

"Most impressive," Nicky said with a grin.

"Always."

"Alright, you two," Torres said, "let's ixnay the lirtingfay until tomorrow and clue this ignorant *muchacha* into what this theosophy business is all about."

Celeste startled and straightened with embarrassment.

Nicky said, "I'll gladly dispense with flirtatious banter until after the operation."

"At any rate..." Celeste threw both her mate and ex-partner a displeased frown. "Theosophy was arguably the most influential occult doctrine at the turn of the century. The alternative spiritual sect drew heavily from Hinduism and Buddhism, as well as from Darwinism and Egyptian spirituality. But the real innovation was its genuine attempt to combine natural science and supernaturalism into a coherent set of teachings."

Torres asked, "What's the connection with the goose-steppers?"

"One of the more obscene aspects to the upstart pseudo-religion was its racialist undercurrent. Although publicly advocating for the universal brotherhood of all races, creeds, castes, and colors, they also aimed at bringing a raising up a root race that was thoroughly Indo-European. A sort of superrace."

"*Dios mío...*" Torres said.

"Hence the Nazi fascination with theosophy," Nicky said. "One of its leading proponents found favor with members of the Third Reich. Rudolph Steiner was the chap. He embraced the reality that a truth stood above the world religions and sought answers to unexplained natural laws and powers within humanity. Which, frankly, as a non-religious sort myself, I sort of fancy."

"Aside from the racialist elements, you mean," Celeste said.

"Most certainly!"

"Just clarifying..."

Nicky cleared his throat and continued, "The Germans sought a truly Germanic religion, where early Romantic writers encouraged the first stirrings of German national feeling through the celebration of German folk traditions and mythology, culminating in a uniting of Germanic paganism with Christianity in ways that were nationalistic to the core."

"In what way?" asked Torres.

"For one, Alfred Schuler propagated a link between the ancient spiritual tradition of Gnosticism, a Christian 14th-century heretical sect called Catharism, and the myth of Atlantis."

"Atlantis?" Celeste said with surprise. "As in the lost city?"

He nodded. "Especially relevant to our operation is the role of this lost civilization. In the theosophic worldview, Thule was the lost city of Atlantis, and it was believed to be the prehistoric source of divine racial and spiritual perfection, with a heavy emphasis on extraterrestrial origins."

A biting wind picked up pace at the revelation, sending a chill through Celeste and the start of a trace connection between the pagan ideology and their operation.

"The Nazis," Nicky continued, "went to great lengths to find this civilization, believing it to hold the keys to a pure Aryan race. It also played a vital role in occult and border scientific theories."

"Border science?" Torres said. "Never heard of it."

"*Grenzwissenschaft.* A kind of religious natural science that stood at the borders of mainstream variations."

"Sounds cuckoo for Cocoa Puffs to me."

Celeste chuckled. "And you sound like you're channeling our friend who is holed up in that castle."

She shrugged. "I miss the blockhead, alright. So sue me."

"Me, too, mate." Celeste wrapped an arm around her shoulder and gave her a squeeze. "But, Nicky, what's this border science nonsense have to do with our operation? More germane: What's it got to do with these recent UFO and alien sightings?"

"Right, I'll get to it," he replied. "On the one hand, the fringe sciences examined unseen forces on the borders of what humans would normally be understood to perceive. Astrology, hand-reading, mediumism, radiesthesia, and the like. But that wasn't all. Border science also sought to manipulate supernatural forces beyond human understanding. This included parapsychology, telepathy, biodynamic agriculture, and the theory that mankind was created from a meteor bearing divine sperm."

Celeste scoffed. "Stuff and nonsense is what this sounds like. A sort of reenchantment of the sciences, I reckon."

"An apt way of putting it. All held together by the view that the paranormal was a legitimate object of scientific inquiry and power. Just as serious, precise, and intensive as any other science, but tapping into unseen forces and knowledge from unseen realms."

"Hence the occultism."

Nicky nodded. "However, those German practitioners believed it belonged to the objective sciences. Which brings us to the germ of what has us standing on this cliff."

"Finally..." Torres sighed.

"A recent review of classified intel from that era reveals a startling connection between this philosophical foundation and the Nazi's pursuit of a miracle weapon."

Celeste leaned toward the man with interest, a whiff of aftershave taking her back in time to their brief partnership. Cedar and coriander. Her favorite.

Her cheeks flushed with memory, and embarrassment.

Clearing her throat, she nodded. "Go on."

"Right, according to this intel," Nicky explained, "Himmler instructed a one Hans Kammler to set up his own secret projects office within the Ahnenerbe."

"Golly..." said Celeste.

"What is this Ah-nano-derby-whatchamacallit?" asked Torres.

Nicky replied, "The Institute for Ancestral Research. Basically, it sought ancient technology, and Kammler set up shop at the Skoda Works Nazi military arsenal where he directed projects on advanced weapons systems. Anti-gravity devices and guided weapons, anti-aircraft lasers and death rays."

"Like, what, lightsabers?"

"Something like that. Kammler's projects ramped up during the final two years of the war with a fevered search for a miracle weapon that would end all weapons, pursuing border scientific weapons inspired by the mythology of the German volkisch movement. One of which was an anti-gravity device. *Die Glocke*."

Torres crossed her arms. "In English, *por favor*."

"The Bell," Celeste said.

Nicky nodded.

"What was it?"

"Reportedly, some sort of nuclear-powered, anti-gravitational device."

"Like a flying saucer?"

Nicky nodded. "One of the lead border scientists claimed the bell or saucer, or whatever, measured twelve to fifteen feet high with two counter-rotating cylinders filled with a liquid, code-named Xerum 525."

"This is nutso to the maxo," said Torres.

Celeste had to agree.

Nicky continued, "According to intelligence reports from that era, the craft was started by a small electric motor with takeoff energy supplied by a power source for an aerial vehicle of saucer-like appearance. When it was tested in the spring of 1945, scientists working on the project reported the flying saucer rose unexpectedly to the ceiling with a blue-green and then a silver-colored glow trailing the craft."

"Crikey..." Celeste said. "Sounds suspiciously like reports from UFO sightings."

Torres added, "Even what Gapinski himself reported."

"Indeed."

"According to some accounts," Nicky went on, "a group of

Americans arrived shortly after the test and took the lead scientists into protective custody when they swept through Germany. They seized all of their research materials under the classified rubric of atomic energy research and the men were never seen from again."

Celeste startled. "Wait a minute. They took Kammler into custody?"

"It isn't entirely clear. However, his scientist compatriots most certainly were."

"Operation Paperclip. The secret American program you told us about to shuttle away Nazi scientists to bolster their own military initiatives."

Nicky nodded. "Perhaps. Kammler and his experiments combined all the border scientific ideas and miracle technologies they had been after. Capturing invisible earth rays, weaponizing electromagnetic forces, their work on atomic energy development, the production of new rocket technologies."

Celeste asked, "Did the Americans use any of it?"

"Not that we know of."

Torres snorted a laugh. "Yeah, right."

"Intelligence reports had always indicated Kammler disappeared before the Americans arrived, without a trace. However, now I'm not so certain about that conjecture."

"Kammler..." Celeste said. "Isn't that the man you saw on Gapinski's photos from the original invasion in Turkey by those hostiles?"

"Precisely," said Nicky.

"Except the man would be well past a hundred, wouldn't he?"

"Perhaps he had a son. Either way, the Nazis banked their final victory on miracle technologies born through their fascination with ancient, possibly extraterrestrial superhumans, who possessed the ability to produce sophisticated weapons, exercise mind control, and wield the power of lightning."

Celeste turned toward the building alighted by a flash of the purplish electric charge from the canopy above. Thunder rumbled on cue, as did a letting of a frigid rain from above slapping against her face.

She said, "All of which was precipitated from that castle, within those stone walls."

Nicky added, "And apparently continued within those walls."

Only one way to find out.

She grabbed one of the black bags and hoisted it on her back. Then took off down a narrow dirt path leading to the castle below.

Time to find some bloomin' answers.

CHAPTER 33

Gapinski was floating in a void of nothingness. Like when he went skinny dipping one April afternoon during high school English class in Grandpappy's backyard pool to cool off during a hella-hot spring in the Deep South. Or swimming through outer space like Sandra Bullock after her shuttle was destroyed. Man was *Gravity* the bomb diggity!

Bomb diggity? Did he say that sort of thing? Maybe after a few too many cans of hefeweizen—hefeweizen? He hated German beer! More like pissweizen it was so bad! But why was it on his mind? Reminded him of his time at Ramstein—and something else...

Hefeweizen...Christmas...blinking skylights.

Couldn't put a finger on it for the life of him. Either way, Gapinski was as happy as a clam in his little world of float-ingness.

Black and dark like a wormhole. Warm and perfectly tuned to his body temperature. Fluidy with the sense of outer space.

Outer space...

The two words struck at something deep inside his noggin.

A memory, or a mission with SEPIO. Something about aliens and UFOs...

He chuckled to himself. Yeah, right. Bet Fox Mulder and Dana Scully had ridden in on white horses to save the day too!

Fox...

Now that sure rang a bell.

Elijah Fox.

Who was that again?

Sounded like an undercover DC Comics superhero. Definitely not in the Marvel Cinematic Universe. Too normal sounding. More Christian Bale as Batman than Christopher Hemsworth as Thor. But whoever he was or whatever he was, this Elijah Fox character, Gapinski didn't have a cotton pickin' clue.

Anywho, where was he?

Ahh, yes, the inside of his head. Which felt like he'd died and gone to be with sweet baby Jesus himself.

A drunken giggle slithered through his consciousness, though it didn't slip past it. Whatever that meant, he wasn't quite sure.

What he was sure of was that he wasn't dead. Just...he didn't quite know. High maybe? Who knew. What he did know was that his throat felt scratchy, like some critter had crawled down inside.

Hey, wasn't there an *X-Files* plot line about aliens climbing inside people through their throats?

A shuddering wave skated through him. Again, more through his consciousness than anything.

But it did remind him of a memory from childhood, when he'd take a spaghetti noodle and swallow it whole while holding onto one end. The thing would slither down his throat like one of his backyard garter snakes, the pasta just chilling down his gullet and reaching all the way down to his stomach. Right up until he slowly pulled the noodle out like a tapeworm.

Grossed his mom and pops out to high heaven! Which made him all the more eager to do it again.

The thought made his throat tickle now. Tried swallowing to chase away the sensation, but no go on that front.

Took a deep breath instead, the smell of a hospital room flooding his senses. Bleach and rubbing alcohol, gauze and Vaseline, the whole nine yards.

And oddly cloves...

Cloves?

Yes, cloves!

The sweet smell was heaven. Cinnamon and nutmeg, joined by the tang of sweet wood swirling into a Nirvana that definitely gave the grassy ganja he'd toked on during high school a run for its money.

Djarum Blacks. Boy, were those the days. When he'd skip school with his best friend Josh, who was a year ahead of him in school and knew where his pops hid the key to his liquor cabinet and cigarettes.

What a memory that was.

Except...

That wasn't the only one his brain's firing synapses flared up at the center of his noggin.

Another memory quickly chased that one. Not sweet. Sour.

And satanic!

The images flashed by in rapid succession, firing off like a pack of cheap 7-Eleven fireworks:

Beer, pizza, lederhosen.

And hefeweizen...

Golf course, 18th hole, frozen grass.

And Christmas...

Lights, trees, triangle.

And blinking skylights!

Then: paralysis, levitation, wicked headache.

It was all coming in at a torrential flood now, the synapses of his wrinkly brain firing away on all cylinders dredging the memories tucked away inside that oversized, bald head of his.

Objects and sensations all flashed by in rapid succession:

Cold metal table, tight leather straps, beeping heart monitor.

German voices, American voices.

Bleach, rubbing alcohol, gauze, Vaseline—

And cloves...

Cloves!

I remember.

I remember!

"*I REMEMBER!!!*" Gapinski screamed with a voice muffled by something jammed down his throat.

He snapped his eyes open with dreadful recollection, as if waking up with the darkest terrors of the night.

Only to find himself floating in another nightmare straight from hell.

With a familiar face staring at him through water and thick glass fogged over from his heavy breathing.

A man with a top hat, smoking a Djarum Black.

With that hair and glasses. That rectangular face and broad forehead. Those beady little down-turned eyes above that straight nose and small cheeks.

From nightmares long buried.

And...something else.

A Presence. Towering behind Top Hat Dude with a mug that would make Fox Mulder squeal!

This isn't happening...Again!

———

THE MAN WITH THE TOP HAT TOOK A LONG DRAG FROM HIS cigarette, held it, then blew ribbons of smoke that curled toward the vaulted ceiling.

Sebastian wanted to retch. What an insufferable habit! He would've blown chunks, too, had the smoke not smelled more of cloves and spice than the bathroom of some Southern diner off Route 66.

Almost said something, the cloud hovering with cancerous threat, the second-hand smoke seeping into his lungs with necrotic intent. How anyone managed it, he hadn't a clue. His brother Silas had picked up the nasty habit after the war. Too bad it hadn't killed him when those raghead Iraqis didn't.

If only…

He coughed, hoping the passive aggressive hint would give the man a clue. It didn't, the American official pulling another drag off the cancer stick with his one good arm and releasing it with a hazy billow that added to the cloud obscuring the chamber lights.

But, again, he said not a peep. The man was too important of an asset to make waves in his plan to destroy the faith that had clung so desperately to the silly notions of a Higher Power.

Instead, the man snorted a laugh as he bent over the hydrochamber bearing the body of the specimen who would soon bear the true Power that would put all those pathetic doctrines of God and theologies of the Creator to rest. For as he discovered, and others before him, the ancient mysteries of the Universe—scientific and arcane—had shown him the better Power.

A Life-Force within the Universe itself that was far more powerful than any silly Spaghetti Monster in outer space.

An ancient Power that had tried to partner with humanity from just after the point Upright Man evolved into Wise Man, pledging to dispense their knowledge of the seen and unseen realms and create a superrace of humans to rule alongside them.

But there were setbacks, and the Power withdrew back into the outer reaches of the Universe only to begin trying anew decades ago. At first in partnership with an ally they assumed would help them rule the world. Then with an unlikely partner who had actually accomplished that aim.

First warning humanity of their destructive pathways, the momentous event of the first nuclear bombing sending the Power into a bit of a frenzied state. Then abducting special people to serve as conduits for their message of peace, prosperity, and progress, only to finally make themselves known with the culmination of their ultimate aim.

Raising up a true race of Homo Deus.

God-Men to bring peace on Earth and further enlightenment to humanity.

And Sebastian would be the one to see it through to the end.

Using his brother to make it happen, his pathetic religious order. By using one of their own...

Another puff, another plume of smoke.

More cloves that set Sebastian's teeth on edge.

The German American bent over the chamber, holding that dreadful cancer stick to his lips for another drag while his other arm lay limp at his side. An old war injury, apparently, during a plane crash in Vietnam.

Sebastian sneered at the imperfection, the uselessness of this man's body and scar on his nature. How the Powers had seen fit to work through such damaged goods was beyond him. And yet, there he was, someone at the top of his career—the US government, even—readying to unleash upon the world the greatest manifestation of human progress since the dawn of *Homo sapiens*.

Running through the final preparations for the Host that

would receive the Power to launch such an endeavor, the German American pulled another drag, held it, then blew it out into the chamber before tossing the butt. Orange sparks skipped across the stone floor, and the final remains lay smoldering.

Disgusting.

Now the tolerable scents of cinnamon and spice were replaced by the acrid smell of an ashtray.

But that wasn't all.

Something sulfuric, something rancid—like the reptile exhibit at the Smithsonian National Zoo.

And then he appeared.

Along with the Force Sebastian had grown to adore.

The hour had arrived. The unveiling of the God-Men was nigh.

A shudder ratcheted down his spine at the thought. Both with trepidation and anticipation.

The man with the top hat turned his head toward the Visitor, acknowledging him with a nod of familiarity.

"My father waited for this day most of his life," he said, returning to the hydrochamber. "I am just wishing he was being around to see it for himself. He was more than ready at the time of his death."

"But is *he* ready?" Sebastian said, gesturing at the subject lying prone inside.

He didn't answer. Instead, he bent toward the glass lid.

A knocking inside drew his attention. Inside the chamber.

Sebastian immediately saw what was wrong.

The SEPIO agent was flailing, as if drowning. The vital sign monitor registered not only a massive spike in his heart rate but also a plummet in his oxygen. They began beeping with protest, the sound filling the stone chamber.

"Dammit, he's choking!"

"I believe it is being time," said the American with that dreadful German accent, "for the next stage of things, anyhow."

A breath caught in Sebastian's chest. For he knew what that meant.

"Prepare the Host for the Power."

Time to unleash the Universe upon humanity.

CHAPTER 34

"Bloody hell..." Celeste cursed as she fussed with the straps of the Osprey body armor hanging loose across her chest, the British equivalent of the Kevlar their Yankish counterparts used for such special operations.

Nicky had supplied both her and Torres with their very own vest, courtesy of Her Majesty's government. She thought it was overkill, especially since that bloomin' strap was stuck, but his intelligence told him to be prepared.

She gave it another yank, the rain steady and cold, soaking her clear through the bone. Another no go, something snagging in the clip.

Huffing, Celeste threw her hands at her head and closed her eyes for a breather. She was cold and wet from the trek down into the valley and across the river, then up through the naked trees barren of leafy protection to the base of the castle walls. The pulsing power within churned her stomach with dread, her very soul wilting under the weight of some unholy presence.

"Here, let me..."

She snapped open her eyes, finding Nicky standing before her and fastening her buckles.

His hot breath plumed in the frigid air, the smell of mint heavy on top of that aftershave again.

She frowned and stepped back, cinching the straps herself and finishing the job.

"Jolly good, Nicky. Thanks for the helping hand."

"My pleasure..."

Torres stepped over bearing some black utensil. "Are we ready to get the show on the road, or what?"

"First things first." Nicky tossed a weapon at Celeste. She caught it with one hand.

An SA80 5.56mm gas-operated assault rifle manufactured by Heckler & Koch. Standard for the British military, as well as those more clandestine operations courtesy of MI6.

Its heft and rubber grip felt good in the hand. Almost made her want to rejoin just to bear that arm again.

Almost...

Torres secured her own weapon around her back and took aim up the side of the wall with her new toy.

"What's that?" Celeste asked.

"A hand-held, gas-powered grappling hook." She grinned wide and jerked a thumb toward Nicky. "Courtesy of Double O Spook, here."

She steadied her aim toward a wrought-iron balcony several stories up.

Celeste looked on, saying, "Don't recall having such help when I worked for the Circus."

"We've innovated since you've left," explained Nicky.

"Apparently..."

A loud *chu-cu* sounded from the utensil, its echo riding above the din of the stream racing from behind. She worried they would be heard rummaging around the base of the castle.

But as the rope sailed high into the sky, and then wrapped securely around the railing, no one came.

"*Te tengo!*" Torres said, making a fist of success. "All set."

"*Buena esa*," Nicky said. "Right, up you go. Celeste will follow, then I will bring up the rear."

Without waiting for confirmation, Naomi secured the rope to a belt wrapped around her waist, then wrapped one end around her arm and gripped it before starting her ascent.

As Silas would say, it was go time.

On the double.

Torres made quick work climbing up the way, the military-grade boots on loan from Her Majesty's government not slipping once. Before long, she was resting on the stone balcony whilst Celeste was making her own way toward the fourth floor.

She climbed with ease, her Secret Intelligence Service training instantly clicking into gear. Helped matters that she was an avid rock climber as well. Soon she joined Naomi and tossed the rope down to Nicky.

Waiting for him to arrive, she inspected the entrance, an original mid-forties piece of work that was securely shut. But also no match for Celeste Bourne, who more than lived up to her surname.

Within seconds, she had popped the lock using a hairpin in time for Nicky to arrive.

"I'll have to try that sometime," Nicky quipped, checking over his H&K rifle. "After you."

He grasped a tiny burnished bronze handle and readied to open the door for her entrance.

Bringing her own SA80 around for the ready, she sucked in a breath and steadied herself to push through.

Moment of truth...

Celeste nodded at Nicky, and in one motion he opened the door and she pushed through white sheer curtains.

Ready for anything.

The room was cold, the air stale. It echoed with her footfalls as she darted inside to sweep for hostiles, joined now by Nicky's and Torres's own approach. There were none.

The space was vast and vaulted, the ceiling high and ornately decorated with gilt whorls and a large, fancy chandelier of small crystal balls anchored at the center. The walls were painted a baby blue, and furniture covered by thick dust clothes were scattered about. Couches, armchairs, end tables. A thin layer of dust across scuffed hardwood floors indicated disuse for some time.

Bringing her rifle against her chest, she exhaled a breath she didn't know she was holding. Relieved to enter without incident.

But far from out of the woods.

Celeste led the way across the floor to a closed door, coming up to it and turning the knob.

It gave without issue.

Holding her breath, she eased it open.

Neglected hinges throwing up a hideous cry.

She held fast, then held her breath—wedging her foot in the open doorway to keep her position but fearing to go any further.

Waiting a beat, then another, she was satisfied no one had paid the sound any mind.

Handing the knob off to Nicky, she nudged the nose of her rifle through the opening into the darkened hallway.

He flung it open to mitigate the hinges' complaint.

They squealed, but that was the end of it.

And all three emerged into a vacant hallway painted faint purple from a floor-to-ceiling window at the end.

"Surprised we haven't met resistance yet," Nicky whispered.

"Likewise," Celeste said, easing down the hallway, the floor moaning in spots but their journey mostly quiet. "Must be busy elsewhere."

"*Sí, muchacha*. But where?"

That was the question, wasn't it...

Another hallway appeared, the other side of the triangle.

The trio padded to the edge.

Celeste held her breath. Waiting, intuiting, discerning any movement beyond the threshold.

Because Nicky was right, it was odd they hadn't met any resistance. Expected at least a passing show of security. But nothing so far.

Perhaps that was a sign of good things to come.

Feeling safe to proceed, she glanced behind for confirmation.

Both Nicky and Torres nodded her onward.

She nodded back and stepped out to round the bend.

And was met by a hulking, bulky figure.

Rising a head above her. All neck with wide shoulders. Arms bulging through a black jumpsuit. Hair blond and wrapped above his head in a bun. Eyes cold and as surprised as her own.

Crikey...

But nothing she couldn't handle.

And nothing that really surprised her.

The hostile reached for a pistol strapped to his side.

Your fault you weren't armed, mate.

Didn't even need to think about what came next.

Letting go of her own weapon, the strap catching it against her neck, she swung her open, stiff palm at his neck.

Swing and chop.

Hard against a bulging Adam's apple.

Once and done. Just as Her Majesty's government had taught her.

The hand reaching for the pistol instantly went to his neck instead, joined by the other.

As well as a hideous choking sound. A pasty gurgle searching for desperate breaths.

The maneuver had crushed that bobbing Adam's apple, lodging it in his windpipe.

He was suffocating. Slowly.

The compassionate side of Celeste chose the next course of action.

Darting around to his back, she kicked the back of his knees.

The man slumped to the floor while she slung one arm around to join those hands. The other reached around his forehead.

In one final motion, she twisted the head sporting that man bun.

A soft *crack* sounded from his neck after it was snapped.

Severing his spinal cord and relieving the man of his suffocation.

Nicky smirked. "Still got it, I see."

"Naturally."

Voices down the corridor startled Celeste into action, along with Nicky.

The pair quickly dragged the body around the corner and edged out of the way.

They stopped halfway down, followed by the turning of a knob and the opening of a door on far-better oiled hinges than their entrance into this bedlam.

Celeste chanced a glance and saw a group of men in white robes entering into a room glowing orange into the hallway. An odd sight that smacked of ceremony.

With two words floating down to her from their conversation.

Power and hosts.

And one more. Not a word. A trio of letters.

E-B-E.

"Extraterrestrial biological entity?" Nicky whispered on a shaky breath.

She spun toward him. "EBE?"

He nodded, tongue licking his lips with anticipatory pleasure.

"If that don't sound like pay dirt," Torres said, "I don't know what does."

Celeste nodded. "Right. I believe we've found our destination."

"Crack on, then," Nicky said, motioning down the corridor with his rifle.

She nodded and rounded the corner, weapon at the ready, but finding no one.

Orange light danced in the hallway and the trace scent of woodsmoke. She led the way toward the open invitation, slowing her pace as soft voices echoed toward her.

Coming up to the entrance, she padded around the threshold, weapon ready for confrontation.

Empty.

The trio entered.

It was a modest room, warmed by a fireplace filled with crackling logs, walls adorned by walnut bookshelves with a large desk of similar wood anchored at the center. A crimson Persian rug with red and green patterns sat atop the same hardwood floors they had found upon entrance. A large window overlooking the town below, faint yellow lights from streetlamps and homes retiring for the night obscured by wet snow.

And a door, standing open and leading into a stone staircase with distant voices echoing their way.

"They must have retired below," Nicky said softly, gesturing with his H&K. "Into the rabbit hole we go..."

Celeste swallowed and nodded, padding across the rug and edging to the hidden entrance leading beneath the castle.

She stopped short, took a breath.

Then plunged down inside.

Swinging her H&K rifle around in one quick motion, she

confirmed the stairwell was empty. Although the voices filtered up to her from down below the winding case of stone stairs.

She took them, one by one, inching ever downward with the cold, rough-cut blocks at her back.

Thunder rolled with a muffle from beyond the stone walls as they made their descent, LED lights along the base of the stairwell wall lighting each step down into the void. What lay beneath was anyone's clue, which Celeste didn't at all fancy. Was never one to launch headlong into an operation without having the full measure of things, especially the full lay of the floor plan for a castle from Hades.

But that was Nicky's way, and it was Silas's as well. Reminding her perhaps she should pay closer mind to the men she partnered with!

The wind howled now as a mixture of rain and heavy, wet snow beat against the thick, interlocking stones of the ancient castle. The voices trailed to nothing as they reached the bottom, finding a subterranean chamber that opened into a vestibule and stretching into a corridor leading toward a glowing chamber.

Greeting them was an unexpected sight.

A statue of a bird-man. Thoth, if Celeste recognized it. The ancient Egyptian god of wisdom. Of revelation. Of divine knowledge.

Of *gnostikos*, the center of Nous's worldview.

The sight of it sent a shiver up Celeste's spine.

It was a perfect replica of the colossal statue artifact she recalled being unearthed near the mortuary temple of Amenhotep III in Luxor decades ago. Towering above the trio in pure, red granite, the ancient ibis face peered down at them beneath a mask of pure gold, with a black onyx beak, flanked by indigo ribbons, and a crown of white and red feathers.

"*Que en el mundo?*" Torres whispered from behind.

"I have to agree with our Latina mate," Nicky voiced. "An odd sight, to be sure."

"Reminds me of the *muy loco* beings Gapinski and Silas said they saw."

Celeste turned to her and nodded, but said nothing, dread growing in her belly.

Voices flared again.

Past Thoth, down through the corridor, and from an open set of heavy doors.

Panicked voices shouting something about drowning before strong commands drew the trio down the hallway.

Celeste padded on careful steps, swinging her H&K rifle around with a tight grip and ready for anything.

The voices grew louder, a vast chamber coming into view just beyond the threshold.

She was not prepared for what she saw.

"Bloody hell..." Nicky said from behind.

Torres joined with a curse of her own: "*Dios mío...*"

The vast circular room was filled with hydrochambers, large, long tubes of green liquid. Had to be forty, perhaps even fifty, of those buggers, it was so bloomin' full of chambers. Straight from a Michael Crichton novel, it was! And floating in the fluid's midst were people. Or so Celeste assumed.

Men, women, what looked like children, even. Naked, with tubes coming out from their mouths and still more jammed in their veins.

They looked peaceful, as if in a womb shielded from the outside world and waiting to be birthed.

Or reborn.

Into what...she could only imagine.

"Celeste!" Torres grabbed her arm and pointed at the center.

Where anchored at the belly of the room was a basin, and lying prone was a familiar face.

Matthew Gapinski.

He was lying curled in the fetal position, the bottom of his feet angled toward them.

And standing over him in a black cloak was a familiar face, hood pulled back and likeness exposed. One who looked like the one she was fancying to marry.

Sebastian Grey.

Except...

It was all wrong! This was a hideous doppelgänger of the man she had seen before. With scaly skin and limbs hulking, head engorged and two bony nubs protruding from a bald skull.

Something had happened to him; something had possessed him!

Something hideous...

Between the seconds that it registered who the man was, he glanced up from Matthew.

Eyes narrowing and fists clenching with rage.

"What are you doing here?" he shouted across the vast space, his voice laced with panic as much as rage.

Others glanced from across the chamber. The same white ceremonial garbs glimpsed earlier, joined by a few in black jumpsuits looking like the bloke she had taken out.

And a man in a top hat. Looking like the chap from the grainy image Gapinski had taken from the dig site after it had been raided.

But that wasn't all.

Some—*thing!* A poltergeist. Tall and towering, with wide shoulders and skin that radiated a scaly iridescence and a humming power.

The Power she had felt from outside. One she had encountered countless times.

And—she couldn't believe she thought this, but...an alien!

Then it was gone. Slunk back into the shadows, or some other dimension of reality.

Same with the man in the top hat, the bloke quickly spinning from view and tearing off toward the back shrouded in shadows.

Just as bullets skipped off from the stone above Celeste's head.

She quickly padded to the closest hydrochamber, letting loose covering fire that sent Sebastian skittering after the bloke who had disappeared through an exit at the far end.

Nicky and Torres let their own weapons roar with a *rat-a-tat-tat* rejoinder.

One, two, three men from the five she glimpsed skittering into the study above flopped to the stone floor with injury.

Or death.

The cost of doing SEPIO business.

More *pop-pop-pops* sounded from beyond the hydrochamber, a woman with a contorted face resting peacefully inside, none the wiser at the melee.

She did catch something disturbing, however.

Her skin. Which was milky white and bumpy. Scaly, even.

Then something else.

Her head. Which was devoid of any hair and oversized, bulbous, like a party balloon.

Perhaps just an illusion from the water. But something told her differently.

She suddenly stirred inside.

Just as a bullet pinged off from the hydrochamber within striking distance of Celeste's own head!

"Bloody hell..."

She ducked below the parapet, waiting for a window to respond.

Nicky popped up instead and sent a *one-two-three* punch sailing across the chamber.

"Victorious!"

And that was that.

She popped her head above the hydrochamber for a look, the chamber empty now of living hostiles.

"Bullocks," she said as she stood. "I quite looked forward to taking out the man who nearly blew my bloomin' head off!"

"Or woman," Torres corrected, "as the case may be."

She raised her H&K. "Indeed."

"Should we tear after him," Nicky said, glancing at the women, "or her?"

A moan and movement from the center of the chamber drew her attention.

"Matthew!"

Ignoring the fleeing hostiles, Celeste ran to Gapinski and knelt at his side. She shook him, averting her eyes from his indecent exposure, but not giving it any thought.

His chest was rising rapidly, so at least he was breathing.

But he was unresponsive. And cold, feeling like the frigid, wet walls they had climbed on their arrival.

"Find a blanket, anything to cover him up!"

"*Aquí...*" Torres was already on it, passing along one of the white robes from one of the downed men.

Celeste threw it across him and gave him another shake. "Matthew, are you with us?"

He shuddered before throwing his eyes open. They darted about as his teeth started chattering.

"Matthew—"

"*Argh!!*" he screamed, the man backing up and hustling away with one hand shielding his face.

"Matthew! It's me, Celeste."

More screaming, high and heady and panicked.

"*Dios mío...*" Torres whispered, putting out a calming hand herself but sending him skittering farther back.

"I dare say," Nicky said, "the man has retired to bloody Bedlam!"

"Jesus, help us..." Celeste prayed.

Which seemed to make a penny drop inside his head.

Gapinski suddenly sat up straighter, his face falling and eyes glazing over before snapping back to life.

Reminded her of that Halloween from senior year of secondary school, when the name of Jesus stayed the hand of a Power coming against her.

So, she wielded it once again.

"Jesus, help Matthew."

Now Gapinski met her eyes, his face brightening and mouth widening into a grin.

"Boy, am I glad to see—"

He stopped short, glancing down at his attire and throwing up a scream.

"Where are my pants?"

Torres laughed. "We were wondering the same thing!"

A zapping spark from the other end of the chamber caught their attention.

Coming from one of the hydrochambers.

Right before one end burst in a spray of sparks that sent flames rising up its side.

Celeste muttered a curse. "Must have been struck during the melee."

"I was just about to suggest we take leave," Nicky said, shuffling over to Gapinski. "Are you alright to walk?"

The SEPIO agent grunted and stood, his robe that was a few sizes too small opening wide for the world to see.

He threw up another scream before shutting the doors.

Another explosion, more flames at the other end, the fire spreading now to the other hydrochambers.

"*Vamos, muchachos!*" Torres encouraged, leading the way toward the exit.

"What about the others?" Celeste said, her instincts screaming for her to save the rest.

"No time, mate," Nicky said.

Another shuddering explosion confirmed it.

The man joined Torres with Celeste guiding Gapinski to follow.

"No, wait..." he said.

Gapinski shuffled over to a hydrochamber with its lid clear open. Perhaps his own, given he was the only one running around.

The thought of him being experimented upon sent a shiver ratcheting down Celeste's spine.

He collapsed to the ground then swiped at something with his large hand.

Torres ran to him and put an arm in the crook of his shoulder, helping him back to his feet.

"Thanks, sister. Now we can go."

"We best get to it," Nicky said, darting back the way they came. "I reckon we don't have much time until this whole bloody thing blows."

"This way." Celeste darted back out into the corridor, her H&K rifle more than at the ready.

It was empty, but for Thoth standing guard.

She raced past, the rest following quickly.

Aiming straight up the well of the stone staircase, she raced with ascension, finger firmly at the trigger and ready for anything as she neared the top.

Almost—

A face suddenly appeared, then a body, connected to the nose of a rifle.

She sent *one-two-three-four* bullets sailing into the figure before ducking back down the well.

His weapon went off, sending a smattering of shots sailing high and wide and pinging off the stone—one sinking into

Celeste's Osprey body armor.

The force of it knocked the wind out of her.

"You alright, love?" Nicky shuffled up to her. "You injured?"

Took a beat, but she caught her breath.

"I'm fine." She stood and heaved another breath, then put a finger in the divot where the piece of lead sunk. "Grateful for the helping hand."

"Thank Her Majesty."

"I'll be sure to do that next time the Queen and I share a cuppa."

The body slumped down a few stairs. Celeste stepped over it, continuing on clear back into the study on toward the door standing wide open.

When two more figures appeared, guns outstretched and ready to—

Menacing *rat-a-tat-tats* exploded.

From behind.

The two bodies slumped to the floor in an instant.

"You're welcome," Nicky said, racing for the door.

"Cracking good shot." Celeste followed, with Torres carrying Gapinski along.

The pair burst through the entrance. Nothing like the element of surprise to throw off any incoming hostiles.

It was empty.

They worked back the way they had come, down the hallway and back to the vacant room. No use getting lost in a former Nazi HQ whilst—

Something deep in the belly of the castle rumbled. An explosion of fire and fury that was surely making its way up top.

Everyone hastened their speed, aiming for the sheer curtains wet with rain and snow and waving like phantoms in the frigid wind.

Nicky arrived at the railing first, the grappling hook still secured. Slinging his rifle around his back, he started his descent.

Torres brought Gapinski, and Celeste asked, "Can you manage rappelling down the face of the wall?"

He inched toward the railing and peered over the edge, an updraft of wind opening his white robe up like a tulip.

"Sonofa—"

Another explosion from behind cut him off, sending him skittering over the edge.

Torres was next, then Celeste.

Before descending, she crossed herself on instinct, then took the plunge.

Didn't take long to reach the bottom. The quartet raced through the forest of barren trees across wet, dead leaves before plunging into the stream winding through the valley.

Ice flooded Celeste's veins as the water flowed past her legs. Thankfully, the military boots Nicky provided kept her legs from going numb. The rest of her body took care of keeping her warm, adrenaline and racing heart doing the heavy lifting.

Halfway on now. They were making good progress.

"Go, go, go!" Nicky cried, waving the group across the stream.

"Don't have to tell me twice," Torres said, leading the charge.

Gapinski said, "Or thrice—"

He faltered a step and fell into the water, throwing up a cry.

Celeste raced to his side. "Up you go..."

She and Torres lifted him back up to his feet.

"I think I twisted my ankle." He winced and muttered a curse.

"Come along, we'll help you manage."

Nicky made it across first, the man gesturing wildly for them to hurry it along. Something that had annoyed her whilst they were partners, the man's tick-tock manner about him that always put her in a rush.

"Watch your step, Matthew," she said, the water at their ankles now. "Almost on to the other—"

An explosion thundered from behind, the blooming force tossing the group from the river against the side of the cliff.

Heat quickly followed. Not scorching, but hot enough to warn of danger.

Without looking, they scrambled up the face of the cliff, helping Gapinski hobble up the path they had traversed at the start of the operation until they all collapsed at the top where they began the whole bloody operation.

Celeste spun toward the castle, the world below painted orange and crimson, shrouded in billowing blackness.

Flames rose high into the midnight sky from the centuries-old structure, the downpour doing nothing to satiate the fires of hell overtaking the old Nazi headquarters. And apparently Nous' base of operations, which was quite the revelation.

Another explosion told her the building was a goner.

"Jolly good, Celeste," Nicky said, out of breath. "You're a cracking good shot, that's for sure. And welcomed back to the Circus anytime you fancy."

Torres scoffed. "What am I, chopped liver?"

"Oh, alright. I'd take you both."

Gapinski moaned, sitting up and rubbing his head. "My head hurts. And I'm hungry. For pizza. An extra-large Pizza Hut stuffed crust, meat lover's."

Now Nicky moaned. "You Yanks and your coronary-inducing fast-food slop."

"With pepperoni, ham, pork, beef, Italian sausage, and bacon."

Torres giggled, her laughter rolling into a guffaw.

"What?" Gapinski furrowed his brow, wincing from the motion. "Was it something I said?"

"Pizza. Of course!" Torres threw her arms around his neck, holding him tight.

Celeste thought she caught a glimpse of tears wetting her face. Or perhaps it was the falling rain. Either way, she understood her burst of sentiment. It was good to hear their friend was back, and to his normal hungry self.

She lay back against the cold, wet grass, taking a moment to recover from the onslaught and also say a prayer of thanksgiving to the Lord for returning Gapinski to the family fold, safe and unharmed.

But she rested only for a moment. Though one of SEPIO's own was now safe, the world was not.

For the true nature of #FirstContact was far different than the world understood.

And demonic.

She had to let Silas know what was happening.

CHAPTER 35
ROME.

S
ilas did a literal double-take with his head at the mention of aliens alongside the biblical sons of God.

Had he heard Elijah right? *Was* Elijah right to associate these rumors of spacecrafts and abductions from extraterrestrials with this other set of beings in the Bible, ones somehow associated with God himself?

Did not compute! Not only the association, but the whole notion of the sons of God. He ran a frustrated hand through his hair, head spinning from the uncertainty that came from this uncharted terrane of knowledge he wished he had a better grasp of.

Did not compute in the slightest...

The other two settled into an as-surprised, as-confused silence, the steady HVAC hum from the Archive's climate control unit the only soundtrack for their whispered discussion.

A cool breeze fell upon his skin from that control system flooding the space, bearing with it the smell of rain and the aftereffects of a thunderstorm. The added scents and sensation were a welcomed balm to his temperature rising from the sudden, unexpected shift in the operation.

Part of him had thought all this talk about aliens was just a metaphor for invasive demons haunting humanity. Like Gina had said they discovered through their work with the FBI. The satanic ritual abuse that was often taken by victims as alien abduction experiences. Maybe even a genuine government conspiracy on the level of *The X-Files* to con humanity into believing in some cosmic super-threat in order to gain and maintain a grip of power over humanity.

Now it seemed Elijah was placing Gapinski's characterization of his experiences in a biblical context, suggesting the Bible itself supported his label. Demonic, sure. But aliens, and from outer space? That was crazy talk!

Again, did not compute.

There was a laugh, a snicker really. From Elijah.

Which made heat race up Silas's neck.

"What's so funny?"

Another snicker before answering, "I just see the fruit of my little truth bomb written all over your face."

"Truth bomb?" he said with a raised brow.

"Bingo. That's what the kids say these days."

Silas sighed and shook his head. They didn't have time for jokes. Not in the middle of an operation with global and theological ramifications. Definitely not in the face of such a proposal that put aliens in a biblical context.

"Perhaps," Gina said, stepping to Silas's side, "we can move this along a bit, Eli. I'm sure Silas is eager to make the connections you're suggesting to their current operation."

Elijah nodded. "Sure. Do you have a Bible?"

"I think something can be arranged," Bartholomew said with a wry grin. "After all, we are in the Vatican Archives."

He left to rummage through the stacks of tomes, then returned with a well-worn, leather-bound volume, black cover faded and page edges stained crimson.

Elijah snatched it and began searching for something else

to read, its crinkled pages whispering as he flipped through the holy book.

"Ah, here we go!" he announced. "Let me read you something—well, several somethings."

Clearing his throat, he read:

God has taken his place in the divine council;
    in the midst of the gods he holds judgment:
    "How long will you judge unjustly
    and show partiality to the wicked?
    Selah
    Give justice to the weak and the orphan;
    maintain the right of the lowly and the destitute.
    Rescue the weak and the needy;
    deliver them from the hand of the wicked."
    They have neither knowledge nor understanding,
    they walk around in darkness;
    all the foundations of the earth are shaken.
    I say, "You are gods,
    children of the Most High, all of you;
    nevertheless, you shall die like mortals,
    and fall like any prince."
    Rise up, O God, judge the earth;
    for all the nations belong to you!

Silas smirked. "Sounds like something straight out of ancient Rome or Greece, with this talk about God ruling over other gods."

Elijah grinned. "Actually, it's from the Holy Scriptures."

"Egads, didn't see that coming," Gina said, shifting and crossing her arms with intrigue.

Silas shifted as well, embarrassment blooming in his cheeks

at missing the Scripture.

Sounded more like something about Zeus or Apollos ruling over the ancient Roman and Greek gods than anything Elijah would bring into a discussion about the Bible. He'd certainly never heard such a thing in Scripture, and yet...

"Where is this from?" he asked, swallowing his pride. Was almost afraid to know the truth of it.

"Psalm 82."

"Really?" He came to Elijah's side now, eyeing the pages of that ancient Jewish poem. "Can't say I recall that psalm. Certainly have never heard mention of some sort of ruling council in heaven. Not in my years studying or teaching—not in my life as a Christian, even."

"That makes two of us," Gina piped up.

Bartholomew nodded as well, the man grabbing his chin and rubbing it with contemplation under narrowed, searching eyes. Silas supposed if the keeper of the Vatican Archives hadn't heard of such a thing, then he shouldn't be too hard on himself.

Elijah just laughed. "Pretty much pegs the state of affairs of modern Christianity. But don't be too embarrassed. Most Christians aren't clued into the supernatural context of the Holy Scriptures and their faith, let alone the Jewish one."

Silas smirked and blurted, "But you're clued in, is that right? The man with the clue?"

He instantly regretted the challenge, realizing he was coming off as a jerk. Felt it was a little too convenient that the man had some special revelation-insight that was missing from Christianity until he came riding in on a white horse to clue in the Christian masses. But he shouldn't have come off like that.

"Not always," he simply said, either missing or ignoring the challenge. "But my people have maintained a tradition that Yahweh rules over a divine council of lesser gods, as I mentioned. You can't deny it. It's in Psalm 82, which is where I first discovered the language. Then when I jumped on my hobbyhorse, connecting with UFO networks and hearing more stories from so-called abductees, I began looking for what the Bible and biblical theology said about it. The last piece of the puzzle was what I read earlier, an obscure Jewish text I had hoped would be buried in the Archives. So thank you, kind sir."

Bartholomew nodded with a smile, then offered another short bow of acknowledgment.

Silas glanced at Bartholomew for confirmation. If there was one other person he trusted to give insight into Elijah's theological and biblical direction, it was their friend from the Vatican Archives.

He just shrugged, crossing his arms and looking over the professor's shoulder as he searched the Bible again.

"Listen to this," Elijah said, "another passage I'd wager you've never considered in light of the divine council." He again read aloud:

Let the heavens praise your wonders, O Lord,
    your faithfulness in the assembly of the holy ones.
    For who in the skies can be compared to the Lord?
    Who among the heavenly beings is like the Lord,
    a God feared in the council of the holy ones,
    great and awesome above all that are around him?
    O Lord God of hosts,
    who is as mighty as you, O Lord?
    Your faithfulness surrounds you.

"That sounds like another psalm," Gina said.

Elijah nodded. "A portion of Psalm 89. And there he is. God, surrounded by a decision-making body of divine beings. The translation I read for 'heavenly beings' is a crappy translation.

Much more accurate to translate the Hebrew *beney elohim* as 'sons of God.'"

"Fascinating..." Silas muttered, wondering why he had never caught that language about sons of God before. And why he was never trained to.

Not that he was an Old Testament guy or biblical scholar. But it irritated him that he was so out-of-the-know, so ignorant of the Bible's original context. Not only as a scholar, and the Master of the Order of Thaddeus even. But as a Christian. Never got that instruction during his childhood catechism, that's for sure! Definitely not from the on-base evangelical Protestant Bible studies in Iraq, either.

"Agree with your translation," Silas said with a nod, "but it's Psalms. Poems for worship and prayer and whatnot. Isn't this language simply poetic? It isn't as if they hold significant theology like the rest of the Bible, like Romans or John's Gospel."

"Oh my cheeps!" Elijah exclaimed. "It isn't as if they hold significant theology like the rest of the Bible?" He closed his eyes and took in a measured breath, then shook his head and muttered, "And you're a Master of a Christian order contending for the faith..."

Before he could offer a defense, the professor continued, "If that little piece of Hebrew poetry doesn't convince you, which has just as much bearing on Christian theology as the rest of the books of the Bible—" He paused, glaring at Silas before adding, "—like Romans and John's Gospel..."

Elijah flipped through several pages in the Bible. "How about we turn to another portion of Scripture that absolutely does hold significant theology, like every part of the Bible."

Another mutter under his breath before Elijah found and read:

Remember the days of old,
  consider the years long past;
  Ask your father, and he will inform you;
  your elders, and they will tell you.
  When the Most High apportioned the nations,
  when he divided humankind,
  he fixed the boundaries of the peoples
  according to the number of the gods;
  the Lord's own portion was his people,
  Jacob his allotted share.

The group gasped and muttered at still more language referencing other gods. Which Silas figured was another way of referencing the sons of God. Then with reference to the nations themselves, somehow being divided among them.

He ran a hand through his hair. This was wild. Completely blew apart his theological categories.

And yet...it also seemed right, true, real. Because there it was. Right there in a plain reading of God's Word. How could he disagree with what the Bible itself seemed to be saying about the unseen, supernatural realm?

"That was the Book of Deuteronomy, chapter 32," Elijah explained. "How about we try one more passage, just to put a cherry on top of our little truth bomb."

He didn't even have to look that passage up. He quoted from memory: *"For our struggle is not against enemies of blood and flesh, but against the rulers, against the authorities, against the cosmic powers of this present darkness, against the spiritual forces of evil in the heavenly places."*

"Ephesians, chapter 6," said Gina.

"Bingo, Gina colada! That language about rulers and authorities, about powers and forces all denotes geographical domain and authority in the New Testament and other Greek literature of the time. Entirely in line with the Deuteronomy 32 worldview I just read, where Yahweh, the Most High God, placed all other nations under the authority of lesser gods. Which Paul also acknowledges in his first letter to the Corinthians, chapter 8: *'indeed there are many gods and many lords...'*"

"Yeah...that's right," said Silas, shifting and crossing his arms, seeing the trace outline of a connection. And yet...

He wasn't quite buying it.

"So, what," he said, raising a challenge he fully expected Elijah to meet, "you're suggesting those beings, those—I can't believe I'm saying this," he muttered, "but those *aliens*, the ones piloting the UFOs or UAPs, or whatever, and then the beings glimpsed by people the past seven decades, like our friend Matt Gapinski—you're saying they are those sons of God?"

"Nope. Not entirely."

"Then what, Eli?" Gina asked. "Maybe we can land this plane, for all our sakes."

Elijah started pacing, bouncing on the balls of his feet with unbounded energy, as if it had been bottled up and now was being unleashed—just like Silas recalled from sitting in on his lecture.

"I believe part of their offspring, the sons of God, are what we could call extraterrestrial biological entities, bearing tremendous power and capabilities that far exceed our own. The Jewish text I read confirms this, which clearly reflects Genesis 6 from the Holy Scriptures, informing the Church that rebellious members of Yahweh's divine council, fallen ones, mated with human women to birth a race of superbeings."

"The *Übermensch*..." Silas muttered. "The sought-after German race of superhumans."

Then he swallowed, making a connection to their present struggles. "That Nous itself has been trying to raise for generations."

"Not a bad way of framing them," Elijah acknowledged. "The fact of the matter is, God has company. Other divine beings form his divine council—the sons of God, they are called. These beings fall under the authority of the God of Israel, but some broke rank, mating with humans near the start of our existence, then were judged, punished, and consigned to the Abyss—"

He suddenly spun around, then bolted for a grouping of furniture. Sad, well-worn pieces of functional, vinyl furniture that had seen better days, but better than nothing.

"I need to sit," he announced, then did so.

Gina and Bartholomew joined him in the chairs, but Silas stood. Needed the blood flowing fully from head to toe to wrap his head around the elephant in the room.

"Get this," Elijah explained, "the unseen world has a hierarchy to it. Problem is, we aren't trained to view this unseen world in this way, like that of a dynastic household ruled by a council of advisors."

"Like the days of Europe?" Gina asked.

"Bingo. Very similar to those ancient European institutions, which were really rooted in millennia of human tradition going all the way back to the kingdoms of Mesopotamia, Babylon and Egypt and whatnot. That context would have set the stage for an Israelite to understand certain terms used in their Scriptures to describe the notion of a hierarchy of divine beings."

"Like the sons of God?" Silas asked.

Elijah nodded. "In the ancient world, *beney elohim,* this Hebrew phrase for 'sons of God' identified divine beings bearing higher-level authority and jurisdictional responsibilities. They ruled with Yahweh on his council until the corrupt *elohim* were punished with death like humans, as Psalm 82 teaches. The end makes it clear that these chastised gods were given a degree of dominion over the nations of the earth, a ruling task at which they failed miserably."

Taking a breath, he continued, "What is important to this discussion is that Yahweh is among the *elohim*, sitting at the head of his divine, heavenly assembly. But know that he is superior to all other gods. He created them, he is their sovereign king. Likewise, since Jesus is Yahweh incarnate, he too stands apart with superiority from the other gods. He is the divine sovereign over all the *beney elohim*."

"Mind blown..." Bartholomew said with a chuckle, making an exploding motion with his fingers at his head. Silas nodded, understanding completely.

"I don't understand," said Gina, "why God needs a council in the first place."

Elijah shrugged. "He doesn't. But Scripture seems to suggest he uses one. A divine administration that serves Yahweh, carrying out his decrees. We're also part of that administrative divine family, you know. Humanity carries a status and function mirroring the heavenly administration we see in Psalms and Deuteronomy. Like the *beney elohim*, the members of the divine council representing God in their assigned tasks, we are also his representatives to accomplish his divine work on Earth."

This was all too wild. Nothing close to what he had learned in graduate school, let alone during his lifetime in the Church! But how did it all connect to these UFOs, to abduction stories —to Gapinski's own experience and the threat these fallen ones posed?

"Granted," Silas said, shifting on unsteady feet with the growing revelation. "That isn't new. At least the notion that we represent God on Earth as his Image Bearers. And, from one former professor to another, I appreciate your insight into this—"

"But..."

He chuckled. "But...how does this factor into our current operation, to these alien sightings or abductions?"

Elijah muttered a chide, to himself it sounded. "Forgive my theological travelogue. That was set up for the Watcher-spirits, the Nephilim offspring which I believe are the very beings who have haunted the memories of countless people across the world, from ages past."

"From Genesis 6, as well as what we read here from the Archives."

"Exactly. We read about the Watchers and their offspring, which were giants."

"Giants?"

Elijah nodded.

"How big," said Gina, glancing at Silas.

"Nearly nine feet tall, and looking like reptiles!"

"Nearly nine-feet tall," Silas added, recollection rising. "That's how our friend Gapinski described the skeletal remains our crew discovered at the Order dig site in Turkey. And—"

He stopped short, swallowing hard, before adding with quivering voice, "That's what I saw at the baseball diamond before Gapinski was taken away..."

"I see..." Elijah sat back and stroked his chin. "Now, one of the more contentious disputes over this passage is the meaning of the word *Nephilim*."

Gina said, "Fallen ones, isn't that right?"

"Bingo again. Which does fit, given how they corrupted humanity and turned them away from Yahweh, blamed for our own fall."

Elijah leaned forward. "However, in the same Mesopotamian context from that era, another supposed divine being, the *apkallus*, similarly mated with women and spawned giant offspring. Likewise, Jewish thinkers in the Second Temple period believed the offspring birthed in Genesis 6 to be giants. This word of ours, *Nephilim*, is found twice in the Old Testament. Here in Genesis 6 and then again in Numbers 13."

"Numbers 13?"

Elijah flipped through the Bible and found another passage.

"When the Israelites came to the Promised Land, they saw strong people who were the descendants of Anak. Then some spies complained..." He read aloud:

"We are not able to go up against this people, for they are stronger than we." So they brought to the Israelites an unfavorable report of the land that they had spied out, saying, "The land that we have gone through as spies is a land that devours its inhabitants; and all the people that we saw in it are of great size. There we saw the Nephilim (the Anakites come from the Nephilim); and to ourselves we seemed like grasshoppers, and so we seemed to them."

"That's right," said Bartholomew, joining the discussion now. "The part when Joshua sent spies into the land of Canaan to scope out the land."

"Very good, Vatican Archives Man," Elijah said. "Israel's holy wars launched against the nations by Yahweh's instructions were meant to rid the Earth of the Nephilim and their offspring, the Anakim. Where the flood did not do the entire trick of eliminating the bastard-born hybrids from Genesis 6, Yahweh's portion, the Israelites, was to eliminate them once and for all. Jewish literature teaches that demons are actually the disembodied souls of dead Nephilim. Watcher-Spirits that continue to plague humanity, as the obscure Jewish text I read says."

Silas sat straighter, it dawning on him now. "You mean the ones who have been visiting Earth for decades?"

Elijah smiled. "Now you're catching on. Better late than never, I suppose."

"Eli..." Gina said, smacking the man's knee.

Silas chuckled. "It's alright. My fiancé says I'm a slow one."

"And who is that?"

"Celeste Bourne."

"Really?" exclaimed Elijah. "What does she see in you?"

Another smack from Gina; a yelp this time from Elijah.

As blunt as ever. "How about we leave my love life alone and stick to what you know about these aliens of ours."

He frowned. "Psalm 82 shows that the status of the sons of God was reduced to mere observers of mankind's affairs, rather than participants. God took away their right to rule over Earth, giving it instead to humanity."

Elijah sat back and brought a hand to his chin, continuing, "So they watched human events unfold, witnessing the divine image pass from one generation to the next—an endless litany of rulers who had been set upon Earth as representatives of the Most High God. And along the way, within the sons of God, within the Watchers there began to well within them a desire for what had been taken away. They sought to reclaim their dominion, desiring their own ruling successors. Until one day they arrived."

"Hashtag first contact..." Silas said on a shaky breath, the picture sharpening with clarity. "The original ones in Genesis 6."

"Bingo. The Watchers descended to Earth in celestial flesh and spent their seed inside the wombs of human women—"

"Eww..." Bartholomew muttered with interruption. Silas had to agree. It was all pretty wild, pretty unbelievable.

"—spawning a ruling class of immortal gods," Elijah continued, "shrouded in the robe of mortal flesh. These rebels did what was unthinkable, unconscionable—breaching the categories of heavenly and earthly beings—rebelling to take back their rightful rule, while humanity embraced them as their gods."

"But Yahweh," Silas said, trying to wrap his mind around Elijah's revelation-insights, "the Most High God, their very Maker, would have none of it. He exiled them to the Abyss and sentenced their bastard offspring to death in the great flood of Genesis 6. It is these half-breeds who were the Nephilim, the giant fallen ones—isn't that right?"

Elijah grinned like a pleased parent. "Nicely done, Master Grey! See, you can be taught. The only other missing piece to the puzzle are the *shedim*."

"What is that meaning?" asked Gina.

"Demons..." answered Silas. "Hebrew for the fallen creatures."

Elijah nodded. "Bingo. The Nephilim bastard-born monstrosities had been exterminated, but they were instantly reborn upon death, becoming as their Watcher forebears: immortal, disembodied, uncontrollable. The Bible reveals that after the flood, more members of his council, the Watchers, the cosmic sons—they rebelled and came to Earth, where humanity was again enraptured. Mankind worshiped them as shamanic teachers, divine healers, powerful saviors. They were gods to them."

Taking a breath, he continued, "Still more bastard-born races arose, known from ancient Hebrew texts as the Anakim, Emim, Rephaim, and Zamzummim. Like those before them they were slaughtered, now by Yahweh's very own portion, the children of Israel, who were sent to conquer the lands occupied by these hybrid beings—blooming the *shedim* to frightening numbers."

"Which have tormented humanity since," Silas added, all of it making perfect sense now. "And manifested themselves in untold ways across the centuries. Including as extraterrestrial biological entities."

"Aliens..." Gina muttered.

Elijah smiled. "Bingo. And these giants were the height you described. Seven or eight, sometimes up to nine feet tall."

Bartholomew smirked. "Sounds like Goliath of Gath, the Giant King David fell with that sling of his."

"You're right on the mark, Vatican Archives Man. He was a remnant of the Anakim that Israel was supposed to drive out of the land of Canaan. Probably a bit over nine feet tall, according to most Hebrew manuscripts of the Old Testament."

"Whoa, that's crazy! Mind blown again..."

Gina smirked. "What would be crazier is if the Watchers were described like those giant reptiles our case studies spoke about. Remember those, Eli, from back in the FBI day?"

He eased back in his chair, smiling. "Actually, there is a Dead Sea Scroll that describes their appearance—4QAmram to be exact. It reveals the Watchers as *fearsome—like a serpent.*"

Silas took a step, leaning against the back of the open chair. "And what did your abductee case studies say about these giants?"

"Quite often," Gina explained, "the apparitions of said abductees have been reptilian in appearance, and especially huge, described as seven or eight feet tall."

"That's crazy..." Bartholomew said.

"But that doesn't speak at all," Silas said, "about the UFOs we witnessed. The—I can't believe I'm saying this, but the spaceships."

Elijah shrugged. "You heard it yourself. Jewish literature suggests the Watchers and their offspring had creative power. In fact, they possessed advanced knowledge that they pledged to pass along to humanity. A higher level of knowledge from the storehouses of the spirit-realm itself. Scientific, engineering, magical."

The room settled into a contemplative silence, the deep-dive into arcane Scripture and biblical theology seemingly numbing everyone's minds.

But Silas's was firing on all cylinders, and Elijah's insights into the Jewish context combined with illuminating parts of Scripture he had never considered before crystalized something for him. Especially what he had been thinking concerning the demonic nature of it all.

"Now that I think about it," he offered, "I suppose it doesn't sound too farfetched, given public belief in extraterrestrials and UFOs. Perhaps the principalities and powers of this dark world have primed people for such an invasion over the decades. And now they are using their creative power to reveal themselves in a way the citizens of the world would immediately recognize and trust."

Now Gina sat forward. "You could be onto something. The alien gods from the stars coming to bring salvation."

Bartholomew added, "And you believe they possessed advanced knowledge for what, UFOs zooming through outer space?"

"Or perhaps," explained Elijah, "they are transporting between spiritual dimensions, not zooming through space itself. Considering there is a Gnostic text with an alternative account of the Genesis flood, there is a ring of truth to it."

"What does that text say?"

"*The Apocryphon of John* suggests humanity was saved not by riding out the flood in Noah's ark, but rather by escaping in a glowing cloud."

"A glowing cloud?" Silas exclaimed.

"Is there an echo in here?" Elijah quipped.

Something was beginning to crystalize in Silas's mind now.

What if, by some fantastical means, the US government had benefited from this knowledge from the Watchers and their offspring, a knowledge so supernatural that it was tapped into somehow—only to be leveraged in military technology so terrifying it was kept secret from the American public, yet glimpsed over the years in equally terrifying ways?

Before he could voice his thoughts, his phone buzzed. He yanked it out. His heart dropped.

Celeste.

Answering, he said, "Tell me you've got good news."

She did. Gapinski was safe, if not shaken. They'd uncovered a weird lab full of equipment filled with beings that looked half human, half—something else.

But there was more.

His brother, Sebastian, had undergone some sort of hideous transformation. Looking like one of those blasted Nephilim Watcher-spirits they'd been studying. Then there was the revelation that Nous's HQ seemed to be located in the German castle. The Order had wondered where their operations had been housed. Nous had proven to be elusive, and Nicky—of all people!—had found them.

"Come to Rome," Silas said, disbelieving what she had uncovered. But also not surprised, given all the crazy SEPIO had faced over the years.

Time to prepare for the final showdown and land this crazy plane.

Or flying saucer, as the case may be.

CHAPTER 36

The smell of blessed black coffee and the warmth of sunlight woke Silas from a deep sleep. As did a crick in his neck and lower back from the single bed and lumpy pillow.

SEPIO may have been the cutting-edge clandestine operation of the Order of Thaddeus, but they still suffered with monastic accommodations, especially in their Rome outpost. A hold-over from their Vatican roots, he supposed. He was all for the vow of poverty, but couldn't they at least get a full-size mattress with decent support?

He stood and stretched, catching a glimpse of the dome crowning St. Peter's Basilica through the tiny window. The sky was a hopeful blue bearing a reassuring sun, with lazy clouds drifting across the expanse without a care. But he knew better. The last few days' events portended darkness and gloom.

Before leaving, the scent of coffee beckoning him onward, now joined by the smell of frying bacon, Silas crouched next to his bed. He stared up at a tiny, unassuming crucifix hanging from a wall of peeling white paint, thanking Christ for enduring the shame and suffering of the cross for even one such as him.

He crossed himself, then prayed the Lord's Prayer he had memorized as a child:

> *Our Father, who art in heaven, hallowed be thy*
> *   name;*
> *Thy kingdom come; thy will be done on earth as it is*
> *   in heaven.*
> *Give us this day our daily bread;*
> *And forgive us our trespasses as we forgive those who*
> *   trespass against us;*
> *And lead us not into temptation, but deliver us from*
> *   evil.*
> *For thine is the kingdom and the power and the glory*
> *   forever.*

"Amen," he said softly. He went to stand, but added: "And Lord, make speed to save your Church this day, make haste to help your servants of justice. Celeste and Torres, Gapinski and me...Elijah and Gina, and—" Couldn't believe he was actually going to say it, but he did. "And even Nicky."

Silas nodded and said *Amen* again. Then he crossed himself, stood, and left to find that coffee and bacon.

His nose brought him through a series of corridors of brick and stone painted beige, and down a winding staircase several stories below. Hadn't been inside the SEPIO's Rome operation in a few years. Not since the Templars had risen to avenge the Church's faithful from the persecuting violence Nous had spread across the world. What a trip that was! He had to ask for directions to the central hub twice from confused agents who hadn't a clue who he was. Not surprised, since he kept a low profile as Order Master.

Eventually, he arrived at a set of heavy steel doors with a keypad. He pressed his hand against the plate of glass, the security measure pulsing blue before turning green. The doors unlocked and he pushed through.

He was greeted by warm air, laden heavy with that coffee and bacon he had smelled earlier, chased by cheesy eggs and berry bread. His stomach rumbled in eager expectation.

Seated around a large horseshoe table in a vast space ringed by workstations and monitoring screens were the ones who had become his family. One in particular sent his pulse soaring. The one who would actually be his family. When he got around to it.

Seeing Celeste made him lose his breath. He grinned. Couldn't help it.

"Nice of you to join us, Mr. Sleepyhead," Gapinski said.

"Hey, Silas," Torres said.

"Good morning, everyone," Silas said, walking toward the group, who were already halfway through their breakfast. "Sorry I'm late. Rough night."

At a workstation, his favorite Italian techie clacked away on a keyboard, joined by an Indian man, Abraham Patel. Silas waved, thankful to have his two best operational support agents joining the rest of his crew.

More than that, he was thankful Matt had been found safe, but maybe not sound, given his experience. And mostly thanks to their new British friend, Nicky, who had also been invited. Joining them were Elijah and Gina, who had flown straight from Grand Rapids after the professor's dentist appointment. Figured SEPIO could use all the help they could get.

So, a full crew of eight, plus himself. Felt like back in the day in Iraq, with all systems go, and everyone coming together to fight the same good fight.

Grabbing his grub, Silas took his spot at the center of the U-shaped table next to Elijah. Then immediately stuffed a forkful of cheesy eggs into his mouth and crunched into a piece of well-salted bacon. He washed it down with black coffee and thought he'd died and gone to Heaven. Nothing in the world like a good old-fashioned American breakfast to get the day going.

But food could wait. Time to get back to it.

Swallowing, Silas cleared his throat. "Thank you for coming, everyone. I think it goes without saying, but we're all thanking the Lord you were rescued without a hitch, Matt. I hope you enjoyed your Pizza Hut pizza."

"Every bite of every piece!" Gapinski said, rubbing his stomach. To which everyone laughed on cue.

"And thanks, Nicky, for your support—both the intelligence and operational. Couldn't have done it without you."

Nicky nodded, saying nothing.

"But we're not out of the woods yet. Zoe, any more chatter on WeShare?"

The petite Italian stood, pushing those baby-blue glasses of hers up the bridge of her nose. "You could say that. Abraham and I have been tracking hundreds of such threads across the social media platform under the #TheTruthIsMe tag. Even more under #FirstContact from WeTube amateur videos."

"That aren't so amateur," added Abraham.

The man put one of them up on the large display anchored behind the pair at one end of the hall. A clear picture of a cloudless evening sky over some small town was visible, the sun having dipped below the horizon and thrown up all sorts of oranges and reds. And in zoomed a familiar delta-shaped craft, with blue and green lights, traveling at erratic and out-of-this world angles and direction.

The room murmured.

"That isn't all," Zoe continued, "I ran the specimen you requested through the test you wanted us to run."

Silas furrowed his brow, confused. "Specimen?"

"Yeah..."

"What are you talking about? I didn't order any test."

Gapinski laughed. "Yeah, about that, chief—"

"Matthew James!" Zoe protested with interruption. "You told me Silas wanted these results, and stat!"

"What are you playing at," Celeste said, "the both of you?"

The Italian huffed and crossed her arms, shoving those glasses back up her nose with irritation.

"I can explain!" Gapinski said.

But Zoe wouldn't let him. "Gapinski handed me a cigarette butt and said you, Silas, wanted it analyzed for DNA. Said it was urgent and to hop to it. Well, I did. For what reason, I can only guess."

That was unlike Gapinski to lie like that. Must be a good reason.

Silas turned to him. "Care to explain."

He shifted. "It's like this. The dude I saw back at that cray-cray castle in Deutschland, the man with the top hat—he was smoking a cigarette when I came to."

"Alright...So why the test?"

Gapinski took a breath before adding, "I remember him from Ramstein." Another breath before: "He was there when I was...experimented on."

Shock rumbled through the room.

"Understand the sentiment. Was as shocked as you are. Suppressed the whole memory of it, until it came back from the dead like a zombie."

"And the test?"

"Recognized the dude from our dig site." He continued, "Same man with the same bad habit. I saw the spent butt when I recovered, just lying there on the floor."

Hope flooded Silas, recognizing this could be the break they were needing.

He looked to Zoe. "Did you get a match?"

She nodded, sliding back into her chair and clattering at her keyboard.

"Sure did. A one Walter Kammler."

"Kammler?" Nicky startled.

Celeste said, "Isn't that the Nazi you had gone on about days ago?"

"Yes. But you said Walter."

Zoe nodded. "That's right."

Nicky made a fist and pounded the table. "I knew it."

"Knew what?" Silas asked.

"That Hans Kammler had indeed lived on, carrying on a life elsewhere."

"And apparently had a son," said Celeste.

"Precisely."

Silas turned to Gapinski. "Nice catch."

He grinned with pride. "That wasn't the only thing I caught."

Swallowing hard and shuddering, as if reliving a memory. He recalled what had happened to him in the chamber. Had felt a Force or Presence or Power, or whatever, and swore he saw it hovering across Kammler's shoulder.

"I glimpsed it as well," Celeste said, her normally steely voice shaky. "Before it sort of evaporated into the aether."

Nicky scoffed. "You're not really claiming to have seen a poltergeist in the bowels of that castle, are you?"

She turned to him, her eyes steely now where her voice was not. "Yes, Nicholas, I am."

He threw up his hands in surrender, muttering, "Well, I certainly saw nothing of the sort!"

Elijah leaned toward Gapinski. "Did it say anything to you?"

He took a breath and shook his head. "Didn't get a chance. He only introduced himself, and then I freaked."

"Introduced himself?" Gina asked.

This was wild. Silas prodded, "As what?"

Elijah said, "Not what, *who*."

"Who then?"

Gapinski answered, "Some dude, or dudette—supposed the alien demon could be a woman."

"Nope. Doesn't work that way," said Elijah.

"Whatever. Anywho, said alien demon introduced himself as something like Semjaza."

Elijah slapped both hands on the table. "Sweet mother of Melchizedek!"

Which made everyone jump.

"Do you think it could have been Shemyaza?"

"Uhh..." Gapinski looked to Silas for help. "That might have been it. Semjaza, Shemyaza. Toe-mahto, to-mayto. All the same alien demon to me!"

Silas asked, "Elijah, what do you have? This name familiar?"

"I'd say!" He muttered something to himself, grinning with marvel.

"Care to share, professor?" Celeste prodded.

"The alien literally named itself," he said. "That's bonkers!"

"Why?"

"Because Semjaza or Shemyaza—Schemchaza, even—is a Watcher listed in that obscure Jewish text we discovered, connected to the Book of Enoch!"

"What?"

"Get out of here..." Silas whispered, the picture drawing clearer.

Elijah continued, "He is the leading figure of the Genesis 6 Watchers episode we uncovered in the Vatican Archives."

"That's right," Silas said. "Wasn't he their leader, of the so-called sons of God?"

"Nope. Not so-called."

"Fine. The sons of God. Wasn't he even said to have given humanity enchantments?"

"Like alien technology?" asked Torres.

"Bingo!" Elijah said with excitement. "There is no way that is a coincidence."

"Then what does this mean," asked Celeste, "for Matthew here?"

"What else, but that he was contacted by a Watcher-spirit, a fallen one—an alien demon, if you prefer."

"Wild..." Silas said.

"Madness is what it is!" Nicky replied.

"Why?"

"Because the idea of some demon popping into our existence is utter rubbish!"

Celeste turned to him with crossed arms. "And aliens visiting us from distant planets isn't?"

Silas continued, "You're the one who brought us the dossier on all this nonsense to begin with, claiming the US government has been secretly continuing its UFO—"

"UAP," Elijah corrected.

Silas frowned, biting back a reply. "Fine, UAP program from decades ago. Why isn't it possible that this technology came from these supernatural beings the professor here says are these Watchers—what if they are the aliens we've been searching for?"

"Not only that," Celeste said, "we have confirmation that the son of one of the leading architects of the Nazi's program to leverage occult magic to supplement their war efforts into discovering a miracle weapon is in charge of it all. Alongside the head of the Church's nemesis, Nous."

That was probably the most surprising part of what Celeste said she discovered in their debrief. The Nazi connection, yes, but also Nous's—his brother's involvement.

Celeste continued, "Of course, Operation Paperclip supplied the US government with a ready-made stream of qualified Nazi scientists, some of whom were directly involved in these occult practices. Quite possibly channeling the enchanted teachings of this Semjaza Watcher."

"Oh my cheeps..." Elijah whispered. "That's it. That's the whole taco."

Gapinski leaned over. "I think what you're looking for is, the whole enchilada."

"Nope. Taco."

"Let me get this straight," interrupted Torres, shifting in her chair. "The US government and other Western nations, perhaps others across the world, have gotten hold of technology that appears alien but is in fact demonic—passed along through Nazis who were secretly working for the American space program. Amiright?"

"Seems to be the long and short of it," Celeste said.

"But how is that possible?"

Elijah said, "One of the things to keep in mind is that these sons of God also share in the Image of God."

That was new. Silas said, "Come again?"

"One of the things to keep in mind is that these sons of God also share in the Image of God—"

"I heard what you said. Now, what do you mean by that? Genesis 1 says humans were made in God's image."

Elijah shook his head. "Nope."

"Yes."

"Nope."

Silas sighed. He wasn't in the mood. "Alright, then what does it say?"

"It says, let us make mankind in *our* image."

"Right. The Trinity."

"Nope."

"What?"

"You're speaking of the sons of God," Celeste said, heading off confrontation, "aren't you?"

Elijah turned to her and smiled. "Bingo. The Image of God refers to a ruling status, something the Watchers themselves possessed before humans were created. Then, when God created mankind, God gave the authority to rule over Earth to humans."

That uneasy feeling returned to Silas's gut. Like everything he had known about his theological understanding of human nature had just gone up in smoke.

"In being given the authority to rule," Elijah went on, "humans—and this goes for the Watchers, too—they were given commands that were connected with abilities. The same creative powers we ourselves use in science and engineering, genetics and technology."

Silas frowned, not understanding the connection. "What is your point?"

"My point is, the Watchers could do anything we could do. But better, at a more advanced level, with a higher level of insight. I don't know, I'm still working that out."

"Like advanced space flight?" asked Gapinski. "Flying saucers, UFOs, UAPs—the whole enchilada?"

Elijah turned to him and grinned. "Bingo."

"If you're right—" Silas paused for a breath, almost afraid to ask, but he did anyway. "If what you're saying is true about these Watchers and their offspring, that there are these supernatural beings also made in Yahweh's image, these fallen ones, much like ourselves but supernatural...Then, well, where does that leave us? What does that do to our own identities as Image Bearers? Doesn't the existence of aliens, intelligent life, threaten our understanding of human nature?"

Elijah jumped to his feet and began to pace, bounding around on the balls of his feet with that unbounded energy again.

"I understand that fear, that acknowledging other beings is thought to necessitate the notion that humanity is not unique. For too long, people, and I include the Church in that group—

too many have defined the Image of God as something to do with intelligence."

"Well, doesn't it?" asked Celeste. "As well as will and emotions, along with cognition?"

"The Image of God isn't something you can qualify merely with humanistic, natural qualities because not all people in various stages of development will manifest those qualities. Unlike all other creatures on Earth, humans were created to be like God. This actually refers to status and not a specific ability."

He quickened his pace, really getting into his impromptu lecture now. Silas let a grin slip, enjoying the show and finding some resonance in what he was saying.

"Think of people with Down's syndrome," Elijah said, spinning around and standing still. "They are still Image Bearers, but they don't exhibit a fully developed sense of intelligence."

Had to give him that one. Seemed to give others in the room pause as well.

"Which means that all of this talk of society eliminating the Down's syndrome disability through selective abortion means instead that society is eliminating Down's syndrome people who bear the Image of God."

Torres snorted a laugh. "Tell that to Iceland."

"Same for us, I suppose, Eli," said Gina. "In our own condition."

Elijah shrugged, glancing at the ceiling and starting in on that tick of his. Thumb to index finger, thumb to middle, thumb to ring finger, thumb to pinkie. But only once.

He said, "Except, why should our autism not reflect some aspect of Yahweh's image? Why do allistic people get to decide what's normal?"

Gapinski raised a brow. "Allistic?"

Gina smiled. "I think we can wait for a deeper discussion on the spectrum until this is over. Didn't mean to sidetrack us."

"Nonetheless," Silas said, "I appreciate the point. What the Imago Dei means is certainly something worth reconsidering. Especially in light of this current operation. Disclosure about other intelligent life will surely change how humans view themselves."

"But it shouldn't!" Elijah continued, "Bearing God's image is about roles, in different places. We image God here on Earth. *They* image God out there, in the spiritual world."

"You mean the Watchers, the sons of God?"

He nodded. "At least they were supposed to. But then many of them fell, same as us, breaching the categories of Heaven and Earth by mating with humanity. And screwing everything up in the process as much as we screwed things up by eating of that dang tree. Sadly, both kinds of the Creator's Image Bearers are fallen ones."

Silas frowned. Ain't that the truth.

Shuffling back to his seat, Elijah slumped down, as if expended of his energy.

He went on, "So what if there is intelligent alien life? Intelligence does not equal Image. Even if intelligent aliens are in the universe, they are not us and we are not them. God does things in the universe that we do not know about."

"But now they are here," Silas said, "manifesting themselves."

"And a Nazi zombie," Gapinski said, "straight out of Castle Wolfenstein is trying to use them to raise up superbeings."

"Reminding us of the intensely spiritual nature of what is going on."

"Remember," Gina said, sliding up to the table and engaging the conversation, "when we worked with the FBI—" She frowned and shook her head, muttering: "Past tense..."

She shook her head again, continuing, "Anyway, what we found was the messaging given to these abductees was incredibly spiritual."

"Gnostic," Elijah added.

Silas clarified, "Meaning, salvation of humanity comes from within."

"And humans are a spark of the divine. The gnostic story is a strong competitor to early Christianity because it used Jesus language."

"For those of us not in the know..." Torres said, brow raised with confusion.

Silas explained, "The gnostic story has the true God creating the Aeon Sophia who then creates the God of the Bible who creates humanity. Yahweh is the bad guy, the serpent from the Garden of Eden in Genesis 3 is the good guy who tries to enlighten humanity regarding our true nature—sparks of the divine. Salvation is not about forgiveness of our rebellious sins and rescue from death, but becoming personally enlightened regarding our true divine nature—leveling up to a higher consciousness."

"This messaging," Gina went on, "is common with many abductee narratives. Lots of overlap between alien narratives and Gnosticism because the whole thing is inherently spiritual."

"Which means," added Celeste, "all of what has been transpiring the past week is inherently spiritual."

"Bingo," Elijah said. "Part of what's going on is that this is about spiritual messaging from spiritual beings who try to direct humanity away from God as spiritual competitors. These are intelligent demonic beings using old lies. Think of Genesis 3, and the promise to become like the gods."

"Like the sons of God..." Silas whispered, it all making sense now. "Which means extraterrestrials would be viewed like gods, coming down to save humanity. Not us, not of Earth or animals, but transcendent. Space equals heaven, right? A transcendent destiny for humanity."

"And yet," Celeste joined in, "all without the God of the

Bible or the pesky accountability that comes from having a Creator. No need to worry about our rebellious sin."

"Pagan Gnosticism dressed in twenty-first century clothes."

"Hate to interrupt..." Zoe said from across the way.

"But you're going to anyway," Elijah said.

Silas smirked. Blunt as usual. "What do you have for us, Zoe?"

"News conference," she said.

Nicky groaned. "Don't tell me London has been overrun by giant alien reptiles."

"Nothing that flashy. Just your run-of-the-mill Pentagon presser responding to the WeShare hysteria."

He scoffed. "About bloody well time!"

Silas asked, "Who's speaking?"

Zoe shrugged. "Check it."

She put up on the large display a familiar scene from the Department of Defense press room. A heavy navy curtain hung behind a row of generals. An image of the Pentagon hung at the center between them, with a man speaking from a podium. A tall man with broad shoulders, face square and jaw set, one arm hanging limp next to his side. Looked like any of the COs Silas might have run into in Iraq.

Gapinski gasped and pointed at the screen. "That's Top Hat Guy!"

"Don't you mean Cigarette Smoking Man?" Gina quipped.

"Who's that?" asked Celeste.

Silas turned to her. "*The X-Files* boogeyman. Matt, who is that?"

"The guy I saw looking straight into my kisser. Both times..."

Celeste said, "The one we discovered through his spent fag as Walter Kammler?"

"Are you sure, Matt?" asked Silas, ice flooding his veins at the implications.

Gapinski nodded, eyes narrowed and jaw set. "Dead to donuts, it's him."

"Googlizing now," replied Elijah, thumbing away on his phone.

Celeste shrugged. "Sort of looks like the bloke I saw slinking away."

"Walter S. Kammler," Elijah said. "Two-star general with the US Air Force."

"*Air Force*," Silas and Celeste said as one.

"Bloody hell..." Nicky said. "Kammler, you say?"

Elijah frowned. "Is there an echo in here? Yes. Two-star Air Force general."

"And the man who probed me..." Gapinski growled, trailing off with clenched jaw and beet-red face.

"Did you say, probed, Hoss?" asked Torres.

He turned to her. "From back in the day, at Ramstein. The memories all came flooding back when I was in that tank."

No one responded to that one, but it was clear they had a massive conspiracy on their hands, stretching back decades. With the supernatural entwined with the natural. The Watchers and Uncle Sam in an unholy tango. This Kammler dude and one of their own.

Celeste said, "I'd say we found our connection to the bloomin' Security Forces from the start of this whole bloody affair."

"I'd say," said Torres.

But what to do about it all...Silas hadn't a clue.

"There is someone who can help." Gina turned to Gapinski with eyes that said he himself knew the answer.

He gave his head a shake before snapping his eyes open. "Harris."

She nodded, saying nothing more.

Silas said, "Wasn't that your old Air Force buddy?"

"The one," added Celeste, "who had the same UFO experience as yourself, Matthew?"

"UAP," corrected Elijah.

"Stuff and nonsense..." she muttered while Gapinski nodded, saying nothing but face draining of color.

"I believe I mentioned it earlier," Gina explained, "but I've been in touch off and on with him through WeShare. Old patient-doctor relationship, you understand. Last I knew, he was working for a defense contractor."

Silas sat straighter at that nugget of information. "Defense contractor?"

"That's right. Works for Aether Aerospace, a defense contractor and aeronautics outfit out of Texas."

Nicky bolted upright. "Wait just a bloody second. Aether Aerospace, you say?"

Silas turned to him. "Didn't your MI6 intelligence source claim they were working on recovered alien UFO—"

Elijah sighed. "UAP."

"Fine, UAP—but wasn't that defense contractor said to be doing something with alien technology?"

Nicky nodded grimly. "Indeed."

The room settled into silent contemplation, the pieces falling together as the Pentagon presser did its best to contain the social media fallout, explaining it all away as it had before.

But now they had a solid lead that might land this crazy plane.

By the grace of the good Lord...

"Aether?" asked Elijah.

Gina nodded, "That's right."

"Interesting."

Silas turned to him. "Why is it interesting?"

"Because in Greek mythology, Aether is one of the primordial deities who is not only a sort of god of space. He also embodies the pure upper air that the gods breathe, as opposed to the normal air breathed by mortals."

"Like the Watchers?"

He nodded, saying nothing more but saying all he needed to say.

Now Silas turned to Gapinski. "We need to have a chat with this ex-airman buddy of yours."

Gapinski frowned. "You think Harris can help?"

Gina shrugged. "Given your shared experience, as well as his relationship with the military industrial complex—a perfect blending of the two, his UAP knowledge combined with his government insiderism. It's worth looking into."

"I should say so," said Celeste.

Silas nodded. "Definitely worth looking into."

"But Harris..." Gapinski sighed, slouching into his chair, the weight of all that'd happened clearly sapping him, combined with the relationship monkey wrench thrown into the mix. "You really think he's in on this nonsense?"

"Only one way to find out," Torres said.

Celeste nodded. "A good SEPIO interrogation should do the trick, I imagine."

"Always something..." Gapinski sighed.

Silas stood. "I guess it's Texas or bust."

Torres joined him. "I hear everything's bigger in Texas."

As did Gapinski. "Including its government conspiracies, I'd wager."

Ain't that the truth.

CHAPTER 37
DALLAS, TEXAS.

Silas drove their rental hard and fast, a Jeep Cherokee that fit like a glove, a familiar ride that drove like his own Jeep Wrangler, but nicer. Not Gapinski-ride nice, but enough to do the job.

He needed something familiar, given all the uncertainty that had been thrown his way.

Saved a few bucks, too, so that should count for something on the TPS report he had to submit to Weiss for expenses, but he wasn't holding his breath.

The drive was an easy one to a suburb north of Dallas. Didn't expect it, given the size of the urban sprawl, but he guessed it was because it was Sunday morning, and everyone was doing their Christian duty, keeping the Sabbath and all.

For Silas's part, he resurrected a Hail Mary from childhood and invoked it for the final leg of their operation—hoping something clicked in place with this Harris character.

Gapinski was still recovering from the hell he'd been through next to him in the passenger's seat, eyes closed and mouth agape with snorts and snores filling the cabin. Figured he'd earned it after all his personal crazy. Torres and Celeste were in the back, with Gina and Elijah half a country away in

Grand Rapids. The good professor needed to get to his dentist appointment, God bless him, which he'd complained loudly about missing. Was able to reschedule an emergency appointment that morning. Something about the dentist owing him a favor. Didn't get it, didn't want to. Probably best to give him a breather while they sussed out the lead in Dallas.

Speaking of which...

Pulling up to the curb, a Lincoln Aviator sat in the driveway of a two-story, red-brick house that looked like all the rest in that cookie-cutter slice of middle-class American suburbia. It gleamed under a fresh coat of wax, the driveway wet and a green hose still snaking from the house.

A good sign Harris was home.

A good start.

Silas parked. Gapinski snorted awake and said he'd take it from there. He was fine with that, and they all got out and walked across the grass.

A noise from the garage caught their attention.

Then a tall, shirtless man with a blond buzz cut sauntered out holding a beer. Stopped short when he saw the SEPIO crew, then craned his neck forward as if disbelieving his eyes.

"Gapinski?" he said.

"The one and only!"

"Can't believe my peepers. What the hell are you doing in Texas? It's been, what, almost two decades?"

He threw back a swig of his Bud Lite and sauntered over, eyeing Silas before his eyes wandered to the ladies—a bit too long for his liking.

Harris gestured with his beer. "Who are they? Jehovah's Witness?"

Gapinski laughed. "Navy SEALs for Jesus, actually."

"Huh?"

"I'll explain inside. Got another beer?"

Harris didn't move, his smile fading. "What's this about, Gapinski?"

He glanced at Silas before saying, "Ramstein. Christmas."

Silas swore he saw the color drain along with that smile. Thought he'd run them out then and there.

Instead, he turned toward the front door. "Forget beer. I've got a big-ass bottle of Stoli vodka for this one. Costco special."

"Even better..." Gapinski said, following him inside.

Celeste whispered to Silas, "Do you think he'll talk?"

"Hope so. Because he's the last lead we got on all this crazy."

Torres snorted a laugh. "So, everything is riding on Gapinski and his war buddy?"

"On a buck and a prayer..."

The inside was an open floor plan rising high to the second floor. Honey-colored wood floors ran throughout, with the same-colored leather furniture anchored on what looked like a genuine bear rug in the living room in front of a chunky stone fireplace. A large moose head with a nice-sized rack hung above the mantle. Rifles from a few centuries ago stood in a glass case on one wall. A kitchen table of reclaimed wood sat next to a large kitchen with granite countertops and craftsman cabinets.

Which was where Harris was, grabbing Gapinski and himself tumblers full of Stoli vodka on ice.

The two of them huddled in the kitchen while Silas and the ladies sat waiting. Probably catching up, probably running through their reason for the visit.

Silas was thinking that Hail Mary might not be enough.

After their ten-minute huddle, the pair returned, drinks in hand. Gapinski handed off a tumbler of whiskey to Silas, which he was most grateful for.

"Gapinski filled me in," Harris said, taking an oversized leather chair flanking the couch, where Gapinski plopped down next to him.

Silas thanked him for the drink in the chair opposite Harris, then got to it.

"We're hoping you can help us out. Fill in the details about what's been going down."

He chuckled and threw back a swig of Stoli. "What's been going down? You mean ETs most recent song and dance."

Silas nodded, throwing back a mouthful of his own drink.

"Where do you want me to start?"

"How about from the top?"

"From the top? Hell, that's a mile-high skyscraper you're looking to climb."

Before Silas could respond, he kept going.

"Because there's David Adaris, who worked on building a secret propulsion system and was invited to Area 51 where he saw a massive engine."

"*The* Area 51?" Torres said.

Harris frowned and whispered, "There another Area 51 I don't know about?"

He sent up a condescending giggle before throwing back more Stoli, surely lubricating his mouth. Whatever worked.

"That's right, little missy. Shook the man to his core."

Throwing back a swig of Stoli, Harris went on, "Then there's Code Name Aurora, under which the military industrial complex produced the stealth fighter Dark Star. Aka Astra. SR–75 was its military code. Many insiders believe it holds secret technology from recovered UFOs. The Skunk-Works Lockheed Martin facility was responsible for the Astra fighter. See if this rings true. The craft is triangular, with nuclear propulsion, noiseless, magnetics emitting a field disruptor, neutralizes the effect of gravity, cannot be detected on radar."

Silas startled. "That's the Astra fighter?"

"No, UAPs. But the tech is being incorporated into these super-secret crafts."

Which sounded to him exactly like what he and Gapinski had seen.

He sat forward, taking another swig of whiskey. "Go on."

"More recently," Harris said, "there was the USS Nimitz events. November 2004, they were. A Tic Tac, cigar-shaped craft traveling off the California coast was spotted by Air Force pilots. Weird speeds and directional shifts were detected. Wasn't seen as hostile, but it wasn't seen as friendly, either, given how close it was traveling to the US mainland coast. Several of them were sighted, acting like flocks of birds."

The man paused, settling back in his chair, staring off past Silas. Where, he didn't know.

Then he said lowly, "Whatever and whoever was driving those bad boys—well, they have the technology to go anywhere they choose. In the water and up into the upper atmosphere and space, defying radar and surveillance. They have the technology we don't. Although, given what I have seen in my line of work, it now seems to be leading to new technology in our own current military craft."

Draining his glass, Harris bolted to his feet and sauntered to the kitchen.

"This is exactly what Elijah was speaking about," Silas said. "The Watchers giving humans advanced technology."

"And you think the US government," Celeste said, "has incorporated it into its own aircraft?"

"Sounds like it to me!"

"How?" asked Torres.

"Through the same pagan nonsense," Gapinski growled, "that almost turned me into an alien..."

The group went silent, the truth of it settling between the SEPIO crew.

Harris sauntered back, fiddling with his phone in one hand and bearing the Stoli bottle in the other. Shoving the phone in his pants pocket, he poured himself a fresh glass.

He said, "Of course, most Americans ain't heard tail nor hide of any of this. From where I sit, the US government has kept a tight lid on UFO information to increase fear over the years."

Silas scoffed. Sounded more like tin-foil hat nonsense than anything.

"You scoff?" Another swig of Stoli, then he pointed at Silas. "You ever heard of Project Sunshine."

"I've heard of *Little Miss Sunshine*," Gapinski quipped.

Harris nodded. "Good movie. But that ain't it."

Silas crossed his arms. "No, I haven't. What of it?"

"During World War II, the Japs, their military gurus and scientists and whatnot, developed these high-altitude balloons. Plan was to send balloons with bioweapons across the Pacific using the upper atmosphere to reach US shores and then explode. A combination of Operation Fugo, which called for sending bombs across the Pacific to set fire to American forests, combined with Unit 731, their fancy-schmancy bioweapons unit."

"And?"

He took a swig and shrugged. "They succeeded during the test phase."

Silas furrowed his brow in confusion. "You mean the Japanese military sent balloons carrying bombs into the sky, they travelled across—what, four- or five-thousand miles of ocean water, then successfully reached the shores and exploded?"

"Righto."

Celeste asked, "I don't ever recall hearing this bit of historical intrigue."

"That's my point!" Harris exclaimed. "The US press was prevented from talking about it by the military. Didn't want to clue the Japs into the fact they succeeded, let alone panic the American public. Pearl Harbor was a bad enough PR disaster.

What'd ya think would happen if the Axis enemy could reach LA with a bio-bomb?"

"Panic," Torres said.

"An all-out rebellion, more like it!" Gapinski added.

Harris nodded. "Righto. So, yeah, way back when Uncle Sam was already developing information-suppression techniques they then further enhanced with Project Blue Book. I assume you know enough to be in the know on that front, right?"

They all said they did.

Silas said, "So you think they're doing that now, still suppressing information about UFOs and aliens?"

"Maybe. Wouldn't put it past them." Harris continued, "Take the case of Huffman, Texas. December 1980. A pair sees something buzzing about on the highway. Betty Cash and Vicki Landrum, their names were. Thought it was the second coming of Christ! They got out of their car and approached the thing resting on the pavement. Almost immediately their skin burns, welts appearing all over, they lose skin and hair."

Celeste said, "Sounds consistent with exposure to radiation."

"You think? Helicopters escorted the vessel away from the highway. To a place that was part of Bergstrom Air Force Base."

Silas sat straight, glancing at Celeste. The Air Force... Another link to that branch of the US government.

Harris poured himself more Stoli and continued, "Richard Dotty, some engineer on base, claimed it was a diamond-shaped vessel using reverse-engineered tech experimenting with nuclear propulsion, and that it had mechanical problems off-base. Ladies were in the wrong place at the wrong time." Another long swig, the man leaning forward and resting on his knees. "The technology is real, man. And being hidden. But not for long."

Gapinski sat straighter. "You're talking disclosure."

"Got that right, brother!"

"By whom?" asked Celeste.

"John Podesta for one."

"Podesta?" Silas said. "As in, what, the former White House Chief of Staff to Clinton?"

"That's right. It all came out in emails that were part of the Russia hack of 2016 and the WikiLeaks unveiling."

Torres scoffed. "WikiLeaks. Now there's a credible source!"

"No, seriously, listen. Tom Delong—"

"And now the Blink-182 frontman?"

"Tom Delong—" Harris said, voice rising and nostrils flaring with irritation. "He and Podesta coordinated UFO intelligence they had gathered in order to release it to the public. Idea was to disclose when Clinton—the missus variety—was elected. Sort of a way for the feds to disclose through coordination with the intel community to release without the government saying so."

"What's the point of it all?" asked Celeste, face dripping with skepticism.

"To get the government to acknowledge the existence of UFOs and ETs and not do anything about it. But if they did that, would that lead to panic? Probably, so the government drips out the intelligence through unofficial channels. Or they use it to panic the public into increasing their power."

That sure sounded familiar to Silas. Panicking the public had been Uncle Sam's MO for almost two decades now. Between the airport security theater and all the coronavirus nonsense that kept people gripped in panic from some respiratory virus, the feds had the corner market on government-sponsored panic porn.

"Inevitable disclosure will happen," Harris went on. "It has to! They'll have to admit we're not alone. For six millennia, humans have been the biggest intelligent cheese on the universe block. Not anymore. How will the world react to the truth that we are not alone? That's the big hairy question no one wants to deal with."

Gapinski said, "Except now it seems to be happening without their control."

Harris nodded. "Which begs the questions no one wants to ask."

"What sorts of questions?" asked Celeste.

"Who are they? Where are they from? What do they want? Why are they here? No one knows or has the answers!"

The man drained his drink and slumped back in his chair, the room going quiet in the face of the questions still begging for answers.

"You know, I've gone back," Harris finally said, still slumped and staring off past Silas again.

Gapinski shook his head. "Gone back..."

"To that forest, outside that golf course at Ramstein."

"No, I didn't know that. What for?"

He shrugged. "Just to feel the place. To stand in the memory of what happened to us."

"Which is why we've gotta talk about it, man. We've got to disclose!"

Harris went to take a swig but saw his glass was empty. "Course, that ain't gonna happen."

"Why not, man?" Gapinski said, then glanced at Silas. "Why not us?"

Harris laughed. "Because even after what's been flying around WeShare—no pun intended—the skeptics will throw up all kinds of arguments." He waved a hand and sloshed more Stoli in his glass. "Not worth it, brother."

"But what can they say?"

Harris answered, "We're alone in the universe, for one. We've been debating for eons whether intelligent life is out there somewhere beyond the deep blue sea. With all we've discovered in recent years, something like 400 exoplanets beyond our solar system, you'd think they'd answer in the affirmative. But nooooo. The evidence could live either way on that front, whether intelligence exists elsewhere. We just don't know yet."

Slurping back a mouthful, Harris went on, "Course, even if it does, skeptics say they're too far away from Earth anyhow. Theory of relativity and all discounts it. Would take some 4,500 Earth years for anything to arrive just from the nearest star system."

Silas said, "So the physical constraints on interstellar travel rule out ETs."

Harris shrugged. "So they say. Computer models say any advanced civilization should have reached Earth long ago, even traveling below the speed of light. How long ago, now that depends on the models. But some suggest within 100 million years."

Another swig before Harris continued, "Visitors from other civilizations *should* be here already. The Fermi Paradox, it's called."

"What's that?"

"Some fancy name for the contradiction between the lack of evidence for extraterrestrial life and high estimate they probably exist."

"In other words," Silas said, "where are they if there's a good chance they exist?"

"Righto, partner. It's like this—" Another swig before explaining, "given how far we've come as a human community in just a few centuries since the scientific revolution, think about how far another civilization might have come in three millennia."

"Or a few million years."

"Righto, partner."

Silas considered this, making the link to all this discussion on the sons of God. Because if they were created before humans, and they visited humans before, according to Genesis 6—well, then maybe they're the missing link.

"Of course," Harris went on, "some wonder if there were aliens, why don't they land on the White House lawn and introduce themselves. Others suggest the world would know definitely by now if ETs were here, given all our fancy-shmancy technology. I don't find them arguments persuasive."

"Why not?"

"It's what Donald Rumsfeld said."

Silas chuckled. "The former Secretary of Defense said something about aliens?"

"Not aliens, per se. It's how he talked about dealing with 'known unknowns' and 'unknown unknowns.'"

He heard a lot of that talk while serving in Iraq. "Makes sense. Go on."

"Same with UFOs and ETs. We don't know what we don't know. But far from proving they don't exist, all anyone up the food chain has done is prove their ignorance."

"Or make it out to appear they are."

Harris pointed at Silas and nodded. "Righto, partner. No one wants to admit what they know. It's better to feign ignorance than speak the truth. After all, if any UFOs *were* discovered to be piloted by other beings from elsewhere in the universe—well, then that would be one of the most important events in world history."

Celeste said, "What's the downside, if it would be so important?"

"Lots! Obviously, admitting to IDing UFOs as alien tech, piloted by bonafide ETs would be admitting to the existence of a powerful threat. Some other civilization reaches Earth—well, obviously they've got vastly superior technology."

"Which means colonization..." said Torres.

"Or even extermination," Gapinski added.

"Righto, partner. How do governments protect their citizens

from that? Which leads to the second dealio in the mix." Another swig of Stoli before explaining, "the tremendous pressure for a one world government."

Silas scoffed. "Doesn't sound too possible, given our modern democratic impulses."

"Maybe, but modern nation-states pride themselves on their sovereignty. Their ability to tax and spend and set zoning laws without the approval of some bureaucrats on some other continent."

"Pretty well sums up Brexit," said Celeste.

"Righto, partner."

"But maybe that's just what's at play here."

"What do you mean?" asked Silas.

She turned to him. "Look at what has transpired the last few years with the pandemic, and the impulse for nation-states to ratchet up restrictions and consolidate power in the face of an existential threat. Facing down the possibility of a colonizing, exterminating alien threat could be just the thing to finally flip the switch on everything the globalists have ever wanted. Give them permission to give it all a go."

Now Harris pointed at Celeste. "You could have something there, little missy. But that gets into the third threat such a thing would pose. The anthropocentric nature of modern sovereignty."

Gapinski twisted up his face. "Antler-pothocary-whatchamacallit?"

"The assumption," Celeste answered, "only we humans have the right to determine our collective fate."

Harris said, "Righto, partner. Mother Nature might put a monkey wrench in things with climate change and coronaviruses, but us *Homo sapiens* decide how we deal with it all."

Torres snorted a laugh. "That's not arrogant at all."

He shrugged. "Maybe, but it beats thinking Nature or the gods are in control of things. It's also how modern governments are able to command the loyalty of their citizens and command their resources—money, time, labor. Just think of how taking UFOs seriously would call this deeply held assumption into question."

"Suppose it would raise doubts," said Gapinski, "about the government being the biggest cheese on the block."

"I'd say! Would raise all sorts of possibilities of something close to the second coming of Jesus Christ himself."

That got Silas's attention. He glanced at Celeste, whose eyes were wide with the same curiosity.

"Go on, then," she said. "What do you mean by that notion?"

"Think about it. With the arrival of ET, who do you think people would give their loyalty to? America, the global super-power who couldn't spot the Death Star coming their way? Please! Serious doubts would be raised whether such govern-ments could survive. The possibility of UFOs and their alien drivers creates a deep insecurity. So governments repress anything relating to UFOs because they fear what it might expose."

"The emperor has no clothes, you mean," Torres said.

"Or the President of the United States," added Silas.

Celeste said, "But this assumes denying the existence of UFOs will automatically maintain anthropocentric rule. Or the reverse, I suppose, that exposure would collapse it into willing servants of a new alien overlord."

"Perhaps," Harris said. "Or it would mean the reverse. It would galvanize individual nation-state citizens into collective action."

Torres said, "A sort of worker bees of the world, unite!"

"Thanks Karl Marx."

"It would sure bring the globalists together," Silas said. "That's for sure."

"Led by a rogue Air Force general," Celeste said, "with ties to both the Nazi-led miracle weapon initiative and religious terrorists bent on world conquest—taking the Church and her theology down with their plan."

Harris did a double take, literally shaking his head and snapping it to Celeste. He turned pale and licked his lips before swallowing.

"Come again, little missy?"

Gapinski clued his war buddy friend into what they had discovered, the connection with Kammler and what they had discovered in Germany. After which Harris promptly downed the rest of his vodka.

"That's some heavy tonnage, right there."

"You're telling me," Gapinski sighed. "If only you could get us into Area 51 with your aerospace contract creds."

Harris sputtered his lips. "Naw, man, Area 51 is totally overrated."

He shifted to the edge of his seat. "But you know where?"

"I've heard rumors in my line of work."

"Then where? We need final proof to blow this all wide open and expose this conspiracy for what it is."

He tilted his head back with contemplation. "Wright-Patterson, that's where."

"What's that?" asked Silas.

"An air force base in Ohio," said Gapinski. "Isn't that right?"

"Yuppers. O-Hi-Ohhh."

"Ohio?" Celeste said, sitting straighter now.

Joined by Torres: "Ohio?"

Harris chuckled. "Is there an echo in here? Yeah, that's what I said."

Silas said, "What part of Ohio?"

"Southwest."

"That's where that news report came from of those UFO sightings."

"And don't forget," Torres said, "all those people waking up in the middle of that field."

Celeste added, "And that hunter stumbling upon them arrayed in a Heaven's Gate-style circle."

Gapinski nodded, jaw set and ready to get to it. "Time to end this ET shucky-ducky." Turning to Harris, he asked, "Can you get us inside?"

"Whoa there, partner," Harris said, throwing his hands up in the air. "This ain't my rodeo to ride in."

"Yes, it is! You were there. Both of us. You saw what happened. Hell, you've been working for the very military industrial complex that's responsible for Kammler!"

"That was not my fault!"

Gapinski took a breath, rubbing a hand across his bald head.

"I know, sorry. But you've got a chance to finish what happened to us way back when. To expose what we both went through, what untold other numbers of people have gone through."

Harris sprang to his feet, shuffling over to a bar and yanking a glass plug from a bottle. He poured himself two fingers' worth of caramel liquid, then raised it to his mouth. Stopping short, he closed his eyes and took a breath, then threw back the entire glass.

He swallowed hard and winced. Something clearly weighing on the man's creased face.

The room waited in silence, a mantle clock beneath the massive moose head ticking by the seconds, then a few minutes while Harris poured himself another tumbler-full of caramel alcohol and threw back yet another mouthful in one fell swoop.

Setting the glass down with a smack, he turned back to the group waiting for his answer, face red and sweaty, eyes dim and sagging of life.

Then he said, "Alright. Let's do this thing."

Gapinski's eyes flashed wide with surprise before narrowing with resolve. He stood and nodded, then sauntered over to his old war buddy.

"Let's get these bastards!"

Harris offered a weak grin. "Yee-haw..."

He put up an open palm. "No, not yee-haw. Hooah, soldier!"

Harris glanced at it and nodded, then clasped it.

The men shared an embrace, then a moment.

Silas sighed with relief, feeling like they were finally about to resolve this whole insane operation.

Time to pay the piper, Kammler.

CHAPTER 38

WRIGHT-PATTERSON AIR BASE.
GREENE COUNTY, OHIO.

Another state, another cornfield. Going on back-to-back operations now. Between Mill Creek Junction and southwest Ohio, Silas would never eat another ear of corn as long as he lived.

Was much more interested in taking the fight to exotic places around the globe. Maybe because of his international roots globetrotting with Dad from military base to military base through most of his childhood, or his own tours with Uncle Sam and travels across Europe during the few times he could take leave. Paris, Rome, London, Frankfurt, even Kiev, which was a trip.

It was also probably because of his snootiness at Midwest living that had little cosmopolitan sense about it. Though his last operation in small-town USA certainly gave him a better appreciation for the simple life, where family, church, and country were pride of place.

Whatever the reason, he was ready for a SEPIO operation to take him overseas again. Maybe find some old saint's bones in Ireland or Germany, or Noah's ark up some mountain in Turkey. Although, they did already have a set of bones from that part of the world, seemingly from that era. Bones that told

a story, one that seemed to confuse our ancestors' development and muddy the waters about our identity. Shoot, maybe
they'd lead them to the Garden of Eden. Wouldn't that be
something!

There'd be time for that. Later, after this operation was
wrapped up.

Now his head needed to be in this game. The one that
Harris had arranged for them, with the man riding shotgun
and leg rapping a mean beat against the floorboards of their
Chevy Suburban with a nervous energy.

Not thrilled about riding in the familiar vehicle that had
been dogging them since that French bistro in Dupont Circle
back in the District. The one where Celeste and him should
have been planning their wedding.

Needed to do something about that, stat. Something he was
fixing to fix once the operation ended and they were home free.

If they ended the operation and were home free, that is.
Because item one on the to-do list was finishing what they
started in that bistro before Nicky McGrath messed things up
to high heaven. They had started putting into motion their
plans to get hitched, and it was about time they tied the knot.

Silas yanked at his collar, undoing the top button of his
white shirt and loosening his tie. Couldn't stand suits. Last time
he'd worn one he'd been dragged into an operation not of his
choosing. There he was again, rumbling toward destiny in the
same getup, along with the rest of his crew. Gapinski, Elijah,
and Harris were sporting the same gear, along with Celeste,
Torres, and Gina in their more feminine counterpart costumes.
Had to look the part to get into the joint.

Rows and rows of corn stretched on toward the horizon
ablaze in the glory of the sun. The sharp tang of manure and
dead leaves rode in on the frigid fall breeze gusting through
Silas's open car window, with the heat blasting and Survivors
'Eye of the Tiger' on repeat, those familiar electric guitar

chords strumming their revving anthem as that piano did its thing while Jimi Jamison did his thing.

It was go time, and Jimi and his power ballad would carry them through to the end after all the crazy—along with the Holy Spirit.

"Here we go, partners." Harris sat straight, the rapping switching to the other leg as he pointed out ahead.

The on-base checkpoint was coming into view. Bright and white, with lights high and shining down with interrogatory intent.

Here we go is right...

Silas buttoned his shirt back up and adjusted his tie, putting his costume back into place. He eased the car up to the red-and-white gate bar that also had a doozy of a color coordinated gate barrier stuck in the middle of the road. Wouldn't get through that with a Mack truck, let alone a Suburban.

Or out, if it came to it...

A Security Forces airman with a narrow gaze stepped to the window, sporting an indigo jumpsuit and menacing M4 rifle slung around wide shoulders across a barrel chest.

"What's your business?"

"Here, pass this along." Harris handed Silas a badge, which he passed through the window.

Leaning toward the window, Harris explained, "Lieutenant Colonel Harris here, with business at NASIC. We all do."

The security grunt eyed the credentials, then asked for everyone's identification.

Silas collected the IDs hot off the press and passed them along. Then promptly threw up a prayer for mercy.

The man had explained his connection to the National Air and Space Intelligence Center through Aether Aeronautics. Apparently, his final rank with the Air Force had landed him a cushy job with the defense contractor that had put him in top-secret circles across a smattering of bases. One of which was

Wright-Patterson, a base with a shadowy history on par with Area 51 that went far deeper and longer than that infamous conspiracy-riven military complex.

Plan was to come under the guise of his contract work. The SEPIO crew had been given similar clearance through some fancy footwork behind the scenes between both Zoe and Nicky. Wasn't thrilled the British spook was in on their operation. Not in the slightest. And he wasn't thrilled to be aiding and abetting a foreign intelligence operative to lift up Uncle Sam's skirt to reveal all their UFO and ET secrets.

But given the stakes, Silas figured all the help they could get was warranted, even if he wondered whether he could fully trust him. Supposed if Celeste could, that was enough. And most of the others were there sitting in that steel sardine box on wheels because others could trust them. Gapinski knew and trusted Gina with his life. Gina swore Elijah was the best there was. And Gapinski had vouched for his war buddy Harris.

Silas just hoped these unknowns pulled through for him, for SEPIO.

For the Church and the world.

"Cleared!" the airman yelled, handing Silas back Harris's badge and the other IDs before waving them on through.

Silas threw the Suburban into *Drive*. That was easy.

Harris guided him as he raced through the base toward an entrance the man used for his assignments with NASIC. Was coy about what exactly he did, claiming top-secret privilege and all. But the man swore what he worked on would be exactly what SEPIO needed to blow open the operation that had sent the world into a tailspin. Not only at the UFO level, but the alien one. The real one where the Watchers' offspring were conspiring with the US government to force a globalist agenda.

Parking, the agents exited the vehicle and followed Harris inside the building. A modest thing of cinder blocks painted white, without any windows and a single door. Looked like a storage unit from one of those 24-hour rentals.

Storing what...Silas could only imagine. Soon they would find out.

He was just thankful the sun had fully set, and they were shrouded in the emerging night's darkness. Not as many lights in these parts either, the more secretive sector of the base not receiving as much security-light love. Fine by him. Less light meant less optics. Crucial for any operation.

The Suburban emptied, and Harris ran through a series of security protocols at the entrance. The door opened to reveal an empty room with another door standing at the center.

Torres asked the obvious: "*Qué es esto?*"

Elijah replied. "Elevator shaft, is what it is."

Harris hustled to another keypad. "Righto, partner."

Silas glanced at Gina, who had gone white but was holding it together. Could tell her breath was labored and brow was breaking out in a line of beading sweat. But she hung in there. A good troop, that's for sure.

"Where does it lead?" asked Celeste.

"Down," Elijah replied.

She turned to him with a raised brow. "You think?"

The door slid open, and Harris hustled inside. "To the golden goose at the end of the rainbow."

Gapinski snorted a laugh. "Mixing metaphors a bit there, aren't you, pal?"

Silas followed the man, and the others filed in after.

"We need to hustle it up," Harris muttered, checking his watch before running through another set of security protocols at a keypad. Palm reader, codes, key fob—the whole nine yards.

Place was locked down tighter than Fort Knox. Which made sense, if whatever lurked below was indeed the golden goose SEPIO had been searching for.

"We're cleared, though, right?" he asked. "Because the

credentials our team created and the magic you worked on your end, we should be good."

Gapinski added, "Plus it's the middle of the night. Everyone knows nobody pays attention to what happens on-base after sunset."

A successful ping sounded, followed by a sudden weightless descent.

"They do on this one, partner," Harris said. "You all ready for what comes next?"

Silas said, "Suppose we have to be. Sort of a captured audience now that we're underground."

"Got that right..." the man muttered, checking his watch again. Curious, but he'd be as nervous as a fox in a henhouse too, Silas wagered, given the stakes. Man could lose his job, his life even, subverting the classified secrets of the US government.

They all could...

Just hoped it was worth it.

Didn't take long before they were slowing to a stop, that weightless feeling giving way to a heavy groundedness before settling.

The elevator door slid open, and everyone gasped as one.

"Holybamoly, Batman..." Gapinski whispered with marvel.

"Oh my cheeps," Elijah agreed with the same.

"Egads," Gina said louder.

"*Dios mío...*" Torres chimed in.

"Crikey," Celeste added.

Silas said nothing. Couldn't. Didn't need to. The rest did the talking for what they were standing before.

All of what they were standing before.

Harris stepped out first, followed quickly by Silas. Figured the others were following in their own way, at their own pace, but didn't break visual with the sight before him to find out.

They had descended into a subterranean chamber that

looked more like a massive hangar. Made sense, given they were on an Air Force base. But this was something out of a movie, it was so vast.

Stretched several stories and at least a mile into the darkness, a series of red lights running down the center blinking far into the maw. Both sides of the subterranean landing strip were lined by a fleet of the familiar delta aircrafts that had been the mainstay of not only UFO sightings stretching back half a century—but they looked similar to the ones he himself had seen.

Strike that.

Exactly like what he had seen.

"Oh, I am *soooo* putting this on my WeTube channel..."

Silas glanced over to find Gapinski holding his phone like a pro vlogger, a tiny LED beam slicing through the dim darkness to capture the science-fiction scene. Torres joined him as well.

Good idea. Maybe they could live-stream their discovery.

Except...looking at his own cellphone, there was zero reception. At least there'd be video evidence. No way Uncle Sam could deny what they'd been covering up.

Silas took a hesitant step, then some more, making his way toward the triangular crafts. They were smooth and undulating with a blue-and-green light pattern around their perimeter. Iridescent, even, the armor plating almost blending into the background. Soundless and hovering without the need of landing gear.

But that wasn't all the vast hangar carried.

Celeste muttered something under her breath, then: "Are those..."

Hydrochambers like the ones she and Torres had reported in Germany lined the back of the chamber. Filled with greenish liquid and—what Silas could only describe as alien beings. Tall and naked, floating in peaceful repose.

Elijah made for those, whispering, "Disembodied spirits of dead Nephilim..."

Gapinski said, "Don't look disembodied to me."

The professor turned to him. "I was speaking about demons. Second Temple Jewish literature understands demons and the demonic forces to be disembodied spirits of dead Nephilim."

Celeste asked, "The ones swept away during the Great Flood?"

Elijah nodded. "And also butchered during the Israelite conquests."

"Across Canaan, you mean?"

"That's right. But this..." The professor swept his hand across the tanks. "These look like an embodiment of those ancient bastard-born beings."

They did. Massive in size with the bulbous heads and sixth digit matching the remains that Gapinski and Torres discovered in Turkey. Could it be true? Did the US government somehow resurrect these beings, with the help of Nazi scientists steeped in the occult?

This wasn't happening...

Yet there it all was. In living color.

Proof.

Only question was, what do they do with it all?

A shuddering clang at the end of the room startled the group, joined by revving engines and stomping feet.

Everyone spun toward the sound.

As a caravan of jeeps and soldiers came barreling their way.

Gapinski cried, "Sonofa—"

"That looks like a platoon of bloody soldiers," Celeste said with interruption.

Silas steeled himself. That it did.

He spun around, searching for options but coming up dry.

Couldn't very well pull out his Beretta on incoming soldiers.

Although, they'd already fired on the feds, so why not add the boys in camo to the list of charges?

With nowhere to go, it didn't take long before familiar beige military vehicles swarmed around them like lions stalking their prey. The open-hatch vehicles skidded to a halt in a circular formation around the group backed in against themselves at the center of the airstrip.

Soldiers leaped from the vehicles and aimed M4 rifles at them all. No doubt ready to put them down hard and cold if any one of them sneezed wrong.

The line parted, and outstepped a familiar face.

The man in the top hat, a cigarette between his lips, with the pleasant scent of cinnamon and cloves riding in on a hazy cloud following the two-star general into the circle.

Walter Kammler.

Dressed in the same military garb they'd seen him in at the press conference. A pressed navy suit typical of the US Air Force, medals tinkling at his chest with every step, what light there was glinting off from two stars affixed to his shoulders.

Gapinski muttered to his friend, "I thought you said we were good to go, buddy."

Harris said nothing, face oddly calm. Perhaps the man had a plan to get them out of this mess.

But then something happened. Something entirely unexpected, but probably predictable.

Harris sauntered out from the line of detention and sided up to Kammler. His jaw set tight and eyes narrowed with steely emotion.

"Crikey, what's this?" asked Celeste, mouth open as if in the same question that was on Silas's mind.

"Always something..." Gapinski growled in a whisper, face reddening and eyes moistening over with betrayal. "You were in on the operation, the whole time?"

Harris said nothing, the man widening his stance and

throwing his hands behind his back. Ready to receive orders from the man who had been dishing them secretly for decades. Probably since he had been abducted, or experimented on, or whatever.

By Kammler, the son of a Nazi war criminal who had been incorporated into the American military industrial complex to leverage advanced aerospace technology straight from the Watchers' offspring—all in order to dominate the world as the biggest hegemonic superpower on the civilization block.

How could Silas have been so stupid not to see it? Harris had seemed too eager to show them the goods, and their entrance seemed paved.

The unlatching of another door interrupted Silas's seething and drew his attention.

To another jeep and another parting of the guards for someone else.

An all too familiar face. One he saw in the mirror every morning.

One Silas hadn't seen since the man's backside was dragged out from that collapsing pagan temple engulfed in flames last year.

Sebastian Grey.

Baby brother.

But one that looked like something from another planet.

Always something is right.

Only question was, how were they going to get out of this SEPIO-made mess?

Again...

CHAPTER 39

Silas's breath seized in his chest at the sight of his brother, the pompous prick sauntering toward him with a wide grin he wanted to slap from here to kingdom come!

Reaching his brother, Sebastian pressed his hands together and offered a slight bow. "Hello, Sy."

The man had swapped his pressed tan pants and a blue button-down with a red bow tie for a black hooded cloak. Celeste had said he looked hideous, with scaly skin and a hulking figure, two horns even on the top of his shaved skill.

Hideous didn't even begin to describe it.

"What happened to you..." Silas managed on a disbelieving breath.

A set of filed teeth filled a wide grin. "Do you like it? The magic of modern science paired with arcane DNA."

"The alien bones from Turkey?" Gapinski said with the same disbelieving breath.

"That's right. You'll recall Rudolf Borg had similar designs for the DNA of Jesus using the Holy Grail—until you stopped him. No matter. We recycled the tech, using the genetic code from the Universe's actual celestial beings. Too bad you'll miss out on the transformation gifted me by the Universe!"

"*Dios mío...*" Torres said, crossing herself.

Silas joined her, something breaking inside of him at the sight of his own flesh and blood. His lungs searched for breath, he even felt a wetness on his cheek. Couldn't help it. The transformation was truly complete. From enthusiastic believer to Doubting Thomas, then a militant pagan bent on decimating the Church to—this *abomination*...

"So it's true then," Celeste said. "You're in cahoots with the American government."

"And me," a deep voice bellowed proudly from behind the line of airmen security.

A man with wide shoulders and hairless olive skin pushed through, with tattoos of symbols marking one side of his face. The man's sandals whispered across the polished concrete beneath a plain, well-tailored white *thawb* cloak. The yang to his brother's yin.

Sha. High Priest of that crazy outfit he called the Church of the Theotites, Church of the Deities.

He joined Sebastian at his side, his mouth widening with gleaming white teeth before he threw his head back and laughed, a wicked sound coming from the depths of his belly. Full of haunting purpose and mocking intent, without any fear or hesitation or consequence.

The sound sent a shiver ratcheting up Silas's spine, along with the sight of his brother paired with that man. There they were. The two enemies of the Order of Thaddeus. And in cahoots with Uncle Sam!

His life had come full circle...

Silas sent a wad of spittle sailing to the floor, the goop landing inches from Sebastian's bare feet.

"Gotta say, surprised to see you still alive, Seba. Last time I saw you two together, he kicked your ass. And where's that lackey of yours, that Chuke character, the one who saved it?"

Sebastian laughed, joined by a low chuckle from Sha. "Yes, well, we've since kissed and made up. Haven't we?"

The Theoti High Priest, or whatever wackadoodle self-made title he was, nodded. "We were realizing that more joined us together than separated us."

His brother stepped forward, jaw set, eyes narrowed, face growing dark. "Like seeing your pathetic religious order come to ruin and that imbecilic, infantile, ignoramus—"

"Sweet mother of Melchizedek!" Elijah sounded from behind with interruption. "How many alliterative adjectives do you need to make your point that the Christian faith is bunk?"

It was like a frog leaped into Sebastian's throat at the slight, his mouth moving up and down to find words but only pasty gasping sounds coming out.

"And who are you being?" Sha said, answering for him.

"Elijah Fox. Ask me again and I'll tell you the same. But are you for real? You look like something from casting in a bad '90s action-adventure flick."

Gapinski snorted a laugh from behind, followed by a nudge from Torres to be quiet. Gina groaned; Celeste giggled.

Silas stood grinning. Way to put those jokers in their place!

Sebastian threw him hateful, seething eyes and was about to respond.

When Kammler stepped forward, muttering something in German. "I believe we should be leaving the reuniting for a later time."

"Gee," said Silas, "and here I brought an apple pie for the reuniting occasion."

The general laughed, blowing a hazy cloud of clove smoke into the air before flicking the butt to the floor.

He stepped closer. "A funny man, you are being. And a worthy opponent. You were giving me and my men quite the run for our money. It took Harris here to bring you to heel. Your blind devotion to your failed cause led to your downfall, your very own eyes not seeing you were being led to your death."

Death? Silas's eyes flashed wide before narrowing and mouth went dry from an adrenaline rush. Had to keep from looking Celeste's way knowing she was in danger, they all were. But if he'd learned anything over the years working with Celeste, and then dating her, she could more than handle this joker. They all could.

At the wave of Kammler's hand, the platoon of airmen took a shuddering aim with their M4 rifles.

Certainly raised the SEPIO stakes.

"How did you know where to find us?" Celeste said.

Torres added, "Yeah, did you text your sugar daddy, or what, *idiota*?"

Kammler nodded. "*Ja.* Harris was sending us a message when you were arriving." He stepped over to Gapinski standing at Silas's side, stale sauerkraut and dill heavy on his breath. "But you, dear friend—you certainly made it easy. Both times."

Gapinski furrowed his brow. "Uh, come again, hombre."

The general grinned a mouth of tarred teeth and pulled out his pack of Djarum Blacks, smacking it against an open palm until another stick came out. Lighting it, he pulled in a long drag, then blew a cloud above his head. The dueling scents of cinnamon and cloves instantly filled the surrounding air again.

He said, "Are you not curious how we were finding you these past days? First in Turkey, then at that Midwest city?"

Gapinski shrugged. "Uh, a good Tarot card reading?"

"Tracker..." Silas whispered, a piece from Gapinski's story coming into sharp focus. He turned to him. "You said when you blinked back to reality after that craft zoomed out of sight in that forest outside of Ramstein—"

He paused, pulling in an angry breath for what he suspected happened to his friend.

"What is it, Silas?" Celeste asked.

Continuing, he explained, "You said you had a wicked headache."

Gapinski nodded. "Yeah. Like a bad batch of Grandpappy's moonshine."

"But then you had some scar at the back of your neck."

His hand went to the back of his head, panic flashing across his face, as if finally understanding what had happened to him all those years ago.

"Did you ever get that checked out?"

Gapinski shook his head, nothing more than a squeak escaping him.

Silas turned to Kammler, stepping forward with a clenched jaw and two clenched fists, ready to go to blows if it came to it.

There was a shuddering show of force from all around, the airmen security snapping to intercept.

Kammler put out a hand, his mouth narrowing into a thin, satisfied smile.

"You tagged him?" Silas said through gritted teeth.

The man shrugged. "Naturally. We were tagging them all. Even Harris here, though he was turning out to be more of an asset for later use than a subject."

"You mean the government's use?"

Another shrug, followed by an acknowledging nod this time.

A rage welled within Silas, so that he couldn't reply. To think the very government he had devoted a good chunk of his life serving—not only as a young adult after the terrorist attacks, putting it all on the line to protect the homeland and deliver justice on behalf of his fellow Americans; but also as a child, being carted across the globe while Dad did the same— to think this government he'd given his life to had been using Matt Gapinski, and countless other American citizens, in some sort of sick experiment paving the way for a consolidation of power and globalist agenda...

Silas's head was spinning, his legs were weakening, his lungs were burning for air with the sheer disbelief of it all.

"Wait a minute," Celeste said, "you said both times. In Turkey and Grand Rapids. What about at the FBI?"

Kammler shrugged. "That wasn't being us. Forces within American government were stopping at nothing to keep their secrets. Such is the American way."

Another drag, another pleasurable scent of cinnamon and cloves alongside the sour revelations.

"Of course," he went on, "our little friend within your outfit was being most useful as well, cluing us to original source that was launching operation to begin with."

Sebastian *tsked*, eyes closing and head shaking briefly before snapping back open, as if the German had let a secret slip.

So, there was a mole. Celeste had been right.

"For what purpose?" she asked, filling the void where Silas was still speechless.

"Why, the next stage in our evolutionary development, *fräulein*."

"The Homo Deus," added Torres. "The God-Man we found in Turkey."

Kammler's eyes flew open, and his face brightened with a wide, wicked grin. "*Ja!* That is exactly what I am saying. My father was being one of the many leading Nazis who were being brought inside to assist the American military program. Scientists, engineers, military commanders—"

"And occult wackadoodles," Gapinski interrupted, finding his voice now, "who worshiped alien demons and worked as conduits to feed Uncle Sam their satanic military technology and designs for human nature. Amiright?"

"The *Übermensch*," Celeste added with a shaky voice, "a

super-race of advanced humans. Forged through arcane, pagan knowledge unearthed by the Nazis..."

Sebastian stepped up to Kammler's side now. "Of course, it was only natural for the good general to partner with us."

"That is being correct," Sha agreed. "For centuries, our religious sect has been committed to divine human mind, the seat of divine intelligence, with the knowledge to be like the gods themselves, as *Ha-Satan* had tried to inform humanity's first ancestors."

"And Nous has wanted to offer an alternative to the Church for centuries, tapping into the natural energies, the natural Powers of the Universe in order to raise humanity up to a higher level of consciousness and usher in the Republic of Heaven. A realm of unlimited human potential across the planet, completely divorced from your silly, dead god's kingdom of heaven."

Silas scoffed. "And how were you planning on doing that?"

Sebastian turned to him and grinned. "Why, using DNA lifted from those bones you discovered, big brother. Fused to the government subjects tracked for later use with the arcane discoveries of Walter's father, Hans. Of which I am the first to benefit!"

Silas spun toward the chambers containing those floating beings. The ones who had been abducted by their government and readied for such a time as this.

"The portal to Edenic perfection," said Sha. "That is the way we have paved, infused by the restless spirits of the dead offspring who had tried to create such a race from ages past."

"This is bloody barbaric!" Celeste exclaimed.

"And *muy loco* in the head," said Torres. "This is what you were using Gapinski for?" She turned to Harris. "What you were allowing your government to do to your friend, your fellow war *compañero*?"

Harris didn't make eye contact, but he also held his head high. Clearly not a remorseful bone in that man's body.

"Except we put all the pieces together," Silas said. "And we've seen your little hangar of horrors. What's going to become of us?"

Sebastian shrugged. "Elimination, naturally."

Fear lanced through Silas. More from the possibility of his teammates facing violence than himself. His fiancé, even.

"Why you—" He launched at Sebastian, smacking him in the face with his forehead.

A hideous crack sounded, and blood instantly bloomed from his nose.

"You broke my blasted nose!" Sebastian whined as he cradled the front of his face.

A strong arm came around from behind to squeeze him tight, holding him fast.

Silas struggled under its might, thrashing for a chance at a second blow.

A thwack to his gut from the butt of a rifle sent him staggering to his knees, a sharp pain slicing through his lower chest. Felt like the bastard fractured a rib.

The arm held him fast as he tried to recover, Silas throwing his arms behind to tear at the threat.

It was no use, the grip tightening at his neck now and threatening to cut off his air.

"On your knees, the rest of you!" Kammler commanded, joined by the sounds of squeaking boots shuffling across the polished cement floor from the soldiers readying to act. "We will be making this as painless as possible. Especially since your government was being so kind to my father back in the day."

There it was. It all made sense.

Senior Kammler had been brought into the military industrial complex through Operation Paperclip, bearing the revelation-knowledge he had received through occult Nazi practices. He had a son, whom he raised in the Air Force to pass along his secrets—where Junior Kammler later fulfilled his father's dream to finish the Nazi cause: not only leveraging Watcher-spirit technology for the US, but raising up a race of superbeings using dead Nephilim DNA.

What were they going to do?

Silas continued to struggle while the others sank to their knees.

Except one.

Instead, Elijah stepped forward.

Horror flashed within. The professor was going to get himself killed! Or Silas and his SEPIO teammates.

He reached for Elijah from the floor, but the arm held him fast.

"No, wait!" he croaked, trying to break free.

Gina voiced her own protest: "Eli, what are you doing?"

But the man scurried from reach, going toe to toe with the son of a Nazi scientist who had tapped into the unseen realm in ways the Church could not have envisioned.

"What's the meaning and purpose of life?" Elijah said matter-of-factly.

Kammler twisted up his face. He growled, "*Was hast du gesagt?*"

"I said, what is the meaning and purpose of life—our life? What is core to our human identity?"

The man chuckled, eying him with suspicion. "I am not understanding what you are meaning."

Elijah started pacing now, on the balls of his feet with that unbounded energy again, his fingers starting in on that tick that seemed to rev up during stressful episodes and when he was excited. Didn't know how the airmen security forces would react, but they seemed to be holding steady.

For now...

"One extreme says this world is all there is. You're born, you go to school, you work, you die — that's it. The only hope we have is to do a little good, while sucking the marrow out of life along the way."

Pivoting, he swung back toward the general. "The other extreme says *all of this just doesn't matter* — heaven is what's important. Many Christians say this, actually. And billionaire techies with too much time on their hands."

"What is being the point of this?" Kammler said in an irritated rush.

"The point is, both have brought incredible confusion to our crucial question. Everything you do right now matters to God. As a human made in his image and likeness, given roles to fulfill as human creatures ruling in his stead."

"Bah!" Sebastian complained. "What a load of crock. Human identity is about our intellectual capacity to shape and bend the world to our will. *Homo sapiens.* Wise, *knowledgeable* man."

"Nope."

"Yes!"

"Nope."

Sebastian sent a sighing huff echoing throughout the vast hangar.

Silas understood the feeling, but now he was appreciating the professor more than ever. Let 'em have it, Eli!

"We've been created by God on purpose and with purpose to enjoy, guard, rule over, and work his physical, seen creation —all of it."

Kammler shook his head and muttered something in German. Didn't know what, but that didn't deter Elijah.

Silas marveled at the man going toe to toe arguing biblical theology with the forces arrayed against the faith— with the son of a Nazi occultist, no less, and his demented brother.

He prayed the Holy Spirit would use him to bring this to an end.

"After creating humanity," he continued, "God tells Mama Eve and Papa Adam to *kabash* the world. To subdue it and enjoy it—growing juicy strawberries, harvesting clay and molding it into works of art, even drinking beer and wine."

"That makes sense," Gapinski said. "After all, beer is proof that God loves us and wants us to be happy."

Elijah frowned. "That's not in the Bible. Who said that?"

"Ben Franklin."

He shook his head and continued. "Alongside this permission to enjoy creation is the command to *shamar* creation. To take care of it, to keep it safe like you would your own home. Guarding and serving creation is one of humanity's first missions on Earth. And God never revokes it."

He started pacing again, that finger tick strumming up with every step.

"Third, *radah*. We rule over creation. Like a king would leave images of themselves to sort of rule over their conquered lands, the Creator has left behind replicas of himself to rule over his land. Us, his Image Bearers, to ensure *shalom*—wholeness, peace, the way God intended his created world to work. We were created to *image* God—to represent him to each other and across Earth."

"What is being the meaning of this?" Kammler screamed again, his patience growing thin.

Elijah stopped and cocked his head. "The meaning? It should be plain. When God breathed all of this into existence, the world was *shalom*. Humanity was supposed to preserve and extend this *shalom* on Earth, this wholeness. Then we royally screwed things up, rebelling against our Creator and plunging the world into chaos and death. Thanks to the very Being you've aligned yourself with."

"No, no, no!" Sebastian sneered. "A higher consciousness is

our destiny—beyond Earth. That is our meaning, and that is what the Power has come to gift us. To drag us from this disaster-riven world into a new destiny beyond!"

"Nope. We are earthlings. God has placed humanity here on purpose and with purpose to rule on his behalf."

"We are divine, meant to rule the stars!"

Elijah frowned. *"Abad.* That's the last thing we're called to do. Work, till, cultivate *this* world, *this* planet. God created this stunning world and told humans to change things. To pick up where he left off by developing the world in distinctly human ways."

Sha scoffed. "And look what we have done with the place! Sebastian is right. We need a higher consciousness to help us save ourselves. To imbue Earth with a new religious consciousness. The Power from the unseen realm Kammler and his ancestors tapped into will lead us there!"

"From the beginning," Elijah said, plowing forward, "God didn't want us to wear animal skins and draw cave paintings the rest of our lives. He meant for us to turn sand into Kindles, take trees and stone and turn them into buildings, to spin wool into cozy sweaters. Bearing God's image means to co-create with God by working, tilling, cultivating this world by discovering, inventing, creating, building things in any number of ways—forever! Not sitting in an eternal yoga position in order to reach a higher mental plain of existence."

Elijah returned to his spot in front of Kammler. "Enjoy, guard, rule over, and work creation. That's what it means to be human. These are *our* roles. Everyone, regardless of gender or ethnicity—whether pre-born, a child, a middle-ager, or an octogenarian. This is what it means to be human, to bear God's image. The one God gave us, not to anything else in creation."

"Enough talk!" the general sneered. "Time to be ending this."

"Except, it is only the beginning for you, Herr Kammler."

CHAPTER 40

W hat the heck was Elijah talking about? What was only the beginning for Kammler? Silas didn't have a clue.

Which could be a good thing or a bad thing!

Hated unknown operation elements, especially when they were introduced by one of his own teammates. But the man had proven himself so far, and his background with the Bureau wasn't something to shake a stick at.

Come on, Elijah. Don't let us down...

Kammler was as confused: "What is it you are meaning?"

Elijah answered, "Between the Armed Services committee hearings in both chambers of Congress, on top of the court-martial that will be must-see CSPAN TV for violating the Insurrection Act—I'd say you'll have your hands full the next few decades."

What was he talking about? Unless President Santos himself came riding in on a white horse to save the day, no way was this guy getting booked.

Kammler took a drag and puffed a hazy blue cloud of those cinnamon and cloves in Elijah's face. A thin smile made him look calm, cool, and collected. But a slight tremor at his hand holding that clove stick betrayed him.

"What is it you are saying?"

Elijah's eyes snapped to Kammler. "Simple. I've been live-streaming this entire conversation from the get-go."

Silas couldn't believe his ears. Live-streaming? How? Now *that* was a truth bomb if he'd ever heard one!

Hope rose within. Perhaps there was still a chance...

Kammler giggled before it rolled into a belly laugh. He sucked another long breath on his stick before tossing it to the floor. The butt sparked before he squished it dead with the heel of his boot.

Then he got in Elijah's face, baring his teeth and growling, "You are lying!"

"Nope. Saw my dentist the other day. Not only because I was due for a cleaning. Your teeth are the best friends you got. Take care of them and they'll take care of you."

"What is being the point of all of this?" Kammler roared, head thrown back and face reddening with rage.

"The point, Herr Kammler, is that I had my dentist install a listening device in my wisdom tooth."

"*Was?*"

"A molar mic, it's called. The latest and greatest in surveillance tech. Developed by the military, actually. A small device that clips to your back teeth. Doubles as both a microphone and speaker, allowing the wearer to transmit recordings without any conspicuous external microphone using high-frequency airwaves that will slice through even ten stories of concrete."

"Brilliant, Eli!" Celeste said with a chuckle. "Cracking good show of things."

"Holybamoly, Batman..." Gapinski whispered.

"Who would've thought," said Torres, "we'd have our very own Double O Spook in SEPIO."

"That's my Eli!" Gina beamed.

Silas had to agree. Who would have thought. Suppose the FBI agent was right. People like her and Elijah would confound his expectations for what they could and couldn't do.

Including whipping up a Plan B behind his back! Was grateful, but would have to circle back to that at some point.

"Granted, there isn't any video," Elijah went on, "but the audio should more than give you a run for your money. And Uncle Sam, I suppose."

"You are being a liar!" Kammler raged.

"Nope. Look." Elijah threw open his mouth, peeling his cheeks back for the general to take a look.

Surprisingly he did, squinting and craning toward his head.

Before snapping back with a start, and his face drained of color.

"Eliminate them!" he screamed, eyes going wide and that hat of his falling to the floor.

The soldiers immediately snapped into motion, hustling to his side and taking aim at SEPIO—the agents and Elijah and Gina.

Not good.

"But not before you see the full power of what we have called forth from the Heavens. The miracle weapon who will save humanity from itself, giving them the knowledge of the gods!"

Kammler's face widened into a wicked Cheshire grin. Silas's gut dropped with anticipation of what came next.

Because there was a hint of it in the man's response.

Miracle weapon.

No, it couldn't be...

The general said, "In the words of a very famous ruler, 'Ecce Homo Deus!'"

Silas immediately recognized those words. The ones

Pontius Pilate said of Jesus Christ when he presented him before the crowds to be crucified.

Behold, the God-Man...

A terrifying roary, snorty, skittering screech sounded through the vast hangar. Small at first before quickly crescendoing, as if emerging from a tear in the fabric of reality itself.

Every hair across his body stood on end.

"What was that?" asked Torres, head going this way and that.

"Sounded like a demon..." said Celeste, surely working from personal memory.

"Always something..." Gapinski growled.

"No, not demon," said Silas, knowing exactly what that was. "Alien demon."

"Nope," corrected Elijah, face betraying not a hint of fear. "Watcher-spirit."

He licked his lips and swallowed hard, steeling himself for a confrontation with something he had never imagined in his wildest dreams.

A Fallen One...

Out of nowhere, something emerged from the shadows—from another dimension, even.

A hulking figure, with a bulbous head resting atop wide shoulders corded with muscle, sauntered toward them. Skin rippled in scaly waves with an iridescent glow. The Being was hideous, horrendous, something straight out of a Stephen King fever dream.

And yet...

Yet there was something attractive about it. Enticing, even. As if it was what Silas had been waiting for his whole life—to give meaning and definition and permission to his identity as a man, as a human.

An Angel of Light. Come to save humanity.

Yesssssss, thaths riiiight....

The Voice erupted from within.

Not his head, his very soul.

"This isn't happening," Silas muttered.

"You see it too?" Celeste whispered on a frightened breath.

He turned to her, his fiancé's eyes wide and transfixed.

"*Dios mío...*" Torres whimpered.

Gapinski looked stunned. Unmoving and unable to voice any sort of recognition, yet his face told all.

He saw what Silas saw. They all did.

The Being slithered from the shadows and planted itself behind Kammler. Who was whose master, it wasn't clear. What was clear was what it said.

With unmoving lips, coming from inside his head!

The time of the Great Unveiling is nigh. For too long, humanity's true identity has lain hidden in the shadows. Its true divine destiny has been denied. No longer! I have come that they might fully know good and evil, SSSSiillassssss...

Silas's heart exploded in his chest and head with a surge of fight-or-flight adrenaline. The Being knew his name. Didn't know what to say to that. Not in the slightest.

Someone responded for him.

"Who are you?"

It was Elijah, commanding the Being.

You know who I am...

"Say it. I want to hear. In the name of Jesus Christ, name yourself."

There was that terrifying roary, snorty, skittering screech again. Livid, even pained.

The Being recoiled from the mention of the Son of God. Its head thrown backward and back arching, arms rising to shield itself—as if it were injured.

Yet it relented. He had to.

SSSSemjazzzzaaa...

Gapinski gasped. "The alien demon from my head!"

"What is it you want?" Elijah asked, eyes fixed on the Being.

And showing not a lick of fear, his jaw clenched and face set.

The Being paused, saying nothing. It only raised an arm, where long fingers curled into a tight fist.

All six of them.

And the tanks started shuddering, the bodies inside banging against the glass trying to escape. There were muffled cries from within, the hosts crying out for their master and seeking the outside world, their wrinkled, deformed hands clawing for release.

Lord Jesus Christ, Son of God, make haste to help us!

The SEPIO crew and Gina all threw up startled cries. Now it really was a Stephen King fever dream!

"What is it you want?" Elijah demanded, taking a step toward the Being now.

To make humanity like the godsssssss. What elssssssee?

"Nope. Not going to happen."

A laugh erupted from the Being, the sound cackling from it like a strangled goat. Bleating and braying, strutting even.

They were doomed...

Until something clangy and screeching caught Silas's attention.

At first, he thought it was coming from the tanks again, the unholy zombies emerging from the green sludge holding them fast after its master showed itself.

But then he realized it was coming from the same direction Kammler and his brother themselves had come.

Seconds later, the same sorts of general personnel vehicles they came riding in on roared toward them, loaded down with men in fatigues and bearing automatic rifles aimed at their position.

"Is that the bloomin' Rangers?" asked Celeste.

Silas wasn't sure, but it was one thing he was sure of.

Help!

The Being spun toward the entourage, Silas certain he caught a frown.

Until we meet againnnn...

"Yes, we shall," Elijah said.

Then it slunk into the shadows, disappearing into the nether, into whatever dimension it had come from.

He added with a mutter: "I'm certain of it..."

Silas collapsed to the floor, drained of energy—physical and spiritual—catching his breath as chaos engulfed him and his SEPIO crew.

Kammler's soldiers fanned out to address whatever was coming at them hot and heavy.

SEPIO skittered back, making for the tanks that had settled now, the only source of protection.

Except Silas saw Kammler scrambling toward one of the jeeps they had come riding in the first time.

He narrowed his eyes and clenched his jaw with resolve.

Not on your life, pal!

Silas darted for the man, hiking his arms and legs up like the good ol' days with the Falls Church Jaguars football team as he chased after the man.

Kammler never had a chance.

He barreled into his back just as he reached a jeep. The man hit the front end hard, his face smacking against the cool aluminum hood and nose blooming with blood.

Silas threw him to the floor and jabbed a knee into his back. The guy struggled, slinging a string of German at him he figured wasn't PG-rated, but he never let go. Held him firm as the newcomers rolled up—an entire military platoon, by the looks of it!

But not before catching sight of Sebastian and Sha slipping into one of the jeeps and tearing off down the runway. Into the maw of darkness that led who knew where. Wanted to go after the bastards, but Kammler was enough. Figured they'd meet again.

One way or another.

The convoy of vehicles came to a screeching halt, and out jumped another platoon of soldiers, larger than the airmen and all in fatigues. Big and bulky and bearing heavy rifles that looked like they'd put their peashooters to shame.

The other soldiers didn't know what to do. Several of the men doubled down on their aim while others set their rifles on the floor and put their hands above their heads.

Parting through the pandemonium was a familiar, clarifying face.

"Nicky?" exclaimed Celeste. "What on earth are you doing here?"

"Saving your bloody backsides, is what!" He sauntered over with someone else in tow. "This here is my complementary equal across the pond."

A tall man with salt-and-pepper hair looking oddly like Nicky nodded, hands stuffed inside a long black overcoat. "Jacob Edwards. Looks like we arrived just in time."

"And you are?" asked Silas, grateful for the backside-saving but thoroughly confused.

"Associate Director of military affairs, managing the relationship between the CIA and armed forces. Nicky McGrath contacted me with an urgent plea for help a few hours ago. Story seemed too fantastical to be true. But, given our history, I trusted the man and assembled a strike team to extract you. Then the live-feed audio playing across WeShare gave us all we needed to get the go ahead and shut this bad boy down."

Gapinski said, "Saved by the Brit spook again, ehh. Whoda thunk it?"

"Double O Spook," Torres corrected. "Whoda thunk it, is right!"

Silas shook his head in disbelief. Had to give it to the man. He saved the day, along with Elijah.

Jerking a thumb over his shoulder, he asked Nicky, "What about all this? The hydrochambers, the—" he glanced at Elijah, emphasizing, "*UAPs*, all of this?"

The MI6 agent looked to his American counterpart. He answered, "We'll clean this up, get these civilians checked out, disassemble these crafts for useful technology."

"I imagine," said Nicky, "your Congress will want to have hearings about it."

Edwards grunted. "Isn't that the truth. Behind closed doors, at least."

Elijah smirked. "So, a cover-up."

The CIA agent drew in a measured breath, saying nothing more before turning away and making for the military grunts.

Just like Uncle Sam to stuff the genie back in the bottle when the moldy cheese hit the fan. Although, given what Elijah pulled, sure would be hard to deny what the Air Force had been pulling all these years. Supposed in the end, Kammler got part of his wish, and that Harris fella. Disclosure.

"What will happen to us?" Celeste called out. "We've glimpsed behind the curtain."

"Your country owes you a debt of gratitude," Edwards shouted with a wave. Then he spun around, adding, "Besides, we'll just erase your memories. Or at least your cellphones."

He grinned and sauntered off.

Silas stuck out his hand, offering it to Nicky. "Thanks. For everything."

Nicky regarded it and gave it a firm shake. "Likewise. Her Majesty is equally grateful for uncovering the American plot."

Not sure he liked the sound of that, but he was just glad it was all over—however it shook out.

Silas watched with satisfaction as Kammler was hauled off to the brig, or wherever they brought two-star generals descended from Nazi war criminals squarely at the center of a political conspiracy with arcane pagan ceremonies channeling alien Watcher-spirits. What happened to his brother was anyone's guess. Both the end result of his escape and the end result of that crazy transformation he underwent channeling the same demonic nonsense.

Too wild for words. All of it.

Par for the SEPIO course...

What he wasn't satisfied with was knowing that Nicky McGrath had indeed saved their backsides once again.

Celeste came up to his side, slipping her hand in his, reminding him he got the girl when the Brit spook didn't.

Supposed that counted for something.

Silas slapped Elijah's back. "You did good, professor."

At which the professor recoiled. Forgot about the personal space issues with the man!

"Sorry about that."

He straightened and took a breath. "No worries. Just glad to be of service."

Silas chuckled. "Of service? You saved our lives! Not to mention broke the conspiracy wide open."

Celeste added, "Airing it for all the world to see!"

He shrugged. "Saw it in a movie once."

Gapinski scoffed. "Hey, how come he gets to use cinematic candy for his operational tactics, but when I do it I get the stink eye?"

"Because yours ended," replied Torres, "with you getting beamed up by aliens."

"That wasn't my fault!"

She grabbed his arm and laughed. "Just glad we got you back alive."

"Thanks for that by the way."

Silas said, "I don't know about you, but I'm ready to go home." He turned to his SEPIO crew, along with Elijah and

Gina. "You did good, team. Did real good."

"So that's it then?" asked Celeste. "You figure the operation is over?"

"Nothing left but the paperwork." He gestured around the hangar. "Imagine someone at the DoD will have their hands full with this for a long time."

"But what about the other remains," Torres said, "the ones supposedly from eons ago?"

Silas shrugged. "What about them?"

"Well, from what I gathered, they clearly showed a coherence between those previous anthropological ancestors and our own."

"What, like our descent from apes?" asked Gapinski.

"We're not talking monkeys," Elijah insisted.

"Be that as it may," Celeste said, "Naomi does have a point."

Silas shook his head. "Not interested in fighting that fight right now."

"Yet the fight has found us, hasn't it?"

Torres added, "Just like ET did."

Silas sighed. Ain't that the truth of it. And he didn't like it one bit, the idea there was still something unresolved from this operation that began in the borderland deserts of Turkey and Iraq. Which he knew was right at the edge of the Fertile Crescent.

The cradle of civilization.

A shiver ratcheted up his spine at the thought. Because the thread that had begun to unspool there, with uncovering those remains—the ones of distant ancestors resting alongside those of the Watchers' offspring—started a fight about the Image of God, manifesting in the seen and unseen realms, connected to Yahweh. To God, the Father Almighty, Creator of Heaven and Earth, as the Church's Creed begins.

A battle that was yet unresolved.

Again, a fight for another day.

He turned to Torres. "Looks like you've got some work to do, then."

She brightened. "Really?"

"Sure thing."

"But that's going to take a whole lot more work, *muchacho*. More digs and more workers and—"

"Mucho dinero," added Gapinski.

Celeste said, "Which Weiss isn't going to love."

Silas smirked, itching for a fight with the overactive board member. "You let me handle Weiss. You just finish what we started."

"And what's that, Master Grey?"

It was Elijah, the man seeming to take an interest in their work.

"You said it yourself, doc. Who are we, where did we come from? What does it mean to be human? Sounds like SEPIO only solved part of the equation."

"The Imago Dei, you mean," replied Elijah. "Our role as image bearers that are distinct from other intelligent life-forms."

Silas pointed at him. "Bingo. In the meantime, I'm taking some leave."

"Leave?" asked Torres. "What for?"

"Yeah, to do what, chief?" Gapinski asked.

Silas smiled, then grabbed Celeste's hand. "To get hitched."

Her cheeks flushed, and she giggled. The sound of angels.

Then she nuzzled into his shoulder. The scent of a garden, her trademark lavender and vanilla, filled his head with delight.

"Come on, darling," he whispered into her ear. "Let's finish planning our wedding."

Off they walked, hand in hand. Past the airmen getting a drumming from their CO—on top of military-issued handcuffs —for their part in the conspiracy. Then up the elevator to the surface where their Chevy Suburban was waiting to take them away.

Not quite riding off into the sunset, but it'd do.

Next stop was walking down the aisle.

After that, who knew.

Weiss was still ticked and the board dead-locked when it came to Silas's performance. This operation would surely give him more fodder in the days ahead, regardless how they saved the day.

The mystery surrounding our human origin and identity was still an open box that needed closing. Something the Church had been wrestling with for centuries but seemed to be ratcheting up to a fevered pitch in recent years. Eden's legacy carried a long shadow.

Whatever. All that could wait. Not his worries; not for the moment.

Because as Jesus said, *'do not worry about tomorrow, for tomorrow will bring worries of its own. Today's trouble is enough for today.'*

Exactly.

All Silas had to worry about was getting to that glorious day when he finally said 'I do' to the most amazing woman God ever created.

Which was no worry at all.

CHAPTER 41

WASHINGTON, DC. THREE DAYS
LATER.

"Where are you taking me?" Elijah asked, his fingers doing that thing again. Thumb to index, thumb to middle, thumb to ring, thumb to pinky. Then rinse and repeat.

Part of Silas understood him. He had his own ways of coping when the moment soured. Counting down from a thousand, concentrating on breathing, yoga. Most of him didn't get him.

He certainly appreciated the guy and his differences. But he was hard to read, was a bit socially awkward, was blunt to a fault. Besides, going rogue during the most critical step in the mission could have tanked the whole operation. More than enough to send him packing back to Grand Rapids.

And yet, Silas hadn't. Instead, he and the professor were on their way to an old SEPIO outpost that had served as a temporary Order HQ. Part of him thought he was crazy for the idea that had been needling him the past week. A vision he'd been toying with since taking over as Master from Rowen Radcliffe a few years ago, yet didn't have the parts in place to make the machinery hum just right.

Now he did, the right one sitting next to him, the other

waiting up ahead. Or at least he hoped they were. Certainly prayed about it, seeking the Lord's guidance and feeling no glaring red-light negatory to his request for divine direction. Mostly, it just felt right after seeing the man in action, both his mind and his hands. Same for his former partner, Gina.

Silas just hoped he was right, that he was reading both the man and the Lord right.

Accompanying them along their trek through DC was the local NPR station, which was quite animated with the latest scandal to rock the capital region. The revelations about the Air Force had blown a hole through the Santos administration—and everyone was ducking for cover and pointing fingers. Typical DC politics.

All that mattered to Silas was that the Order had come through unscathed. Which had taken some of the pressure off from Weiss, given what they achieved. Not out of the woods yet, but close.

Hopefully. Who knew...

"Where are you taking me?" Elijah asked again, louder, more insistent.

Breezing through a yellow light, he answered, "Don't worry, partner. I think you'll like the surprise."

"I hate surprises."

"You'll like this one. At least, I hope you will."

"It better not be ice cream. I'm allergic."

Silas turned to him with a raised brow. "Allergic? Like lactose intolerant or something?"

"No, it's the milk protein. So the surprise better not be ice cream. I'll wheeze and vomit, sometimes even get the hives."

"Don't worry. It's not ice cream."

"Then what is it? I hate surprises!"

Silas shook his head. Boy, did he know it.

"Just a few more minutes and it will all make sense."

Elijah sighed and settled back, those fingers going at it

again. Felt bad putting him through the anxiety that came with the unknown, but he was glad to see the guy could at least handle some ambiguity when it arose. Because his little surprise would carry a whole heck of a lot of it in the coming months.

Took some cajoling, and a bit of enticing using the Order's vaults of historic relics, but the professor had spent the night then joined Silas for the jaunt across town. Gina was riding in another car driven by Celeste that Silas had sent on ahead of them, with Gapinski and Torres accompanying them. None of them knew what he was planning, and he hoped they would welcome it, all of them, Gina included.

Because from where Silas sat, the fate of the world depended on it.

Arriving at their destination, he pulled into a looping driveway off Michigan Avenue and turned into a service entrance on the westside of the Basilica of the National Shrine of the Immaculate Conception. The access driveway ran behind a stone wall and a thick hedgerow, leading to a keycard entrance into the old outpost.

Waiting for them was the other car and SEPIO crew.

Celeste stepped out of her silver BMW, along with Gapinski, Torres, and the other newcomer, Gina.

"What is she doing here?" Elijah asked with surprise.

Silas threw his Jeep into *Park* and threw him a grin. "Part of the surprise."

"I hate surprises."

"Come on, Eli. I think you'll like what I've cooked up."

"Better not be pork schnitzel. Hate schnitzel. Hate all German food, really."

Silas chuckled to himself, glad they shared culinary tastes.

"Nice of you to show yourselves," said Celeste. "We were beginning to worry you'd been abducted by our new friends."

Silas laughed. "Nope, just traffic."

"Should've let me drive," Gapinski said.

"Not if you want to live..." Torres quipped.

"Heard that!"

"Let's leave the ribbing for later, alright?" said Silas, leading them to a steel door with a palm-reading keypad. "We've got business to discuss."

Celeste leaned against the stone wall near the keypad. "And what, pray tell, is this business of ours, hmm?"

He threw her a grin. "It's a surprise."

"I hate surprises," Elijah complained from behind.

She pushed off and huffed. "You and me both, mate..."

Placing his hand on the security pad, the door unlocked, and Silas pushed through. A short, sterile-white hallway led to an elevator. The group stepped inside and traveled three stories beneath the Catholic church and former SEPIO outpost.

After a bell chimed, the elevator doors revealed a red-brick hallway completely void of any activity. Air was stale, too, with a layer of dust covering the floor. Even caught some cobwebs in the ceiling corners.

"This way," Silas instructed as he hastened forward through the hallway to a set of double doors at the end.

Another palm-reading keypad stood guard, waiting for his hand. When one door unlocked, he opened it to reveal a modest space in disuse.

Flipping a switch, dimmed recess lighting flitted to life around the perimeter, shining down upon narrow tables lining the dark walls commanded by workstations. Back in the day, they would have been manned by agents dutifully executing on SEPIO orders. Now they lay dormant, dust coating the surface and more webs spun between hibernating monitors. A massive dormant screen hung at one end, no longer tracking critical mission updates and relevant news footage. A raised platform with a few chairs stood at the center awaiting someone's control.

A certain someone Silas prayed said yes to a project burning in his heart the past year. One that seemed all the more urgent given the stakes of this past mission.

The six men and women gathered inside the hibernating room, their footfalls wandering the space echoing and throwing up more dust. The air was stale and staid, smelling of settled plaster and the musty scent of an ill attended basement, the HVAC not having been used in ages.

"Why did you bring me here?" Elijah finally asked, getting down to business.

Silas appreciated his no-nonsense approach to life. Was never one for BS himself, so he got to it.

"I brought you here," he explained, "because I have a proposition for you."

"What kind of proportion."

"A job proposition."

Elijah's eyes snapped to his. He held a stare for a beat, as if he were both surprised and intrigued.

"I already have a job," he said matter-of-factly.

Silas smiled. "I know, but I'm hoping you'll accept my offer."

"What offer?"

"To help lead a new project I'm launching for the Order."

"Project?" the Order trio said as one.

He nodded. "That's right. Both you and Gina. Something I'm calling Group X."

"Group X?" asked Celeste, brow furrowed.

"For *inexplicitus.*"

"Latin for unexplainable," Elijah said.

Silas nodded, "And inexplicable, incomprehensible, inconceivable."

Torres snorted a laugh. "Quite the alteration there, chief."

"Why is everything Order-related always in Latin?" asked Gapinski.

Ignoring him, Silas continued, "The X also has the advantage of symbolizing the name of Christ."

"The Greek letter *Chi*," said Elijah.

"That's right."

"What's the point of...this Group X? What's its purpose."

"To work the same magic you helped us out with this past mission. One of the things I realized after everything went down was that the Order has been missing a crucial element to our mission to preserve and contend for the once-for-all faith entrusted to God's holy people."

"Jude 3," said Elijah.

Silas nodded.

"And what are we missing?" Torres asked, folding her arms and squinting with skepticism.

"Yeah, chief," Gapinski joined in. "SEPIO's mission kicking butt and taking names seems to be working just fine."

Celeste folded her arms as well and widened her stance, face creasing with confusion. Of all the Order agents, she might be the most difficult to convince. After all, the new project came close to stepping on her own turf as director of operations for Project SEPIO. So what she would think—what she would *say*...well, it was anyone's guess.

"I must say," she said, "I'm intrigued. What do you propose?"

Silas cleared his throat and answered, "An investigative arm to the Order. That's what we're missing."

"We've got ourselves such an arm."

"Hello..." Gapinski said. "A little thing called S-E-P-I-O."

Silas took a breath. Here we go...

"SEPIO is a special-ops arm," he explained, "supplying the Church with muscle to make more kinetic responses to the threats against Christianity."

Gina smirked. "Nice euphemism there for *violent* responses."

"Forceful responses," Silas corrected.

"Tomato, potato."

"Like I said," Gapinski added, "kicking butt and taking names."

"What's the alternative suggestion?" asked Celeste. "If not a kinetic response, then what?"

Gapinski and Torres stared at him without a word. Even Elijah and Gina were standing by.

Silas cleared his throat. "Given what we dealt with in this operation, I thought it was time the Order took more seriously our struggle against this present darkness. To wage war against the fallen ones still ravaging this world, and then investigate the supernatural struggle making itself known in ways humanity hasn't seen before. Like Paul says in his letter to the Ephesians."

"You mean Ephesians 6," Elijah said.

"That's right."

Elijah closed his eyes and tipped his head back. "*For our struggle is not against enemies of blood and flesh,*" he intoned, quoting from Paul's letter, "*but against the rulers, against the authorities, against the cosmic powers of this present darkness, against the spiritual forces of evil in the heavenly places.*"

Silas nodded. "After everything went down in this mission, and given some of what we've faced in previous operations, it's become clear to me that the dynamics at play here are way beyond the flesh-and-blood kind."

"You're speaking of spiritual warfare," said Celeste.

"That's exactly what I mean."

"Like, Harry Potter-style?" Gapinski asked.

Torres smacked his arm. "Harry Potter is kiddie magic, *muchacho!*"

"Spiritual warfare is about fulfilling one task," Silas continued, "setting captive people free from the grip of this present supernatural darkness through the gospel of Jesus Christ. Both individual and societal."

Elijah went to respond, but snapped his mouth closed. Seemed to consider this angle of the job. Gave him pause.

Silas understood the silent stare. Respected it even, Elijah neither folding nor fleeing at his request. He understood what he was inviting the professor into was far more dangerous than what he'd even been asked to join by Radcliffe—given the supernatural aspect of the gig. Going against the cosmic powers Paul spoke about, in the more overt, confrontational, stand-your-ground way Silas was envisioning for Group X—well, it would be a whole level beyond SEPIO's current engagement, and his own.

But Silas knew Elijah could handle it—and Gina, the pair of them confronting this present darkness overtaking the world. He just knew it. He hoped it, anyway.

And prayed they would...

"Why me?" Elijah finally asked.

The question instantly brought Silas back to a moment when he was approached by Radcliffe—who stroked his ego a bit, saying Silas had everything needed to fight the good SEPIO fight.

How could Silas have said no after that? But he had. Said he would pray about it, but that Radcliffe shouldn't hold his breath. Which was the Christian way of telling him to go fly a kite.

For Radcliffe's part, he said the Holy Spirit could be a powerful, convincing force when activated by prayer. Eventually he caved, dragged kicking and screaming by the power of the Holy Spirit!

But Silas didn't have the luxury of waiting for the Third Person of the Trinity to work his magic. Neither did the Church. He needed an answer, now.

Silas widened his stance and folded his arms. "You know, I

asked the same thing when I was approached about joining the Order as a SEPIO agent. And I'll tell you what a wise man once told me. Why not you?"

This seemed to put him back on his heels. Elijah actually took a step back and then matched Silas's pose, crossing his arms and widening his stance.

"I don't follow."

"Look, Eli, you've clearly got the academic chops, both in biblical theology and the Jewish worldview sitting at the backdrop to the Christian one. Then there's your time with the FBI. Someone who can handle a weapon when the moment calls for it is always a welcomed skill around here. With this new initiative, you've got a real chance to do something—"

"I'm already doing something. I'm a professor."

Silas couldn't help but smile. Had literally said the exact same thing to Radcliffe. Was angry, even, at his suggestion that all he had been doing wasn't enough—teaching his students, giving them enough of a compelling experience of Christianity to take an interest in it. Radcliffe had even suggested he'd traded fighting for something bigger than himself for a pleasurable life of comfort and tenure. That definitely ticked him off!

"I'll say one more thing," he started, "and then I'll leave it alone for you to give me a yes or no—"

"I've already made my decision."

Silas's heart sank, figuring what he had decided, but pressed on anyway.

"If I may, another word from my old friend. He said the sort of life offered at universities, the life of—" He stopped himself, smiling at what he was about to suggest, but doing it anyway. "Of, well, comfort and tenure. Anyway, neither are bad in their own right. But only when the world is right and evil isn't knocking on the door. It's in the midst of good people's cozy comfort that wickedness blooms."

There was that look of regard again, as if Elijah was sizing him up.

He said, "You're saying bad men need nothing more to accomplish their ends, than that good men should look on and do nothing."

Now Silas laughed. "That was what the old Order Master told me when I resisted joining the fight for the faith."

"John Stuart Mills is a tedious, if not cliché, chestnut. But it serves a purpose from time to time."

"But it's true, isn't it?" Silas put up a hand before Elijah could object with his own objection from back in the day. "And I know you're not sitting on your butt. You're a professor, raising up pastors for goodness' sake! That's an admirable calling."

"I know it is."

"I just think there could be something else in store for you. Not at all a coincidence you have the experience Group X needs to get off the ground. And the fact we met, and you helped us crack the case...No, brother, I dare say it's all providential."

Elijah stiffened at that suggestion. "Something the Holy Spirit orchestrated."

Silas nodded, silence falling between them. Not much more to say than: "So what do you say?"

The professor stared off, and those fingers started up again.

But only once this time before he snapped back his gaze to Silas. Looked like he'd made up his mind. One way or another.

He held his breath, praying in the moment as the seconds ticked by for the Holy Spirit to tune his heart toward what Silas believed the Lord himself was calling the Order to undertake.

"Well, I for one think it's a splendid idea."

Wasn't at all the voice Silas expected. Or, frankly, the response.

It was Celeste, voicing her approval. Grinning, even!

"I agree," added Gapinski. "With all the wackadoodle stuff

being thrown at the Order lately—and not all of it from this world, from Nous—we could use all the help we can get."

Torres nodded. "*Sí*, I agree. Another pair of hands would sure help. Or four, if our new FBI friend wants in on the action."

Gina offered a smile and turned to Elijah. "Sounds like our old gig, partner. Investigating the paranormal, the stuff of Ephesians 6, and all."

"Sure does," Elijah simply said, the man starting in on his finger-strumming tick again.

"So what do you say? I'm in if you are."

Silas held his breath. If he couldn't convince the man, maybe his old partner could.

Moment of truth...

Another beat later, he answered with a nod. "Sounds good."

Silas threw Celeste a glance, who offered a smile and thumbs up. Gapinski and Torres both nodded. Glad SEPIO was onboard!

Now he smiled. "What, just like that?"

"Just like that."

Celeste asked, "You're not sure you want to pray about it?"

"Who says I haven't?"

"If there's one person I know," said Gina, "who is dialed into the movement of the Holy Spirit in his life, it's Eli Fox."

"Good to know."

"When I see an open door," Elijah explained, "I go through it. No questions asked. That's something you're going to have to get used to."

"Fair enough." Silas nodded and stuck out his hand with a grin. "Welcome aboard."

At which the man promptly looked down with wide eyes.

That's right! Physical touch wasn't his thing. For a minute, he regretted the gesture. Was still getting used to Elijah's unique needs. Respected them, just didn't get them.

But the professor did something that surprised him.

Elijah slapped his hand against Silas's. Just a brief smack, their skin skating past one another with the barest of touch. A beat later, his hand was back at his side. But it was something. A gesture of solidarity, of friendship.

And a start to what Silas hoped would be a fruitful partnership in contending for the Church and struggling against the supernatural forces arrayed against it.

For the good of the faith and glory of Christ.

ENJOY FALLEN ONES?

A big thanks for joining Silas Grey and the rest of SEPIO on their adventure saving the Church! **Here's what's next:**

If you're ready for another adventure, you can get a full-length novel in the series for free! Join the insider's group to be notified of specials and new releases by going to this link: www.jabouma.com/free

Want to join Elijah Fox and Gina Anderson solving supernatural mysteries? Dive into the Group X spin-off series: www.groupxcases.com.

If you loved the book and have a moment to spare, **a short review is much appreciated.** Nothing fancy, just your honest take. Spreading the word is probably the #1 way you can help independent authors like me and help others enjoy the story.

AUTHOR'S NOTE
THE HISTORY BEHIND THE STORY…

Probably goes without saying, but with all the references to *The X-Files*, I'm a major fanboy! I've watched through the entire series at least three times. My wife even humored me early in our marriage with one of those run-throughs, though we skipped the Monster of the Week episodes and only watched through the mythology ones. Elijah Fox and Gina Anderson were certainly nods to the show's main characters—Fox Mulder, played by David Duchovny; Gillian Anderson, who played Dana Scully. As was the Djarum smoking man who was a top-hat wearing fill-in for the Cigarette Smoking Man nemesis.

Even if you never watched the show, there were certainly plenty of conspiracies racing through the '90s surrounding Area 51 and supposed UFO sightings and alien encounters. Robert Stack offered plenty of grist on *Unsolved Mysteries*, as did the alien autopsy flick. Can't say I was necessarily a believer in all the hubbub, but it certainly raised all sorts of questions about the sightings and stories, not to mention what the Bible might say about it all, if anything.

Hadn't really thought about it all again until the past few years, when *The New York Times* broke open a story in 2017 about continued efforts by the US government to catalogue and track UFO sightings. Then still more stories surfaced in the last year, spurring Congress to commission a report from the Pentagon on the nature of the UFO threat—or UAP, rather, as Elijah would surely correct!

Figured it was the perfect time to throw SEPIO into a political conspiracy leveraging the history surrounding the phenomenon, and all the questions it raises about the nature of human identity, as well as the nature of God himself and other celestial beings. The story went in a different direction than I originally intended. The other half of it will wrap up with Book 12, where I will close the loop on understanding our identity as Image Bearers (that's where those other bones factor in). But suffice it to say, there was plenty in this book to noodle on, on top of the adventure.

Now to the book's research and deeper themes. As with all of my books, I like to add a note at the end with what went into the story. I definitely aim to craft an entertainment-first tale, but I also like to add a bit of insight and inspiration for faith. So, if you care to learn more about the foundation of this episode in the Order of Thaddeus, here is some of what I discovered that made its way into SEPIO's latest adventure.

What Does it Mean to Be Human?

That's the question that originally launched this book, a story that went in a very different direction than I had planned and is yet unfinished (more on that below). I had originally envisioned the scene from chapter 3, where SEPIO uncovers a number of bones that confuses our human ancestry and identity, with the ancient *Homo* lines mixed with those from the Bronze Age and our Nephilim friend. That mixture was meant to dive deep into issues of human origins, our nature, and identity. I only got half the story in this one, where the answer to the question centered on the possibilities of other intelligent beings in the universe, and what that revelation would do to our own status in the universe.

Because as Elijah Fox explained, even if there are other intelligent beings—aliens, if you will—who cares? Doesn't matter in the slightest to our unique, unrivaled status as Image Bearers of God who have been specially crafted to represent his rule and reign on Earth. Using those four Hebrew words in the bunker on Wright-Patterson Air Force Base, the good professor revealed our true human identity is rooted in enjoying, guarding, ruling over, and working creation. That's what it means to be human.

Everyone, regardless of gender or ethnicity—whether pre-born, a child, a middle-ager, or an octogenarian—is a Statue of God, an Image Bearer who has been placed on Earth as God's representative. Rather than intelligence or will, emotion or socialization, human nature is rooted in our *status* and *role* as Image Bearers of the Most High God, created in his image and likeness, as Genesis 1:26 explains. This is why signing two characters up to the SEPIO operation who might fall outside the normal definition of Image Bearer was so important for me. Elijah Fox and Gina Anderson bear the Image of God, regardless of their perceived challenges that falls outside emotional, social, and even intelligence norms as autistic people.

I will say, it is always a risk for any writer to represent characters from certain walks of life that are far outside their own. Naomi Torres is one such character, a Latino woman. Elijah and Gina were two more, autistic people whose characters came to me in the writing process. I spent time reading autistic people's stories and getting to know their experiences in the world to get them right. I particularly wanted to listen to their pain points when it comes to representation in the media, not wanting to fall into the same traps.

Hopefully, I represented them justly, writing unique, individual characters that shed some light on how they image their Creator in the world and their unique challenges expressing their personhood. However, if I fell down on the mark, and you yourself are autistic who can offer me insight into better representation, do contact me and help me understand how I can better write the stories of autistic Image Bearers. Because I plan to continue with Elijah's and Gina's stories as investigators in the Church's struggle against this present supernatural darkness—more on that below!

The History of UFOs and Alien Abductions.

I won't rehash the history surrounding UFOs and alien abductions. Everything I covered in chapters 4, 5, 12, and 37 is historically accurate as far as the historical record and eyewitness testimony are concerned. Yes, Project Blue Book was a thing, as well as the Robertson Panel that sought to debunk the stories—even signing up Disney and Walter Cronkite for its efforts! MK-Ultra is also a stain on our American history, which provided a plausible backdrop for what happened to Matt Gapinski with the tests he himself underwent at the hand of a faction within the US government.

His personal encounter with unidentified aerial phenomenon was based on an actual account from another military base, from Christmas 1980 in Rendlesham Forest outside the RAF Bentwaters/Woodbridge complex in England. Gapinski's story was adapted from the account given in Leslie Kean's book *UFOs: Generals, Pilots, and Government Officials Go on the Record*, chapter 18. I modified it a bit, throwing in the abduction angle that connected to the larger conspiracy surrounding raising up a superrace of alien hybrids.

Kean's book is especially remarkable, as it offers a journalistic lens upon the phenomenon, letting experts—military, scientific, political—speak to what is clearly a modern phenomenon largely beginning around the end of World War II. Which offered the perfect entrance into the Nazi connection at the foundation of my own SEPIO conspiracy. Everything recounted in chapter 32 by Nicky McGrath concerning Nazi technology and occult border science is factual, drawn from Eric Kurlander's *Hitler's Monsters: A Supernatural History of the Third Reich*. Although it might be a stretch to say their technological insights were downloaded from Watcher-spirits, the clear occult roots offered a plausible springboard for the prologue and continued conspiracy that began in Germany and ended up in America.

Hans Kammler was a real high-ranking operative who worked on such projects as *der Glocke*, a supposed flying saucer known as The Bell. He set up shop at the Skoda Works Nazi military arsenal where he directed projects on advanced weapons systems. Anti-gravity devices and guided weapons, anti-aircraft lasers and death rays were some of those pursuits. Kammler did disappear without a trace, as well, though he most likely died without a family. Certainly no son Walter Kammler, a two-star general in the US Air Force whom I invented! However, the history surrounding Operation Paperclip allowed for the possibility of Senior Kammler being brought into the military industrial complex, having a son, and passing along his secrets—where Junior Kammler later sought to fulfill his father's dream to finish the Great Cause: raising up a race of superbeings using dead Nephilim DNA.

Which brings us to the biblical and spiritual angle of my story, like all of my books.

Ancient Sons of God and the Unseen Realm

If you've been raised in the Church and are familiar with Christianity, perhaps you could relate to Silas. I know I could! I was born and bread on the Bible, went to Bible college, studied to be a pastor, and possess two shiny graduate and post-graduate diplomas in Divinity and Theology. And yet, the notion of a divine council and the sons of God from Genesis 6, Deuteronomy 32, Psalms 82, and elsewhere was completely new to me.

If you read these sections of Scripture—especially those Elijah focused on at the Vatican, Psalms 82 and 89, Deuteronomy 32, 1 Corinthians 8—and take them at face value, believing what they simply say reflects God's reality, perhaps you will shift in your own view of the unseen realm as I have in this writing project. We Christians, and even other spiritually interested and religious people, already understand other supernatural players are on the field. Angels, demons, seraphim, Satan himself. Why not the Sons of God, which the Bible explicitly mentions? The portions of 1 Enoch Elijah read in the Vatican Archives speak to this reality from Genesis 6. The "obscure Jewish text connected to the Enoch tradition" is actually a chapter toward the end of the Book of Enoch. I just used it for my purposes to put the pieces together, which certainly reveals the Fallen Ones, the giants, as evil spirits causing chaos on earth.

I'm still working it through myself, seeking to understand the Jewish backdrop to the Bible, Old and New Testaments alike. I'm especially seeking to take seriously the supernatural assumptions of the Bible and its teachings and worldview, which our post-Enlightenment, hypermodern twenty-first century world dismisses out right. Perhaps this story can be an introduction into this supernatural conversation.

I have Michael Heiser to thank for that introduction, whose material in *Unseen Realms*, *Reversing Hermon*, and *Demons* really opened my eyes to the Jewish worldview at the center of not only the Hebrew Scriptures (more commonly called the Old Testament) but also the New Testament. Many have tilled similar fields in the past few decades, seeking to reclaim the

Jewishness of Jesus, Paul, and the rest of the New Testament (specifically the likes of N.T. Wright). Though the idea of a divine council, over which Yahweh, the Most High God of Israel, rules both the heavens and the earth, might be new for you—it certainly was for me!—the scholarship in recent years has trended in this direction.

Elijah's commentary on both the divine council and the sons of God was largely drawn from Heiser's insights, appearing in chapters 23, 28, 31, 35, and 36, which the good professor distilled for our SEPIO adventurers. Same for Heiser's remarkable insights into Genesis 6 and the Watchers, along with their Nephilim offspring, who still impact our world as their demonic disembodied souls wage war from the unseen realm. A particularly enlightening lecture on aliens and demons helped fill in the gaps, especially in chapters 23 and 36 (www.faithlifetv.com/items/479903). Heiser's fictional book, *The Façade*, also connected the dots between what might be happening with contactees experiences and the demonic realm —a plausible connection made in this story.

The Bible, UFOs, and Aliens

So what does the Bible say about UFOs—again, I hear Elijah's complaint: *UAPs!*—and aliens? Well, not much! But the connections I make between the Book of Enoch and its Watcher worldview that begins in Genesis 6 and carries through to Deuteronomy 32 could be a start. This worldview explains the Sons of God or Watchers were celestial beings created by Yahweh, the Most High God. They rebelled and fell, being bound in the Abyss until later being released at the Apocalypse —which I make use of in my end times, apocalyptic science fiction series *Ichthus Chronicles*. This thread is picked up specifically in Season 2, *Apocalypse Rising*.

The Watchers possessed supernatural insight into science,

technology, and other realms of knowledge that could be conveyed to their offspring, born through their copulation with human women. I understand this idea is fantastical, but God's Word seems to indicate such a relationship between the unseen and seen realms occurred at some point in human history. Supernatural beings breached the veil between the supernatural realm and the natural one, birthing hybrid beings known as the Nephilim. In fact, it would seem their kind—the supernatural Fallen Ones who manifest themselves as demons in our natural realm—still possess such insight into heavenly powers. Perhaps they have conveyed aspects of this revelation-insight to those who have sought their help—like the Nazis in their search for a miracle weapon to win the war. That's the fictional conjecture, anyway.

More likely—which Gina Anderson gets at with her insights as a parapsychologist who has interviewed and studied abductee testimony—these demons pose as aliens to blind the hearts and minds of humans and turn them away from Jesus Christ. The actors in the unseen realm are creative, powerful, and cunning. No reason they could not use our fascination with space visitors, perpetuated and amplified by Hollywood and the media, to trick people into believing in extraterrestrial beings from outer space—especially given the clear anti-Christian messaging steeped in a pagan Gnostic worldview, as is the case with abductees. The remarks about the cultic nature of alien abduction stories are factual, drawn from Michael Heiser's own research and side-hobby fascination with such stories. Professor John Mack of Harvard did indeed put together an MIT conference in 1982, and one of the papers connected alien abductee stories with satanic ritual abuse.

Either way, as the time for Christ's second coming draws near, and the Church continues its mission of sharing the radical, revolutionary story of God's crazy, rescuing love in Jesus, I can imagine the unseen realm will be breaking into our natural realm in remarkable, mysterious, and supernaturally dark ways.

Which requires an investigative arm of the Church to solve those supernatural mysteries!

Group X and the Future of the Order of Thaddeus

First of all, let me just make it clear the Order and Project SEPIO aren't going anywhere! Neither are their stories. I love the SEPIO gang and the adventures they live, and I imagine I will continue telling their stories for years to come. The exhortation found in Jude 3 is as vital as ever, and we need a group contending for the once-for-all faith entrusted to God's holy people now more than ever! Besides, I love a good gunfight and car chase, and who doesn't love blowing things up?

Second, yes, Group X is a new Order of Thaddeus subgroup! I am thrilled to branch out a bit into the paranormal, supernatural suspense genre and tell thrilling stories steeped in issues of faith. Elijah Fox and Gina Anderson are pairing up to solve cases that demand a more investigatory touch. And where my SEPIO Order of Thaddeus stories tend to focus on global disaster conspiracies, I envision their work confronting the unseen realm, the cosmic powers of this present darkness. Group X stories will trend toward smaller and localized, far more personal and timely.

Where Jude 3 is the basis for the Order broadly and SEPIO's more kinetic response to worldly, flesh-and-blood threats, Ephesians 6:12 anchors Group X and its more procedural investigations—revealing that our ultimate struggle is against the spiritual forces of evil in the unseen realm.

Follow Elijah's and Gina's mysterious cases at www.groupx cases.com!

Research is an important part of my process for creating compelling stories that entertain, inform, and inspire. Here are a few resources I used to research the history behind the UFO and alien phenomenon:

- Heiser, Michael. *Unseen Realms: Recovering the Supernatural Worldview of the Bible.* Bellingham, WA: Lexham Press, 2015. www.bouma.us/ufo1
- _____ . *Reversing Hermon: Enoch, the Watchers & the Forgotten Mission of Jesus Christ.* Crane, MO: Defending Publishing, 2017. www.bouma.us/ufo2
- _____ . *Demons: What the Bible Really Says about the Powers of Darkness.* Bellingham, WA: Lexham Press, 2020. www.bouma.us/ufo3
- _____ . *Aliens & Demons: Evidence of an Unseen Realm* lecture. https://faithlifetv.com/items/479903.
- Kean, Leslie. *UFOs: Generals, Pilots, and Government Officials Go on the Record.* New York: Three Rivers Press, 2010. www.bouma.us/ufo4
- Kurlander, Eric. *Hitler's Monsters: A Supernatural History of the Third Reich.* New Haven, CT: Yale University Press, 2017. www.bouma.us/ufo5
- Vallee, Jacques. *Messengers of Deception: UFO Contacts and Cults.* Brisbane: Daily Grail Publishing, 1979. www.bouma.us/ufo6

GET YOUR FREE THRILLER

Building a relationship with my readers is one of my all-time favorite joys of writing! Once in a while I like to send out a newsletter with giveaways, free stories, pre-release content, updates on new books, and other bits on my stories.

Join my insider's group for updates, giveaways, and your free novel—a full-length action-adventure story in my *Order of Thaddeus* thriller series. Just tell me where to send it.

Follow this link to subscribe:
www.jabouma.com/free

ALSO BY J. A. BOUMA

Nobody should have to read bad religious fiction—whether it's cheesy plots with pat answers or misrepresentations of the Christian faith and the Bible. So J. A. Bouma tells compelling, propulsive stories that thrill as much as inspire, offering a dose of insight along the way.

Order of Thaddeus Action-Adventure Thriller Series

Holy Shroud • Book 1

The Thirteenth Apostle • Book 2

Hidden Covenant • Book 3

American God • Book 4

Grail of Power • Book 5

Templars Rising • Book 6

Rite of Darkness • Book 7

Gospel Zero • Book 8

The Emperor's Code • Book 9

Deadly Hope • Book 10

Fallen Ones • Book 11

The Eden Legacy • Book 12

Silas Grey Collection 1 (Books 1-3)

Silas Grey Collection 2 (Books 4-6)

Silas Grey Collection 3 (Books 7-9)

Backstories: Short Story Collection 1

Martyrs Bones: Short Story Collection 2

Group X Cases **Supernatural Suspense Series**

Not of This World • Book 1

The Darkest Valley • Book 2

Against These Powers • Book 3

Luck Be the Ladies • Novelette

End Times Chronicles **Sci-Fi Apocalyptic Series**

Apostasy Rising / Season 1, Episode 1

Apostasy Rising / Season 1, Episode 2

Apostasy Rising / Season 1, Episode 3

Apostasy Rising / Season 1, Episode 4

Apostasy Rising / Full Season 1 (Episodes 1 to 4)

Apocalypse Rising / Season 2, Episode 1

Apocalypse Rising / Season 2, Episode 2

Apocalypse Rising / Season 2, Episode 3

Apocalypse Rising / Season 2, Episode 4

Apocalypse Rising / Full Season 2 (Episodes 1 to 4)

Faith Reimagined **Spiritual Coming-of-Age Series**

A Reimagined Faith • Book 1

A Rediscovered Faith • Book 2

Mill Creek Junction **Short Story Series**

The New Normal • Collection 1

My Name's Johnny Pope • Collection 2

Joy to the Junction! • Collection 3

The Ties that Bind Us • Collection 4

A Matter of Justice • Collection 5

Get all the latest short stories at: www.millcreekjunction.com

Find all of my latest book releases at: www.jabouma.com

ABOUT THE AUTHOR

J. A. Bouma believes nobody should have to read bad religious fiction—whether it's cheesy plots with pat answers or misrepresentations of the Christian faith and the Bible. So he tells compelling, propulsive stories that thrill as much as inspire, while offering a dose of insight along the way.

As a former congressional staffer and pastor, and award-nominated bestselling author of over forty religious fiction and nonfiction books, he blends a love for ideas and adventure, exploration and discovery, thrill and thought. With graduate degrees in Christian thought and the Bible, and armed with a voracious appetite for most mainstream genres, he tells stories you'll read with abandon and recommend with pride—exploring the tension of faith and doubt, spirituality and culture, belief and practice, and the gritty drama that is our collective pilgrim story.

When not putting fingers to keyboard, he loves vintage jazz vinyl, a glass of Malbec, and an epic read—preferably together. He lives in Grand Rapids with his wife, two kiddos, and rambunctious boxer-pug-terrier.

www.jabouma.com • jeremy@jabouma.com

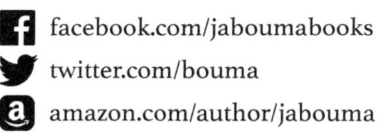

facebook.com/jaboumabooks
twitter.com/bouma
amazon.com/author/jabouma